ON FINDING THE WRITER'S VOICE:

"Each new novel or story demands its *own* voice, I think, and the genesis of each remains mysterious—a long, patient process of discovery."

—Andrea Barrett

"I would urge upon all young writers this axiom: Find the material, and the voice will take care of itself. . . . A preening voice, which enjoys itself too much, becomes quickly tedious, whereas a voice that delivers a tale, full of human pulse and recognizable circumstances, strikes us as mellifluous."

—John Updike

"I guess the most important thing I can say about my writing voice, or voices, is that they're the smartest voices I have, often teaching me things I didn't know I knew."

—Judith Rossner

"I don't believe most writers can or should choose a voice. . . . For most of us I believe the voice gradually emerges, coming out of all that we have read . . . from the exquisite discipline of writing itself, and from who we are at the most fundamental level, from our souls, if you will."

—Frank Conroy

"For the writer who has been writing for a period of years, there can be no day, no hour, no epiphany of a moment, when he or she discovers his or her 'voice'. . . . The challenge for the writer—at times a challenge that evokes intense anxiety—is to discover and to refine the voice that is unique to that work."

—Joyce Carol Oates

A Literary Guild Alternate Section

AMERICAN VOICES

BEST SHORT FICTION BY CONTEMPORARY AUTHORS

•

WITH COMMENTS BY THE AUTHORS

SELECTED BY

SALLY ARTESEROS

WASHINGTON SQUARE PRESS
PUBLISHED BY POCKET BOOKS
New York London Toronto Sydney Tokyo Singapore

A Washington Square Press Publication of
POCKET BOOKS, a division of Simon & Schuster Inc.
1230 Avenue of the Americas, New York, NY 10020

Cover design by John Gall
Front cover illustration by Coco Masuda

Published by arrangement with Hyperion, an imprint of the Walt Disney Book Publishing Group, Inc.

American voices : best short fiction by contemporary authors/ selected by Sally Arteseros.
p. cm.
ISBN 0-671-78315-7
1. Short stories, American. 2. American fiction—20th century.
I. Arteseros, Sally.
[PS648.S5A56 1993]
813'.0108—dc20 92-30087
CIP

First Washington Square Press trade paperback printing May 1993

10 9 8 7 6 5 4 3 2 1

Printed in the U.S.A.

CONTENTS

Comments by the authors precede their stories

CONTENTS

INTRODUCTION

I was delighted when the Literary Guild invited me to assemble a new collection of short fiction for its members, and also when, soon afterward, this became a joint project with the new publishing house Hyperion. The idea was to bring together in one volume stories by some of the most interesting and exciting people writing short fiction in America today—writers a well-informed reader should know. While other excellent story anthologies exist, often they are focused around a particular theme: the best stories published in a certain year, or by writers from a specific background or area of the country; stories about family, about love. But here was a chance to collect *the best*—a sort of "required reading" of some of the finest short fiction written in America in the last fifteen years.

I turned to this task with enthusiasm, as I have been been reading, editing, and studying short stories for decades. As a Senior Editor at Doubleday I edited fiction and story collections by some outstanding writers, and I was involved for many years with the publication of *Prize Stories: The O. Henry Awards,* edited by William Abrahams. Over my years of reading there were certain treasures that stood out, and these I was eager to share—stories such as John Updike's "Separating" and Alice Adams's "Roses, Rhododendron"; Frank Conroy's "Midair," Bobbie Ann Mason's "Shiloh," and Amy Tan's "Rules of the Game," the tale of a chess-playing girl who taps into her own "invisible strength."

Creating this collection has also given me the opportunity to read the work of some brilliant writers I had not known before.

I have tried to choose stories that resonate in the memory—perhaps because of a single moment or scene, as in Raymond Carver's unforgettable tale of a child and a birthday cake. I wanted stories that are deeply rooted in a particular time and place, but that are also universal, that distill life's events to the essence.

Some of the stories take place during a short period of time; they are marvelously compressed and contained. John Sayles's "The Halfway Diner" is set on a bus trip as women are traveling to see their men in prison. Jane Smiley's "Lily" happens over the course of a weekend: three old friends meet in the home of one of them, and the gathering changes their lives forever. Tobias Wolff's "The Rich Brother" unfolds during a car ride, as a man picks up his younger, shiftless, yet still innocent and trusting brother from the community from which he has been expelled.

Christopher Tilghman's "In a Father's Place" occurs over the course of a weekend on the Eastern Shore of Maryland, as a young man brings his girlfriend home to meet his family. Judith Rossner's "116th Street Jenny," set during a summer in Italy, describes a young woman's relationship to a painting of herself: an inventive twist on *The Picture of Dorian Gray*.

While these stories take place during a short period of time, we see how their characters' lives stretch out before and after, irrevocably changed.

Many of the stories contain powerful images that are also very sensual: the roses and rhododendron of Alice Adams, the cups of tea made by Harriet Doerr's Edie to comfort the motherless children; those children, for the rest of their lives, without quite understanding why, would always love tea.

Since the time I studied and taught the short story at the University of Connecticut in the late 1950s, there has been a remarkable ripening, an increasing diversity, in the stories being written and published in the United States. Today, exciting new voices are coming into and enriching the mainstream of American fiction. I have included some of those voices here—stories by writers who are black, Mexican American, Chinese American.

I think many readers are interested in the idea of "voice," of how and when a writer finds his or her own distinctive voice and taps into his own "invisible strength," writing stories that only he or she could have written—stories with an individual thumbprint, a signature.

Preceding the stories are comments from the authors, introducing themselves and saying something about how the story came to be. These comments are personal, honest, and illuminating, and I believe they will be of value both to readers and to other writers of fiction.

For some, stories come through visual images. As John Updike comments: "The voice of fiction speaks in images, and I find mine when the images come abundantly, and interweave to make a continuous music." All of the authors acknowledge that they have to work hard to "get it right," and some are surprised at where a story can take them. Joyce Carol Oates says: "The writer often labors, through successive revisions, to create the very prose style that is 'characteristic'—just as the story, when completed, is virtually never the story that was imagined at the outset. The act of writing the story propels us beyond it." And Dennis McFarland adds: "Every story is an investigation. As you investigate who a character is, you experiment with what he must sound like; and as you hear what he sounds like, you begin to understand more about who he is. Given this floundering process, it's a miracle that anything ever comes out right. And I think it's why our best stories are never entirely smooth, but tend to have rough edges."

In addition to a distinctive voice, what many of these stories have in common is a sense of mystery—the mystery of life, of what goes on in a person's heart, of why people are moved to do what they do.

The dance critic Arlene Croce wrote a book called *Afterimages*, the title referring to the vision that we are left with when a dance is over and the dancer has left the stage. I think it is fair to say that many of the stories in this volume will have strong "afterimages" for readers—they will linger in the memory long after the book is closed.

I like to think that if a person had just one collection of contemporary American stories to take with him to a desert island, it would be this one—for there are sustaining riches here, to be enjoyed and savored, again and again.

For inspiration and help I want to thank Barbara Greenman, Jaye Isler, and Diana Klemin at the Literary Guild; Leslie Wells at Hyperion; Jane Rosenman at Washington Square Press; Wendy Weil, Fran Kiernan, Kate Medina, Robin Metz, Barbara Broadhurst and William Abrahams; and most of all, the writers included here.

—SALLY ARTESEROS

AMERICAN VOICES

ALICE ADAMS

" 'Roses, Rhododendron' was one of a group of stories that I began writing in the early seventies, not long after my father died. (The deaths of parents, dreadful and sad as they are, do I think to an extent free writers.) I was thinking about my childhood best friend, Judith, and her connection to my parents and me—they were crazy about her too. And it occurred to me to try to write a story about us from her point of view. And, with radical changes of course, that is how this story came about. It was both interesting and instructive to do—and it did turn out to be a story that people in general have liked. I guess everyone had a best friend, and we all feel nostalgic about that friendship.

"Its publishing history was odd, I thought: it went to *The New Yorker*, got turned down; went to *McCall's*, again turned down. At which point I rewrote it slightly, sent it back to *The New Yorker*, which took it.

"I'm not sure about developing a voice. It's not something of which one is conscious, I think. When I first began publishing stories people began to tell me that they could recognize a story by me right away, and I could never quite see how. I still don't."

ROSES, RHODODENDRON

For Judith

ONE dark and rainy Boston spring of many years ago, I spent all my after-school and evening hours in the living room of our antique-crammed Cedar Street flat, writing down what the Ouija board said to my mother. My father, a spoiled and rowdy Irishman, a sometime engineer, had run off to New Orleans with a girl, and my mother hoped to learn from the board if he would come back. Then, one night in May, during a crashing black thunderstorm (my mother was both afraid and much in awe of storms), the board told her to move down South, to North Carolina, taking me and all the antiques she had been collecting for years, and to open a store in a small town down there. That is what we did, and shortly thereafter, for the first time in my life, I fell violently and permanently in love: with a house, with a family of three people, and with an area of countryside.

Perhaps too little attention is paid to the necessary preconditions of "falling in love"—I mean the state of mind or place that precedes one's first sight of the loved person (or house or land). In my own case, I remember the dark Boston afternoons as a precondition of love. Later on, for another important time, I recognized boredom in a job. And once the fear of growing old.

In the town that she had chosen, my mother, Margot (she picked out her own name, having been christened Margaret), rented a small house on a pleasant back street. It had a big surrounding screened-in porch, where she put most of the antiques, and she put a discreet sign out in the front yard: "Margot—Antiques." The store was open only in the afternoons. In the mornings and on Sundays, she drove around the countryside in our ancient and spacious Buick, searching for trophies among the area's country stores and farms and barns. (She is nothing if not enterprising; no one else down there had thought of doing that before.)

Although frequently embarrassed by her aggression—she thought nothing of making offers for furniture that was in use in a family's rooms—I often drove with her during those first few weeks. I was excited by the novelty of the landscape. The red clay banks that led up to the thick pine groves, the swollen brown creeks half hidden by flowering tangled vines. Bare, shaded yards from which rose gaunt, narrow houses. Chickens that scattered, barefoot children who stared at our approach.

"Hello there. I'm Mrs. John Kilgore—Margot Kilgore—and I'm interested in buying old furniture. Family portraits. Silver."

Margot a big brassily bleached blonde in a pretty flowered silk dress and high-heeled patent sandals. A hoarse and friendly voice. Me a scrawny, pale, curious girl, about ten, in a blue linen dress with smocking across the bodice. (Margot has always had a passionate belief in good clothes, no matter what.)

On other days, Margot would say, "I'm going to look over my so-called books. Why don't you go for a walk or something, Jane?"

And I would walk along the sleepy, leafed-over streets, on the unpaved sidewalks, past houses that to me were as inviting and as interesting as unread books, and I would try to imagine what went on inside. The families. Their lives.

The main street, where the stores were, interested me least. Two-story brick buildings—dry-goods stores, with dentists' and lawyers' offices above. There was also a drugstore, with round marble tables and wire-backed chairs, at which wilting ladies sipped at their Cokes (this was to become a favorite haunt of Margot's). I preferred the civic monuments: a pre-Revolutionary Episcopal chapel of yellowish cracked plaster, and several tall white statues to the Civil War dead—all of them quickly overgrown with ivy or Virginia creeper.

These were the early nineteen-forties, and in the next few years the town was to change enormously. Its small textile factories would be given defense contracts (parachute silk); a Navy preflight school would be established at a neighboring university town. But at that moment it was a sleeping village. Untouched.

My walks were not a lonely occupation, but Margot worried that they were, and some curious reasoning led her to believe that a bicycle would help. (Of course, she turned out to be right.) We went to Sears, and she bought me a big new bike—blue, with balloon tires—on which I began to explore the outskirts of town and the countryside.

The house I fell in love with was about a mile out of town, on top of a hill. A small stone bank that was all overgrown with tangled roses led up to its yard, and pink and white roses climbed up a trellis to the roof of the front porch—the roof on which, later, Harriet and I used to sit and exchange our stores of erroneous sexual information. Harriet Farr was the daughter of the house. On one side of the house, there was what looked like a newer wing, with a bay window and a long side porch, below which the lawn sloped down to some flowering shrubs. There was a yellow rosebush, rhododendron, a plum tree, and beyond were woods—pines, and oak and cedar trees. The effect was rich and careless, generous and somewhat mysterious. I was deeply stirred.

As I was observing all this, from my halted bike on the dusty white hilltop, a small, plump woman, very erect, came out of the front door and went over to a flower bed below the bay window. She sat down very stiffly. (Emily, who was Harriet's mother, had some terrible, never diagnosed trouble with her back; she generally wore a brace.) She was older than Margot, with very beautiful white hair that was badly cut in that butchered nineteen-thirties way.

From the first, I was fascinated by Emily's obvious dissimilarity to Margot. I think I was also somehow drawn to her contradictions—the shapeless body held up with so much dignity, even while she was sitting in the dirt. The lovely chopped-off hair. (There were greater contradictions, which I learned of later—she was a Virginia Episcopalian who always voted for Norman Thomas, a feminist who always delayed meals for her tardy husband.)

Emily's hair was one of the first things about the Farr family that I mentioned to Margot after we became friends, Harriet and Emily and I, and I began to spend most of my time in that house.

"I don't think she's ever dyed it," I said, with almost conscious lack of tact.

Of course, Margot was defensive. "I wouldn't dye mine if I thought it would be a decent color on its own."

But by that time Margot's life was also improving. Business was fairly good, and she had finally heard from my father, who began to send sizable checks from New Orleans. He had found work with an oil company. She still asked the Ouija board if she would see him again, but her question was less obsessive.

The second time I rode past that house, there was a girl sitting on the front porch, reading a book. She was about my age. She looked up. The next time I saw her there, we both smiled. And the time after that (a Saturday morning in late June) she got up and slowly came out to the road, to where I had stopped, ostensibly to look at the view—the sweep of fields, the white highway, which wound down to the thick greenery bordering the creek, the fields and trees that rose in dim and distant hills.

"I've got a bike exactly like that," Harriet said indifferently, as though to deny the gesture of having come out to meet me.

For years, perhaps beginning then, I used to seek my antithesis in friends. Inexorably following Margot, I was becoming a big blonde, with some of her same troubles. Harriet was cool and dark, with long, gray eyes. A girl about to be beautiful.

"Do you want to come in? We've got some lemon cake that's pretty good."

Inside, the house was cluttered with odd mixtures of furniture. I glimpsed a living room, where there was a shabby sofa next to a pretty, "antique" table. We walked through a dining room that contained a decrepit mahogany table surrounded with delicate fruit-wood chairs. (I had a horrifying moment of imagining Margot there, with her accurate eye—making offers in her harsh Yankee voice.) The walls were crowded with portraits and with nineteenth-century oils of bosky landscapes. Books overflowed from rows of shelves along the walls. I would have moved in at once.

We took our lemon cake back to the front porch and ate it there, overlooking that view. I can remember its taste vividly. It was light and tart and sweet, and a beautiful lemon color. With it, we drank cold milk, and then we had seconds and more milk, and we discussed what we liked to read.

We were both at an age to begin reading grownup books, and there was some minor competition between us to see who had read more of them. Harriet won easily, partly because her mother reviewed books for the local paper, and had brought home Steinbeck, Thomas Wolfe, Virginia Woolf, and Elizabeth Bowen. But we also found in common an enthusiasm for certain novels about English children. (Such snobbery!)

"It's the best cake I've ever had!" I told Harriet. I had already adopted something of Margot's emphatic style.

"It's very good," Harriet said judiciously. Then, quite casually, she added, "We could ride our bikes out to Laurel Hill."

We soared dangerously down the winding highway. At the bridge across the creek, we stopped and turned onto a narrow, rutted dirt road that followed the creek through woods as dense and as alien as a jungle would have been—thick pines with low sweeping branches, young leafed-out maples, peeling tall poplars, elms, brambles, green masses of honeysuckle. At times, the road was impassable, and we had to get off our bikes and push them along, over crevices and ruts, through mud or sand. And with all that we kept up our somewhat stilted discussion of literature.

"I love Virginia Woolf!"

"Yes, she's very good. Amazing metaphors."

I thought Harriet was an extraordinary person—more intelligent, more poised, and prettier than any girl of my age I had ever known. I felt that she could become anything at all—a writer, an actress, a foreign correspondent (I went to a lot of movies). And I was not entirely wrong; she eventually became a sometimes-published poet.

We came to a small beach, next to a place where the creek widened and ran over some shallow rapids. On the other side, large gray rocks rose steeply. Among the stones grew isolated, twisted trees, and huge bushes with thick green leaves. The laurel of Laurel Hill. Rhododendron. Harriet and I took off our shoes and waded into the warmish water. The bottom squished under our feet, making us laugh, like the children we were, despite all our literary talk.

Margot was also making friends. Unlike me, she seemed to seek her own likeness, and she found a sort of kinship with a woman named Dolly Murray, a rich widow from Memphis who shared many of Margot's superstitions—fear of thunderstorms, faith in the Ouija board. About ten years older than Margot, Dolly still dyed her hair red; she was a noisy, biassed, generous woman. They drank gin and gossiped together, they met for Cokes at the drugstore, and sometimes they drove to a neighboring town to have dinner in a restaurant (in those days, still a daring thing for unescorted ladies to do).

I am sure that the Farrs, outwardly a conventional family, saw me as a neglected child. I was so available for meals and overnight visits. But that is not how I experienced my life—I simply felt free. And an important thing to be said about Margot as a mother is that she never made me feel guilty for doing what I wanted to do. And of how many mothers can that be said?

There must have been a moment of "meeting" Emily, but I have forgotten it. I remember only her gentle presence, a soft voice, and my own sense of love returned. Beautiful white hair, dark deep eyes, and a wide mouth, whose corners turned and moved to express whatever she felt—amusement, interest, boredom, pain. I have never since seen such a vulnerable mouth.

I amused Emily; I almost always made her smile. She must have seen me as something foreign—a violent, enthusiastic Yankee (I used forbidden words, like "God" and "damn"). Very unlike the decorous young Southern girl that she must have been, that Harriet almost was.

She talked to me a lot; Emily explained to me things about the South that otherwise I would not have picked up. "Virginians feel superior to everyone else, you know," she said, in her gentle (Virginian) voice. "Some people in my family were quite shocked when I married a man from North Carolina and came down here to live. And a Presbyterian at that! Of course, that's nowhere near as bad as a Baptist, but only Episcopalians really count." This was all said lightly, but I knew that some part of Emily agreed with the rest of her family.

"How about Catholics?" I asked her, mainly to prolong the conversation. Harriet was at the dentist's, and Emily was sitting at her desk answering letters. I was perched on the sofa near her, and we both faced the sweeping green view. But since my father, Johnny Kilgore, was a lapsed Catholic, it was not an entirely frivolous question. Margot was a sort of Christian Scientist (her own sort).

"We hardly know any Catholics." Emily laughed, and then she

sighed. "I do sometimes still miss Virginia. You know, when we drive up there I can actually feel the difference as we cross the state line. I've met a few people from South Carolina," she went on, "and I understand that people down there feel the same way Virginians do." (Clearly, she found this unreasonable.)

"West Virginia? Tennessee?"

"They don't seem Southern at all. Neither do Florida and Texas—not to me."

("Dolly says that Mrs. Farr is a terrible snob," Margot told me, inquiringly.

"In a way." I spoke with a new diffidence that I was trying to acquire from Harriet.

"Oh.")

Once, I told Emily what I had been wanting to say since my first sight of her. I said, "Your hair is so beautiful. Why don't you let it grow?"

She laughed, because she usually laughed at what I said, but at the same time she looked surprised, almost startled. I understood that what I had said was not improper but that she was totally unused to attentions of that sort from anyone, including herself. She didn't think about her hair. In a puzzled way, she said, "Perhaps I will."

Nor did Emily dress like a woman with much regard for herself. She wore practical, seersucker dresses and sensible, low shoes. Because her body had so little shape, no indentations (this must have been at least partly due to the back brace), I was surprised to notice that she had pretty, shapely legs. She wore little or no makeup on her sun- and wind-weathered face.

And what of Lawrence Farr, the North Carolina Presbyterian for whom Emily had left her people and her state? He was a small, precisely made man, with fine dark features (Harriet looked very like him). A lawyer, but widely read in literature, especially the English nineteenth century. He had a courtly manner, and sometimes a wicked tongue; melancholy eyes, and an odd, sudden, ratchety laugh. He looked ten years younger than Emily; the actual difference was less than two.

•

"Well," said Margot, settling into a Queen Anne chair—a new antique—on our porch one stifling hot July morning, "I heard some really interesting gossip about your friends."

Margot had met and admired Harriet, and Harriet liked her, too—Margot made Harriet laugh, and she praised Harriet's fine brown hair. But on some instinct (I am not sure whose) the parents had not met. Very likely, Emily, with her Southern social antennae, had somehow sensed that this meeting would be a mistake.

That morning, Harriet and I were going on a picnic in the woods to the steep rocky side of Laurel Hill, but I forced myself to listen, or half listen, to Margot's story.

"Well, it seems that some years ago Lawrence Farr fell absolutely madly in love with a beautiful young girl—in fact, the orphaned daughter of a friend of his. Terribly romantic. Of course, she loved him, too, but he felt so awful and guilty that they never did anything about it."

I did not like this story much; it made me obscurely uncomfortable, and I think that at some point both Margot and I wondered why she was telling it. Was she pointing out imperfections in my chosen other family? But I asked, in Harriet's indifferent voice, "He never kissed her?"

"Well, maybe. I don't know. But of course everyone in town knew all about it, including Emily Farr. And with her back! Poor woman," Margot added somewhat piously but with real feeling too.

I forgot the story readily at the time. For one thing, there was something unreal about anyone as old as Lawrence Farr "falling in love." But looking back to Emily's face, Emily looking at Lawrence, I can see that pained watchfulness of a woman who has been hurt, and by a man who could always hurt her again.

In those days, what struck me most about the Farrs was their extreme courtesy to each other—something I had not seen before. Never a harsh word. (Of course, I did not know then about couples who cannot afford a single harsh word.)

Possibly because of the element of danger (very slight—the slope was gentle), the roof over the front porch was one of the places Harriet and

I liked to sit on warm summer nights when I was invited to stay over. There was a country silence, invaded at intervals by summer country sounds—the strangled croak of tree frogs from down in the glen; the crazy baying of a distant hound. There, in the heavy scent of roses, on the scratchy shingles, Harriet and I talked about sex.

"A girl I know told me that if you do it a lot your hips get very wide."

"My cousin Duncan says it makes boys strong if they do it."

"It hurts women a lot—especially at first. But I knew this girl from Santa Barbara, and she said that out there they say Filipinos can do it without hurting."

"Colored people do it a lot more than whites."

"Of course, they have all those babies. But in Boston so do Catholics!"

We are seized with hysteria. We laugh and laugh, so that Emily hears and calls up to us, "Girls, why haven't you-all gone to bed?" But her voice is warm and amused—she likes having us laughing up there.

And Emily liked my enthusiasm for lemon cake. She teased me about the amounts of it I could eat, and she continued to keep me supplied. She was not herself much of a cook—their maid, a young black girl named Evelyn, did most of the cooking.

Once, but only once, I saw the genteel and opaque surface of that family shattered—saw those three people suddenly in violent opposition to each other, like shards of splintered glass. (But what I have forgotten is the cause—what brought about that terrible explosion?)

The four of us, as so often, were seated at lunch. Emily was at what seemed to be the head of the table. At her right hand was the small silver bell that summoned Evelyn to clear, or to bring a new course. Harriet and I across from each other, Lawrence across from Emily. (There was always a tentativeness about Lawrence's posture. He could have been an honored guest, or a spoiled and favorite child.) We were talking in an easy way. I have a vivid recollection only of words that began to career and gather momentum, to go out of control. Of voices raised. Then Harriet rushes from the room. Then Emily's face reddens dangerously, the corners of her mouth twitch downward, and Lawrence, in an exquisitely icy voice, begins to lecture me on the virtues of reading Trollope. I am supposed to help him pretend that nothing has happened, but I can hardly hear what he is saying. I am in shock.

That sudden unleashing of violence, that exposed depth of terrible emotions might have suggested to me that the Farrs were not quite as I had imagined them, not the impeccable family in my mind—but it did not. I was simply and terribly—and selfishly—upset, and hugely relieved when it all seemed to have passed over.

During that summer, the Ouija board spoke only gibberish to Margot, or it answered direct questions with repeated evasions:

"Will I ever see Johnny Kilgore again, in this life?"

"Yes no perhaps."

"Honey, that means you've got no further need of the board, not right now. You've got to think everything out with your own heart and instincts," Dolly said.

Margot seemed to take her advice. She resolutely put the board away, and she wrote to Johnny that she wanted a divorce.

I had begun to notice that these days, on these sultry August nights, Margot and Dolly were frequently joined on their small excursions by a man named Larry—a jolly, red-faced man who was in real estate and who reminded me considerably of my father.

I said as much to Margot, and was surprised at her furious reaction. "They could not be more different, they are altogether opposite. Larry is a Southern gentleman. You just don't pay any attention to anyone but those Farrs."

A word about Margot's quite understandable jealousy of the Farrs. Much later in my life, when I was unreasonably upset at the attachment of one of my own daughters to another family (unreasonable because her chosen group were all talented musicians, as she was), a wise friend told me that we all could use more than one set of parents —our relations with the original set are too intense, and need dissipating. But no one, certainly not silly Dolly, was around to comfort Margot with this wisdom.

The summer raced on. ("Not without dust and heat," Lawrence several times remarked, in his private ironic voice.) The roses wilted on the roof and the banks next to the road. The creek dwindled, and beside it honeysuckle leaves lay limply on the vines. For weeks, there was no rain, and then, one afternoon, there came a dark torrential thunderstorm. Harriet and I sat on the side porch and watched its violent start—the black clouds seeming to rise from the horizon, the cracking, jagged streaks of lightning, the heavy, welcome rain. And, later, the clean smell of leaves and grass and damp earth.

Knowing that Margot would be frightened, I thought of calling her, and then remembered that she would not talk on the phone during storms. And that night she told me, "The phone rang and rang, but I didn't think it was you, somehow."

"No."

"I had the craziest idea that it was Johnny. Be just like him to pick the middle of a storm for a phone call."

"There might not have been a storm in New Orleans."

But it turned out that Margot was right.

The next day, when I rode up to the Farrs' on my bike, Emily was sitting out in the grass where I had first seen her. I went and squatted beside her there. I thought she looked old and sad, and partly to cheer her I said, "You grow the most beautiful flowers I've ever seen."

She sighed, instead of smiling as she usually did. She said, "I seem to have turned into a gardener. When I was a girl, I imagined that I would grow up to be a writer, a novelist, and that I would have at least four children. Instead, I grow flowers and write book reviews."

I was not interested in children. "You never wrote a novel?"

She smiled unhappily. "No. I think I was afraid that I wouldn't come up to Trollope. I married rather young, you know."

And at that moment Lawrence came out of the house, immaculate in white flannels.

He greeted me, and said to Emily, "My dear, I find that I have some rather late appointments, in Hillsboro. You won't wait dinner if I'm a trifle late?"

(Of course she would; she always did.)

"No. Have a good time," she said, and she gave him the anxious look that I had come to recognize as the way she looked at Lawrence.

Soon after that, a lot happened very fast. Margot wrote to Johnny (again) that she wanted a divorce, that she intended to marry Larry. (I wonder if this was ever true.) Johnny telephoned—not once but several times. He told her that she was crazy, that he had a great job with some shipbuilders near San Francisco—a defense contract. He would come get us, and we would all move out there. Margot agreed. We would make a new life. (Of course, we never knew what happened to the girl.)

I was not as sad about leaving the Farrs and that house, that town, those woods as I was to be later, looking back. I was excited about San Francisco, and I vaguely imagined that someday I would come back and that we would all see each other again. Like parting lovers, Harriet and I promised to write each other every day.

And for quite a while we did write several times a week. I wrote about San Francisco—how beautiful it was: the hills and pastel houses, the sea. How I wished that she could see it. She wrote about school and friends. She described solitary bike rides to places we had been. She told me what she was reading.

In high school, our correspondence became more generalized. Responding perhaps to the adolescent mores of the early nineteen-forties, we wrote about boys and parties; we even competed in making ourselves sound "popular." The truth (my truth) was that I was sometimes popular, often not. I had, in fact, a stormy adolescence. And at that time I developed what was to be a long-lasting habit. As I reviewed a situation in which I had been ill-advised or impulsive, I would reënact the whole scene in my mind with Harriet in my own role—Harriet cool and controlled, more intelligent, prettier. Even more than I wanted to see her again, I wanted to *be* Harriet.

Johnny and Margot fought a lot and stayed together, and gradually a sort of comradeship developed between them in our small house on Russian Hill.

I went to Stanford, where I half-heartedly studied history. Harriet was at Radcliffe, studying American literature, and writing poetry.

We lost touch with each other.

Margot, however, kept up with her old friend Dolly, by means of Christmas cards and Easter notes, and Margot thus heard a remarkable piece of news about Emily Farr. Emily "up and left Lawrence without so much as a by-your-leave," said Dolly, and went to Washington, D.C., to work in the Folger Library. This news made me smile all day. I was so proud of Emily. And I imagined that Lawrence would amuse himself, that they would both be happier apart.

By accident, I married well—that is to say, a man whom I still like and enjoy. Four daughters came at uncalculated intervals, and each is remarkably unlike her sisters. I named one Harriet, although she seemed to have my untidy character.

From time to time, over the years, I would see a poem by Harriet Farr, and I always thought it was marvellous, and I meant to write her. But I distrusted my reaction. I had been (I was) so deeply fond of Harriet (Emily, Lawrence, that house and land) and besides, what would I say—"I think your poem is marvellous?" (I have since learned that this is neither an inadequate nor an unwelcome thing to say to writers.) Of course, the true reason for not writing was that there was too much to say.

Dolly wrote to Margot that Lawrence was drinking "all over the place." He was not happier without Emily. Harriet, Dolly said, was traveling a lot. She married several times and had no children. Lawrence developed emphysema, and was in such bad shape that Emily quit her job and came back to take care of him—whether because of feelings of guilt or duty or possibly affection, I didn't know. He died, lingeringly and miserably, and Emily, too, died a few years later—at least partly from exhaustion, I would imagine.

Then, at last, I did write Harriet, in care of the magazine in which I had last seen a poem of hers. I wrote a clumsy, gusty letter, much too long, about shared pasts, landscapes, the creek. All that. And as soon as I had mailed it I began mentally rewriting, seeking more elegant prose.

When for a long time I didn't hear from Harriet, I felt worse and worse, cumbersome, misplaced—as too often in life I had felt before. It did not occur to me that an infrequently staffed magazine could be at fault.

Months later, her letter came—from Rome, where she was then living. Alone, I gathered. She said that she was writing it at the moment of receiving mine. It was a long, emotional, and very moving letter, out of character for the Harriet that I remembered (or had invented).

She said, in part: "It was really strange, all that time when Lawrence was dying, and God! so long! and as though 'dying' were all that he was doing—Emily, too, although we didn't know that—all that time the picture that moved me most, in my mind, that moved me to tears, was not of Lawrence and Emily but of you and me. On our bikes at the top of the hill outside our house. Going somewhere. And I first thought that that picture simply symbolized something irretrievable, the lost and irrecoverable past, as Lawrence and Emily would be lost. And I'm sure that was partly it.

"But they were so extremely fond of you—in fact, you were a rare area of agreement. They missed you, and they talked about you for years. It's a wonder that I wasn't jealous, and I think I wasn't only because I felt included in their affection for you. They liked me best with you.

"Another way to say this would be to say that we were all three a little less crazy and isolated with you around, and, God knows, happier."

An amazing letter, I thought. It was enough to make me take a long look at my whole life, and to find some new colors there.

A postscript: I showed Harriet's letter to my husband, and he said, "How odd. She sounds so much like you."

Alice Adams is the author of seven novels, including the best-selling *Superior Women* and *Caroline's Daughters*. Her stories have appeared frequently in *Prize Stories: The O. Henry Awards*, and she was editor of *The Best American Short Stories 1991*. Her most recent collection of stories is *After You've Gone*. Ms. Adams lives in San Francisco but she grew up in North Carolina, where "Roses, Rhododendron" is set.

JOHN UPDIKE

"I was born in 1932, in the small town of Shillington, Pennsylvania. My father was a high-school math teacher and my mother a frustrated writer—frustrated, that is, by her inability to crack the short-story market of the thirties and forties, though she received some encouragement from editors. Her typewriter was part of the scenery of my infancy, and perhaps I was less attracted to the art of writing than to the fun of using the typewriter. The first narrative of mine that I can recall involved cavepersons with names like Moogmoog and made it less than halfway down the page, single-spaced. Up to my college years I really was more zealous as a would-be cartoonist and light-verse poet than as a fictionist, though during several summer vacations I did begin novels—one a mystery novel, one what I now know is called a *Bildungsroman*. Neither got past page 100. In college I took courses that obliged me to turn in completed stories, and a kind of light dawned when one of my instructors, Kenneth Kempton, read aloud to us some then brand-new stories by J. D. Salinger. This kind of shapely shapelessness, with every casual sentence burnished to a subtle glow, seemed to me to fit life as I knew it, in the early fifties.

"My first story accepted for publication in a national magazine *(The New Yorker)* was written the June I got out of college. Titled 'Friends from Philadelphia,' it was one of a number I submitted in my early twenties; the difference between it and the many that came back was not blindingly apparent to me as I wrote it. I was conscious, however, of letting the material—Shillington, basically, in its innocent complexity; the undercurrents of family life; the animating force of sexual desire behind polite appearances—speak here a little more directly than hitherto, in a language of visualized acts and things, and I would urge upon all young writers this axiom: find the material, and the voice will take care of itself. As in human conversation, a preening voice, which enjoys itself too much, becomes quickly tedious, whereas a voice that delivers a tale, full of human pulse and recognizable circumstance, strikes us as mellifluous. In the matter of short stories, I have found that where the material feels solid under me the voice—the sentences, each with subject and predicate—naturally arises, and insists upon its own reverberations and integrity.

"While writing 'Separating,' which was composed in a week or so of mornings on Martha's Vineyard, in the coming-and-going company of several of my children, on a typewriter in my lap, all I had to do was let my characters speak, inserting in my own voice a few pictures like the fixed lock near the beginning and the lit window toward the end. The horizontal fluting on the aluminum side of the train that brings Dickie home, the tear-blurred matches that little John keeps lighting—these stick in my mind as moments when my voice sings out. The voice of fiction speaks in images, and I find mine when the images come abundantly, and interweave to make a continuous music."

SEPARATING

THE day was fair. Brilliant. All that June the weather had mocked the Maples' internal misery with solid sunlight—golden shafts and cascades of green in which their conversations had wormed unseeing, their sad murmuring selves the only stain in Nature. Usually by this time of the year they had acquired tans; but when they met their elder daughter's plane on her return from a year in England they were almost as pale as she, though Judith was too dazzled by the sunny opulent jumble of her native land to notice. They did not spoil her homecoming by telling her immediately. Wait a few days, let her recover from jet lag, had been one of their formulations, in that string of gray dialogues—over coffee, over cocktails, over Cointreau—that had shaped the strategy of their dissolution, while the earth performed its annual stunt of renewal unnoticed beyond their closed windows. Richard had thought to leave at Easter; Joan had insisted they wait until the four children were at last assembled, with all exams passed and ceremonies attended, and the bauble of summer to console them. So he had drudged away, in love, in dread, repairing screens, getting the mowers sharpened, rolling and patching their new tennis court.

The court, clay, had come through its first winter pitted and windswept bare of redcoat. Years ago the Maples had observed how often, among their friends, divorce followed a dramatic home improvement, as if the marriage were making one last effort to live; their own worst crisis had come amid the plaster dust and exposed plumbing of a kitchen renovation. Yet, a summer ago, as canary-yellow bulldozers gaily churned a grassy, daisy-dotted knoll into a muddy plateau, and a crew of pigtailed young men raked and tamped clay into a plane, this transformation did not strike them as ominous, but festive in its impudence; their marriage could rend the earth for fun. The next spring, waking each day at dawn to a sliding sensation as if the bed were being tipped, Richard found the barren tennis court—its net and tapes still rolled in the barn—an environment congruous with his mood of purposeful desolation, and the crumbling of handfuls of clay into cracks and holes (dogs had frolicked on the court in a thaw; rivulets had eroded trenches) an activity suitably elemental and interminable. In his sealed heart he hoped the day would never come.

Now it was here. A Friday. Judith was re-acclimated; all four children were assembled, before jobs and camps and visits again scattered them. Joan thought they should be told one by one. Richard was for making an announcement at the table. She said, "I think just making an announcement is a cop-out. They'll start quarrelling and playing to each other instead of focusing. They're each individuals, you know, not just some corporate obstacle to your freedom."

"O.K., O.K. I agree." Joan's plan was exact. That evening, they were giving Judith a belated welcome-home dinner, of lobster and champagne. Then, the party over, they, the two of them, who nineteen years before would push her in a baby carriage along Fifth Avenue to Washington Square, were to walk her out of the house, to the bridge across the salt creek, and tell her, swearing her to secrecy. Then Richard Jr., who was going directly from work to a rock concert in Boston, would be told, either late when he returned on the train or early Saturday morning before he went off to his job; he was seventeen and employed as one of a golf-course maintenance crew. Then the two younger children, John and Margaret, could, as the morning wore on, be informed.

"Mopped up, as it were," Richard said.

"Do you have any better plan? That leaves you the rest of Saturday to answer any questions, pack, and make your wonderful departure."

"No," he said, meaning he had no better plan, and agreed to hers, though to him it showed an edge of false order, a hidden plea for control, like Joan's long chore lists and financial accountings and, in the days when he first knew her, her too-copious lecture notes. Her plan turned one hurdle for him into four—four knife-sharp walls, each with a sheer blind drop on the other side.

All spring he had moved through a world of insides and outsides, of barriers and partitions. He and Joan stood as a thin barrier between the children and the truth. Each moment was a partition, with the past on one side and the future on the other, a future containing this unthinkable *now*. Beyond four knifelike walls a new life for him waited vaguely. His skull cupped a secret, a white face, a face both frightened and soothing, both strange and known, that he wanted to shield from tears, which he felt all about him, solid as the sunlight. So haunted, he had become obsessed with battening down the house against his absence, replacing screens and sash cords, hinges and latches—a Houdini making things snug before his escape.

The lock. He had still to replace a lock on one of the doors of the screened porch. The task, like most such, proved more difficult than he had imagined. The old lock, aluminum frozen by corrosion, had been deliberately rendered obsolete by manufacturers. Three hardware stores had nothing that even approximately matched the mortised hole its removal (surprisingly easy) left. Another hole had to be gouged, with bits too small and saws too big, and the old hole fitted with a block of wood—the chisels dull, the saw rusty, his fingers thick with lack of sleep. The sun poured down, beyond the porch, on a world of neglect. The bushes already needed pruning, the windward side of the house was shedding flakes of paint, rain would get in when he was gone, insects, rot, death. His family, all those he would lose, filtered through the edges of his awareness as he struggled with screw holes, splinters, opaque instructions, minutiae of metal.

Judith sat on the porch, a princess returned from exile. She regaled them with stories of fuel shortages, of bomb scares in the Underground, of Pakistani workmen loudly lusting after her as she walked past on her way to dance school. Joan came and went, in and out of the house, calmer than she should have been, praising his struggles with the lock as if this were one more and not the last of their long succession of shared chores. The younger of his sons for a few minutes held the rickety screen door while his father clumsily hammered and chiseled, each blow a kind of sob in Richard's ears. His younger daughter, having been at a slumber party, slept on the porch hammock through all the noise—heavy and pink, trusting and forsaken. Time, like the sunlight, continued relentlessly; the sunlight slowly slanted. Today was one of the longest days. The lock clicked, worked. He was through. He had a drink; he drank it on the porch, listening to his daughter. "It was so sweet," she was saying, "during the worst of it, how all the butchers and bakery shops kept open by candlelight. They're all so plucky and cute. From the papers, things sounded so much worse here—people shooting people in gas lines, and everybody freezing."

Richard asked her, "Do you still want to live in England forever?" *Forever:* the concept, now a reality upon him, pressed and scratched at the back of his throat.

"No," Judith confessed, turning her oval face to him, its eyes still childishly far apart, but the lips set as over something succulent and satisfactory. "I was anxious to come home. I'm an American." She was a woman. They had raised her; he and Joan had endured together to raise her, alone of the four. The others had still some raising left in them. Yet it was the thought of telling Judith—the image of her, their first baby, walking between them arm in arm to the bridge—that broke him. The partition between his face and the tears broke. Richard sat down to the celebratory meal with the back of his throat aching; the champagne, the lobster seemed phases of sunshine; he saw them and tasted them through tears. He blinked, swallowed, croakily joked about hay fever. The tears would not stop leaking through; they came not through a hole that could be plugged but through a permeable spot in a membrane, steadily, purely, endlessly, fruitfully. They became, his tears, a shield for himself against these others—their faces, the fact of their assembly, a last time as innocents, at a table where he sat the last time as head. Tears dropped from his nose as he broke the lobster's back; salt flavored his champagne as he sipped it; the raw clench at the back of his throat was delicious. He could not help himself.

His children tried to ignore his tears. Judith, on his right, lit a cigarette, gazed upward in the direction of her too energetic, too sophisticated exhalation; on her other side, John earnestly bent his face to the extraction of the last morsels—legs, tail segments—from the scarlet corpse. Joan, at the opposite end of the table, glanced at him surprised, her reproach displaced by a quick grimace, of forgiveness, or of salute to his superior gift of strategy. Between them, Margaret, no longer called Bean, thirteen and large for her age, gazed from the other side of his pane of tears as if into a shop window at something she coveted—at her father, a crystalline heap of splinters and memories. It was not she, however, but John who, in the kitchen, as they cleared the plates and carapaces away, asked Joan the question: *"Why is Daddy crying?"*

Richard heard the question but not the murmured answer. Then he heard Bean cry, "Oh, no-oh!"—the faintly dramatized exclamation of one who had long expected it.

John returned to the table carrying a bowl of salad. He nodded tersely at his father and his lips shaped the conspiratorial words "She told."

"Told what?" Richard asked aloud, insanely.

The boy sat down as if to rebuke his father's distraction with the example of his own good manners. He said quietly, "The separation."

Joan and Margaret returned; the child, in Richard's twisted vision, seemed diminished in size, and relieved, relieved to have had the bogieman at last proved real. He called out to her—the distances at the table had grown immense—"You knew, you always knew," but the clenching at the back of his throat prevented him from making sense of it. From afar he heard Joan talking, levelly, sensibly, reciting what they had prepared: it was a separation for the summer, an experiment. She and Daddy both agreed it would be good for them; they needed space and time to think; they liked each other but did not make each other happy enough, somehow.

Judith, imitating her mother's factual tone, but in her youth off-key, too cool, said, "I think it's silly. You should either live together or get divorced."

Richard's crying, like a wave that has crested and crashed, had become tumultuous; but it was overtopped by another tumult, for John, who had been so reserved, now grew larger and larger at the table. Perhaps his younger sister's being credited with knowing set him off. "Why didn't you *tell* us?" he asked, in a large round voice quite unlike his own. "You should have *told* us you weren't getting along."

Richard was startled into attempting to force words through his tears. "We *do* get along, that's the trouble, so it doesn't show even to us —" *That we do not love each other* was the rest of the sentence; he couldn't finish it.

Joan finished for him, in her style. "And we've always, *especially*, loved our children."

John was not mollified. "What do you care about *us?*" he boomed. "We're just little things you *had.*" His sisters' laughing forced a laugh from him, which he turned hard and parodistic: "Ha ha *ha.*" Richard and Joan realized simultaneously that the child was drunk, on Judith's homecoming champagne. Feeling bound to keep the center of the stage, John took a cigarette from Judith's pack, poked it into his mouth, let it hang from his lower lip, and squinted like a gangster.

"You're not little things we had," Richard called to him. "You're the whole point. But you're grown. Or almost."

The boy was lighting matches. Instead of holding them to his cigarette (for they had never seen him smoke; being "good" had been his way of setting himself apart), he held them to his mother's face, closer and closer, for her to blow out. Then he lit the whole folder—a hiss and then a torch, held against his mother's face. Prismed by tears, the flame filled Richard's vision; he didn't know how it was extinguished. He heard Margaret say, "Oh stop showing off," and saw John, in response, break the cigarette in two and put the halves entirely into his mouth and chew, sticking out his tongue to display the shreds to his sister.

Joan talked to him, reasoning—a fountain of reason, unintelligible. "Talked about it for years . . . our children must help us . . . Daddy and I both want . . ." As the boy listened, he carefully wadded a paper napkin into the leaves of his salad, fashioned a ball of paper and lettuce, and popped it into his mouth, looking around the table for the expected laughter. None came. Judith said, "Be mature," and dismissed a plume of smoke.

Richard got up from this stifling table and led the boy outside. Though the house was in twilight, the outdoors still brimmed with light, the lovely waste light of high summer. Both laughing, he supervised John's spitting out the lettuce and paper and tobacco into the pachysandra. He took him by the hand—a square gritty hand, but for its softness a man's. Yet, it held on. They ran together up into the field, past the tennis court. The raw banking left by the bulldozers was dotted with daisies. Past the court and a flat stretch where they used to play family baseball stood a soft green rise glorious in the sun, each weed and species of grass distinct as illumination on parchment. "I'm sorry, so sorry," Richard cried. "You were the only one who ever tried to help me with all the goddam jobs around this place."

Sobbing, safe within his tears and the champagne, John explained, "It's not just the separation, it's the whole crummy year, I *hate* that school, you can't make any friends, the history teacher's a scud."

They sat on the crest of the rise, shaking and warm from their tears but easier in their voices, and Richard tried to focus on the child's sad year—the weekdays long with homework, the weekends spent in his room with model airplanes, while his parents murmured down below, nursing their separation. How selfish, how blind, Richard thought; his eyes felt scoured. He told his son, "We'll think about getting you transferred. Life's too short to be miserable."

They had said what they could, but did not want the moment to heal, and talked on, about the school, about the tennis court, whether it would ever again be as good as it had been that first summer. They walked to inspect it and pressed a few more tapes more firmly down. A little stiltedly, perhaps trying now to make too much of the moment, Richard led the boy to the spot in the field where the view was best, of the metallic blue river, the emerald marsh, the scattered islands velvety with shadow in the low light, the white bits of beach far away. "See," he said. "It goes on being beautiful. It'll be here tomorrow."

"I know," John answered, impatiently. The moment had closed.

Back in the house, the others had opened some white wine, the champagne being drunk, and still sat at the table, the three females, gossiping. Where Joan sat had become the head. She turned, showing him a tearless face, and asked, "All right?"

"We're fine," he said, resenting it, though relieved, that the party went on without him.

In bed she explained, "I couldn't cry I guess because I cried so much all spring. It really wasn't fair. It's your idea, and you made it look as though I was kicking you out."

"I'm sorry," he said. "I couldn't stop. I wanted to but couldn't."

"You *didn't* want to. You loved it. You were having your way, making a general announcement."

"I love having it over," he admitted. "God, those kids were great. So brave and funny." John, returned to the house, had settled to a model airplane in his room, and kept shouting down to them, "I'm O.K. No sweat." "And the way," Richard went on, cozy in his relief, "they never questioned the reasons we gave. No thought of a third person. Not even Judith."

"That *was* touching," Joan said.

He gave her a hug. "You were great too. Very reassuring to everybody. Thank you." Guiltily, he realized he did not feel separated.

"You still have Dickie to do," she told him. These words set before him a black mountain in the darkness; its cold breath, its near weight affected his chest. Of the four children, his elder son was most nearly his conscience. Joan did not need to add, "That's one piece of your dirty work I won't do for you."

"I know. I'll do it. You go to sleep."

Within minutes, her breathing slowed, became oblivious and deep. It was quarter to midnight. Dickie's train from the concert would come in at one-fourteen. Richard set the alarm for one. He had slept atrociously for weeks. But whenever he closed his lids some glimpse of the last hours scorched them—Judith exhaling toward the ceiling in a kind of aversion, Bean's mute staring, the sunstruck growth in the field where he and John had rested. The mountain before him moved closer, moved within him; he was huge, momentous. The ache at the back of his throat felt stale. His wife slept as if slain beside him. When, exasperated by his hot lids, his crowded heart, he rose from bed and dressed, she awoke enough to turn over. He told her then, "Joan, if I could undo it all, I would."

"Where would you begin?" she asked. There was no place. Giving him courage, she was always giving him courage. He put on shoes without socks in the dark. The children were breathing in their rooms, the downstairs was hollow. In their confusion they had left lights burning. He turned off all but one, the kitchen overhead. The car started. He had hoped it wouldn't. He met only moonlight on the road; it seemed a diaphanous companion, flickering in the leaves along the roadside, haunting his rearview mirror like a pursuer, melting under his headlights. The center of town, not quite deserted, was eerie at this hour. A young cop in uniform kept company with a gang of T-shirted kids on the steps of the bank. Across from the railroad station, several bars kept open. Customers, mostly young, passed in and out of the warm night, savoring summer's novelty. Voices shouted from cars as they passed; an immense conversation seemed in progress. Richard parked and in his weariness put his head on the passenger seat, out of the commotion and wheeling lights. It was as when, in the movies, an assassin grimly carries his mission through the jostle of a carnival—except the movies cannot show the precipitous, palpable slope you cling to within. You cannot climb back down; you can only fall. The synthetic fabric of the car seat, warmed by his cheek, confided to him an ancient, distant scent of vanilla.

A train whistle caused him to lift his head. It was on time; he had hoped it would be late. The slender drawgates descended. The bell of approach tingled happily. The great metal body, horizontally fluted, rocked to a stop, and sleepy teen-agers disembarked, his son among them. Dickie did not show surprise that his father was meeting him at this terrible hour. He sauntered to the car with two friends, both taller than he. He said "Hi" to his father and took the passenger's seat with an exhausted promptness that expressed gratitude. The friends got in the back, and Richard was grateful; a few more minutes' postponement would be won by driving them home.

He asked, "How was the concert?"

"Groovy," one boy said from the back seat.

"It bit," the other said.

"It was O.K.," Dickie said, moderate by nature, so reasonable that in his childhood the unreason of the world had given him headaches, stomach aches, nausea. When the second friend had been dropped off at his dark house, the boy blurted, "Dad, my eyes are killing me with hay fever! I'm out there cutting that mothering grass all day!"

"Do we still have those drops?"

"They didn't do any good last summer."

"They might this." Richard swung a U-turn on the empty street. The drive home took a few minutes. The mountain was here, in his throat. "Richard," he said, and felt the boy, slumped and rubbing his eyes, go tense at his tone, "I didn't come to meet you just to make your life easier. I came because your mother and I have some news for you, and you're a hard man to get ahold of these days. It's sad news."

"That's O.K." The reassurance came out soft, but quick, as if released from the tip of a spring.

Richard had feared that his tears would return and choke him, but the boy's manliness set an example, and his voice issued forth steady and dry. "It's sad news, but it needn't be tragic news, at least for you. It should have no practical effect on your life, though it's bound to have an emotional effect. You'll work at your job, and go back to school in September. Your mother and I are really proud of what you're making of your life; we don't want that to change at all."

"Yeah," the boy said lightly, on the intake of his breath, holding himself up. They turned the corner; the church they went to loomed like a gutted fort. The home of the woman Richard hoped to marry stood across the green. Her bedroom light burned.

"Your mother and I," he said, "have decided to separate. For the summer. Nothing legal, no divorce yet. We want to see how it feels. For some years now, we haven't been doing enough for each other, making each other as happy as we should be. Have you sensed that?"

"No," the boy said. It was an honest, unemotional answer: true or false in a quiz.

Glad for the factual basis, Richard pursued, even garrulously, the details. His apartment across town, his utter accessibility, the split vacation arrangements, the advantages to the children, the added mobility and variety of the summer. Dickie listened, absorbing. "Do the others know?"

"Yes."

"How did they take it?"

"The girls pretty calmly. John flipped out; he shouted and ate a cigarette and made a salad out of his napkin and told us how much he hated school."

His brother chuckled. "He did?"

"Yeah. The school issue was more upsetting for him than Mom and me. He seemed to feel better for having exploded."

"He did?" The repetition was the first sign that he was stunned.

"Yes. Dickie, I want to tell you something. This last hour, waiting for your train to get in, has been about the worst of my life. I hate this. *Hate* it. My father would have died before doing it to me." He felt immensely lighter, saying this. He had dumped the mountain on the boy. They were home. Moving swiftly as a shadow, Dickie was out of the car, through the bright kitchen. Richard called after him, "Want a glass of milk or anything?"

"No thanks."

"Want us to call the course tomorrow and say you're too sick to work?"

"No, that's all right." The answer was faint, delivered at the door to his room; Richard listened for the slam that went with a tantrum. The door closed normally, gently. The sound was sickening.

Joan had sunk into that first deep trough of sleep and was slow to awake. Richard had to repeat, "I told him."

"What did he say?"

"Nothing much. Could you go say goodnight to him? Please."

She left their room, without putting on a bathrobe. He sluggishly changed back into his pajamas and walked down the hall. Dickie was already in bed, Joan was sitting beside him, and the boy's bedside clock radio was murmuring music. When she stood, an inexplicable light—the moon?—outlined her body through the nightie. Richard sat on the warm place she had indented on the child's narrow mattress. He asked him, "Do you want the radio on like that?"

"It always is."

"Doesn't it keep you awake? It would me."

"No."

"Are you sleepy?"

"Yeah."

"Good. Sure you want to get up and go to work? You've had a big night."

"I want to."

Away at school this winter he had learned for the first time that you can go short of sleep and live. As an infant he had slept with an immobile, sweating intensity that had alarmed his babysitters. In adolescence he had often been the first of the four children to go to bed. Even now, he would go slack in the middle of a television show, his sprawled legs hairy and brown. "O.K. Good boy. Dickie, listen. I love you so much, I never knew how much until now. No matter how this works out, I'll always be with you. Really."

Richard bent to kiss an averted face but his son, sinewy, turned and with wet cheeks embraced him and gave him a kiss, on the lips, passionate as a woman's. In his father's ear he moaned one word, the crucial, intelligent word: *"Why?"*

Why. It was a whistle of wind in a crack, a knife thrust, a window thrown open on emptiness. The white face was gone, the darkness was featureless. Richard had forgotten why.

JOHN UPDIKE

John Updike, one of America's greatest living writers, has twice won the Pulitzer Prize—for *Rabbit Is Rich* in 1981 and, in 1991, for *Rabbit at Rest*, the concluding volume in the much-acclaimed quartet whose publication spanned thirty years. In addition to his novels, volumes of essays, poems, memoir, and children's books, Mr. Updike has published eight collections of short stories. He lives in Massachusetts.

JUDITH ROSSNER

"My mother wanted me to be a writer and academic and not to get bogged down, as she had, in nonsense like getting married, having children and engaging in domestic activities. I began dictating poetry to her before I entered school and, once I'd begun, never stopped writing, which earned me praise both at home and in school. At the age of nineteen I dropped out of C.C.N.Y., married, learned how to cook and sew, had children, gardened and so on, without ever ceasing to write.

"The moral of this story is that, handled correctly, children will do what their parents want them to do. And/or the opposite.

"I guess the most important thing I can say about my writing voice, or voices, is that they're the smartest voices I have, often teaching me things I didn't know I knew. A writer character in my novel *His Little Women* calls herself the Ouija Broad. She's stealing one of my lines. More than once I've begun a book meaning to tell some story from a character's point of view, only to have some other story, or character, take over from her.

"I'd always been fascinated by libel, and my novel *August* began life as the story of a writer who is being sued for libel by a woman he had lived with. He consults a psychoanalyst, Lulu Shinefeld, who is familiar with such cases, and has a love affair with her. After about 120 pages I got bored with the love story. Since the libel suit wasn't coming into my head, and since their work is the most interesting part of most people, I decided to show Dr. Shinefeld with one of her patients. The next morning I sat down at my typewriter (You heard me. Typewriters and first husbands have their flaws but life was surely easier then.) and caused a patient to enter the doctor's office. She must have been waiting there all the while, because she promptly took over the book.

"It wasn't the last time this sort of thing would happen to me. Having written '116th Street Jenny' and determined that I would next go back to the *August* sequel I'd been meaning to write, I found myself, instead, picking up at the point where '116th Street Jenny' left off."

116TH STREET JENNY

AT the beginning of the seventies my parents and my sister and brother were all stable, married and teaching in universities, so that even if the sixties hadn't provided me with the rhetoric to explain dropping out or smoking dope, I might have felt the need to distinguish myself by doing both. In the middle of my sophomore year at Oberlin, I returned to Manhattan and with four friends moved into an apartment on the Lower East Side that was to be a sort of urban commune, a group disengaged from life's crude competitions and petty quarrels, unmoved by the need to plan for the future or take account of the past. Our arrangement lasted into the following autumn only because each of us was away for much of the time during the warm months.

In the early winter, I asked my parents if I could come home. They consented, on the condition that I return to college, Barnard or Columbia's School of General Studies. They both taught at Columbia (my mother, modern art, my father, twentieth-century European history) so that aside from the schools' other virtues, they would not have to pay tuition. Although I didn't yet know this, my parents had applied for joint grants that would take them to the Orient during the following academic year. They were concerned about renting to strangers or allowing the apartment to remain vacant and were delighted to find, once I'd moved back in, that I had calmed down, was not interested in sharing my living quarters with friends for more than an occasional night, and was willing to act, at least for a while, as though I valued a college degree.

I had grown up in that apartment, one of those huge Riverside Drive aeries built in the days when most large apartments had some provision for a maid, that is to say, for a person without the space and comfort requirements of the normal human being. There were four good-sized bedrooms off a back hallway, then a tiny one next to the kitchen. Moving back, I suggested to my parents that since I'd been away and we'd all had more privacy, it might be just as well for me to sleep in the tiny room; the large bedroom that was still more or less mine could be a study and a second guest room. Of the rooms that had been my sister's and brother's, one had been furnished to suit the housekeepers they hired periodically then fired because they were inadequate as cooks.

My parents had an extremely strong interest in good food. Women hired in spite of their unfamiliarity with our favorites were given a certain length of time to learn them and were fired if they had not. From an early age I had exhibited a strong affinity for the domestic, a tendency to be in the kitchen while everyone else in the family was off at a desk. As I grew up I had become increasingly helpful in the matter of training new housekeeper-cooks, increasingly capable of making a good meal myself. It had been a puzzle to me when I was young, and remained a source of disgruntlement as I grew up, that my parents, for all their culinary obsessiveness, could not accept the notion of food's drawing me more powerfully than academic subjects did.

That summer, while visiting their friends, the painters Eleanora and Jason Stonepark at their home outside Florence (They'd become friendly when Eleanora was my mother's student), my parents had found and hired to come home with them a woman named Anna Cherubini. Anna's children were running the family's mom-and-pop style restaurant in Florence, for which Anna had been the chef until her husband died the year before. For reasons having to do with the wife of one of her sons, Anna had begun to feel superfluous. After some deliberation she had consented to come to the States to work for my parents "for a little while," tending the apartment and preparing her lovely meals.

In the course of learning from Anna how to cook her specialties, which included fresh pasta (still unknown in New York outside of the West Village, East Harlem and a couple of high-priced restaurants), and of helping her to translate the recipes for my parents' other favorites, I not only became a much better cook than I'd been, but also learned to speak a decent Italian. Then, in the spring of 1974, Anna got a call from her family saying she was needed at the restaurant. *Rapido*. She went.

All this is by way of explaining how it came to be that on a weekday night when Eleanora and Jason (Her maiden name was Stein, she'd married the person then named Jason Park, and in those days when the debate over keeping one's "own" name, that is to say, one's father's name, hadn't even begun, they had legally changed their last names to Stonepark) were coming to dinner and both my parents had heavy teaching schedules, I cooked and served the meal. When Jason, learning it was my work, congratulated me in Italian and I answered in kind, he asked, still in Italian, whether I had spent time in Italy.

I liked Jason and did not attempt to impress him with the extent of the rebelliousness that had encouraged my parents to send me to camp instead of taking me on their travels, as they had my sister and brother. I was a change-of-life baby, born to a mother whose two real children had been civilized academics almost from birth. I told Jason I'd gone to camp with my friends.

He nodded. "I can understand that. Do your friends share your interest in Italy?"

I grinned. "Pizza's about it."

I wasn't even certain it was legitimate for *me* to claim an affinity. I had become fluent in Italian because of my interest in food and the amount of time I spent with Anna. The food romance and the big-city romance had yet to marry, taking New Yorkers on the honeymoon, and exotic, or even just plain foreign, foods were not available throughout Manhattan as they would be in another few years. Anna, during her first weeks in New York, had always been looking for ingredients she did not, when they were located, deem satisfactory. My parents had initiated her to Zabar's, and Zabar's was all right for cheese and coffee beans (although she would not acknowledge that the Reggiano bought there was identical to the Parmesan she'd grated in Italy), and she would make do with canned tomatoes when the real ones ("*pommadori nostrani*") went out of season. But it was I who had brought her to the Village and lower Second Avenue for sausages, fresh herbs and bread she judged good enough to eat, not to speak of vegetables like finocchio and broccoli rabe that would remain unknown in non-Italian neighborhood stores until the Koreans took them over. My Italian had come in the learning of the food even as I would become facile with Spanish, which I'd studied in school but never used outside it, when Cuban-Chinese restaurants began to flourish along Broadway. I never learned French because I didn't know anyone who spoke it and the cookbooks were available in English.

Jason asked if I knew that he and Eleanora had a home and vineyard in Gaiole that my parents occasionally visited. When I told him I'd heard about the place, which sounded wonderful, he said, "Perhaps you'll come and visit us sometime and see for yourself." I smiled, dismissing the remark as a pleasantry, but as it turned out, he had something quite specific in mind. The following week I accepted an invitation to Sunday lunch at his home. When I asked my father if he knew why I'd been invited, he shrugged and said that I had impressed Jason. When I pushed him to speculate, he said that one of the things he liked about Jason was that if the other man had something to discuss with me, he'd bring it up directly with me. I might bear in mind that my mother had a very high opinion of Eleanora Stonepark's talent. Eleanora was one of a minuscule number of students she'd ever chosen to see after graduation.

Thus did my father inform me (I would understand it this way only later) that I was on my own but in a place where I must not dishonor my family.

The Stoneparks lived in the building on Park Avenue where Jason had been raised. The rooms were large and pleasant, the walls full of paintings by Jason *or* Eleanora. That is to say, their paintings did not share rooms. Jason's huge oils, hung in the living room with its big, soft chairs and sofas in shades of teal and gray, were powerful and somber abstracts in black, brown, and gray, easier to describe than to look at, impossible to trace, at least with this viewer's brain, to the gentle soul who took an interest in other humans his wife did not appear to share. On the other hand, it became apparent as I followed him from the living room, through a long hallway with hundreds of family photographs, into a large, bright room hung with Eleanora's paintings which was clearly the place where the family spent most of its time, that what *he* did not share with *her* was a talent for painting wonderful pictures.

The walls, the curtains, and the chair upholstery were all a soft yellow that seemed to provide sunshine even on a day as gray as this one. The floor was covered by a sisal rug. Tall windows looked out on a terrace that ran around two sides of the room. Aside from those windows and their curtains, Eleanora's paintings and sketches were the only objects at eye level or higher.

I'm not sure whether I actually gasped as I entered the room and saw them, or whether memory has me dramatizing a real reaction, but I found them wonderful. Along with many watercolors (Later, seeing Chianti country, my first thought was that the landscape was almost as beautiful as it had been in her paintings) were several oils, a few drawings of the (naked) female form, and a couple of portraits of (dressed) men. When I try now to remember specific pictures, I see one vast swirl of brilliant color.

I was standing at the room's entrance, thunderstruck—artstruck, if you will—with Jason just ahead and slightly to one side of me, when I heard a child's voice mimicking an engine's sound, and at the same moment was knocked into Jason by that child as he barged past us into the room, thrusting before him the largest toy engine I'd ever seen.

Jason straightened us out and said, as we watched the boy, who was then eight, circling the room, still making his engine noises, "Well, now you've met Evan, and I'm sure if you've survived at all, you're the better for it . . . You are all right, aren't you?"

"Mmm," I said. "I'm fine, thank you."

My eyes returned to the nearest paintings while my brain wished for a few minutes alone with them before I was required to talk or to deal with Evan. It was not to be.

"Who're you?" the boy asked.

"My name is Caroline," I said.

"Are you my mother's friend or my father's?" he asked.

I replied with a straight face that actually *my* mother and father were friends of *his* mother and father.

"So how come you're the one who's here?" he asked.

Now I allowed myself to smile. "They invited me."

"They must want you to do something," he said. "Are you a good baby-sitter?"

Beside me Jason groaned good-naturedly and without serious concern.

"I don't know if I'm a good one or a bad one because I've never done it," I replied.

"Oh, well," Evan said. "You will if you come to Italy with us."

I turned to Jason and was about to tell him I hoped his invitation wasn't about that because I'd promised my parents I'd go to summer school when Eleanora Stonepark breezed into the room in a flowing black velvet hostess gown of a sort I'd never seen before. Eleanora never wore anything but black, a phenomenon in those days in a way that it isn't now.

I find myself, as I try to describe the condition of my brain at that moment, going to a framed page of Eleanora's ink drawings I would see only later, as we sat at lunch. There was a tree in full leaf and flower. Next to it stood the same tree, recognizable but beginning to break into cubes and other less specific forms. And next to that a mad swirl unrecognizable as the tree in any way you could specify but that you understood to represent its soul.

Eleanora fixed on me one of her more dazzling smiles. (Later I would grade them as Earth and Sky Light Up; Earth Only; The Neighborhood; The Room. Her mouth made the same motions with each of them, yet the range in effect was staggering.) "So," she said, "are we thinking it all might work?"

I stared at her. I had the feeling gates had closed behind me.

"My dear," Jason said, moving to her side, putting a protective arm around her although I was quite certain it was I who required protection, "Caroline has just arrived and I haven't told her about our idea."

"Oh, God," said Eleanora, a model of adorable dismay, "I hope I haven't ruined things."

"You have never in your entire life ruined anything," Jason assured her. "You have simply made it desirable for me to explain why we've invited Caroline to lunch though we don't know her very well." He turned to me. "May I offer you a glass of wine? The food will be ready any moment."

I nodded.

He pressed a buzzer on the wall and a maid appeared. She was asked to bring us some white wine. Eleanora had settled into an easy chair with a copy of *Vogue,* which she was flipping through as though some question had been answered and she could go back to thinking about whatever really concerned her. When the maid brought our wine, Evan said he wanted to have lunch with us. Eleanora, without looking up from her *Vogue,* said in Italian that this didn't seem like a good idea (I don't know if this is the time to mention that Eleanora was an upper-middle-class Jewish girl from Manhattan who was then thirty-eight years old, to her husband's fifty), at which point Jason steered the protesting child into the kitchen.

"Let me tell you about the farmhouse in Gaiole," he said when the three of us had settled at the table. Our first course, prosciutto and melon, was in front of us. "It's an easy drive from Florence and we do it often. We spend as much time as we can at the house, we both have studios right there, and when Evan's on vacation, we're normally there. Our usual help, or at least those of our help who've had the care of Evan, generally accompany us. But now, for a variety of reasons, we'd like to change that. Aside from any other consideration, he hasn't been learning Italian in the natural, you might say, manner we'd hoped he might. In the way you yourself did."

Jason explained that it hadn't occurred to him to look for someone like me until the night of our dinner, when it had come to seem that each and every problem they had in Italy, beginning with the language matter, going on to the way they liked to eat (the female half of the live-in couple was "a Sicilian with an exceedingly limited repertory," but transporting another cook to and home from the farm was a nuisance, aside from the matter of many Italian women's balking at trying French dishes), and ending with the matter of having someone look after Evan whom he could actually enjoy, might be solved if I would come to Italy with them. This summer was particularly important because Eleanora was having her first major show the following winter and would be working even harder than she usually did.

"Now," Jason said, "you're not even to try to make a decision immediately. You are to think about the possibilities and enjoy your lunch."

But the two were mutually exclusive: Was I allowed to explain about my parents' insistence that I go to summer school to make up for lost time, or would I find out when I reached home that this had been a breach of faith?

In between the melon and prosciutto and our main course, a lovely fish salad I could barely choke down, Eleanora began sketching, using a piece of paper from a pile and a pencil from a mug filled with sharp ones that rested on top of it near her place at the table. A couple of times I thought I felt her glancing at me and as we ate (Periodically she put down her fork and sketched for a moment) I became convinced that I was her subject. My indecision about how to find out was made keener by the fact that there was very little conversation about anything, and no apparent sense, on anyone else's part, of something missing.

I had grown up at a table where four active academics reviewed aloud what they were doing, frequently with a sense of competition and/or urgency. Now, with my sister and brother gone, my parents discussed whatever concerned the two of them. I knew many details of their current grant proposals, geared to their eagerness to go together to Japan: My mother wanted to study the influence of Japanese art on Impressionism between the two World Wars; my father's proposal had to do with relations between Germany and Japan. Here, Eleanora's very presence made table chat superfluous, although Jason volunteered an occasional comment or offered me food.

I contained myself until I'd finished my fish salad but then I leaned over to see what was on her paper.

"You have a good face," Eleanora said. "I'd love to paint you some time." She smiled winsomely, turning around the paper to show me a pencil sketch instantly recognizable as the Real Me.

I was dumbstruck.

"She's upset by my picture," Eleanora said gravely to Jason.

"Oh, no," I croaked, gasped, "It's wonderful! I can't believe you just . . ."

She had *seen* me in some way that my parents, never mind my parents, *my best friends* did not. I was viewed by my friends as easy to get along with. It was my enjoyable peculiarity to be interested in what girls had once *thought* they were interested in—most particularly, of course, in cooking. My friends' mothers had gone to Barnard, Vassar, and Radcliffe then married, learned to cook, read good books, and joined the PTA. Their daughters, whether because they'd been galvanized by the new Women's Movement or because they had some specific interest, intelligence, and/or drive, wanted to be lawyers (mostly), doctors (practicing down South or serving in the Peace Corps), or, in one case, to run for Congress. When we had group sleepovers, I cooked. If they apologized for putting me to work, I told them I didn't mind. But saying I didn't mind had nothing to do with being *agreeable;* it was the *truth.* I found the preparation of the food as compelling as the gossip, which I also enjoyed. Because the other girls did not share my pleasure in cooking, they attributed my willingness to virtue.

Eleanora Stonepark, in the most casual way imaginable, had seen my dark side. The face she'd drawn was of a quirky and difficult human being whose mouth had a distinctly sardonic turn—as my fleshly one did not. At the same time, the flaws in the person she had portrayed, perhaps because that person seemed intelligent and self-possessed, were tolerable to me in a way that the flaws in her model were not.

After lunch, Eleanora picked up the piece of paper with my soul on it and appeared to be about to leave the table.

"May I have it?" I asked without debating whether it was acceptable to do this. My voice trembled and I was sure that I would cry if she said no, while I could not imagine why she would want to hold on to it.

"Of course you may," Eleanora said graciously. "But first . . . I want to play with it for a while, you know?"

I nodded, mesmerized.

"What I think," she said, suddenly playful, "is that by the time we've had our lovely summer, I'll be ready to part with it. For all I know, I'll have done a painting, by then."

I could barely breathe.

"You don't understand," I gasped. "I'd *love* to go to Gaiole." I probably would have wanted to go even without this cleverly mounted bait. Whether it was a judgment about her work or a reaction to her presence, or both, I had been conquered by Eleanora Stonepark, a woman who could do something extraordinary that no one else I knew could do. And then, of course, there was Jason, a moderate and easy person who would always be around if Eleanora's artistic temperament or my own somewhat anti-authoritarian bias should pose any problems. "I just *can't.* I promised my parents I'd go to summer school."

"Are you telling us," Eleanora asked gravely, "that the only thing standing between you and a summer in Gaiole is your parents?"

I nodded.

Eleanora, who understood better than I her power over my parents, not to say over me and various others, smiled.

That evening my parents began the conversation that would end in my receiving permission to go to Gaiole by saying that they understood the only thing preventing me from working for the Stoneparks was their own "perhaps foolish" insistence that I push through six credits in school, and ended it by extracting a promise from me—as though I'd pleaded with them to go—to work harder than I otherwise would have during the term that followed.

This is not a story about my summer with the Stoneparks, which, if it wasn't always easy, was tolerable for a variety of reasons.

Gaiole was hot but very beautiful and there was a large pool on the land in back of the house. (Most of the vineyard was on a hillside across a winding dirt road, the road that led to the *autostrada* on which we drove to Florence.) The household was run around Eleanora's preparation for her show. (It was understood that Jason was not under similar pressure, but unless I'm mistaken, there was always some reason for the house's being run around Eleanora.) It worked because most of her time was spent in the studio. My primary job was to keep Evan out of her way when he wasn't with his father. This became easier as Evan forgot about my being a hired hand and came actually to enjoy my company.

My absorption in the physical matter of everyday life made it easier in a variety of ways for me to get along with Eleanora. When I was challenged about food (or almost anything else), I became intent upon solving the problem. This also worked with Evan, who got hooked into kitchen matters and began to learn Italian from me very much as I had learned it from Anna. Finally, I was fascinated by the operation of the vineyard, and my fascination led to a very agreeable affair with Angelo Ferrante, who managed that vineyard and several others owned by non-residents. (The Stoneparks' had its own beautiful label, designed by Eleanora. Framed in gold and printed in brilliant colors, its central image was a goblet of red wine standing on a rock in front of a green shrub.)

Angelo, a lively-homely man of thirty-one given to pronouncements like, "All American girls are spoiled"—always in Italian, of course—had a wife and five children in Sicily, and was casually flirtatious but became friendly when I spoke a non-touristy Italian he could readily understand. (He had English but wouldn't use it.) Our affair began less than two weeks after I'd arrived at the beginning of June, but our friendship commenced on the day I told him, in Italian, of course, that he should not judge all American women by Eleanora Stonepark.

Angelo stopped in his tracks. We'd been walking between two rows of vines set on the big old tree branches that were his favorite stakes. He turned to me, hands on hips, and said something that translates as, "Ah, finally! I thought there must be something wrong with you, that you never complain about the bitch!"

I felt more defensive than conspiratorial—yet, oddly, it was Eleanora, not myself, I felt compelled to defend, with a little speech about how artists couldn't be held to the same standard as the rest of us. This infuriated Angelo, who said that artist or no artist, he'd kick the shit out of me if I ever acted like that.

I don't want to convey the impression that I precisely *liked* Eleanora, whose behavior was very much that of the royal personage. But my sense of her as an artist whose work gave me great pleasure dominated my reactions, muted them when required. She was the way artists were *supposed* to be. And then of course there was my powerful desire, never voiced but with me every day of my life in Gaiole, to own the promised drawing or—too much really to hope for—the painting she might choose to do.

Whether because veneration prevented me from getting angry at otherwise insufferable words and deeds, or because of the convenience Evan's attachment to me afforded, or because of my increasing skill at cooking Italian haute cuisine, or because I didn't happen to have any of the habits that got under Eleanora's skin and turned her into a screeching lunatic (talking a lot, saying *gezundheit* or God bless you when someone sneezed, and spending more than a few seconds gnawing the meat remaining on bones when most had been cut off are crimes I remember offhand), Eleanora's behavior toward me was very much the same when we reached the middle of August as it had been in June.

It had been understood when I took the job that I would leave Gaiole a week before the family did to register for my classes. As the time for my departure drew close, Angelo grew melancholy over the prospect of my disappearance, *la mia sparizione.* An early member of the first generation of females more scared of falling in love than of getting pregnant, I had assured myself, the first time I allowed him to show me an absent neighbor's villa, that it was OK to go to bed because I wasn't going to fall in love with him. Now, as he pressed me to delay my leavetaking, I was finding that whether or not you called it love, if you liked it, you didn't want it to end.

Jason had taken Evan into town on some errand. Angelo and I were lying on a tarp at the far end of the vineyard. The sunset was particularly beautiful and the aroma of ripening grapes filled the air. I told him that I didn't actually have to be at school until the end of that week and he said he had business in Sicily, we could drive down the coast together. He would bring me to the airport down there. Nobody (Nobody was always Eleanora, whose name he was loathe to pronounce) would even have to know. He would exchange my ticket, which Jason had already given me. I could tell the Stoneparks that he, Angelo, was taking me to the airport. He began immediately to plan for our trip to Palermo, where he had wine business. He'd always said that Sicily was *un altro mondo,* and it was a world I had to see.

I did not mention our trip in explaining to Jason that I wouldn't require transportation to the airport. Attempting to avoid a direct lie, I said something like, "Angelo is going to drive me." Jason simply nodded, but that evening, which was a week before the date I was scheduled to leave, Eleanora joined Jason, Evan, and me for dinner for the first time in days.

I had been wondering more and more whether she remembered about my picture, and if so, whether she would give it to me. I had a strong enough sense of her to know that I was best off not being the one to raise the issue; nothing riled Eleanora more than the suggestion of an act outside forces required her to perform. But I also knew that I was not going to leave without making a strong effort to get what I'd been promised. (I spent a great deal of time trying to decide which I'd prefer, the drawing or a watercolor. In one fantasy, she gave me both because she was so pleased with my summer's work. In another, she painted a marvelous portrait, parting with it reluctantly because she loved it—me—so much.)

Eleanora, a master of psychology when it might effect some improvement in her life, spent a lot of time praising the green soup I'd made the day before, yawning, and telling us that no matter how exhausted she was, she simply had to go back to work after dinner, she couldn't believe she had only two weeks left in Gaiole. Jason ate doggedly during this monologue but at some point he put down his soup spoon. He looked perturbed. He did not meet my eyes—or Eleanora's.

"I'm not sure which upsets me more," Eleanora said, looking directly at me for the first time since she'd begun, "my having to leave in two weeks or your leaving in one."

Evan looked up from his soup. "One? One? What do you mean, leaving in one?"

I smiled uncomfortably. "I thought your parents must have told you already," I said. "I have to be in school the week before you do."

"I am the guilty party," Eleanora announced bravely as Evan looked from her to his father and back. "It was too awful. I didn't even remind myself and I certainly never thought to tell anyone. Not that I've been able to think about anything except the paintings. I don't have three-quarters . . . No, that's not true . . . I'm lying to myself . . . I don't have *half* the number of pictures I promised Bruce and Leon. I really don't know what I'm going to do." Her eyes brimmed with tears and her voice shook.

In what might have been the masterstroke of his entire childhood, Evan picked this moment not only to deliver a monologue that was at once a tribute to me and a threat about his behavior when/if I left, but to do it *in Italian*, which he normally refused to employ when his parents were around, but saved for the time when we were alone. Weeks earlier I had given Jason permission to spy on us to determine that this was true. Not only was it true, but I was aware that Evan occasionally looked up words to save as surprises. He had developed a crush on me, and I had a more difficult day if he happened to see me talking to Angelo.

"I don't believe this is happening now," he declaimed in patchy but adequate Italian. "Tell me you're kidding around. Tell me the plans I've made don't have to be thrown away. All the things we wanted to do that we didn't have time for . . . All the . . . And I can't believe you didn't even *tell* me!"

"I thought you knew, love," I responded, also in Italian. "And I have to tell you, I'm impressed with your vocabulary, and I bet your folks are, too."

"Impressed! Impressed!" Eleanora said dramatically. "But what good will it do if you're not here to talk with him?"

This was classic Eleanora, unable to imagine a use for his Italian, now that he had it, beyond keeping him busy and out of her way. I started to respond, if only for Evan's sake, saying I thought it would do a great deal of good because he enjoyed it, as witness the vocabulary he had, which meant he was—when Eleanora interrupted to ask me on which day I was actually required to register and Evan went around the table to sit on his father's lap.

I stopped dead in my verbal tracks, unable to answer because I hadn't thought out a lie and the truth would tell her I had an extra few days I could choose to remain.

"The truth is," I lied, "I don't exactly remember. I think it's the fourth, but—"

"Would you like to call home and ask?" Eleanora interrupted.

"Uh, no, uh, not really," I said. "I mean, even if it's a couple of days later, I need some time to get myself organized, buy some clothes, that kind of thing."

I looked at Jason, who was toying with his piece of bread, embarrassed, I believe, at what his wife was doing to me. Which didn't mean he was about to jump in on my side, a reality I was mulling over even as Eleanora began to speak.

"Well, I was just thinking . . . I have to admit I was thinking about it because Jason mentioned your leaving, and I was looking at that little sketch of you, you know, I have it on the bulletin board over my drafting table . . . Or maybe you don't . . . I don't know how recently you've been in the studio . . ." (I had been in the studio once at the beginning of the summer but had not been invited again.) "Anyway, what I was thinking was about how I meant to do a little watercolor portrait, you were so pleased with the sketch, and now I won't have time to do it."

I thought—I might have imagined it because it's so perfect but I don't actually believe I did—I thought I saw Jason blush, although he didn't look up. Perhaps if he hadn't been a witness I would have caved in at that moment, promised to stay if Eleanora would do the watercolor. Evan was looking back and forth between us, not commenting on the transaction, which he already understood to be just that, and one in which his interests coincided with his mother's.

"How's Angelo?" she asked.

My breath was taken away. It was the first time she'd ever so much as mentioned Angelo, who dealt only with Jason.

"He seems to be fine," I said stiffly.

"Is Angelo the reason you don't need us to take you to the airport?" she asked.

"Yes," I said, trying to figure out what I would do if she asked any more questions.

She was smart enough not to. After a pause, she pushed away her plates, set both elbows on the table, her chin on her hands. "OK. Here's the deal I have to offer. Stay till we go and I'll do the watercolor."

I couldn't breathe, much less cry, though I had a strong desire to do both. Something prevented me from caving in right away. I turned to Evan and told him that no matter what I decided, I cared about him and would stay in touch when we were all in New York. Eleanora's words were repeating themselves in my head, and when I had delivered this message to him, I turned back to his mother.

"You said you'd do it," I pointed out. "You didn't say it would be mine."

She smiled. "My goodness, love, you've gotten so suspicious. Of course it will be yours. I'm only doing it for you."

Note the tense; if I did not assume she would have her way, Eleanora already did. And of course she'd forgotten her original notion that my face was too fascinating *not* to paint.

The stumbling block was Angelo. While I wanted the painting even more than I wanted to drive south with him, I was scared of his reaction when I told him I couldn't go. With Jason's permission, I called my parents, who would be leaving for Japan in between the time I'd been supposed to arrive and the time I would if I stayed, to ask if one of them would register for me if I remained in Gaiole until the Stoneparks left. It is fair to say they were happier to do it for this reason than they would have been for another. Then I told Eleanora that I would remain if she would give me the picture before that extra week arrived. Until then, I would hold on to the ticket Jason had already given me, for the earlier flight out of Florence.

"Trusting little soul, aren't you," Eleanora commented, at once pleased by her work's importance to me and irritated by the doubt that was implicit in my condition.

"I trust," I said calmly (I'd been preparing the line from the moment I awakened that morning), "that your work is the most important thing to you and that you'll do whatever you have to do to keep it going."

She let out a hearty laugh, and slammed a hand down on the table.

"Is that the one you had waiting?" she asked. "Is that why Jason got Evan out of here?"

In fact, Evan was angry with me, which was why he had chosen to go to the tennis court with Jason. I'd explained to him about school and about how the whole arrangement had been made before I even really *knew* him and had nothing to do with anything but preparing for school, but my explanation hadn't altered his feelings. That evening, when Eleanora had capitulated, telling me that if I wasn't "too busy," I should visit her studio in the evening, I told Evan I hoped to be able to remain with him in Gaiole until the end, after all. He became provisionally friendly without displaying any interest in how or why this had been arranged. Informed that we were all set, he became affectionate again.

Angelo was even less easily mollified, my explanation of why I could not go down the coast being greeted by an extraordinary diatribe punctuated by references to secrets he hadn't told me yet that he would have revealed on the trip and curses I hadn't learned yet but could identify as such. It was only when he expressed incredulity that I should care about anything done by that *puttana*, and I told him maybe *I* was the whore because her paintings were worth big money in the States (a lie I didn't yet know would turn into the truth), that his rage diminished and he became interested in the matter of what her work was worth.

At nine o'clock, when Evan had gone to his room with his father, I walked around the grounds for a few minutes, then went into the house and upstairs to the back, which faced north and held Eleanora's studio. (Jason's faced south. He was said not to mind the summer heat or to need the northern light preferred by painters.) I knocked twice and waited for what seemed like a very long time until she called to me to enter. I did so.

It was a breathtaking room, even at night, when the glass wall at its far end was no longer letting in the entire countryside and all the (indirect) light in the world. Eleanora's unfinished paintings were propped against the otherwise bare walls, giving the lie to her suggestion that she worked on only one at a time. Finished works stood in racks against one wall. Her easel and worktable were near the window. She sat at the former, facing it and nearly invisible to me.

"Sit down," she ordered. "I'll be with you in a minute."

Was she going to make a great show, I wondered, of rushing to finish the painting she really *should* be working on in order to deal with my selfish demands? I decided I couldn't anticipate all the possibilities and simply had to remain firm. My terms were my terms. I relaxed somewhat into this posture and spent my waiting time admiring the unfinished pictures, surreptitiously watching her work, wondering what she was painting. It's probably easy to imagine how I felt when after perhaps fifteen or twenty minutes, her left hand came around the easel to beckon to me, and I walked, nearly on tiptoe, to the easel, and she brought me around to stand beside her, and I was looking at a delicate and still-damp watercolor that had obviously begun in the pencil sketch of me.

I gasped.

There I was. My straight brown hair, my murky brown-green eyes, the blue turtleneck sweater I'd worn to their house for lunch months earlier and hadn't worn since but which she'd apparently remembered as she apparently remembered every visual detail she'd once taken in, and, most importantly, the sense of her subject's power that had first captivated me, perhaps even more emphatic than it had been in the drawing.

I couldn't have minded less. That is to say, if she had been looking for a little revenge upon the youngster who was extracting a price, she'd failed to find it. In any event, I doubt she could have made me look bad enough to anger me and I don't believe she'd actually tried. Her artistic conscience, surely the strongest of any of the kinds of conscience she might have possessed, would not have allowed her to turn me into anyone substantially more monstrous than I was. I prepared to have her hand me the painting and wave me out of the room, but if I was already more than satisfied with the work, she was not. I sat for more than an hour as she painted and fussed and finally, when she'd announced that she was finished and I, with tears in my eyes, had told her it was wonderful, she promised to look in the attic the next morning for a frame that fit. I could have it in the evening.

I did.

I had it and I treasured it. Even if the summer had been far more difficult, possessing my picture would have made it worthwhile. When we all went to Florence that weekend for our farewell visit to Evan's favorite restaurant, I picked up a large, touristy satchel whose sole virtue was that it would safely hold the painting (between two pieces of corrugated board) during the trip home. On the plane I sat stiffly with the bag in back of me, the corrugated board cushioned in turn by laundry on both sides. I was unwilling to put it under the seat in front lest it slide away. Reaching home (my parents had left two days earlier), I decided to return to the big bedroom that had once been mine and use the maid's room for my guests. The apparent reason was that, with my parents gone, most of the apartment was unoccupied. The real reason was that, fond as I was of the little room, it had no wall that could do justice to my painting.

I hung it so that it faced me as I lay in my bed in the big room. Had it been feasible, I would have removed not only all other decoration but the two narrow bookcases standing against that wall. I did set them as far as possible from one another. The portrait of the interesting human being perceived by Eleanora Stonepark hung solitary, nearly regal, between them. It would not be exaggerating to say that although I didn't think about her all the time, the world scared me less when she was with me than it did when I was alone. She was my promise that somewhere inside me there was a real person who might someday do something interesting.

I'd returned to school the previous year because it was my side of an agreement, not because academia had come to seem more inviting. I felt alienated from the younger students by what I'd learned out in the real world, but I lacked the desire to pass on reality's wisdom (Dope or no dope there were dishes to be washed, and so on). With all the time

I'd spent congratulating myself on not thinking that I was in love with Angelo, I was dismayed to find, as I walked around the campus looking at scraggly-haired Jewish suburbanites and Midwestern blonds who rolled reefers as easily as they'd once caught pop flies, that I missed him more than I'd dreamed I might in the days when I was giving up his company to acquire my painting.

Not that I ever regretted the exchange. It was, after all, my future self, as revealed to me by Eleanora's painting, who assured me of being a real person with interests I would develop, if only I were allowed to do so. In fact, at some point during the autumn it occurred to me that it was no coincidence that the person who had portrayed me as an interesting human being was also a person who seriously appreciated my cooking.

I began to daydream about attending the Culinary Institute in upstate New York, a fantasy that seemed a little more realistic than the notion of getting my parents to pay my tuition at one of the great cooking schools in France. Eventually the very possession of a daydream about something I wanted to do diminished my sense of being empty and uninteresting enough to allow me to make a few new friends.

Perhaps it's simplest for me to quote the letter from the Root-Pierson Gallery, dated November 21st of that year, in its entirety.

Dear Miss Weiss:

As you probably know, the Root-Pierson Gallery is planning an exhibition of the paintings of Eleanora Stonepark to open in New York on January 1st of next year and, after a month here, to travel to Boston and Washington.

We understand from Mrs. Stonepark that you own one of her few watercolor portraits, *116th Street Jenny,* which we would like to include in the exhibition. We would need to have it in the gallery by December 20th. We would, of course, take care of all transportation and insurance costs.

We very much look forward to hearing from you, at which time we will send the Gallery's formal loan agreement. And of course we hope you will attend the opening. Eleanora Stonepark will be present.

We will be sending you the announcement and invitation at a later date.

Sincerely,
Bruce Pierson

It took me very little time to frame my response:

Dear Mr. Pierson:
I have your letter asking me to lend you my picture. I am sorry that I cannot do this.

Sincerely,
Caroline Weiss

There was no question of my being willing to risk the kind of damage that might be done to my precious picture. I hesitated only over the matter of explaining my need to live with the person I did not and never would think of as 116th Street Jenny. But the phrases that came to my mind when I considered such an explanation were at once so precise and so melodramatic ("I'm sorry, I can't live without her, she is my promise of a future") that I decided to forgo an explanation.

At the beginning of the school term Evan had called, wanting me to spend that Saturday afternoon with him. I'd been unable to do this. When I'd called him a couple of Saturdays later because I had some time, Jason had told me Evan was visiting a friend. He went on to say that they thought of me often and felt the summer had been very good for Evan. I'd not talked to either father or son since then, but now I had a call from Jason. The matter of lending the painting had left my mind completely once my letter was mailed, and when I heard his voice, I assumed he was calling because I had failed to do so.

"Hi," I said, "I want you to know, it's not that I haven't been thinking about him, but I'm so busy, and when you said he was getting along, I guess I just . . ."

"I wasn't actually calling about Evan," Jason said. "I was calling about the business of lending the painting."

"Oh, yes," I said quickly, still far from understanding the nature of the ground I was treading upon. "I can understand why they want it, but . . . If anyone knows how much I love it, how important it is to me . . ."

"Yes, of course," Jason said. "That was why Eleanora gave it to you. She could see how you felt about the work."

I did not awaken to the gravity of the matter. Nor did it occur to me to point out that her motives had been somewhat more complex and selfish than he was suggesting.

"Mmm," I said. "I mean, I love all her stuff, but then there's the business of . . . I mean, she *saw* me, you know? I never felt as though anyone knew who I was, I didn't know *myself,* and then Eleanora *saw* me."

"Ah, yes," Jason said after a moment. "Well, what she's seeing at the moment is a young woman who won't lend her back her own painting when she needs it desperately for a show."

Now I heard him. It did not cross my mind that I should part with my portrait, but I realized, finally, that my refusal was not a simple matter.

"I don't," I began after a while. "I don't . . ." My voice cracked. I had no way to finish the sentence. For the first time since they'd gone overseas, I wished desperately that my parents were home. Maybe they'd have come to my aid, explained to Jason better than I could how the painting . . . I began to cry, covering the receiver so he would not hear me.

"Caroline?" he said after a moment. "Are you there?"

"Yes," I said, sobbing.

"Can you tell me . . . Are you afraid you won't get it back at the end of the show?"

I was afraid of not surviving its absence, but I knew this was crazy and I mustn't say it.

"What I really . . . It's the only thing on the wall. The wall will be . . . I mean, I look at it all the time. She's *with* me. I can't imagine . . . I mean, it's a very long time, Jason." Until then the difference between three days and three months had seemed unimportant. Without realizing it, I had begun to bargain. "You know, I only took the job because I loved her work so much."

"Well," Jason said after a long pause, "what if we gave you one of Eleanora's sketches to keep on the wall while we had the painting?"

"Gave me?" I repeated moronically. "Sketches?"

He misunderstood, thought me in better command than I was of the conversation's content and bargaining for a better offer.

"I'd offer you another watercolor, but the whole problem is that there are only a few watercolors Eleanora feels are good enough for the show, and there's no other portrait, and she hasn't been working in watercolor, and she usually works very slowly, that painting was a freak, in a sense, and she's particularly fond of it. She didn't want to let go of it when she finished, but she never would have dreamed of failing to honor her part of your bargain."

Particularly since I wouldn't have stayed the extra week if she hadn't.

The thought passed through my brain but once again made no effort to drop into my mouth. In fact, I was silent as I tried to absorb what he was saying and understand what it meant to me and my portrait. Jason, a sophisticated slave to the Empress Eleanora, waited for me to grasp the magnitude of what she had done for me, the ignominious nature of my response.

"I'm sorry," I finally said, not apologizing but expressing regret at the difficulty of our situation.

"Well," Jason said, "I accept your apology, but of course you haven't accepted my solution to our problem."

My problem was his telephone call, which I wanted desperately to be finished with.

"I have an idea," Jason said in a different, perhaps artificially hearty voice. "I think you and I should go to Eleanora's studio, where you'll be able to look at her sketches and the paintings that won't be in the show and find one you'd like to put in Jenny's place. How does that sound?"

"OK," I managed to say after a very long time in which my brain hadn't accepted the notion, but had come to understand I had to go along with it.

"All right, then," Jason said. "There's someone waiting for me and I have to go, now, but I'll be in touch in a day or two. Bye."

I said good-bye and hung up, then returned to my room, stretched out on the bed, looked at my picture, and gradually allowed my saner self to come into control of my brain. Loving the picture didn't mean I had to see it every day of my life. I loved people I didn't see for years at a time and then, there they were again, and it was just as it had been before. If I missed my girl (Her name was not and never would be Jenny, damn it, much less the demeaning 116th Street Jenny; if I'd had to be given a name other than Caroline, at least I might have been consulted) terribly, I could visit the gallery . . . at least the one in New York. And it wasn't as though I would miss her because of a space on the wall. Someone—or something—would be there, keeping her place for her and for me. I could almost feel good about Jason's solution. Certainly I could wish it had come more easily. In any event, it would be exciting, to visit Eleanora's studio. I could almost look forward to hearing from Jason.

But two days later there was another letter from Bruce Pierson that made me regret having opened myself to the whole idea.

Dear Miss Weiss:

This is to confirm your telephone conversation with Jason Stonepark in which you agreed that you would go to Mrs. Stonepark's studio to select a substitute for the watercolor you will lend to the Root-Pierson Gallery's exhibition of her work, January 1st through March 31st.

We have enclosed a loan form which we ask you to return to us as soon as possible so the pick-up can be arranged. Thanks so much for your cooperation in this matter.

Sincerely,
Bruce Pierson

I was as angry as though I'd never agreed to the substitution plan. Did they really believe I was going to turn over my painting and then sit around waiting for a phone call? What kind of an idiot did they think I was? Even if Eleanora Stonepark hadn't been a difficult and duplicitous human being, Jason a subservient one who would say anything to appease her, I would have been a fool to consent to such an arrangement. I sat down and fired off a letter to Pierson that I can't bear to quote here, but which began with the suggestion that they were treating me not only like a child, but a dumb one, and ended by saying there were no circumstances under which I would permit my painting to leave and I didn't want to hear from any of them again.

I did not.

Eleanora's show opened to great acclaim, remained open for a month in New York, closed. I paid little attention. I was determined to do enough schoolwork so my parents wouldn't claim I'd failed to keep my side of our bargain, and I had a reasonable social life by this time. When my summer money had run out, I'd taken a four-night-a-week baby-sitting job with a neighborhood mother, Jackie Liebman, a working divorcée who was attending night school. I got along with Jackie as well as with her children (she couldn't get over the fact that I happily cooked meals and baked bread and cookies with the children) and in the spring, she told me she and some friends had rented a house on Fire Island for the summer and needed a responsible housekeeper-babysitter. I explained that I would be in summer school but could make a weekend—perhaps even a three- or four-day weekend arrangement. Jackie found someone who would take the other days until the week in August when I finished school. That week coincided with my parents' return from Japan. I did not see them, although we spoke on the phone, until I returned to New York with the Liebmans after Labor Day.

They were pleased with the way I'd kept the apartment, satisfied with what I told them of school, and glad I'd found a job that did not interfere with my schoolwork. (I would return to part-time baby-sitting for Jackie.) I judged them unready for a conversation about cooking school, nor did I have any reason to rush. I had applied to the Culinary Institute of America but knew there were many more applications than there were places and I was far from certain I'd be admitted. They admired Eleanora's painting and exclaimed over her generosity in having given it to me. I told them I'd made a deal with her, but the story of the deal appeared not to alter their vision of her virtue, and I could not make myself confess to what had happened later. My natural reluctance combined with the obligations accumulated during their year in the Orient to delay the day of reckoning.

Then, on a Sunday evening in late autumn, when my father and I were reading the *Times* in the living room, my mother came in with a funny expression on her face and, leaning against the wall next to the entrance, asked, "What happened with the Stoneparks?"

Startled, terribly anxious, I tried to remember what I'd decided to say when this question arose. All I could think of was my father's telling me, a zillion years ago, what a high opinion my mother had of Eleanora.

"The Stoneparks," I repeated.

My father looked up.

"What happened . . . basically . . . is . . . they wanted my painting."

"*Your* painting?" my mother said. "You mean *her* painting that she was so extraordinarily generous as to give you?"

"She wasn't exactly being generous," I said, feeling the muddy water come up around my eyes. "We made a deal where she would give it to me if—"

"Did you or did you not refuse to let her borrow her own painting for her show?"

I nodded. This was going to be even worse than I'd feared. My mother's eyes closed and her body—could it be my imagination?—sagged. After a moment she felt her way along the wall to the nearest chair, a stiff-backed uncomfortable job she occasionally piled magazines on but that none of us ever sat in. My father had put down his newspaper.

"I didn't exactly refuse," I said. "At least I wasn't *going* to. I mean, I was, then I wasn't, and then I got this awful letter." They were staring at me in horror. I had begun to plead. "You don't know what went on with that painting. You don't know what I went through to get it. It was the only reason I took the job in the first place, she sort of promised it, and then when I finally got it, I mean, I had to stay an extra week and not take a trip I wanted to take and then I only—"

"Maybe," my father said, "you had better bring us the letter."

"Letters," I corrected automatically.

"Letters," he said.

My mother's eyes were still closed. Her mouth trembled. I went to my room, finding the correspondence easily since it wasn't with all the stuff I kept on the top of my desk because I might need to look at it again. Now I could see that was wishful thinking. I was going to have to make clear the extent of the picture's importance to me; it wasn't just the idea of the promise, I cared about the *picture.* If they didn't understand that, they'd never forgive me for angering their friends. They'd kick me out of the house before I ever mentioned the Culinary Institute!

I returned to the living room. They were sitting together on the sofa, my father's arm around my mother. They looked as though they'd come from a funeral.

"There's something I want to explain before I give you the letters," I said.

"You can explain later," my father said.

I handed them over. He did not look at me, nor did my mother. I turned to leave the room and was ordered, in a voice I'd seldom heard, to sit down. I sat in the chair my mother had used earlier and waited, trying, with only limited success, to breathe.

"Oh, my God," was the only thing my mother said—so quickly that I thought there must be some mistake.

When they had finished, they looked up at me. They appeared to be considerably more astonished than John Hinckley's parents would be, some years later, upon learning of their son's attempt to kill Ronald Reagan.

"What on earth possessed you?" my mother asked, her voice breaking. "How could you possibly . . ." But she trailed off, failing to find the words to describe so heinous a crime.

"That's what I was trying to explain," I said. "I couldn't imagine doing without it. I hardly had it on the wall when they wanted it back and I couldn't . . ." My voice broke as I pleaded for understanding. "I love her. It. I couldn't imagine parting with her. She was my company when I was alone here. I—"

"Of *course* you love it," my mother broke in. "Of *course* you . . ." But she was still unable to cope with the enormity of my offense and once again, her words trailed off.

"The issue is not whether you love the painting," my father said.

"The issue is whether you have the right to refuse an artist the chance to show her own work."

I was silenced. My brain hadn't framed it that way at any point. It didn't change the way I felt about Eleanora or the painting but it gave me something to think about. In truth, I hadn't thought of it as hers but as my own. What my father was saying was that even if it was *my* painting, it was *her* work. It had become mine without ever ceasing to be hers.

"Well," he finally said, "as long as we're having this painful conversation, you might as well tell us your version of the story so we can figure out what we can possibly say to Eleanora."

With some difficulty, I told them about the summer, reminding them of that first Sunday, when I'd come home dazzled by the sketch she'd promised me. I said that dealing with Eleanora had been the most difficult part of my job but I hadn't minded because of my respect for her as an artist. I told them about the friend I'd made in Gaiole who was going to show me southern Italy and how, as I planned to leave exactly when I'd said before I consented to take the job that I had to leave, she had bribed me with the picture to stay.

"But you didn't have to leave," my mother interrupted. "You said you were going to take a trip with your friend."

"That's not the issue," my father said wearily. "Let's stay with the issue."

I was no longer certain what the issue was, but I proceeded with the stuff I'd been sure of before this matter of who owned a painting had arisen, my tale of the imperious Eleanora and the servant who wanted to please because she valued the reward.

"All right," my father finally said. "So, you made your bargain and you got your picture. Eleanora kept her side of your bargain."

"I got the picture first. I was afraid—"

"Yes, yes." He waved a hand in the air. "You told us about all that. You hung your picture. And then you got the letter from Bruce Pierson. You did not understand, I gather, that it is the overriding custom to give an artist back her own work whenever she wants to show it. I have never until now heard of anyone's refusing such a request."

I hung my head in shame. Tears rolled down my cheeks and dropped onto my cotton T-shirt.

"So, you wrote your unacceptable letter, saying you could not do this, at which point Pierson spoke to Jason, who called you and made the extraordinarily generous offer to let you have something else while this was in the show."

"I accepted!" I pointed out eagerly. "I was going to do it. Jason said he'd bring me to the studio, and I could choose something to stay in its place, something she didn't need for the show, and I was still miserable about parting with my picture, but I was going to do it!"

"And then?"

"And then I got the letter."

"This one." My father held up Pierson's letter saying that after I'd signed the form, my painting would be picked up.

I nodded.

"And?"

"Look at it!" I pleaded. "I promise to give them my picture as soon as they want it and all they promise is that at some later date I'll receive a call and go to the studio! They could have taken the picture the next day and let me replace it a week before the show got back! I could have had a bare wall for months! I wasn't sure I'd ever get it back!"

My father was looking at the correspondence again. My mother was staring at me as though trying to figure out how she'd managed, for all these years, not to notice the degree of monstrousness of the creature to whom she'd given birth.

"The loan agreement," my father said, "specifies a pick-up/delivery date of December 22nd or 23rd, that is, a week before the show opens, and a return date of two or three days after it returns to New York. Why should you think for a moment that they wouldn't honor it?"

I stared at him, thunderstruck. Whatever he was reading was utterly foreign to me. It wasn't that I'd forgotten. I'd never seen it! Was it possible I'd never even looked at the agreement that came with the letter? Yes, I had to admit, not only was it possible, but I could almost remember slamming down the letter and the papers stapled to it without a glance at anything past the first page.

"Why do you look so surprised?" my father asked. Beside him, my mother, her arms wrapped around herself, keened like a captain's wife upon hearing that the ship has gone down. "Is it possible that you never even bothered to look at the agreement?"

"Bothered isn't right," I cried out—before crying in. "It wasn't about *bothering.*" I hadn't even looked at the contract but had been relieved to have an excuse—an arbitrariness to the letter—to go back on my promise to Jason. "It's that I freaked when I thought about it, and when I read the letter, I just . . . It was as though . . . I couldn't let someone like that have me. I mean, the picture of me!"

My mother, unable to tolerate this babble, stood up and walked out of the living room. My father sat, shaking his head, looking down at the papers in his hand and then back at me as though some new indictment of my behavior had presented itself and he needed only to find a way to frame it. Finally he stood, walked over to me holding the papers like something that might give him a disease, and handed them to me.

"I can only hope," he said, "that you have a somewhat better understanding of the trust involved in holding an artist's work than you did before. Not that I have reason to believe it will help. Our friendship with Eleanora is probably lost, and it would be difficult to exaggerate how painful that will be for us if it turns out to be true. You might want to try writing her a letter, now that you realize what they had every right to expect of you. If you decide to write, you'd better show me the letter before you send it."

Who could tell what I, a monster of no sensibility, might say to further offend the Lady Eleanora? There was no danger, in any event, of my writing to her. If I'd been told I would have to leave home if I failed to write, I think I would have returned to my room and packed my bags instead of locking the door, throwing myself down on the bed and crying, as I did, until I fell asleep. I don't know what I dreamed, but I remember quite precisely the moment when, having slowly awakened and gradually pulled myself together just enough to get up and head for the bathroom, I realized that I had walked past my picture—*the* picture—without once looking in its direction. That is to say, I had looked at the floor to make sure I would *not* see it.

Gradually, over a period of months, Jenny ceased to cause me pain when I glanced her way. But I could not recapture the pleasure of looking. Where once I'd played games with her—peeking, for example, to see if her eyes followed me when I walked across the room, as the Mona Lisa's eyes were said to follow one—now she was just there, like a lot of other people. 116th Street Jenny. If she was the person I would become, it was ridiculous to have assumed that I would like that person. I would live with her the way one lived with, or at least dealt with, a lot of people one wasn't crazy about.

Life went on. Gradually my parents became civil, then casual, and finally friendly enough so that I didn't skitter into my bedroom at every free moment but might hang around for some conversation or a meal. The process was assisted immeasurably when my mother published a monograph from a lecture on women artists she had given at Columbia in which she claimed there was no painter on the American scene more talented than Eleanora Stonepark. I could not swear that it was only after the monograph's publication in *Art News* that the two couples became friendly again. I do know it was then that the name Stonepark (as in Dinner 8-Stoneparks) began to appear on the calendar hanging on the refrigerator door.

I broached to my parents the notion that cooking school, not a university, was where I belonged, and they told me that while they were not unsympathetic, university, not cooking school, was what they would support. I resisted pointing out that they didn't *have* to support Columbia. I tried arguing with them on the grounds that they, with their active devotion to good food, should find it not simply reasonable but utterly delightful that I wanted to become a chef. They said that as far as they could see, I was already a chef and could improve my skills as much as I needed to at home. Home was for cooking and school was for learning the subjects that would enrich my mental life and provide me with a profession suitable to a young woman from an academic family. When I asked if that wasn't a snobbish argument, serving some notion of who I was supposed to be rather than who I was, my father smiled complacently and said, "Guilty," thus putting an end to the discussion.

•

The issue was not joined again until a spring evening when we were at dinner. That weekend I'd baby-sat for Jackie while she investigated sharing a summer house in Westhampton, a new location. When I returned on Sunday evening, they were eating in the kitchen. My mail, which included a notice of acceptance from the Culinary Institute, was at my place. I flushed when I saw the envelope. When I had opened and read it, I smiled sadly, put it back in its envelope without speaking and helped myself to some of the cold leftovers on the table.

"Do I gather," my father asked after a while, "that you have applied for admission to this . . . uh . . ."

"School," I said, expressionless. "It's a very good school for cooking. It's called the Culinary Institute of America."

"Indeed," he said. "And have you been accepted?"

"Yes," I said. "I have been accepted. But I can't afford it."

I had been trying to figure out a way, a set of ways, that I could raise the money to attend, but the fee was daunting to someone who had managed to put aside a negligible amount of money. If I'd felt that pleading could get me someplace, I surely would have done it, but I had no hope at all.

"Your mother and I have been talking," my father said to me the following evening. "You know our feelings about paying for—"

"You've told me," I broke in.

"Yes," he said. "Well, we still feel the same way, but it occurred to us . . ."

I looked up, hearing the opening for the first time.

". . . that there was room for negotiation on the matter."

"Where?" I asked. "What? What do I have to do?"

"Well," he said slowly, "what occurred to us is that while we have the money but don't want to spend it that way, there is another way that we might spend it, without, you might say, compromising our principles. That is, we might spend it to buy something we wanted."

I stared at him uncomprehendingly. He waited. *Something they wanted.* When I finally understood that he was talking about my painting, it was only because there was no other possibility.

He smiled. My mother smiled. They had not been so wrapped up in their work and their social-artistic life as to fail to notice that I was unhappy. Now they were pleased to have found a way to let me do what I wanted to do without compromising their academic principles and while obtaining a painting they would love to own. I was, after all, the only member of the family who possessed an Eleanora Stonepark. They knew from the place in my room to which Jenny had long since been moved that I did not want to look at her.

I could not smile back because my mind, long before it had a reasonable explanation for doing so, refused even to consider letting them have her.

Their smiles faded. I doubt they believed that I would give up the Culinary Institute before I would part with my picture. But it was occurring to them for the first time that I might not jump at their offer. When I told them days later that even if it meant giving up the Institute, I could not accept, they smiled at each other in sad confirmation: I had always been contrary.

Surely I needed to find a way to be my own person rather than theirs —or, as they would have it, to be contrary. But I don't think contrariness made me cling to my painting. I was beginning to suspect that I would not remain in my parents' home long enough to get a degree. I had no clear idea of what I would do when I left, that is to say, of how close it would be to something I *wanted* to do. I didn't know which of the friends I'd made at school I would keep or whether I would make new ones, nor did I have any assurance that my parents, the fixed point in my life whether I was being my own person or theirs or trying to find some reasonable combination of the two, would remain friendly as I floundered around, looking for a life. But the person in the picture was my assurance that I would find one, and whether I liked her or not, whether or not she made me happy, I needed to keep with me the difficult young woman another difficult woman had named 116th Street Jenny.

Judith Rossner, who lives in New York City, has published a number of stories and articles. She is the author of eight novels, including *Looking for Mr. Goodbar, Emmeline,* and *August,* and she is at work on a new novel.

TOBIAS WOLFF

"I was spending Christmas with my brother Geoffrey and his family in Vermont back in the early seventies. One day Geoffrey got a call from a man with whom he'd briefly shared a room in a ski lodge some twenty years earlier and hadn't seen since. Dan, his name was. He called to say that he'd just come back from Peru, and that he had a business proposition to make. It couldn't wait. He was calling from the village store, after spending ten hours hitching up from New York in the snow.

"My brother and I picked Dan up and took him to an empty house that Geoffrey had once rented and still had the keys to. It was cold. The three of us sat around with our coats on while this pathetic, haunted-looking creature with frozen pantlegs and wet street shoes and half his teeth missing tried to interest us in buying into a gold mine. He had brought no shares with him, and no printed description of the venture. He simply wanted us to give him money. We heard him out, politely said no, and took him back to the store. Later, Geoffrey told me that Dan had been one of the most graceful skiers he'd ever seen, devilishly handsome, and a great ladies' man. He was also a thief. The last time my brother laid eyes on him was the day Dan took off with several of his shirts and a cherished jacket. Geoffrey never brought this up during their reunion, and treated the man with patience and courtesy.

"The incident wouldn't leave me alone. I first tried writing it pretty close to the event, but it wouldn't flower. It was merely conventional and sad, a cautionary tale of youthful beauty and promise marked for ruin by a weak character. Then, and this is my usual procedure, I threw history to the winds and invented like crazy, and gradually the pattern of the story began to reveal itself to me. Its true subject, I saw, was not the desperation of a self-betrayed man, but the difficulties of brotherhood. I had given a lot of thought to this subject; it meant something to me, called on my deepest feelings, as Dan's situation did not. What I did, then, was use the original event as port of entry to a story that gave those feelings free play. That is the beauty of fiction. Through its agency, we can sometimes write more truly than when we stick to the facts."

THE RICH BROTHER

THERE were two brothers, Pete and Donald.

Pete, the older brother, was in real estate. He and his wife had a Century 21 franchise in Santa Cruz. Pete worked hard and made a lot of money, but not any more than he thought he deserved. He had two daughters, a sailboat, a house from which he could see a thin slice of the ocean, and friends doing well enough in their own lives not to wish bad luck on him. Donald, the younger brother, was still single. He lived alone, painted houses when he found the work, and got deeper in debt to Pete when he didn't.

No one would have taken them for brothers. Where Pete was stout and hearty and at home in the world, Donald was bony, grave, and obsessed with the fate of his soul. Over the years Donald had worn the images of two different Perfect Masters around his neck. Out of devotion to the second of these he entered an ashram in Berkeley, where he nearly died of undiagnosed hepatitis. By the time Pete finished paying the medical bills Donald had become a Christian. He drifted from church to church, then joined a pentecostal community that met somewhere in the Mission District to sing in tongues and swap prophecies.

Pete couldn't make sense of it. Their parents were both dead, but while they were alive neither of them had found it necessary to believe in anything. They managed to be decent people without making fools of themselves, and Pete had the same ambition. He thought that the whole thing was an excuse for Donald to take himself seriously.

The trouble was that Donald couldn't content himself with worrying about his own soul. He had to worry about everyone else's, and especially Pete's. He handed down his judgments in ways that he seemed to consider subtle: through significant silence, innuendo, looks of mild despair that said, *Brother, what have you come to?* What Pete had come to, as far as he could tell, was prosperity. That was the real issue between them. Pete prospered and Donald did not prosper.

At the age of forty Pete took up sky diving. He made his first jump with two friends who'd started only a few months earlier and were already doing stunts. They were both coked to the gills when they jumped but Pete wanted to do it straight, at least the first time, and he was glad that he did. He would never have used the word "mystical," but that was how Pete felt about the experience. Later he made the mistake of trying to describe it to Donald, who kept asking how much it cost and then acted appalled when Pete told him.

"At least I'm trying something new," Pete said. "At least I'm breaking the pattern."

Not long after that conversation Donald also broke the pattern, by going to live on a farm outside of Paso Robles. The farm was owned by several members of Donald's community, who had bought it and moved there with the idea of forming a family of faith. That was how Donald explained it in the first letter he sent. Every week Pete heard how happy Donald was, how "in the Lord." He told Pete that he was praying for him, he and the rest of Pete's brothers and sisters on the farm.

"I only have one brother," Pete wanted to answer, "and that's enough." But he kept this thought to himself.

In November the letters stopped. Pete didn't worry about this at first, but when he called Donald at Thanksgiving Donald was grim. He tried to sound upbeat but he didn't try hard enough to make it convincing. "Now listen," Pete said, "you don't have to stay in that place if you don't want to."

"I'll be all right," Donald answered.

"That's not the point. Being all right is not the point. If you don't like what's going on up there, then get out."

"I'm all right," Donald said again, more firmly. "I'm doing fine."

But he called Pete a week later and said that he was quitting the farm. When Pete asked him where he intended to go, Donald admitted that he had no plan. His car had been repossessed just before he left the city, and he was flat broke.

"I guess you'll have to stay with us," Pete said.

Donald put up a show of resistance. Then he gave in. "Just until I get my feet on the ground," he said.

"Right," Pete said. "Check out your options." He told Donald he'd send him money for a bus ticket, but as they were about to hang up Pete changed his mind. He knew that Donald would try hitchhiking to save the fare. Pete didn't want him out on the road all alone where some head case could pick him up, where anything could happen to him.

"Better yet," he said. "I'll come and get you."

"You don't have to do that. I didn't expect you to do that," Donald said. He added, "It's a pretty long drive."

"Just tell me how to get there."

But Donald wouldn't give him directions. He said that the farm was too depressing, that Pete wouldn't like it. Instead, he insisted on meeting Pete at a service station called Jonathan's Mechanical Emporium.

"You must be kidding," Pete said.

"It's close to the highway," Donald said. "I didn't name it."

"That's one for the collection," Pete said.

The day before he left to bring Donald home, Pete received a letter from a man who described himself as "head of household" at the farm where Donald had been living. From this letter Pete learned that Donald had not quit the farm, but had been asked to leave. The letter was written on the back of a mimeographed survey form asking people to record their response to a ceremony of some kind. The last question said:

What did you feel during the liturgy?

a) Being

b) Becoming

c) Being and Becoming

d) None of the Above

e) All of the Above

Pete tried to forget the letter. But of course he couldn't. Each time he thought of it he felt crowded and breathless, a feeling that came over him again when he drove into the service station and saw Donald sitting against a wall with his head on his knees. It was late afternoon. A paper cup tumbled slowly past Donald's feet, pushed by the damp wind.

Pete honked and Donald raised his head. He smiled at Pete, then stood and stretched. His arms were long and thin and white. He wore a red bandanna across his forehead, a T-shirt with a couple of words on the front. Pete couldn't read them because the letters were inverted.

"Grow up," Pete yelled. "Get a Mercedes."

Donald came up to the window. He bent down and said, "Thanks for coming. You must be totally whipped."

"I'll make it." Pete pointed at Donald's T-shirt. "What's that supposed to say?"

Donald looked down at his shirt front. "Try God. I guess I put it on backwards. Pete, could I borrow a couple of dollars? I owe these people for coffee and sandwiches."

Pete took five twenties from his wallet and held them out the window.

Donald stepped back as if horrified. "I don't need that much."

"I can't keep track of all these nickels and dimes," Pete said. "Just pay me back when your ship comes in." He waved the bills impatiently. "Go on—take it."

"Only for now." Donald took the money and went into the service station office. He came out carrying two orange sodas, one of which he gave to Pete as he got into the car. "My treat," he said.

"No bags?"

"Wow, thanks for reminding me," Donald said. He balanced his drink on the dashboard, but the slight rocking of the car as he got out tipped it onto the passenger's seat, where half its contents foamed over before Pete could snatch it up again. Donald looked on while Pete held the bottle out the window, soda running down his fingers.

"Wipe it up," Pete told him. "Quick!"

"With what?"

Pete stared at Donald. "That shirt. Use the shirt."

Donald pulled a long face but did as he was told, his pale skin puckering against the wind.

"Great, just great," Pete said. "We haven't even left the gas station yet."

Afterwards, on the highway, Donald said, "This is a new car, isn't it?"

"Yes. This is a new car."

"Is that why you're so upset about the seat?"

"Forget it, okay? Let's just forget about it."

"I said I was sorry."

Pete said, "I just wish you'd be more careful. These seats are made of leather. That stain won't come out, not to mention the smell. I don't see why I can't have leather seats that smell like leather instead of orange pop."

"What was wrong with the other car?"

Pete glanced over at Donald. Donald had raised the hood of the blue sweatshirt he'd put on. The peaked hood above his gaunt, watchful face gave him the look of an inquisitor.

"There wasn't anything wrong with it," Pete said. "I just happened to like this one better."

Donald nodded.

There was a long silence between them as Pete drove on and the day darkened toward evening. On either side of the road lay stubble-covered fields. A line of low hills ran along the horizon, topped here and there with trees black against the gray sky. In the approaching line of cars a driver turned on his headlights. Pete did the same.

"So what happened?" he asked. "Farm life not your bag?"

Donald took some time to answer, and at last he said, simply, "It was my fault."

"What was your fault?"

"The whole thing. Don't play dumb, Pete. I know they wrote to you." Donald looked at Pete, then stared out the windshield again.

"I'm not playing dumb."

Donald shrugged.

"All I really know is they asked you to leave," Pete went on. "I don't know any of the particulars."

"I blew it," Donald said. "Believe me, you don't want to hear the gory details."

"Sure I do," Pete said. He added, "Everybody likes the gory details."

"You mean everybody likes to hear how someone else messed up."

"Right," Pete said. "That's the way it is here on Spaceship Earth."

Donald bent one knee onto the front seat and leaned against the door so that he was facing Pete instead of the windshield. Pete was aware of Donald's scrutiny. He waited. Night was coming on in a rush now, filling the hollows of the land. Donald's long cheeks and deep-set eyes were dark with shadow. His brow was white. "Do you ever dream about me?" Donald asked.

"Do I ever dream about you? What kind of a question is that? Of course I don't dream about you," Pete said, untruthfully.

"What do you dream about?"

"Sex and money. Mostly money. A nightmare is when I dream I don't have any."

"You're just making that up," Donald said.

Pete smiled.

"Sometimes I wake up at night," Donald went on, "and I can tell you're dreaming about me."

"We were talking about the farm," Pete said. "Let's finish that conversation and then we can talk about our various out-of-body experiences and the interesting things we did during previous incarnations."

For a moment Donald looked like a grinning skull; then he turned serious again. "There's not that much to tell," he said. "I just didn't do anything right."

"That's a little vague," Pete said.

"Well, like the groceries. Whenever it was my turn to get the groceries I'd blow it somehow. I'd bring the groceries home and half of them would be missing, or I'd have all the wrong things, the wrong kind of flour or the wrong kind of chocolate or whatever. One time I gave them away. It's not funny, Pete."

Pete said, "Who did you give the groceries to?"

"Just some people I picked up on the way home. Some field-workers. They had about eight kids with them and they didn't even speak English—just nodded their heads. Still, I shouldn't have given away the groceries. Not all of them, anyway. I really learned my lesson about that. You have to be practical. You have to be fair to yourself." Donald leaned forward, and Pete could sense his excitement. "There's nothing actually wrong with being in business," he said. "As long as you're fair to other people you can still be fair to yourself. I'm thinking of going into business, Pete."

"We'll talk about it," Pete said. "So, that's the story? There isn't any more to it than that?"

"What did they tell you?" Donald asked.

"Nothing."

"They must have told you something."

Pete shook his head.

"They didn't tell you about the fire?" When Pete shook his head again Donald regarded him for a time, then said, "I don't know. It was stupid. I just completely lost it." He folded his arms across his chest and slumped back into the corner. "Everybody had to take turns cooking dinner. I usually did tuna casserole or spaghetti with garlic bread. But this one night I thought I'd do something different, something really interesting." Donald looked sharply at Pete. "It's all a big laugh to you, isn't it?"

"I'm sorry," Pete said.

"You don't know when to quit. You just keep hitting away."

"Tell me about the fire, Donald."

Donald kept watching him. "You have this compulsion to make me look foolish."

"Come off it, Donald. Don't make a big thing out of this."

"I know why you do it. It's because you don't have any purpose in life. You're afraid to relate to people who do, so you make fun of them."

"Relate," Pete said softly.

"You're basically a very frightened individual," Donald said. "Very threatened. You've always been like that. Do you remember when you used to try to kill me?"

"I don't have any compulsion to make you look foolish, Donald—You do it yourself. You're doing it right now."

"You can't tell me you don't remember," Donald said. "It was after my operation. You remember that."

"Sort of." Pete shrugged. "Not really."

"Oh yes." Donald said. "Do you want to see the scar?"

"I remember you had an operation. I don't remember the specifics, that's all. And I sure as hell don't remember trying to kill you."

"Oh yes," Donald repeated, maddeningly. "You bet your life you did. All the time. The thing was, I couldn't have anything happen to me where they sewed me up because then my intestines would come apart again and poison me. That was a big issue, Pete. Mom was always in a state about me climbing trees and so on. And you used to hit me there every chance you got."

"Mom was in a state every time you burped," Pete said. "I don't know. Maybe I bumped into you accidentally once or twice. I never did it deliberately."

"Every chance you got," Donald said. "Like when the folks went out at night and left you to baby-sit. I'd hear them say good night, and then I'd hear the car start up, and when they were gone I'd lie there and listen. After a while I would hear you coming down the hall, and I would close my eyes and pretend to be asleep. There were nights when you would stand outside the door, just stand there, and then go away again. But most nights you'd open the door and I would hear you in the room with me, breathing. You'd come over and sit next to me on the bed—you remember, Pete, you have to—you'd sit next to me on the bed and pull the sheets back. If I was on my stomach you'd roll me over. Then you would lift up my pajama shirt and start hitting me on my stitches. You'd hit me as hard as you could, over and over. And I would just keep lying there with my eyes closed. I was afraid that you'd get mad if you knew I was awake. Is that strange or what? I was afraid that you'd get mad if you found out that I knew you were trying to kill me." Donald laughed. "Come on, you can't tell me you don't remember that."

"It might have happened once or twice. Kids do those things. I can't get all excited about something I maybe did twenty-five years ago."

"No maybe about it. You did it."

Pete said, "You're wearing me out with this stuff. We've got a long drive ahead of us and if you don't back off pretty soon we aren't going to make it. You aren't, anyway."

Donald turned away.

"I'm doing my best," Pete said. The self-pity in his own voice made the words sound like a lie. But they weren't a lie! He was doing his best.

The car topped a rise. In the distance Pete saw a cluster of lights that blinked out when he started downhill. There was no moon. The sky was low and black.

"Come to think of it," Pete said, "I did have a dream about you the other night." Then he added, impatiently, as if Donald were badgering him. "A couple of other nights too. I'm getting hungry," he said.

"The same dream?"

"Different dreams. I only remember one of them well. There was something wrong with me, and you were helping out. Taking care of me. Just the two of us. I don't know where everyone else was supposed to be."

Pete left it at that. He didn't tell Donald that in this dream he was blind.

"I wonder if that was when I woke up," Donald said. He added, "I'm sorry I got into that thing about my scar. I keep trying to forget it but I guess I never will. Not really. It was pretty strange, having someone around all the time who wanted to get rid of me."

"Kid stuff," Pete said. "Ancient history."

They ate dinner at a Denny's on the other side of King City. As Pete was paying the check he heard a man behind him say, "Excuse me, but I wonder if I might ask which way you're going?" and Donald answered, "Santa Cruz."

"Perfect," the man said.

Pete could see him in the fish-eye mirror above the cash register: a red blazer with some kind of crest on the pocket, little black mustache, glossy black hair combed down on his forehead like a Roman emperor's. A rug, Pete thought. Definitely a rug.

Pete got his change and turned. "Why is that perfect?" he asked.

The man looked at Pete. He had a soft ruddy face that was doing its best to express pleasant surprise, as if this new wrinkle were all he could have wished for, but the eyes behind the aviator glasses showed signs of regret. His lips were moist and shiny. "I take it you're together," he said.

"You got it," Pete told him.

"All the better, then," the man went on. "It so happens I'm going to Santa Cruz myself. Had a spot of car trouble down the road. The old Caddy let me down."

"What kind of trouble?" Pete asked.

"Engine trouble," the man said. "I'm afraid it's a bit urgent. My daughter is sick. Urgently sick. I've got a telegram here." He patted the breast pocket of his blazer.

Pete grinned. Amazing, he thought, the old sick daughter ploy, but before he could say anything Donald got into the act again. "No problem," Donald said. "We've got tons of room."

"Not that much room," Pete said.

Donald nodded. "I'll put my things in the trunk."

"The trunk's full," Pete told him.

"It so happens I'm traveling light," the man said. "This leg of the trip anyway. In fact I don't have any luggage at this particular time."

Pete said, "Left it in the old Caddy, did you?"

"Exactly," the man said.

"No problem," Donald repeated. He walked outside and the man went with him. Together they strolled across the parking lot, Pete following at a distance. When they reached Pete's car Donald raised his face to the sky, and the man did the same. They stood there looking up. "Dark night," Donald said.

"Stygian," the man said.

Pete still had it in mind to brush him off, but he didn't do that. Instead he unlocked the door for him. He wanted to see what would happen. It was an adventure, but not a dangerous adventure. The man might steal Pete's ashtrays but he wouldn't kill him. If Pete got killed on the road it would be by some spiritual person in a sweatsuit, someone with his eyes on the far horizon and a wet Try God T-shirt in his duffel bag.

As soon as they left the parking lot the man lit a cigar. He blew a cloud of smoke over Pete's shoulder and sighed with pleasure. "Put it out," Pete told him.

"Of course," the man said. Pete looked into the rear-view mirror and saw the man take another long puff before dropping the cigar out the window. "Forgive me," he said. "I should have asked. Name's Webster, by the way."

Donald turned and looked back at him. "First name or last?"

The man hesitated. "Last," he said finally.

"I know a Webster," Donald said. "Mick Webster."

"There are many of us," Webster said.

"Big fellow, wooden leg," Pete said.

Donald gave Pete a look.

Webster shook his head. "Doesn't ring a bell. Still, I wouldn't deny the connection. Might be one of the cousinry."

"What's your daughter got?" Pete asked.

"That isn't clear," Webster answered. "It appears to be a female complaint of some nature. Then again it may be tropical." He was quiet for a moment, and then added: "If indeed it *is* tropical, I will have to assume some of the blame myself. It was my own vaulting ambition that first led us to the tropics and kept us in the tropics all those many years, exposed to every evil. Truly I have much to answer for. I left my wife there."

Donald said quietly, "You mean she died?"

"I buried her with these hands. The earth will be repaid, gold for gold."

"Which tropics?" Pete asked.

"The tropics of Peru."

"What part of Peru are they in?"

"The lowlands," Webster said.

Pete nodded. "What's it like down there?"

"Another world," Webster said. His tone was sepulchral. "A world better imagined than described."

"Far out," Pete said.

The three men rode in silence for a time. A line of trucks went past in the other direction, trailers festooned with running lights, engines roaring.

"Yes," Webster said at last, "I have much to answer for."

Pete smiled at Donald, but Donald had turned in his seat again and was gazing at Webster. "I'm sorry about your wife," Donald said.

"What did she die of?" Pete asked.

"A wasting illness," Webster said. "The doctors have no name for it, but I do." He leaned forward and said, fiercely, "*Greed.*" Then he slumped back against his seat. "My greed, not hers. She wanted no part of it."

Pete bit his lip. Webster was a find and Pete didn't want to scare him off by hooting at him. In a voice low and innocent of knowingness, he asked, "What took you there?"

"It's difficult for me to talk about."

"Try," Pete told him.

"A cigar would make it easier."

Donald turned to Pete and said, "It's okay with me."

"All right," Pete said. "Go ahead. Just keep the window rolled down."

"Much obliged." A match flared. There were eager sucking sounds.

"Let's hear it," Pete said.

"I am by training an engineer," Webster began. "My work has exposed me to all but one of the continents, to desert and alp and forest, to every terrain and season of the earth. Some years ago I was hired by the Peruvian government to search for tungsten in the tropics. My wife and daughter accompanied me. We were the only white people for a thousand miles in any direction, and we had no choice but to live as the Indians lived—to share their food and drink and even their culture."

Pete said, "You knew the lingo, did you?"

"We picked it up." The ember of the cigar bobbed up and down. "We were used to learning as necessity decreed. At any rate, it became evident after a couple of years that there was no tungsten to be found. My wife had fallen ill and was pleading to be taken home. But I was deaf to her pleas, because by then I was on the trail of another metal—a metal far more valuable than tungsten."

"Let me guess," Pete said. "Gold?"

Donald looked at Pete, then back at Webster.

"Gold," Webster said. "A vein of gold greater than the Mother Lode itself. After I found the first traces of it nothing could tear me away from my search—not the sickness of my wife nor anything else. I was determined to uncover the vein, and so I did—but not before I laid my wife to rest. As I say, the earth will be repaid."

Webster was quiet. Then he said, "But life must go on. In the years since my wife's death I have been making the arrangements necessary to open the mine. I could have done it immediately, of course, enriching myself beyond measure, but I knew what that would mean—the exploitation of our beloved Indians, the brutal destruction of their environment. I felt I had too much to atone for already." Webster paused, and when he spoke again his voice was dull and rushed, as if he had used up all the interest he had in his own words. "Instead I drew up a program for returning the bulk of the wealth to the Indians themselves. A kind of trust fund. The interest alone will allow them to secure their ancient lands and rights in perpetuity. At the same time, our investors will be rewarded a thousandfold. Two-thousandfold. Everyone will prosper together."

"That's great," Donald said. "That's the way it ought to be."

Pete said, "I'm willing to bet that you just happen to have a few shares left. Am I right?"

Webster made no reply.

"Well?" Pete knew that Webster was on to him now, but he didn't care. The story had bored him. He'd expected something different, something original, and Webster had let him down. He hadn't even tried. Pete felt sour and stale. His eyes burned from cigar smoke and the high beams of road-hogging truckers. "Douse the stogie," he said to Webster. "I told you to keep the window down."

"Got a little nippy back there."

Donald said, "Hey, Pete. Lighten up."

"Douse it!"

Webster sighed. He got rid of the cigar.

"I'm a wreck," Pete said to Donald. "You want to drive for a while?"

Donald nodded.

Pete pulled over and they changed places.

Webster kept his counsel in the back seat. Donald hummed while he drove, until Pete told him to stop. Then everything was quiet.

Donald was humming again when Pete woke up. Pete stared sullenly at the road, at the white lines sliding past the car. After a few moments of this he turned and said, "How long have I been out?"

Donald glanced at him. "Twenty, twenty-five minutes."

Pete looked behind him and saw that Webster was gone. "Where's our friend?"

"You just missed him. He got out in Soledad. He told me to say thanks and goodbye."

"Soledad? What about his sick daughter? How did he explain her away?" Pete leaned over the seat. Both ashtrays were still in place. Floor mats. Door handles.

"He has a brother living there. He's going to borrow a car from him and drive the rest of the way in the morning."

"I'll bet his brother's living there," Pete said. "Doing fifty concurrent life sentences. His brother and his sister and his mom and his dad."

"I kind of liked him," Donald said.

"I'm sure you did," Pete said wearily.

"He was interesting. He'd been places."

"His cigars had been places, I'll give you that."

"Come on, Pete."

"Come on yourself. What a phony."

"You don't know that."

"Sure I do."

"How? How do you know?"

Pete stretched. "Brother, there are some things you're just born knowing. What's the gas situation?"

"We're a little low."

"Then why didn't you get some more?"

"I wish you wouldn't snap at me like that," Donald said.

"Then why don't you use your head? What if we run out?"

"We'll make it," Donald said. "I'm pretty sure we've got enough to make it. You didn't have to be so rude to him," Donald added.

Pete took a deep breath. "I don't feel like running out of gas tonight, okay?"

Donald pulled in at the next station they came to and filled the tank while Pete went to the men's room. When Pete came back, Donald was sitting in the passenger's seat. The attendant came up to the driver's window as Pete got in behind the wheel. He bent down and said, "Twenty-two fifty-five."

"You heard the man," Pete said to Donald.

Donald looked straight ahead. He didn't move.

"Cough up," Pete said. "This trip's on you."

Donald said, softly, "I can't."

"Sure you can. Break out that wad."

Donald glanced up at the attendant, then at Pete. "Please," he said. "Pete, I don't have it anymore."

Pete took this in. He nodded, and paid the attendant.

Donald began to speak when they left the station but Pete cut him off. He said, "I don't want to hear from you right now. You just keep quiet or I swear to God I won't be responsible."

They left the fields and entered a tunnel of tall trees. The trees went on and on. "Let me get this straight," Pete said at last. "You don't have the money I gave you."

"You treated him like a bug or something," Donald said.

"You don't have the money," Pete said again.

Donald shook his head.

"Since I bought dinner, and since we didn't stop anywhere in between, I assume you gave it to Webster. Is that right? Is that what you did with it?"

"Yes."

Pete looked at Donald. His face was dark under the hood but he still managed to convey a sense of remove, as if none of this had anything to do with him.

"Why?" Pete asked. "Why did you give it to him?" When Donald didn't answer, Pete said, "A hundred dollars. Gone. Just like that. I *worked* for that money, Donald."

"I know, I know," Donald said.

"You don't know! How could you? You get money by holding out your hand."

"I work too," Donald said.

"You work too. Don't kid yourself, brother."

Donald leaned toward Pete, about to say something, but Pete cut him off again.

"You're not the only one on the payroll, Donald. I don't think you understand that. I have a family."

"Pete, I'll pay you back."

"Like hell you will. A hundred dollars!" Pete hit the steering wheel with the palm of his hand. "Just because you think I hurt some goof-ball's feelings. Jesus, Donald."

"That's not the reason," Donald said. "And I didn't just *give* him the money."

"What do you call it, then? What do you call what you did?"

"I *invested* it. I wanted a share, Pete." When Pete looked over at him Donald nodded and said again, "I wanted a share."

Pete said, "I take it you're referring to the gold mine in Peru."

"Yes," Donald said.

"You believe that such a gold mine exists?"

Donald looked at Pete, and Pete could see him just beginning to catch on. "You'll believe anything," Pete said. "Won't you? You really will believe anything at all."

"I'm sorry," Donald said, and turned away.

Pete drove on between the trees and considered the truth of what he had just said—that Donald would believe anything at all. And it came to him that it would be just like this unfair life for Donald to come out ahead in the end, by believing in some outrageous promise that would turn out to be true and that he, Pete, would reject out of hand because he was too wised up to listen to anybody's pitch anymore except for laughs. What a joke. What a joke if there really was a blessing to be had, and the blessing didn't come to the one who deserved it, the one who did all the work, but to the other.

And as if this had already happened Pete felt a shadow move upon him, darkening his thoughts. After a time he said, "I can see where all this is going, Donald."

"I'll pay you back," Donald said.

"No," Pete said. "You won't pay me back. You can't. You don't know how. All you've ever done is take. All your life."

Donald shook his head.

"I see exactly where this is going," Pete went on. "You can't work, you can't take care of yourself, you believe anything anyone tells you. I'm stuck with you, aren't I?" He looked over at Donald. "I've got you on my hands for good."

Donald pressed his fingers against the dashboard as if to brace himself. "I'll get out," he said.

Pete kept driving.

"Let me out," Donald said. "I mean it, Pete."

"Do you?"

Donald hesitated. "Yes," he said.

"Be sure," Pete told him. "This is it. This is for keeps."

"I mean it."

"All right. You made the choice." Pete braked the car sharply and swung it to the shoulder of the road. He turned off the engine and got out. Trees loomed on both sides, shutting out the sky. The air was cold and musty. Pete took Donald's duffel bag from the back seat and set it down behind the car. He stood there, facing Donald in the red glow of the taillights. "It's better this way," Pete said.

Donald just looked at him.

"Better for you," Pete said.

Donald hugged himself. He was shaking. "You don't have to say all that," he told Pete. "I don't blame you."

"Blame me? What the hell are you talking about? Blame me for what?"

"For anything," Donald said.

"I want to know what you mean by blame me."

"Nothing. Nothing, Pete. You'd better get going. God bless you."

"That's it," Pete said. He dropped to one knee, searching the packed dirt with his hands. He didn't know what he was looking for; his hands would know when they found it.

Donald touched Pete's shoulder. "You'd better go," he said.

Somewhere in the trees Pete heard a branch snap. He stood up. He looked at Donald, then went back to the car and drove away. He drove fast, hunched over the wheel, conscious of the way he was hunched and the shallowness of his breathing, refusing to look at the mirror above his head until there was nothing behind him but darkness.

Then he said, "A hundred dollars," as if there were someone to hear.

The trees gave way to fields. Metal fences ran beside the road, plastered with windblown scraps of paper. Tule fog hung above the ditches, spilling into the road, dimming the ghostly halogen lights that burned in the yards of the farms Pete passed. The fog left beads of water rolling up the windshield.

Pete rummaged among his cassettes. He found Pachelbel's Canon and pushed it into the tape deck. When the violins began to play he leaned back and assumed an attentive expression as if he were really listening to them. He smiled to himself like a man at liberty to enjoy music, a man who has finished his work and settled his debts, done all things meet and due.

And in this way, smiling, nodding to the music, he went another mile or so and pretended that he was not already slowing down, that he was not going to turn back, that he would be able to drive on like this, alone, and have the right answer when his wife stood before him in the doorway of his home and asked, Where is he? Where is your brother?

Tobias Wolff is the author of the highly acclaimed memoir *This Boy's Life;* he has also published a novel, *The Barracks Thief,* winner of the 1985 PEN Faulkner Award, and two collections of stories. "The Rich Brother" is from his collection *Back in the World.* He teaches at Syracuse University.

JOYCE CAROL OATES

"For the writer who has been writing for a period of years, there can be no day, no hour, no epiphany of a moment, when he or she discovers his or her 'voice.' Rather, we work through a succession of voices, some overlapping and imbricating, others seemingly unrelated to what has preceded, or will follow. Each work of fiction has its own distinctive voice and the challenge for the writer—at times a challenge that evokes intense anxiety—is to discover and to refine the voice that is unique to that work.

"It will be said that the writer's characteristic prose style *is* that voice; and that, in even the most virtuoso of experimental writers, a reader with a sharp ear can discern rhythms, cadences, turns of speech, above all favored words, that make the prose immediately recognizable. It may be said that, even behind a pseudonym, none of us can really hide; our language is as irremediably our own as our voice—and fingerprints.

"And yet, extraordinary as it might seem as a claim, the writer often labors, through successive revisions, to create the very prose style that is 'characteristic'—just as the story, when completed, is virtually never the story that was imagined at the outset. The act of writing the story propels us beyond it. So 'The Swimmers,' a story I had thought was about a woman and a man and their unresolved love, becomes, in retrospect, as if from a vantage point of both distance and time, a story about the questing, yearning, intensely romantic 'I' who tells it—that core of being, with which many who are not writers might identify, that invests in the world around it a powerful mystery and passion that is surely the equivalent of erotic love, and may outlive such love."

THE SWIMMERS

THERE are stories that go unaccountably wrong and become impermeable to the imagination. They lodge in the memory like an old wound never entirely healed. This story of my father's younger brother Clyde Farrell, my uncle, and a woman named Joan Lunt, with whom he fell in love, years ago, in 1959, is one of those stories.

Some of it I was a part of, aged 13. But much of it I have to imagine.

It must have been a pale, wintry, unflattering light he first saw her in, swimming laps in the early morning in the local Y.M.C.A. pool, but that initial sight of Joan Lunt—not her face, which was obscured from him, but the movement of her strong, supple, creamy-pale body through the water, and the sureness of her strokes—never faded from Clyde Farrell's mind.

He'd been told of her; in fact, he'd come to the pool that morning to observe her, but still you didn't expect to see such serious swimming, 7:45 A.M. of a weekday, in the antiquated white-tiled "Y" pool, light slanting down from the wired glass skylight overhead, a sharp medicinal smell of chlorine and disinfectant pinching your nostrils. There were a few other swimmers in the pool, ordinary swimmers, one of them an acquaintance of Clyde's who waved at him, called out his name when Clyde appeared in his swim trunks on the deck, climbed up onto the diving board, then paused to watch Joan Lunt swimming toward the far end of the pool . . . just stood watching her, not rudely but with a frank, childlike interest, smiling with the spontaneous pleasure of seeing another person doing something well, with so little waste motion. Joan Lunt in her yellow bathing suit with the crossed straps in back and her white rubber cap that gleamed and sparked in the miniature waves: an attractive woman in her mid-30s, though she looked younger, with an air of total absorption in the task at hand, swimming to the limit of her capacity, maintaining a pace and a rhythm Clyde Farrell would have been challenged to maintain himself, and Clyde was a good swimmer, known locally as a very good swimmer, a winner, years before, when he was in his teens, of county and state competitions. Joan Lunt wasn't aware of him standing on the diving board watching her, or so it appeared. Just swimming, counting laps. How many she'd done already he couldn't imagine. He saw that she knew to cup the water when she stroked back, not to let it thread through her fingers like most people do; she knew as if by instinct how to take advantage of the element she was in, propelling herself forward like an otter or a seal, power in her shoulder muscles and upper arms, and the swift scissors kick of her legs, feet flashing white through the chemical-turquoise glitter of the water. When Joan Lunt reached the end of the pool, she ducked immediately down into the water in a well-practiced maneuver, turned, used the tiled side to kick off from, in a single graceful motion that took her a considerable distance, and Clyde Farrell's heart contracted when, emerging from the water, head and shoulders and flashing arms, the woman didn't miss a beat, just continued as if she hadn't been confronted with any limit or impediment, any boundary. It was just water, and her in it, water that might go on forever, and her in it, swimming, sealed off and invulnerable.

Clyde Farrell dived into the pool, and swam vigorously, keeping to his own lane, energetic and single-minded, too, and when, after some minutes, he glanced around for the woman in the yellow bathing suit, the woman I'd told him of meeting, Joan Lunt, he saw, to his disappointment, that she was gone.

His vanity was wounded. He thought, She never once looked at me.

My father and my uncle Clyde were farm boys who left the farm as soon as they were of age: joined the U.S. Navy out of high school, went away, came back and lived and worked in town, my father in a small sign shop and Clyde in a succession of jobs. He drove a truck for a gravel company, he was a foreman in a local tool factory, he managed a sporting-goods store; he owned property at Wolf's Head Lake, 20 miles to the north, and spoke with vague enthusiasm of developing it someday. He wasn't a practical man and he never saved money. He liked to gamble at cards and horses. In the Navy, he'd learned to box and for a while after being discharged, he considered a professional career as a welterweight, but that meant signing contracts, traveling around the country, taking orders from other men. Not Clyde Farrell's temperament.

He was good-looking, not tall, about 5′9″, compact and quick on his feet, a natural athlete, with well-defined shoulder and arm muscles, strong, sinewy legs. His hair was the color of damp sand, his eyes a warm liquid brown, all iris. There was a gap between his two front teeth that gave him a childlike look and was misleading.

No one ever expected Clyde Farrell to get married, or even to fall seriously in love. That capacity in him seemed missing, somehow: a small but self-proclaimed absence, like the gap between his teeth.

But Clyde was powerfully attracted to women, and after watching Joan Lunt swim that morning, he drifted by later in the day to Kress's, Yewville's largest department store, where he knew she'd recently started to work. Kress's was a store of some distinction, the merchandise was of high quality, the counters made of solid, burnished oak; the overhead lighting was muted and flattering to women customers. Behind the counter displaying gloves and leather handbags, Joan Lunt struck the eye as an ordinarily pretty woman, composed, intelligent, feminine, brunette, with a brunette's waxy-pale skin, carefully made up, even glamourous, but not a woman Clyde Farrell would have noticed, much. He was 32 years old, in many ways much younger. This woman was too mature for him, wasn't she? Probably married or divorced, very likely with children. Clyde thought, In her clothes, she's just another one of them.

So Clyde walked out of Kress's, a store he didn't like anyway, and wasn't going to think about Joan Lunt, but one morning a few days later, there he was, unaccountably, back at the Y.M.C.A., 7:30 A.M. of a weekday in March 1959, and there, too, was Joan Lunt in her satiny-yellow bathing suit and gleaming white cap. Swimming laps, arm over strong, slender arm, stroke following stroke, oblivious of Clyde Farrell and of her surroundings, so Clyde was forced to see how her presence in the old, tacky, harshly chlorinated pool made of the place something extraordinary that lifted his heart.

That morning, Clyde swam in the pool for only about ten minutes, then left and hastily showered and dressed and was waiting for Joan Lunt out in the lobby. Clyde wasn't a shy man, but he could give that impression when it suited him. When Joan Lunt appeared, he stepped forward and smiled and introduced himself, saying, "Miss Lunt? I guess you know my niece Sylvie? She told me about meeting you." Joan Lunt hesitated, then shook hands with Clyde and said in that way of hers that suggested she was giving information meant to be clear and unequivocal, "My first name is Joan." She didn't smile but seemed prepared to smile.

Joan Lunt was a good-looking woman with shrewd dark eyes, straight dark eyebrows, an expertly reddened mouth. There was an inch-long white scar at the left corner of her mouth like a sliver of glass. Her thick, shoulder-length dark-brown hair was carefully waved, but the ends were damp; although her face was pale, it appeared heated, invigorated by exercise.

Joan Lunt and Clyde Farrell were nearly of a height, and comfortable together.

Leaving the Y.M.C.A., descending the old granite steps to Main Street that were worn smooth in the centers, nearly hollow with decades of feet, Clyde said to Joan, "You're a beautiful swimmer—I couldn't help admiring you in there," and Joan Lunt laughed and said, "And so are you—I was admiring you, too," and Clyde said, surprised, "Really? You saw me?" and Joan Lunt said, "Both times."

It was Friday. They arranged to meet for drinks that afternoon, and spent the next two days together.

In Yewville, no one knew who Joan Lunt was except as she presented herself: a woman in her mid-30s, solitary, very private, seemingly unattached, with no relatives or friends in the area. No one knew where exactly she'd come from, or why; why here of all places, Yewville, New York, a small city of fewer than 30,000 people, built on the banks of the Eden River, in the southwestern foothills of the Chautauqua Mountains. She had arrived in early February, in a dented rust-red 1956 Chevrolet with New York State license plates, the rear of the car piled with suitcases, cartons, clothes. She spent two nights in Yewville's single good hotel, The Mohawk, then moved into a tiny furnished apartment on Chambers Street. She spent several days interviewing for jobs downtown, all of which you might call jobs for women specifically, and was hired at Kress's, and started work promptly on the first Monday morning following her arrival. If it was sheerly good luck, the job at Kress's, the most prestigious store in town, Joan Lunt seemed to take it in stride, the way a person would who felt she deserved as much. Or better.

The other saleswomen at Kress's, other tenants in the Chambers Street building, men who approached her—no one could get to know her. It was impossible to get beyond the woman's quick, just slightly edgy smile, her resolute cheeriness, her purposefully vague manner. Asked where she was from, she would say, "Nowhere you'd know." Asked was she married, did she have a family, she would say, "Oh, I'm an independent woman, I'm well over eighteen." She'd laugh to suggest that this was a joke, of a kind, the thin scar beside her mouth white with anger.

It was observed that her fingers were entirely ringless.

But the nails were perfectly manicured, polished an enamel-hard red.

It was observed that, for a solitary woman, Joan Lunt had curious habits.

For instance, swimming. Very few women swam in the Y.M.C.A. pool in those days. Sometimes Joan Lunt swam in the early morning, and sometimes, Saturdays, in the late morning; she swam only once in the afternoon, after work, but the pool was disagreeably crowded, and too many people approached her. A well-intentioned woman asked, "Who taught you to swim like *that?*" and Joan Lunt said quietly, "I taught myself." She didn't smile and the conversation was not continued.

It was observed that, for a woman in her presumed circumstances, Joan Lunt was remarkably arrogant.

It seemed curious, too, that she went to the Methodist church Sunday mornings, sitting in a pew at the very rear, holding an opened hymnbook in her hand but not singing with the congregation; and that she slipped away afterward without speaking to anyone. Each time, she left a neatly folded dollar bill in the collection basket.

She wasn't explicitly unfriendly, but she wasn't friendly. At church, the minister and his wife tried to speak with her, tried to make her feel welcome, *did* make her feel welcome, but nothing came of it, she'd hurry off in her car, disappear. In time, people began to murmur that there was something strange about that woman, something not right, yes, maybe even something wrong; for instance, wasn't she behaving suspiciously? Like a runaway wife, for instance? A bad mother? A sinner fleeing Christ?

Another of Joan Lunt's curious habits was to drink, alone, in the early evening, in the Yewville Bar & Grill, or the White Owl Tavern, or the restaurant-bar adjoining the Greyhound Bus Station. If possible, she sat in a booth at the very rear of these taverns where she could observe the front entrances without being seen herself. For an hour or more she'd drink bourbon and water, slowly, very slowly, with an elaborate slowness, her face perfectly composed but her eyes alert. In the Yewville Bar & Grill, there was an enormous sectioned mirror stretching the length of the taproom, and in this mirror, muted by arabesques of frosted glass, Joan Lunt was reflected as beautiful and mysterious. Now and then, men approached her to ask if she were alone. Did she want company? How's about another drink? But she responded coolly to them and never invited anyone to join her. Had my uncle Clyde approached her in such a fashion, she would very likely have been cool to him, too, but my uncle Clyde wasn't the kind of man to set himself up for any sort of public rejection.

One evening in March, before Joan Lunt met up with Clyde Farrell, patrons at the Yewville Bar & Grill, one of them my father, reported with amusement hearing an exchange between Joan Lunt and a local farmer who, mildly drunk, offered to sit with her and buy her a drink, which ended with Joan Lunt's saying, in a loud, sharp voice, "You don't want trouble, mister. Believe me, you don't."

Rumors spread, delicious and censorious, that Joan Lunt was a man-hater. That she carried a razor in her purse. Or an ice pick. Or a lady's-sized revolver.

It was at the Y.M.C.A. pool that I became acquainted with Joan Lunt, on Saturday mornings. She saw that I was alone, that I was a good swimmer, might have mistaken me for younger than I was (I was 13), and befriended me, casually and cheerfully, the way an adult woman might befriend a young girl to whom she isn't related. Her remarks were often exclamations, called across the slapping little waves of the turquoise-tinted water, "*Isn't* it heavenly!"—meaning the pool, the prospect of swimming, the icy rain pelting the skylight overhead while we, in our bathing suits, were snug and safe below.

Another time, in the changing room, she said almost rapturously, "There's nothing like swimming, is there? Your mind just *dissolves.*"

She asked my name, and when I told her, she stared at me and said, "*Sylvie*—I had a close friend once named Sylvie, a long time ago. I loved that name, and I loved *her.*"

I was embarrassed, but pleased. It astonished me that an adult woman, a woman my mother's age, might be so certain of her feelings and so direct in expressing them to a stranger. I fantasized that Joan Lunt came from a part of the world where people knew what they thought and announced their thoughts importantly to others. This struck me with the force of a radically new idea.

I watched Joan Lunt covertly, and I didn't even envy her in the pool—she was so far beyond me. Her face that seemed to me strong and rare and beautiful and her body that was a fully developed woman's body—prominent breasts, shapely hips, long firm legs—all beyond me. I saw how the swiftness and skill with which Joan Lunt swam made other swimmers, especially the adults, appear slow by contrast; clumsy, ill-coordinated, without style.

One day, Joan Lunt was waiting for me in the lobby, hair damp at the ends, face carefully made up, her lipstick seemingly brighter than usual. "Sylvie," she said, smiling, "let's walk out together."

So we walked outside into the snow-glaring, windy sunshine, and she said, "Are you going in this direction? Good, let's walk together." She addressed me as if I were much younger than I was, and her manner was nervous, quick, alert. As we walked up Main Street, she asked questions of me of a kind she'd never asked before, about my family, about my "interests," about school, not listening to the answers and offering no information about herself. At the corner of Chambers and Main, she asked eagerly if I would like to come back to her apartment to visit for a few minutes, and although out of shyness I wanted to say "No, thank you," I said "Yes" instead, because it was clear that Joan Lunt was frightened about something, and I didn't want to leave her.

Her apartment building was shabby and weather-worn, as modest a place as even the poorest of my relatives lived in, but it had about it a sort of makeshift glamour, up the street from the White Owl Tavern and the Shamrock Diner, where motorcyclists hung out, close by the railroad yards on the river. I felt excited and pleased to enter the building and to climb with Joan Lunt—who was chatting briskly all the while—to the fourth floor. On each floor, Joan would pause, breathless, glancing around, listening, and I wanted to ask if someone might be following her, waiting for her. But, of course, I didn't say a thing. When she unlocked the door to her apartment, stepped inside and whispered, "Come in, Sylvie," I seemed to understand that no one else had ever been invited in.

The apartment was really just one room with a tiny kitchen alcove, a tiny bathroom, a doorless closet and a curtainless window with stained, injured-looking Venetian blinds. Joan Lunt said with an apologetic little laugh, "Those blinds—I tried to wash them, but the dirt turned to a sort of paste." I was standing at the window peering down into a weedy back yard of tilting clotheslines and wind-blown trash, curious to see what the view was from Joan Lunt's window, and she came over and drew the blinds, saying, "The sunshine is too bright, it hurts my eyes."

She hung up our coats and asked if I would like some coffee or fresh-squeezed orange juice. "It's my half day off from Kress's," she said. "I don't have to be there until one." It was shortly after 11 o'clock.

We sat at a worn dinette table, and Joan Lunt chatted animatedly and plied me with questions, as I drank orange juice in a tall glass, and she drank black coffee, and an alarm clock on the window sill ticked the minutes briskly by. Few rooms in which I've lived even for considerable periods of time are as vividly imprinted in my memory as that room of Joan Lunt's, with its spare, battered-looking furniture (including a sofa bed and a chest of drawers), its wanly wallpapered walls bare of any hangings, even a mirror, and its badly faded shag rug laid upon painted floor boards. There was a mixture of smells—talcum powder, perfume, cooking odors, insect spray, general mustiness. Two opened suitcases were on the floor beside the sofa bed, apparently unpacked, containing underwear, toiletries, neatly folded sweaters and blouses, several pairs of shoes. A single dress hung in the closet, and a shiny black raincoat, and our two coats Joan had hung on wire hangers. I stared at the suitcases thinking how strange, she'd been living here for weeks but hadn't had time yet to unpack.

So this was where the mysterious Joan Lunt lived! The woman of whom people in Yewville spoke with such suspicion and disapproval! She was far more interesting to me, and in a way more real, than I was to myself; shortly, the story of the lovers Clyde Farrell and Joan Lunt, as I imagined it, would be infinitely more interesting, and infinitely more real, than any story with Sylvie Farrell at its core. (I was a fiercely introspective child, in some ways perhaps a strange child, and the solace of my life would be to grow, not away from but ever more deeply and fruitfully into my strangeness, the way a child with an idiosyncratic, homely face often grows into that face and emerges, in adulthood, as "striking," "distinctive," sometimes even "beautiful.") It turned out that Joan liked poetry, and so we talked about poetry, and about love, and Joan asked me in that searching way of hers if I were "happy in my life," if I were "loved and prized" by my family, and I said, "Yes—I guess so," though these were not issues I had ever considered before, and would not have known to consider if she hadn't asked. For some reason, my eyes filled with tears.

Joan said, "The crucial thing, Sylvie, is to have precious memories." She spoke almost vehemently, laying her hand on mine. "That's even more important than Jesus Christ in your heart, do you know why? Because Jesus Christ can fade out of your heart, but precious memories never do."

We talked like that. Like I'd never talked with anyone before.

I was nervy enough to ask Joan how she'd gotten the little scar beside her mouth, and she touched it, quickly, and said, "In a way I'm not proud of, Sylvie." I sat staring, stupid. The scar wasn't disfiguring in my eyes but enhancing. "A man hit me once," Joan said. "Don't ever let a man hit you, Sylvie."

Weakly, I said, "No, I won't."

No man in our family had ever struck any woman that I knew of, but it happened sometimes in families we knew. I recalled how a ninth-grade girl had come to school that winter with a blackened eye, and she'd seemed proud of it, in a way, and everyone had stared—and the boys just drifted to her, staring. Like they couldn't wait to get their hands on her themselves. And she knew precisely what they were thinking.

I told Joan Lunt that I wished I lived in a place like hers, by myself, and she said, laughing, "No you don't, Sylvie, you're too young." I asked where she was from and she shrugged, "Oh—nowhere," and I persisted, "But is it north of here, or south? Is it the country? Or a city?" and she said, running her fingers nervously through her hair, fingering the damp ends, "My only home is *here, now,* in this room, and, sweetie, that's more than enough for me to think about."

It was time to leave. The danger had passed, or Joan had passed out of thinking there was danger.

She walked with me to the stairs, smiling, cheerful, and squeezed my hand when we said goodbye. She called down after me, "See you next Saturday at the pool, maybe—" but it would be weeks before I saw Joan Lunt again. She was to meet my uncle Clyde the following week and her life in Yewville that seemed to me so orderly and lonely and wonderful would be altered forever.

Clyde had a bachelor's place (that was how the women in our family spoke of it) to which he brought his women friends. It was a row house made of brick and cheap stucco, on the west side of town, near the old, now defunct tanning factories on the river. With the money he made working for a small Yewville construction company, and his occasional gambling wins, Clyde could have afforded to live in a better place, but he hadn't much mind for his surroundings and spent most of his spare time out. He brought Joan Lunt home with him because, for all the slapdash clutter of his house, it was more private than her apartment on Chambers Street, and they wanted privacy, badly.

The first time they were alone together, Clyde laid his hands on Joan's shoulders and kissed her, and she held herself steady, rising to the kiss, putting pressure against the mouth of this man who was virtually a stranger to her so that it was like an exchange, a handshake, between equals. Then, stepping back from the kiss, they both laughed —they were breathless, like people caught short, taken by surprise. Joan Lunt said faintly, "I—I do things sometimes without meaning them," and Clyde said, "Good. So do I."

Through the spring, they were often seen together in Yewville; and when, weekends, they weren't seen, it was supposed they were at Clyde's cabin at Wolf's Head Lake (where he was teaching Joan Lunt to fish) or at the Scholharie Downs race track (where Clyde gambled on the standardbreds). They were an attractive, eye-catching couple. They were frequent patrons of local bars and restaurants, and they turned up regularly at parties given by friends of Clyde's, and at all-night poker parties in the upstairs, rear, of the Iroquois Hotel—Joan Lunt didn't play cards, but she took an interest in Clyde's playing, and, as Clyde told my father, admiringly, she never criticized a move of his, never chided or teased or second-guessed him. "But the woman has me figured out completely," Clyde said. "Almost from the first, when she saw the way I was winning, and the way I kept on, she said, 'Clyde, you're the kind of gambler who won't quit, because, when he's losing, he has to get back to winning, and when he's winning, he has to give his friends a chance to catch up.' "

In May, Clyde brought Joan to a Sunday gathering at our house, a large, noisy affair, and we saw how when Clyde and Joan were separated, in different rooms, they'd drift back together until they were touching, literally touching, without seeming to know what they did, still less that they were being observed. So that was what love was! Always a quickness of a kind was passing between them, a glance, a hand squeeze, a light pinch, a caress, Clyde's lazy fingers on Joan's neck beneath her hair, Joan's arm slipped around Clyde's waist, fingers hooked through his belt loop. I wasn't jealous, but I watched them covertly. My heart yearned for them, though I didn't know what I wanted of them, or for them.

At 13, I was more of a child still than an adolescent girl: thin, long-limbed, eyes too large and naked-seeming for my face and an imagination that rarely flew off into unknown territory but turned, and turned, and turned, upon what was close at hand and known, but not altogether known. Imagination, says Aristotle, begins in desire: But what *is* desire? I could not, nor did I want to, possess my uncle Clyde and Joan Lunt. I wasn't jealous of them, I loved them both. I wanted them to *be.* For this, too, was a radically new idea to me, that a man and a woman might be nearly strangers to each other, yet lovers; lovers, yet nearly strangers; and the love passing between them, charged like electricity, might be visible, without their knowing. Could they know how I dreamt of them!

After Clyde and Joan left our house, my mother complained irritably that she couldn't get to know Joan Lunt. "She's sweet-seeming, and friendly enough, but you know her mind isn't there for you," my mother said. "She's just plain *not there.*"

My father said, "As long as the woman's there for Clyde."

He didn't like anyone speaking critically of his younger brother apart from himself.

But sometimes, in fact, Joan Lunt wasn't there for Clyde: He wouldn't speak of it, but she'd disappear in her car for a day or two or three, without explaining very satisfactorily where she'd gone, or why. Clyde could see by her manner that wherever Joan had gone had, perhaps, not been a choice of hers, and that her disappearances, or flights, left her tired and depressed; but still he was annoyed, he felt betrayed. Clyde Farrell wasn't the kind of man to disguise his feelings. Once, on a Friday afternoon in June before a weekend they'd planned at Wolf's Head Lake, Clyde returned to the construction office at 5:30 P.M. to be handed a message hastily telephoned in by Joan Lunt an hour before: CAN'T MAKE IT THIS WEEKEND. SORRY. LOVE, JOAN. Clyde believed himself humiliated in front of others, vowed he'd never forgive Joan Lunt and that very night, drunk and mean-spirited, he took up again with a former girlfriend . . . and so it went.

But in time they made up, as naturally they would, and Clyde said, "I'm thinking maybe we should get married, to stop this sort of thing," and Joan, surprised, said, "Oh, that isn't necessary, darling—I mean, for you to offer that."

Clyde believed, as others did, that Joan Lunt was having difficulties with a former man friend or husband, but Joan refused to speak of it; just acknowledged that, yes, there was a man, yes, of course he was an *ex* in her life, but she resented so much as speaking of him; she refused to allow him re-entry into her life. Clyde asked, "What's his name?" and Joan shook her head, mutely, just no; no, she would not say, would not utter that name. Clyde asked, "Is he threatening you? Now? Has he ever shown up in Yewville?" and Joan, as agitated as he'd ever seen her, said, "He does what he does, and I do what I do. And I don't talk about it."

But later that summer, at Wolf's Head Lake, in Clyde's bed in Clyde's hand-hewn log cabin on the bluff above the lake, overlooking wooded land that was Clyde Farrell's property for a mile in either direction, Joan Lunt wept bitterly, weakened in the aftermath of love, and said, "If I tell you, Clyde, it will make you feel too bound to me. It will seem to be begging a favor of a kind, and I'm not begging."

Clyde said, "I know you're not."

"I don't beg favors from anyone."

"I know you don't."

"I went through a long spell in my life when I did beg favors, because I believed that was how women made their way, and I was hurt because of it, but not more hurt than I deserved. I'm older now. I know better. The meek don't inherit the earth and they surely don't deserve to."

Clyde laughed sadly and said, "Nobody's likely to take you for meek, Joan honey."

Making love, they were like two swimmers deep in each other, plunging hard. Wherever they were when they made love, it wasn't the place they found themselves in when they returned, and whatever the time, it wasn't the same time.

The trouble came in September: A cousin of mine, another niece of Clyde's, was married, and the wedding party was held in the Nautauga Inn, on Lake Nautauga, about ten miles east of Yewville. Clyde knew the inn's owner, and it happened that he and Joan Lunt, handsomely dressed, were in the large public cocktail lounge adjacent to the banquet room reserved for our party, talking with the owner-bartender, when Clyde saw an expression on Joan's face of a kind he'd never seen on her face before—fear, and more than fear, a sudden sick terror—and he turned to see a stranger approaching them, not slowly, exactly, but with a restrained sort of haste: a man of about 40, unshaven, in a blue seersucker sports jacket now badly rumpled, tieless, a muscled but soft-looking man with a blunt, rough, ruined-handsome face, complexion like an emery board, and this man's eyes were too bleached a color for his skin, unless there was a strange light rising in them. And this same light rose in Clyde Farrell's eyes, in that instant.

Joan Lunt was whispering, "Oh, no—*no,*" pulling at Clyde's arm to turn him away, but naturally, Clyde Farrell wasn't going to step away from a confrontation, and the stranger, who would turn out to be named Robert Waxman, Rob Waxman, Joan Lunt's former husband, divorced from her 15 months before, co-owner of a failing meat-supplying company in Kingston, advanced upon Clyde and Joan smiling as if he knew them both, saying loudly, in a slurred but vibrating voice, "Hello, hello, hello!" and when Joan tried to escape, Waxman leapt after her, cursing, and Clyde naturally intervened, and suddenly, the two men were scuffling, and voices were raised, and before anyone could separate them, there was the astonishing sight of Waxman, with his gravelly face and hot eyes, crouched, holding a pistol in his hand, striking Clyde clumsily about the head and shoulders with the butt and crying, enraged, "Didn't ask to be born! Goddamn you! I didn't ask to be born!" And "I'm no different from you! Any of you! *You!* In my heart!" There were screams as Waxman fired the pistol point-blank at Clyde, a popping sound like a firecracker, and Waxman stepped back to get a better aim—he'd hit his man in the fleshy part of a shoulder—

and Clyde Farrell, desperate, infuriated, scrambled forward in his wedding-party finery, baboon style, not on his hands and knees but on his hands and feet, bent double, face contorted, teeth bared, and managed to throw himself on Waxman, who outweighed him by perhaps 40 pounds, and the men fell heavily to the floor, and there was Clyde Farrell straddling his man, striking him blow after blow in the face, even with his weakened left hand, until Waxman's nose was broken and his nostrils streamed blood, and his mouth, too, was broken and bloody, and someone risked being struck by Clyde's wild fists and pulled him away.

And there on the floor of the breezy screened-in barroom of the Nautauga Inn lay a man, unconscious, breathing erratically, bleeding from his face, whom no one except Joan Lunt knew was Joan Lunt's former husband; and there, panting, hot-eyed, stood Clyde Farrell over him, bleeding, too, from a shoulder wound he was to claim he'd never felt.

Said Joan Lunt repeatedly, "Clyde, I'm sorry. I'm so sorry."

Said Joan Lunt carefully, "I just don't know if I can keep on seeing you. Or keep on living here in Yewville."

And my uncle Clyde was trying hard, trying very hard, to understand.

"You don't love me, then?" he asked several times.

He was baffled, he wasn't angry. It was the following week and by this time he wasn't angry, nor was he proud of what he'd done, though everyone was speaking of it, and would speak of it, in awe, for years. He wasn't proud because, in fact, he couldn't remember clearly what he'd done, what sort of lightning-swift action he'd performed; no conscious decision had been made that he could recall. Just the light dancing up in a stranger's eyes, and its immediate reflection in his own.

Now Joan Lunt was saying this strange, unexpected thing, this thing he couldn't comprehend. Wiping her eyes, and, yes, her voice was shaky, but he recognized the steely stubbornness in it, the resolute will. She said, "I do love you. I've told you. But I can't live like that any longer."

"You're still in love with *him.*"

"Of course I'm not in love with him. But I can't live like that any longer."

"Like what? What I did? I'm not *like* that."

"I'm thirty-six years old. I can't take it any longer."

"Joan, I was only protecting you."

"Men fighting each other, men trying to kill each other—I can't take it any longer."

"I was only protecting you. He might have killed you."

"I know. I know you were protecting me. I know you'd do it again if you had to."

Clyde said, suddenly furious, "You're damned right I would. If that son of a bitch ever—"

Waxman was out on bail and returned to Kingston. Like Clyde Farrell, he'd been treated in the emergency room at Yewville General Hospital; then he'd been taken to the county sheriff's headquarters and booked on charges of assault with a deadly weapon and reckless endangerment of life. In time, Waxman would be sentenced to a year's probation: He had no prior record except for traffic violations; he was to impress the judge with his air of sincere remorse and repentance. Clyde Farrell, after giving testimony and hearing the sentencing, would never see the man again.

Joan Lunt was saying, "I know I should thank you, Clyde. But I can't."

Clyde splashed more bourbon into Joan's glass and into his own. They were sitting at Joan's dinette table beside a window whose grimy and cracked Venetian blinds were tightly closed. Clyde smiled and said, "Never mind thanking me, honey: Just let's forget it."

Joan said softly, "Yes, but I can't forget it."

"It's just something you're saying. Telling yourself. Maybe you'd better stop."

"I want to thank you, Clyde, and I can't. You risked your life for me. I know that. And I can't thank you."

So they discussed it, like this. For hours. For much of a night. Sharing a bottle of bourbon Clyde had brought over. And eventually, they made love, in Joan Lunt's narrow sofa bed that smelled of talcum powder, perfume and the ingrained dust of years, and their lovemaking was tentative and cautious but as sweet as ever, and driving back to his place early in the morning, at dawn, Clyde thought surely things were changed; yes, he was convinced that things were changed. Hadn't he Joan's promise that she would think it all over, not make any decision, they'd see each other that evening and talk it over then? She'd kissed his lips in goodbye, and walked him to the stairs, and watched him descend to the street.

But Clyde never saw Joan Lunt again.

That evening, she was gone, moved out of the apartment, like that, no warning, not even a telephone call, and she'd left only a brief letter behind with CLYDE FARRELL written on the envelope. Which Clyde never showed to anyone and probably, in fact, ripped up immediately.

It was believed that Clyde spent some time, days, then weeks, into the early winter of that year, looking for Joan Lunt; but no one, not even my father, knew exactly what he did, where he drove, whom he questioned, the depth of his desperation or his yearning or his rage, for Clyde wasn't, of course, the kind of man to speak of such things.

Joan Lunt's young friend Sylvie never saw her again, either, nor heard of her. And this hurt me, too, more than I might have anticipated.

And over the years, once I left Yewville to go to college in another state, then to begin my own adult life, I saw less and less of my uncle Clyde. He never married; for a few years, he continued the life he'd been leading before meeting Joan Lunt—a typical "bachelor" life, of its place and time; then he began to spend more and more time at Wolf's Head Lake, developing his property, building small wood-frame summer cottages and renting them out to vacationers, and acting as caretaker for them, an increasingly solitary life no one would have predicted for Clyde Farrell.

He stopped gambling, too, abruptly. His luck had turned, he said.

I saw my uncle Clyde only at family occasions, primarily weddings and funerals. The last time we spoke together in a way that might be called forthright was in 1971, at my grandmother's funeral: I looked up and saw through a haze of tears a man of youthful middle age moving in my general direction, Clyde, who seemed shorter than I recalled, not stocky but compact, with a look of furious compression, in a dark suit that fitted him tightly about the shoulders. His hair had turned not silver but an eerie metallic blond, with faint tarnished streaks, and it was combed down flat and damp on his head, a look here, too, of furious constraint. Clyde's face was familiar to me as my own, yet altered: The skin had a grainy texture, roughened from years of outdoor living, like dried earth, and the creases and dents in it resembled animal tracks; his eyes were narrow, damp, restless; the eyelids looked swollen. He was walking with a slight limp that he tried, in his vanity, to disguise; I learned later that he'd had knee surgery. And the gunshot wound to his left shoulder he'd insisted at the time had not given him much, or any, pain gave him pain now, an arthritic sort of pain, agonizing in cold weather. I stared at my uncle thinking, *Oh, why? Why?* I didn't know if I were seeing the man Joan Lunt had fled from or the man her flight had made.

But Clyde sighted me and hurried over to embrace me, his favorite niece, still. If he associated me with Joan Lunt—and I had the idea he did—he'd forgiven me long ago.

Death gives to life, to the survivors' shared life, that is, an insubstantial quality. It's like an image of absolute clarity reflected in water —then disturbed, shattered into ripples, revealed as mere surface. Its clarity, even its beauty, can resume, but you can't any longer trust in its reality.

So my uncle Clyde and I regarded each other, stricken in that instant with grief. But, being a man, *he* didn't cry.

We drifted off to one side, away from the other mourners, and I saw it was all right between us, it was all right to ask, so I asked if he had ever heard from Joan Lunt after that day. Had he ever heard of her? He said, "I never go where I'm not welcome, honey," as if this were the answer to my question. Then added, seeing my look of distress, "I stopped thinking of her years ago. We don't need each other the way we think we do when we're younger."

I couldn't bear to look at my uncle. *Oh, why? Why?* Somehow, I must have believed all along that there was a story, a story unknown to me, that had worked itself out without my knowing, like a stream tunneling its way underground. I would not have minded not knowing this story could I only know that it *was*.

Clyde said, roughly, "*You* didn't hear from her, did you? The two of you were so close."

He wants me to lie, I thought. But I said only, sadly, "No, I never hear from her. And we weren't close."

Said Clyde, "Sure you were."

The last I saw of Clyde that day, it was after dark and he and my father were having a disagreement just outside the back door of our house. My father insisted that Clyde, who'd been drinking, wasn't in condition to drive his pickup truck back to the lake, and Clyde was insisting he was, and my father said, "Maybe yes, Clyde, and maybe no," but he didn't want to take a chance, why didn't *he* drive Clyde home, and Clyde pointed out truculently that, if my father drove him home, how in hell would he get back here except by taking Clyde's only means of transportation? So the brothers discussed their predicament, as dark came on.

Joyce Carol Oates is one of America's most gifted and most prolific writers. Among her recent novels are *Because It Is Bitter and Because It Is My Heart*, and *You Must Remember This*. Her newest collection of stories is *Heat*, in which "The Swimmers" appears. For *Prize Stories 1991: The O. Henry Awards* she commented: " 'The Swimmers' belongs to a gathering of stories I think of half consciously as having happened 'back there'—'back then.' It's the world of my childhood and young girlhood, in the countryside south of Lockport, New York; an environment very much like that of 'The Swimmers,' as I was, at least in memory, very much like the young girl narrator. . . . My writing as a whole divides, without my intending it so, into areas that seem to me almost geographical—there is the present, there is the entirely fictional, there is 'back then' and 'back there.' Naturally, my heart is most attached to the last named, where recent novels of mine . . . most obviously occur." Miss Oates is Distinguished Professor in the Humanities at Princeton University.

FRANK CONROY

"I began writing short stories as a kid—seventeen and eighteen years old—bumming around Europe. I wrote several stories in Paris, where I lived in the Arab quarter. At Haverford College I was lucky enough to run into a fine teacher willing to do line-by-line editing. I learned a great deal from Professor Ashmead, and in fact sold my first story before graduation. I've continued to work in the short form ever since, but only occasionally. The stories seem to find me rather than the reverse, and I never attempt one unless I feel I really must.

"The spark for 'Midair' came from a single moment. I was in an elevator in Washington, D.C., and saw a delivery boy who looked like my son. For months I pondered the strength and emotional complexity of that moment, and eventually the whole story grew backwards from it.

"I don't believe most writers can or should choose a voice. (There are some remarkable exceptions—Mailer and Doctorow come to mind. They change voices depending on the work. Very great masters, both of them.) For most of us I believe the voice gradually emerges, coming out of all that we have read (I don't mean mimicry, of course, rather the combined influence of thousands of voices), from the exquisite discipline of writing itself, and from who we are at the most fundamental level, from our souls, if you will. In other words, when I'm working, I don't think about it."

MIDAIR

A sunny, windy day on the Lower East Side of New York. The year is 1942. Sean, aged six, is being more or less pulled along the sidewalk by his father, who has shown up from nowhere to take him home from school. Sean tries to keep the pace, although he does not remember the last time he has seen this big, exuberant man, nor is he altogether sure that he trusts him. Mary, on the other side, is nine. Her legs are longer, and she seems happy, skipping every now and then, shouting into the wind, calling him Daddy. Sean cannot hear what they're saying except in fragments—the wind tears at the words. His hand, wrist, and part of his forearm are enclosed in his father's fist. The big man strides along, red-faced, chin jutting forward proudly, his whole carriage suggesting the eagerness and confidence of a soldier marching forward to receive some important, hard-won medal.

He is not a soldier, as Sean's mother has recently explained. He is not in the Army (although a war is going on) but in something called a rest home, where people go in order to rest. He does not seem tired, Sean thinks.

"It'll be a different story now, by God," his father says as they turn the corner onto Seventh Street. "A completely different story." Energy seems to radiate from the man like an electrical charge. His body carries a pale-blue corona, and when he speaks his white teeth give off white lightning. "What a day!" He lets go of the children's hands and makes a sweeping gesture. "An absolute pip of a day. Look at that blue sky! The clouds! Seventh Street! Look how vivid the colors are!"

Sean cannot look. He is preoccupied with the unnatural force of his father's enthusiasm. It is as if all that has been pointed out is too far away to be seen. The boy's awareness is focused on the small bubble of space immediately surrounding himself, his father, and his sister. Within that area he sees clearly—as if his life depended on it—and there is no part of him left over to see anything else.

They reach the tenement building and climb the stoop. His father hesitates at the door.

"The key," he says.

"Mother has it," Mary says.

"You haven't got it?" He rolls his head in exasperation.

"I'm sorry." Mary is afraid she has failed him. "I'm sorry, Daddy."

Sean is uneasy with her use of the word "Daddy." It sounds strange, since they never use it. It is not part of their domestic vocabulary. On those extremely rare occasions when Sean, Mary, and their mother ever mention the man, the word they have always used is "Father."

Mrs. Rosenblum, second floor rear, emerges from the house.

"Good morning," his father says, smiling, catching the door. "In you go, children."

Mrs. Rosenblum has never seen this big man before but recognizes, from his expensive clothes and confident manner, that he is a gentleman, and the father of the children. A quick glance at Mary, smiling as he touches her head, confirms everything.

"Nice," Mrs. Rosenblum says. "Very nice."

Inside, Sean's father takes the steps two at a time. The children follow up to the top floor—the fourth—and find him standing at the door to the apartment, trying the knob.

"No key here, either, I suppose."

"It's the same one," Mary says.

He gives the door a hard push, as if testing. Then he steps back, looks around, and notices the iron ladder leading up to the hatch and the roof.

"Aha! More than one way to skin a cat." He strides over to the ladder and begins to climb. "Follow me, buckos. Up the mainmast!"

"Daddy, what are you doing?" Mary cries.

"We'll use the fire escape." He pushes up the hatch and sunlight pours down. "Come on. It's fun!"

Sean can hear the wind whistling up there as his father climbs through. Mary hesitates an instant and then mounts the ladder. As she approaches the top, Sean follows her. He ascends into the sunshine and the wind.

The big man moves rapidly across the tarred roof to the rear of the building and the twin hoops of the fire-escape railing. He shouts back at the children, but his words are lost. He beckons, turns, and grabs the railings. His feet go over the edge and he begins to descend. Then he stops—his head and shoulders visible—and shouts again. Mary moves forward, the big man sinks out of sight, and Sean follows.

The boy steps to the edge and looks over. His father is ten feet below, on the fire-escape landing, red face up-turned.

"Come on!" The white teeth flash. "The window's open."

The wind whips Mary's skirt around her knees as she goes over. She has to stop and push the hair out of her eyes. When she reaches the landing below, Sean grabs the hoops. Five floors down, a sheet of newspaper flutters across the cement at the bottom of the airshaft. It seems no bigger than a page from a book. He climbs down. Pigeons rise from the airshaft and scatter. On the landing, he sees his father, already inside, lifting Mary through the kitchen window. He follows quickly on his own.

The kitchen, although entirely familiar in every detail, seems slightly odd in its totality. The abruptness of the entry—without the usual preparation of the other rooms—tinges the scene with unreality. Sean follows his father and sister through the kitchen, into the hall, and to the doorway of his mother's room. His father does not enter but simply stops and looks.

"Have you been here before?" Sean asks.

"Of course he has, silly," Mary says rapidly.

His father turns. "Don't you remember?"

"I don't think so," Sean says.

As they pass the main door to the apartment, toward the front of the hall, his father pauses to slip on the chain lock.

For more than an hour they have been rearranging the books on the living-room shelves, putting them in alphabetical order by author. Sean's father stops every now and then, with some favorite book, to do a dramatic reading. The readings become more and more dramatic. He leans down to the children to emphasize the dialogue, shouting in different voices, gesticulating with his free arm in the air, making faces. But then, abruptly, his mood changes.

"The windows are filthy," he says angrily, striding back and forth from one to another, peering at the glass. The books are forgotten now as he goes to the kitchen. Mary quickly pushes them over to the foot of the bookcase. Sean helps. While doing this, they look very quickly, almost furtively, into each other's eyes. It takes a fraction of a second, but Sean understands. He is aware that his father's unexplained abandonment of an activity in which he had appeared to be so deeply involved has frightened Mary. His own feelings are complex—he is gratified that she is scared, since in his opinion she should have been scared all along, while at the same time his own fear, because of hers, escalates a notch.

"What's going to happen?" Sean asks quietly.

"Nothing. It's OK." She pretends not to be afraid.

"Get Mother." The sound of water running in the kitchen.

Mary considers this. "It's OK. She'll come home from work the way she always does."

"That's a long time. That's too long."

The big man returns with a bucket and some rags. His face seems even more flushed. "We'll do it ourselves. Wait till you see the difference." He moves to the central window, and they are drawn in his wake. Sean recognizes a shift in the atmosphere: before, with the books, there was at least a pretense of the three of them doing something together—a game they might all enjoy—but now his father's attention has narrowed and intensified onto the question of the windows. He seems barely aware of the children.

He washes the panes with rapid, sweeping movements. Then he opens the lower frame, bends through, turns, and sits on the sill to do the outside. Sean can see his father's face, concentrated, frowning, eyes searching the glass for streaks.

Sean begins to move backward.

"No," Mary says quickly. "We have to stay."

The boy stops beside the rocking chair where his mother sits after dinner.

The big man reenters, and steps back to regard the results of his work. "Much better. Much, much better." He moves on to the next window. "Fresh water, Mary. Take the bucket."

Mary obeys, and goes back to the kitchen.

The big man stares down at the street. Sean stays by the rocking chair.

"You don't remember," the big man says. "Well, that's all right. Time is different for children. In any case, the past is behind us now. What counts is the future." He gives a short, barking laugh. "Another cliché rediscovered! But that's the way it is. You have to penetrate the clichés, you have to live them out to find out how true they are. What a joke!"

Mary brings the bucket of water to his side. Suddenly he moves closer to the window. He has seen something on the street.

"God damn." He moves back rapidly. He turns and runs down the hall to the kitchen. Sean and Mary can see him closing and locking the rear windows. "Bastards!" he shouts.

Mary moves sideways to glance through the window to the street.

"What is it?" Sean asks.

"An ambulance." Her voice is beginning to quaver. "It must be that ambulance."

Now he comes back into the living room and paces. Then he rushes to the newly washed window, opens it, and tears the gauzy curtains from the rod and throws them aside. Sean can see Mary flinch as the curtains are torn. The big man moves from one window to the next, opening them and tearing away the curtains. Wind rushes through the room. Torn curtains rise from the floor and swirl about.

He gathers the children and sits down on the couch, his arms around their shoulders. Sean feels crushed and tries to adjust his position, but his father only tightens his grip. The big man is breathing fast, staring into the hall, at the door.

"Daddy," Mary says. "It hurts."

A slight release of pressure, but Sean is still held so tightly to the man's side he can barely move.

"Oh, the bastards," his father says. "The tricky bastards."

The buzzer sounds. Then, after a moment, a knock on the door. The big man's grip tightens.

Another knock. The sound of a key. Sean watches the door open a few inches until the chain pulls it short. He sees the glint of an eye.

"Mr. Kennedy? This is Dr. Silverman. Would you open the door, please?"

"Alone, are you, Doctor?" An almost lighthearted tone.

A moment's pause. "No. I have Bob and James here with me." A calm voice, reassuring to Sean. "Please let us in."

"The goon squad," his father says.

"Bob in particular is very concerned. And so am I."

"Bob is a Judas."

"Mr. Kennedy. Be reasonable. We've been through this before, after all."

"No, no." As if correcting a slow student. "This is different. I'm through with you people. I'm through with all of that. I've come home, I'm here with my children, and I'm going to stay."

A pause. "Yes. I can see the children."

"We've been having a fine time. We've been washing the windows, Doctor." An almost inaudible chuckle.

"Mr. Kennedy, I implore you to open the door. We simply must come in. We must discuss your plans."

"I'm not going to open the door. And neither are you. What we have here, Doctor, is a Mexican standoff. Do you get my meaning?"

"I'm very sorry to hear you say that." Another pause—longer this time. "Bob would like a word with you."

"Mr. Kennedy? This is Bob." A younger voice.

"I'm not coming back, Bob. Don't try any crap with me. I know why you're here."

"I'm worried about you. You're flying. You know that."

"Got the little white jacket, eh, Bob? The one with the funny sleeves?"

"Look, if you don't come back they'll assign me to Mr. Farnsworth. You wouldn't do that to me. Please."

"Cut the crap, Bob."

"Listen. I'm with you. You know that. I mean, how many times have we talked about your—"

A tremendous crash as the door is kicked in, the frame splintering where the chain has come away. Sean is aware that things are happening very fast now, and yet he can see it all with remarkable clarity. Wood chips drift lazily through the air. Three men rush through the door—two in white uniforms, one in ordinary clothes. He knows they are running toward the couch as fast as they can—their faces frozen masks of strain—but time itself seems to have slowed down.

Still clamped to his father's side, Sean feels himself rise up into the air. He sees his father's other hand make a grab for Mary, who is trying to escape. He gets hold of her hair, but she twists away with a yell. Sean feels betrayed that she has gotten away. She was the one calling him Daddy. The wind roars as the big man rushes to the window and climbs out on the sill.

"Stop where you are!" he shouts back at the men.

Sean cannot see, but he senses that the men have stopped. He can hear Mary crying, hear the wind, and hear the sound of his father's heart racing under the rough tweed of his jacket. He stares down at the street, at the cracks in the sidewalk. With the very limited motion available to his arms, he finds his father's belt and hangs on with both fists.

"You bastards," his father shouts. "What you don't realize is I can do anything. Anything!"

Something akin to sleepiness comes over Sean. As time passes he realizes—a message from a distant outpost—that he has soiled himself. Finally, they are pulled back in, with great speed and strength, and fall to the floor. His father screams as the men cover him.

In college, his father long dead, and all memory of his father's visit in 1942 completely buried, Sean looks for a wife. He is convinced that if he doesn't find someone before he graduates, he will have missed his chance for all time. The idea of living alone terrifies him, although he is not aware that it terrifies him. He lives as if he did not have a past, and so there is a great deal about himself of which he is not aware. He is entirely ignorant of his lack of awareness, and believes himself to be in full control of his existence. He zeroes in on a bright, rather guarded girl he meets in Humanities 301, and devotes himself to winning her hand. It is a long campaign, and the odds are against him—her family disapproves vehemently, for reasons that are never made clear, and she is more intelligent than Sean, and ambitious, in a way he is not, for power in some as yet unnamed career. She is older than he is. She is not afraid of living alone. Yet in the end his tenacity prevails. Graduate school provides no route for her ambition, she drifts for a bit, and finally capitulates over the telephone. Sean is exultant.

They are married by a judge in her parents' midtown brownstone. Sean is six feet two inches tall, weighs a hundred and thirty-three pounds, and appears, with his Irish, slightly acned face, to be all of seventeen. (He is actually twenty-two.) His wife is struck by the irony of the fact that more than half of the relatives watching the event are divorced. Sean is impressed by the activity outside the window during the ceremony. The New York Foundling Hospital is being torn down—the wrecker's ball exploding walls even as the absurdly short judge drones on. For both of them—in a moment of lucidity whose importance they are too young to recognize—the ceremony is anticlimactic, and faintly ridiculous.

Four years pass, and nothing happens. They both have a small monthly income from trust funds. She dabbles in an occasional project or temporary job but always retreats in mysterious frustration to the safety of their apartment. He writes a book, but it contains nothing, since he knows very little about people, or himself. He remains a boy; the marriage that was to launch him into maturity serves instead to extend his boyhood. Husband and wife, they remain children. They live together in good will, oddly sealed off from one another, and from the world. He dreams of people jumping out of windows, holding hands, in eerie accord. He has no idea what the dreams mean, or where they come from. She confesses that she has never believed in romantic love. They are both frightened of the outside, but they respond differently. She feels that what is out there is too dangerous to fool with. He feels that, however dangerous, it is only out there that strength can be found. In some vague, inchoate way, he knows he needs strength.

Privately, without telling him, she decides to have children. Philip is born. John is born. Sean is exultant.

A summer night in 1966. Sean drives down from Harlem, where he has gotten drunk in a jazz club. The bouncer, an old acquaintance, has sold him an ounce of marijuana. Sean carries it in a sealed envelope in his back pocket. He turns off the Henry Hudson Parkway at Ninety-sixth Street, slips along Riverside Drive for a couple of blocks, turns, and pulls up in front of Judy's house. It's a strange little building—five floors with a turret up the side, a dormer window on her top-floor apartment, bits of crenellation and decoration, like some miniature castle. A Rapunzel house.

He had met her on the sidelines during a soccer game. Kneeling on the grass, he had turned his head to follow the fullback's kick, and found himself looking instead at the slender, blue-jeaned thigh of the girl standing next to him. Perhaps it was the suddenness, the abrupt nearness of the splendid curve of her backside, the images sinking into him before he had time to protect himself. The lust he felt was so pure it seemed, for all its power, magically innocent, and he got to his feet and began talking to her. (She was eventually to disappear into medical school, but never, as it turned out, from his memory.)

He stares up at the dark window. Behind the window is a room, and in the room a bed, in which for a year he has been making love to Judy. She is gone now, away for a month, driving around France in a *deux-chevaux* Citroën leased by him as a gift. The room is dark and empty, and yet he has to go in. He does not question the urge. He simply gets out of the car and approaches the building. Once he is in motion, a kind of heat suffuses him. He experiences something like tunnel vision.

Inside, he scans the mailboxes. A few letters are visible behind the grille in hers. He opens the door with his key and runs up the stairs—turning at landings, climbing, turning, climbing, until he is there, at the top floor. It is midnight, and the building is silent. He slips the key into the lock, turns and pushes. The door will not open. He has forgotten the police lock, the iron bar she'd had installed before she left—with a separate locking mechanism. He doesn't have that key. He leans against the door for a moment, and the faint scent of the room inside reaches him. He is dizzy with the scent, and the door suddenly enrages him. The scent is inside, and he must get inside.

He pounds his shoulder against the glossy black wood in a steady rhythm, putting all his weight against it. The door shakes in its hinges, but he can feel the solidity of the iron bar in the center. There is not an iota of movement in the bar. He moves back in the hallway—halfway to the rear apartment—runs forward, raises his right leg, and kicks the central panel of the door. A terrific crash, but the door does not yield. He continues to run and kick, in a frenzy, until he starts falling down.

Out of breath, he sits on the stairs to the roof and looks at Judy's door. He cannot believe there is no way to get it open. The wood is cracked in several places. Finally, as his breathing slows, he gives up. The iron bar will never move.

Slowly, swirling like smoke, an idea emerges. He turns and looks up the stairs, into the darkness. After a moment he stands up, mounts the stairs, opens the hatch, and climbs out onto the roof. The air cools him—he is drenched with sweat. Purple sky. Stars. He crosses the flat part of the roof to the front of the building, where it suddenly drops off in a steep slope—a Rapunzel roof, tiled with overlapping slate. There is a masonry ridge, perhaps an inch high, at the bottom edge, fifteen feet down. He moves sideways until he comes to a place he estimates lies directly above the dormer window. He gets down on his belly and carefully slides his legs over onto the tiles, lowering more and more of himself onto the steep incline, testing to see if he can control his downward motion. Sufficient control seems possible, and, very slowly, he releases his grip on the roof and begins to slide. His face presses against the slate, and he can feel the sweat from his cheek on the slate. From somewhere off toward Amsterdam Avenue comes the sound of a siren.

He descends blindly and stops when his toes touch the ridge. Beyond the ridge, there is empty space and a clear drop to the sidewalk, but he is unafraid. He remains motionless for several moments, and his noisy brain falls still. He is no longer drunk. A profound calm prevails, a sense of peacefulness—as sweet, to him, as water to some traveler in the desert. Carefully, he slides down sideways until his entire body lies along the ridge. He raises his head and looks at the deserted street below—the pools of light under the street lamps, the tops of the parked cars, the square patterns of the cracks in the sidewalk—and there is a cleanness and orderliness to things. He becomes aware that there is a reality that lies behind the appearance of the world, a pure reality he has never sensed before, and the knowledge fills him with gratitude.

He moves his head farther out and looks for the dormer window.

There it is. He had thought to hang on to the edge of the roof and swing himself down and into the window. In his mind, it had been a perfectly straightforward procedure. In his mind, he had known he could do anything—anything he was capable of imagining. But now, as he looks at the dormer window—too far away, full of tricky angles—he sees that the plan is impossible. He immediately discards the plan, as if he had been caught up in a story that ended abruptly. He no longer has any interest in getting into the apartment.

Moving slowly and carefully, as calm in his soul as the calmness in the great purple sky above him, he retreats. Using the friction of his arms and legs, of his damp palms and the sides of his shoes, he inches his way up the sloping roof. He reaches the top of the building.

Once inside, he closes the roof door behind him and descends rapidly. He passes the door to the apartment without a glance.

As his children are born, Sean begins to write a book about his past. At first he is ebullient, possessed by gaiety. He doesn't remember much—his childhood all jumbled, without chronology. There are only isolated scenes, places, sights and sounds, moods, in no apparent order. It seems a small thing to write down these floating memories, to play with them at a distance. It seems like fun.

His children, simply by coming into the world, have got him started. As the work gets difficult, the fact of his children sustains him in some roundabout fashion. His gaiety changes to a mood of taut attentiveness, as the past he had trivialized with his amnesia begins, with tantalizing slowness, to reveal itself. He knows hard work for the first time in his life, and he is grateful. Soon he finds himself in a kind of trance; after hours of writing he will look down at a page or two with a sense of awe, because the work is better than anything he could reasonably have expected of himself. He will live this way for four years. In his mind, his writing, his ability to write at all, is connected to his children.

He develops a habit of going into their room late at night. Blue light from the street lamp outside angles through the large windows to spill on the waxed wooden floor. Philip is three, sleeping on his side, his small hand holding a rubber frog. Sean crosses the room and looks at John, aged two. Behind delicate eyelids, his eyes move in a dream.

Sean goes to a spot equidistant from both beds and sits down on the floor, his legs folded. He stares at the pale-blue bars of light on the floor and listens. He hears the children breathe. When they move, he hears them move. His mind clears. After half an hour he gets up, adjusts their blankets, and goes to bed.

At a small dinner party with his wife, in Manhattan, he becomes aware that the host and hostess are tense and abstracted. The hostess apologizes and explains that she should have cancelled the dinner. There had been a tragedy that afternoon. The young couple living directly above, on the eighth floor, had left a window open, and their baby girl had somehow pulled herself up and fallen through to her death.

"You're white as a ghost," his wife says as they leave the table. "Sean, you're trembling!"

They forgo coffee, with apologies, and go home immediately. Sean drives fast, parks by a hydrant, and runs up the stoop into the house.

"It's OK, it's OK," his wife says.

He nods to the sitter in the living room and keeps on going, up the stairs, to the children's room. They are asleep, safe in their beds.

"We have to get guardrails," he says, going to the windows, locking them. "Bars—those things—whatever they are."

"Yes. We will," his wife whispers. "OK."

"All the windows. Front and back."

"Yes, yes. Don't wake them, now."

That night he must sleep in their room.

Sean lies full length in the oversize bathtub, hot water to his chin. When he comes home from work (he writes in a small office a mile away), he almost always takes a bath. Philip and John push the door open and rush, stark naked, to the tub. They're about to be put to bed, but they've escaped. Sean doesn't move. Philip's head and shoulders are visible, while John, shorter, shows only his head. Their faces are solemn. Sean stares into their clear, intelligent eyes—so near—and waits, showing no expression, so as to draw the moment out. The sight of them is a profound refreshment.

"Do it, Daddy," Philip says.

"Do what?"

"The noise. When you wash your face."

Sean rises to a sitting position. He washes his face, and then rinses by bending forward and lifting cupped handfuls of water. He simultaneously blows and moans into the handfuls of water, making a satisfying noise. The boys smile. The drama of Daddy-in-the-bath fascinates them. They can't get enough of it.

Sean reaches out and lifts first one and then the other over the edge and into the tub. His hands encompass their small chests, and he can feel the life in them. The boys laugh and splash about, slippery as pink seals fresh from the womb. They hang on his neck and slide over his chest.

His wife comes in and pulls them up, into towels. They go off to bed. Later, in the kitchen, she says, "I wish you wouldn't do that."

"What?"

"In the bath like that."

He is nonplussed. "Good heavens. Why not?"

"It could scare them."

"But they love it!"

"It's icky."

"Icky," he repeats. He goes to the refrigerator for some ice. He can feel the anger starting, his face beginning to flush. He makes a drink and goes into the living room. The anger mounts as he hears the sounds of her working in the kitchen, making dinner. Abruptly, he puts down his drink, goes into the hall, down the stairs, and out the front door. He spends the evening in a bar frequented by writers and returns home drunk at three in the morning.

A few years later, Sean drives home from the office. He has worked late, missed dinner. He thinks about his boys, and begins to weep. He pulls off the expressway and parks in the darkness by the docks. It occurs to him that he is in bad trouble. The weeping has come out of nowhere, to overwhelm him, like some exotic physical reflex, and it could as well have happened on the street or in a restaurant. There is more pressure in him than he can control, or even gauge, his pretenses to the contrary notwithstanding. As he calms down, he allows himself to face the fact that his wife has begun to prepare for the end: a whisper of discreet activity—ice-skating with a male friend on weekends, veiled references to an unknown future, a certain coyness around the house. When he goes, he will have to leave the children. He starts the car, and the boys are in his mind; he feels the weight of their souls in his mind.

He unlocks the front door of the house, hangs his coat in the closet, and climbs the stairs. Silence. A fire burns in the fireplace in the empty living room. The kitchen and dining room are empty. He moves along the landing and starts up the second flight of stairs.

"Daddy." Philip is out of sight in his bedroom, but his voice is clear, his tone direct, as if they'd been talking together, as if they were in the middle of a conversation.

"I'm coming." Sean wonders why the house is so quiet. His wife must be up in the attic. John must be asleep.

"Why were you crying?" Philip asks.

Sean stops at the top of the stairs. His first thought is not how the boy knows but if the knowledge has scared him. He goes into the room, and there is Philip, wide awake, kneeling at the foot of his bed, an expectant look on his face.

"Hi." Sean can see the boy is not alarmed. Curious, focused, but not scared.

"Why?" the boy asks. He is six years old.

"Grownups cry sometimes, you know. It's OK."

The boy takes it in, still waiting.

"I'm not sure," Sean says. "It's complicated. Probably a lot of things. But it's OK. I feel better now."

"That's good."

Sean senses the boy's relief. He sits down on the floor. "How did you know I was crying?" He has never felt as close to another human being as he does at this moment. His tone is deliberately casual.

The boy starts to answer, his intelligent face eager, animated. Sean watches the clearly marked stages: First, Philip draws a breath to begin speaking. He is confident. Second, he searches for language to frame what he knows, but, to his puzzlement, it isn't there. Third, he realizes he can't answer the question. He stares into the middle distance for several moments. Sean waits, but he has seen it all in the boy's face.

"I don't know," the boy says. "I just knew."

"I understand."

After a while the boy gives a sudden large yawn, and gets under the covers. Sean goes downstairs.

The time arrives when he must tell the boys he is going away. Philip is eight, and John almost seven. They go up into the attic playroom. Sean masks the storm in his heart and explains that no one in the family is at fault. He has no choice—he must leave, and not live in the house anymore. As he says this, the boys glance quickly at each other—almost furtively—and Sean feels a special sharp, mysterious pang.

Twelve years later, Sean stands on line at Gate 6 in Boston's Logan Airport, waiting to check in for Eastern's 7:45 A.M. flight to Philadelphia. He is gray-haired, a bit thick around the middle, wears reading glasses low on his nose, and walks, as he moves closer to the desk, with a slight limp, from a cartilage operation on his right knee. He wears a dark suit and a trenchcoat, and carries a soft canvas overnight bag hanging from his shoulder.

"Morning." The attendant is a black woman with whom he has checked in every Monday morning for the last two years. "It's nowhere near full," she says. "I'll upgrade you now." Sean commutes weekly between the two cities, and the airline has provided him with a special card. When first class is not full, he gets a first-class seat at no extra charge. She hands him his boarding pass, and he nods as he moves away.

He sits down and waits for the boarding call. Businessmen surround him, two military officers, three stewardesses, a student carrying a book bag from the university in Boston where Sean teaches. He doesn't recognize the student but watches him abstractedly. Philip and John are that age now. Sean recalls that when his boys entered college, in Washington and Chicago, he found himself easing up on his own students in Boston, softening his style despite himself.

The flight is called. He surrenders his ticket and moves down the enclosed walkway to the open door of the plane. The stewardess recognizes him and takes his coat. He settles down in seat 2-A and accepts a cup of coffee. The ritual is familiar and reassuring. Sean is at ease.

It had not always been thus. When he'd begun commuting, Sean was tense in the air. It had been difficult for him to look out the window without a flash of panic. In his fear, he was abnormally sensitive to the other passengers—controlling his anger at loud conversations, conscious of any intrusion, however minute, into the space allotted to him. Expansive people irritated him the most. He could not abide the way they threw their elbows about, or thoughtlessly stretched their legs, or clumsily bumped into his seat. He found himself hating the other passengers, cataloguing their faults like a miser counting money. But eventually, as he got used to flying, he began to recognize the oddness, the almost pathological oddness of his hatred, and it went away. Only on very rough flights did it recur.

Now he can gaze down through miles of empty space without fear. He wonders why, and concludes that both his former fear of heights and his present lack of fear are inexplicable. The stewardess brings breakfast, and his right knee cracks painfully as he adjusts his position.

The tenth summer of Sunday softball. The game Sean helped to organize had become a tradition in the town of Siasconset. Philip and John began as small boys and grew to young men playing the infield. Sean's second wife had taken pictures from the start, and the effect was that of time-lapse photography—a collapsed history in which the father grew older, the sons grew taller and stronger, and everyone else stayed more or less the same. Sean stood on the mound with a one-run lead, runner at first, and two outs. The batter was Gino, a power hitter. Sean threw an inside pitch and watched Gino's hips come around, watched the bat come around, and heard the snap of solid contact. The ball disappeared in speed toward third base. Sean turned to see John frozen in the air, impossibly high off the ground, feet together, toes pointed down, his legs and torso perfectly aligned in a smooth curve, a continuous brushstroke, his long arm pointing straight up at full extension, and there, nestled deep in the pocket of his glove, the white ball.

Sean gave a shout of joy, dimly aware of pain in his knee, shouting all the way down as he fell, twisting, utterly happy, numb with pleasure.

The stewardess clears away his breakfast. Below, New York City slips past. He finds the old neighborhood, even the street, but he can't make out the house where his first wife still lives. They have retained good relations, and talk on the phone every month or so. His second, younger wife approves of the first, and vice versa. Sean is absurdly proud of this.

"Do you ever dream about me?" he had once asked her on the phone. "I mean, do I ever appear in your dreams?"

Slightly taken aback, she had laughed nervously. "No. What an odd question."

"I only ask because you crop up in mine. What is it—eleven years now, twelve? You still show up now and then."

The plane lands smoothly at the Philadelphia airport. Looping his bag over his shoulder, Sean is out the door, through the building, and into a cab.

"Downtown. The Drexler Building."

In his late forties, to his amazement, and through a process he never completely understood, the board of the Drexler Foundation had asked him to direct that part of their organization which gave money to the arts. It is work he enjoys.

He pays the driver and stares up at the Drexler Building—seventy stories of glass reflecting the clouds, the sky. Pushing through the big revolving door, he crosses the lobby, quickening his step as he sees the express elevator ready to leave. He jumps through just as the doors close behind him, pushes the button for the sixty-fifth floor, and turns.

For a split second he is disoriented. Philip, his older son, stands before him on the other side of the elevator, facing front. Sean's heart lurches, and then he sees that it is a young man of Philip's age, size, and general appearance, delivering a large envelope to Glidden & Glidden, on sixty-four. For a moment the two ideas overlap—the idea of Philip and the idea of the young man—and in that moment time seems to slow down. It is as if Sean had seen his son across a supernatural barrier—as if he, Sean, were a ghost haunting the elevator, able to see the real body of his son but unable to be seen by him. An almost unbearable sadness comes over him. As he emerges from this illusion, he knows full well that his son is hundreds of miles away at college, and yet he finds within himself a pressure of love for the young man so great it is all he can do to remain silent. The elevator ascends, and Sean regains control of himself. Now he can see the young man clearly —alert, a little edgy, clear blue eyes, a bit of acne.

"I hate elevators," the young man says, his eyes fixed on the lights above the door indicating the floors.

"I'm not crazy about them, but it beats walking."

The elevator approaches sixty-four, but then the lights go out, the emergency light comes on, and it stops between sixty-three and sixty-four. A slight bump downward. Sean grabs the rail involuntarily. Under the flat white light of the emergency bulb, the young man is pale, gaunt-looking.

"Oh my God," he says.

They fall a few feet more.

The young man presses himself into a corner. His eyes are wild.

Sean is utterly calm.

"Oh God oh God oh God." The young man's voice begins to rise.

"This has happened to me several times," Sean lies. "In Chicago. Once in Baltimore. The elevators have brakes, non-electrical, separate from all the other systems, which automatically engage if the elevator exceeds a certain speed." This, he thinks, is the truth. "Do you understand what I'm saying?"

The young man's mouth is open, as if to scream. He looks in all directions, finally at Sean.

"It can't fall. It can't. Do you understand?"

"Yes." The young man swallows hard.

"We're perfectly safe."

Sean watches the young man as several minutes go by. He remains silent, remembering his own panic in airplanes, his own need for privacy on those occasions, guessing that the boy feels likewise. After another minute, however, he can see the fear rising again in the young man's face. Sean shrugs off his bag and crosses the space between them.

"Listen," he says quietly, "it's going to be OK."

The young man is breathing fast. He stares at Sean without seeing him. Sean reaches out and takes the young man's head in his hands.

"I want you to listen to me, now. We are quite safe. Focus on me, now. I know we are safe, and if you focus on me *you* will know we are safe." The young man sees him now. He moves his head slightly in Sean's hands.

"Hypnotism," he whispers.

"No, for Christ's sake, it isn't hypnotism," Sean says. "We're going to stay like this until the lights come on. We're going to stay like this until the door opens, or they come get us, or whatever." Sean can feel the young man begin to calm down. He holds the boy's head gently and stares into his eyes. "Good. That's good."

After a while the lights come on, the elevator rises, and the doors open. The boy jumps out. "Come on, come on!" he cries.

Sean smiles. "This is sixty-four. I'm going to sixty-five."

The young man moves forward, but the door closes. The elevator goes up one floor, and Sean gets out.

That night, as he lies in bed waiting for sleep, Sean goes over the entire incident in his mind. He laughs aloud, remembering the young man's expression when he realized Sean was going to stay in the elevator.

Then he remembers the day in 1942 when his father showed up unexpectedly, took him home from school, washed the windows, and carried him out on the windowsill. He remembers looking down at the cracks in the sidewalk. Here, in the darkness, he can see the cracks in the sidewalk from more than forty years ago. He feels no fear—only a sense of astonishment.

Frank Conroy, Director of the University of Iowa Writers Workshop, is the author of the classic autobiography *Stop-Time,* and of a collection of stories, *Midair.*

HARRIET DOERR

"One of the best things about aging is being able to watch imagination overtake memory. A childhood once considered unremarkable is now revealed packed with fascinating incidents and people.

"In their astonishing hats, my relatives wave gloved hands from the running boards of touring cars. Trailed by children, they sweep down the aisles of Majestic Opera Houses to see *Chu Chin Chow* or of Orpheums to see Houdini. They sit fully clothed on beaches, and in their guest rooms hang a framed poem that starts, "A garden is a lovesome thing, God wot."

"Did I actually ride the roller coaster fifteen consecutive times in order to have every fifth ride free? Is it true we were allowed to drive a car at thirteen and forbidden to see *The Sheik*?

"Even more recent recollections have begun to tilt toward myth. In a Mexican village, did the mayor shoot himself and his mistress with a single bullet on the front seat of his old Chevrolet? Did every ditch in Mexico turn pink with wild cosmos during the summer rains?

"Most incredible of all is my finding a few of the right words for images, putting them down, and eventually seeing them printed and published.

"The story 'Edie: A Life' is fiction. Its scenes, situations, and characters, except for Edie herself, are invented and have no connection with real life, if there is such a thing."

EDIE: A LIFE

IN the middle of an April night in 1919, a plain woman named Edith Fisk, lifted from England to California on a tide of world peace, arrived at the Ransom house to raise five half-orphaned children.

A few hours later, at seven in the morning, this Edith, more widely called Edie, invited the three eldest to her room for tea. They were James, seven; Eliza, six; and Jenny, four. Being handed cups of tea, no matter how reduced by milk, made them believe that they had grown up overnight.

"Have some sugar," said Edie, and spooned it in. Moments later she said, "Have another cup." But her h's went unspoken and became the first of hundreds, then thousands, which would accumulate in the corners of the house and thicken in the air like sighs.

In an adjoining room the twins, entirely responsible for their mother's death, had finished their bottles and fallen back into guiltless sleep. At the far end of the house, the widower, Thomas Ransom, who had spent the night aching for his truant wife, lay across his bed, half awake, half asleep, and dreaming.

The three children sat in silence at Edie's table. She had grizzled hair pulled up in a knot, heavy brows, high cheeks, and two long hairs in her chin. She was bony and flat, and looked starched, like the apron she had tied around her. Her teeth were large and white and even, her eyes an uncompromising blue.

She talked to the children as if they were her age, forty-one. "My father was an ostler," she told them and they listened without comprehension. "My youngest brother died at Wipers," she said. "My nephew was gassed at Verdun."

These were places the children had never heard of. But all three of them, even Jenny, understood the word, die.

"Our mother died," said James.

Edie nodded.

"I was born, oldest of eight, in Atherleigh, a town in Devon. I've lived in five English counties," she told them, without saying what a county was. "And taken care of thirty children, a few of them best forgotten."

"Which ones?" said James.

But Edie only talked of her latest charges, the girls she had left to come to America.

"Lady Alice and Lady Anne," said Edie, and described two paragons of quietness and clean knees who lived in a castle in Kent.

Edie didn't say "castle," she said "big brick house." She didn't say "lake," she said "pond." But the children, dazzled by illustrations in Cinderella and King Arthur, assumed princesses. And after that, they assumed castle, tower, moat, lake, lily, swan.

Lady Alice was seven and Lady Anne was eight when last seen immaculately crayoning with their ankles crossed in their tower overlooking the lake.

Eliza touched Edie's arm. "What is gassed?" she said.

Edie explained.

Jenny lifted her spoon for attention. "I saw father cry," she said. "Twice."

"Oh, be quiet," said James.

With Edie, they could say anything.

After that morning, they would love tea forever, all their lives, in sitting rooms and restaurants, on terraces and balconies, at sidewalk cafes and whistle stops, even under awnings in the rain. They would drink it indiscriminately, careless of flavor, out of paper cups or Spode, with lemon, honey, milk, or cream, with spices or with rum.

Before Edie came to the Ransom house, signs of orphanhood were everywhere—in the twins' colic, in Eliza's aggravated impulse to pinch Jenny, in the state of James' sheets every morning. Their father, recognizing symptoms of grief, brought home wrapped packages in his overcoat pockets. He gave the children a Victrola and Harry Lauder records.

"Shall we read?" he would ask in the evening, and take Edward Lear from the shelf. "There was an Old Man with a beard," read

Thomas Ransom, and he and his children listened solemnly to the unaccustomed voice speaking the familiar words.

While the twins baffled everyone by episodes of weight loss and angry tears, various efforts to please were directed toward the other three. The cook baked cakes and frosted their names into the icing. The sympathetic gardener packed them into his wheelbarrow and pushed them at high speeds down sloping paths. Two aunts, the dead mother's sisters, improvised weekly outings—to the ostrich farm, the alligator farm, the lion farm, to a picnic in the mountains, a shell hunt at the beach. These contrived entertainments failed. None substituted for what was needed: the reappearance at the piano or on the stairs of a young woman with freckles, green eyes, and a ribbon around her waist.

Edie came to rescue the Ransoms through the intervention of the aunts' English friend, Cissy. When hope for joy in any degree was almost lost, Cissy wrote and produced the remedy.

The aunts brought her letter to Thomas Ransom in his study on a February afternoon. Outside the window a young sycamore, planted by his wife last year, cast its sparse shadow on a patch of grass.

Cissy wrote that all her friends lost sons and brothers in the war and she was happy she had none to offer up. Wherever one went in London wounded veterans, wearing their military medals, were performing for money. She saw a legless man in uniform playing an accordion outside Harrod's. Others, on Piccadilly, had harmonicas wired in front of their faces so they could play without hands. Blind men, dressed for parade, sang in the rain for theatre queues.

And the weather, wrote Cissy. Winter seemed to be a state of life and not a season. How lucky one was to be living, untouched by it all, in America, particularly California. Oh, to wake up to sunshine every morning, to spend one's days warm and dry.

Now she arrived at the point of her letter. Did anyone they knew want Edith Fisk, who had taken care of children for twenty-five years and was personally known to Cissy? Edie intended to live near a cousin in Texas. California might be just the place.

The reading of the letter ended.

"Who is Cissy?" said Thomas Ransom, unable to foresee that within a dozen years he would marry her.

James, who had been listening at the door, heard only the first part of the letter. Long before Cissy proposed Edie, he was upstairs in his room, trying to attach a harmonica to his mouth with kite string.

Edie was there within two months. The aunts and Thomas Ransom began to witness change.

Within weeks the teasing stopped. Within months the nighttime sheets stayed dry. The twins, male and identical, fattened and pulled toys apart. Edie bestowed on each of the five equal shares of attention and concern. She hung their drawings in her room, even the ones of moles in traps and inhabited houses burning to the ground. Samples of the twins' scribblings remained on permanent display. The children's pictures eventually occupied almost all one wall and surrounded a framed photograph of Lady Alice and Lady Anne, two small light-haired girls sitting straight-backed on dappled ponies.

"Can we have ponies?" Eliza and Jenny asked their father, but he had fallen in love with a woman named Trish and, distracted, brought home a cage of canaries instead.

Edie and the Ransom children suited each other. It seemed right to them all that she had come to braid hair, turn hems, push swings, take walks; to apply iodine to cuts and embrace the cry that followed, to pinch her fingers between the muddy rubber and the shoe. Edie stopped nightmares almost before they started. At a child's first gasp she would be in the doorway, uncombed and toothless, tying on her wrapper, a glass of water in her hand.

The older children repaid this bounty with torments of their own devising. They would rush at her in a trio, shout, "We've 'idden your 'at in the 'all," and run shrieking with laughter, out of her sight. They crept into her room at night, found the pink gums and big white teeth where they lay floating in a mug and, in a frenzy of bad manners, hid them in a hat box or behind the books.

Edie never reported these lapses of deportment to Thomas Ransom. Instead she would invoke the names and virtues of Lady Alice and Lady Anne.

"They didn't talk like roustabouts," said Edie. "They slept like angels through the night."

Between spring and fall the nonsense ceased. Edie grew into the Ransoms' lives and was accepted there, like air and water and the food they ate. From the start, the children saw her as a refuge. Flounder as they might in the choppy sea where orphans and half-orphans drown, they trusted her to save them.

Later on, when their father emerged from mourning, Edie was the mast they clung to in a squall of stepmothers.

Within a period of ten years Thomas Ransom, grasping at the outer fringe of happiness, brought three wives in close succession to the matrimonial bed he first shared with the children's now sainted mother. He chose women he believed were like her, and it was true that all three, Trish, Irene, and Cissy, were small-boned and energetic. But they were brown-eyed and, on the whole, not musical.

The first to come was Trish, nineteen years old and porcelain-skinned. Before her arrival Thomas Ransom asked the children not to come knocking at his bedroom door day and night, as they had in the past. Once she was there, other things changed. The children heard him humming at his desk in the study. They noticed that he often left in mid-morning, instead of at eight, for the office where he practiced law.

Eliza asked questions at early morning tea. "Why are they always in their room, with the door locked?"

And Jenny said, "Yes. Even before dinner."

"Don't you know anything?" said James.

Edie poured more pale tea. "Hold your cups properly. Don't spill," she told them, and the lost *h* floated into the steam rising from the pot.

Trish, at nineteen, was neither mother nor sister to the children. Given their priorities of blood and birth and previous residence, they inevitably outdistanced her. They knew to the oldest steamer trunk and the latest cookie the contents of the attic and larder. They walked oblivious across rugs stained with their spilled ink. The hall banister shone with the years of their sliding. Long ago they had enlisted the cook and the gardener as allies. Three of them remembered their mother. The other two thought they did.

Trish said good morning at noon and drove off with friends. Later she paused to say goodnight in a rustle of taffeta on Thomas Ransom's arm as they left for a dinner or a dance.

James made computations. "She's nine years older than I am," he said, "and eighteen years younger than father."

"He keeps staring at her," said Eliza.

"And kissing her hand," said Jenny.

Edie opened a door on a sliver of her past. "I knew a girl once with curly red hair like that, in Atherleigh."

"What was her name?" James asked, as if for solid evidence.

Edie bit off her darning thread. She looked backward with her inward eye. Finally she said, "Lily Stiles. The day I went into service in Dorset, Lily went to work at the Rose and Plough."

"The Rose and Plough," repeated Eliza. "What's that?"

"It's a pub," said Edie, and she explained what a public house was. Immediately this establishment, with its gleaming bar and its game of darts, was elevated in the children's minds to the mysterious realm of Lady Alice and Lady Anne and set in place a stone's throw from their castle.

At home, Trish's encounters with her husband's children were brief. In passing, she waved to them all and patted the twins on their dark heads. She saw more of the three eldest on those Saturday afternoons when she took them, along with Edie, to the movies.

Together they sat in the close, expectant dark of the Rivoli Theatre, watched the shimmering curtains part, shivered to the organist's opening chords and, at the appearance of an image on the screen, cast off their everyday lives to be periled, rescued, rejected, and adored. They sat spellbound through the film and when the words, The End, came on, rose depleted and blinking from their seats to face the hot sidewalk and full sun outside.

Trish selected the pictures and, though they occasionally included Fairbanks films and ones that starred the Gishes, these were not her favorites. She detested comedies. To avoid Harold Lloyd, they saw

Rudolph Valentino in "The Sheik." Rather than endure Buster Keaton, they went to "Gypsy Blood," starring Alla Nazimova.

"I should speak to your father," Edie would say later on at home. But she never did. Instead, she only remarked at bedtime, "It's a nice change, going to the pictures."

Trish left at the end of two years, during which the children according to individual predispositions, grew taller and developed the hands and feet and faces they would always keep. They learned more about words and numbers, they began to like oysters, they swam the Australian crawl. They survived crises. These included scarlet fever, which the twins contracted and recovered from, and James' near electrocution as a result of his tinkering with wires and sockets.

Eliza and Jenny, exposed to chicken pox on the same day, ran simultaneous fevers and began to scratch. Edie brought ice and invented games. She cleared the table between their beds and knotted a handkerchief into arms and legs and a smooth, round head. She made it face each invalid and bow.

"This is how my sister Frahnces likes to dahnce the fahncy dahnces," Edie said, and the knotted handkerchief waltzed and two-stepped back and forth across the table.

Mesmerized by each other, the twins made few demands. A mechanical walking bear occupied them for weeks, a wind-up train for months. They shared a rocking horse and crashed slowly into one another on tricycles.

James, at eleven, sat in headphones by the hour in front of a crystal radio set. Sometimes he invited Edie to scratch a chip of rock with wire and hear a human voice advance and recede in the distance.

"Where's he talking from?" Edie would ask, and James said, "Oak Bluff. Ten miles away."

Together they marveled.

The two aunts, after one of their frequent visits, tried to squeeze the children into categories. James is the experimenter, they agreed. Jenny, the romantic. The twins, at five, too young to pigeon-hole. Eliza was the bookish one.

A single-minded child, she read while walking to school, in the car on mountain curves, on the train in tunnels, on her back on the beach at noon, in theatres under dimming lights, between the sheets by flashlight. Eliza saw all the world through thick lenses adjusted for fine print. On Saturdays, she would often desert her invited friend and choose to read by herself instead.

At these times Edie would approach the bewildered visitor. Would she like to feed the canaries? Climb into the tree house?

"We'll make tiaras," she told one abandoned guest and, taking Jenny along, led the way to the orange grove.

"We're brides," announced Jenny a few minutes later, and she and Eliza's friend, balancing circles of flowers on their heads, stalked in a barefoot procession of two through the trees.

That afternoon, Jenny, as though she had never seen it before, inquired about Edie's ring. "Are you engaged?"

"I was once," said Edie, and went on to expose another slit of her past. "To Alfred Trotter."

"Was he killed at Wipers?"

Edie shook her head. "The war came later. He worked for his father at the Rose and Plough."

In a field beyond the grove, Jenny saw a plough, ploughing roses.

"Why didn't you get married?"

Edie looked at her watch and said it was five o'clock. She brushed off her skirt and got to her feet. "I wasn't the only girl in Atherleigh."

Jenny, peering into the past, caught a glimpse of Lily Stiles behind the bar at the Rose and Plough.

After Trish left, two more years went by before the children's father brought home his third wife. This was Irene, come to transplant herself in Ransom ground. Behind her she trailed a wake of friends, men with beards and women in batik scarves, who sat about the porch with big hats between them and the sun. In a circle of wicker chairs, they discussed Cubism, Freud, Proust, and Schoenberg's twelve-tone row. They passed perfumed candies to the children.

Irene changed all the lampshades in the house from white paper to red silk, threw a Persian prayer rug over the piano, and gave the children incense sticks for Christmas. She recited poems translated from the Sanskrit and wore saris to the grocery store. In spite of efforts on both sides, Irene remained an envoy from a foreign land.

One autumn day, not long before the end of her tenure as Thomas Ransom's wife, she took Edie and all five children to a fortune teller at the county fair. A pale-eyed, wasted man sold them tickets outside Madame Zelma's tent and pointed to the curtained entrance. Crowding into the stale air of the interior, they gradually made out the fortune teller's veiled head and jewelled neck behind two lighted candelabra on a desk.

"Have a seat," said Madame.

All found places on a bench or hassocks, and rose, one by one, to approach the palmist as she beckoned them to a chair facing her.

Madame Zelma, starting with the eldest, pointed to Edie.

"I see children," said the fortune teller. She concentrated in silence for a moment. "You will cross the ocean. I see a handsome man."

Alfred Trotter, thought Jenny. Us.

Madame Zelma, having wound Edie's life backward from present to past, summoned Irene.

"I see a musical instrument," said Madame, as if she knew of Irene's guitar and the chords in minor keys that were its repertory. "Your flower is the poppy. Your fruit, the pear." The fortune teller leaned closer to Irene's hand. "Expect a change of residence soon."

Edie and the children listened.

And so the fortunes went, the three eldest's full of prizes and professions, talents and awards, happy marriages, big families, silver mines and fame.

By the time Madame Zelma reached the twins, she had little left to predict. "Long lives," was all she told them. But what more could anyone divine from the trackless palms of seven-year-olds?

By the time Cissy, the next wife, came, James' voice had changed and his sisters had bobbed their hair. The twins had joined in painting an oversized panorama titled, "After the Earthquake." Edie hung it on her wall.

Cissy, the children's last stepmother, traveled all the way from England, like Edie. Introduced by the aunts through a letter, Thomas

Ransom met her in London, rode with her in Hyde Park, drove with her to Windsor for the day, then took her boating on the upper reaches of the Thames. They were married in a registry, she for the third, he for the fourth time, and spent their honeymoon on the Isle of Skye in a long, gray drizzle.

"I can hardly wait for California," said Cissy.

Once there, she lay about in the sun until she blistered. "Darling, bring my parasol, bring my gloves," she entreated whichever child was near.

"Are the hills always this brown?" she asked, splashing rose water on her throat. "Has that stream dried up for good?"

Cissy climbed mountain paths looking for wildflowers and came back with toyon and sage. Twice a week on her horse, Sweet William, she rode trails into the countryside, flushing up rattlesnakes instead of grouse.

On national holidays which celebrated American separation from Britain, Cissy felt in some way historically at fault. On the day before Thanksgiving, she strung cranberries silently at Edie's side. On the Fourth of July they sat together holding sparklers six thousand miles from the counties where their roots, still green, were sunk in English soil.

During the dry season of the year, from April to December, the children sometimes watched Cissy as she stood at a corner of the terrace, her head turning from east to west, her eyes searching the implacable blue sky. But for what? An English bird? The smell of fog?

By now the children were half grown or more, and old enough to recognize utter misery.

"Cissy didn't know what to expect," they told each other.

"She's homesick for the Sussex downs," said Edie, releasing the *h* into space.

"Are you homesick, too, for Atherleigh?" asked Eliza.

"I am not."

"You knew what to expect," said Jenny.

Edie said, "Almost."

The children discussed with her the final departure of each stepmother.

"Well, she's gone," said James, who was usually called to help carry out bags. "Maybe we'll have some peace."

After Cissy left, he made calculations. "Between the three of them, they had six husbands," he told the others.

"And father's had four wives," said one of the twins. "Six husbands and four wives make ten," said the other.

"Ten what?" said James.

"Poor souls," said Edie.

At last the children were as tall as they would ever be. The aunts could no longer say, "How are they ever to grow up?" For here they were, reasonably bright and reasonably healthy, survivors of a world war and a great depression, durable relics of their mother's premature and irreversible defection and their father's abrupt remarriages.

They had got through it all—the removal of tonsils, the straightening of teeth, the first night at camp, the first dance, the goodbyes waved from the rear platforms of trains that, like boats crossing the Styx, carried them away to college. This is not to say they were the same children they would have been if their mother had lived. They were not among the few who can suffer anything, loss or gain, without effect. But no one could point to a Ransom child's smile or frown or sleeping habits, and reasonably comment, "No mother."

Edie stayed in the Ransom house until the twins left for college. By now, Eliza and Jenny were married, James married, divorced, and remarried. Edie went to all the graduations and weddings.

On these occasions the children hurried across playing fields and lawns to reach and embrace her.

"Edie!" they said. "You came!" They introduced their fellow graduates and the persons they had married. "This is Edie. Edie, this is Bill, Terry, Peter, Joan," and were carried off in whirlwinds of friends.

As the Ransom house emptied of family, it began to expand. The bedrooms grew larger, the hall banister longer, the porch too wide for the wicker chairs. Edie took leave of the place for want of children in 1938. She was sixty years old.

She talked to Thomas Ransom in his study, where his first wife's portrait, painted in pastels, had been restored to its place on the wall facing his desk. Edie sat under the green-eyed young face, her unfaltering blue glance on her employer. Each tried to make the parting easy. It was clear, however, that they were dividing between them, top to bottom, a frail, towering structure of nineteen accumulated years, which was the time it had taken to turn five children with their interminable questions, unfounded terrors, and destructive impulses, into mature adults who could vote, follow maps, make omelets, and reach an accord of sorts with life and death.

Thinking back over the intervening years, Thomas Ransom remembered Edie's cousin in Texas and inquired, only to find that Texas had been a disappointment, as had America itself. The cousin had returned to England twelve years ago.

"Would you like that?" he asked Edie. "To go back to England?"

She had grown used to California, she said. She had no one in Atherleigh. So, in the end, prompted by the look in his first wife's eyes, Thomas Ransom offered Edie a cottage and a pension to be hers for the rest of her life.

Edie's beach cottage was two blocks back from the sea and very small. On one wall she hung a few of the children's drawings, including the earthquake aftermath. Opposite them, by itself, she hung the framed photograph of Lady Alice and Lady Anne, fair and well-seated astride their ponies. Edie had become the repository of pets. The long-lived fish swam languidly in one corner of her sitting room, the last of the canaries moulted in another.

Each Ransom child came to her house once for tea, pulling in to the curb next to a mailbox marked Edith Fisk.

"Edie, you live so far away!"

On their first Christmas apart, the children sent five cards, the next year four, then two for several years, then one, or sometimes none.

During the first September of Edie's retirement, England declared war on Germany. She knitted socks for the British troops and, on one occasion four years after she left it, returned briefly to the Ransom house. This was when the twins were killed in Europe a month apart at the age of twenty-four, one in a fighter plane over the Baltic, the other in a bomber over the Rhine. Two months later Thomas Ransom asked

Edie to dispose of their things and she came back for a week to her old, now anonymous, room.

She was unprepared for the mass of articles to be dealt with. The older children had cleared away childhood possessions at the time of their marriages. But here were all the books the twins had ever read, from Dr. Doolittle to Hemingway, and all their entertainments, from a Ouija board to skis and swim fins. Years of their civilian trousers, coats, and shoes crowded the closets.

Edie first wrapped and packed the bulky objects, then folded into cartons the heaps of clothing, much of which she knew. A week was barely time enough to sort it all and reach decisions. Then, suddenly, as though it had been a matter of minutes, the boxes were packed and at the door. Edie marked each one with black crayon. Boys' Club, she printed, Children's Hospital, Red Cross, Veterans.

That afternoon, she stood for a moment with Thomas Ransom on the porch, the silent house behind them. The November air was cold and fresh, the sky cloudless.

"Lovely day," said Edie.

Thomas Ransom nodded, admiring the climate while his life thinned out.

If the three surviving children had written Edie during the years that followed, this is what she would have learned.

At thirty-five, James, instead of having become an electrical engineer or a master mechanic, was a junior partner in his father's law firm. Twice divorced and about to take a new wife, he had apparently learned nothing from Thomas Ransom, not even how to marry happily once. Each marriage had produced two children, four intended cures that failed. James' practice involved foreign corporations and he was often abroad. He moved from executive offices to board rooms and back, and made no attempt to diagnose his discontent. On vacations at home, he dismantled and reassembled heaters and fans, and wired every room of his house for sound.

Whenever he visited England, he tried, and failed, to find time to send Edie a card.

Eliza had been carried off from her research library by an archaeologist ten years older and three inches shorter than she. He took her first to Guatemala, then to Mexico, where they lived in a series of jungle huts in Chiapas and Yucatán. It was hard to find native help and the clothes Eliza washed often hung drying for days on the teeming underbrush. Her damp books, on shelves and still in boxes, began to mildew. She cooked food wrapped in leaves over a charcoal fire. On special days, like her birthday and Christmas, Eliza would stand under the thatch of her doorway and stare northwest through the rain and vegetation in the direction of the house where she was born and first tasted tea.

Edie still lived in the house when Jenny, through a letter from her last stepmother, Cissy, met the Englishman she would marry. Thin as a pencil and pale as parchment, he had entered the local university as an exchange fellow. Jenny was immediately moved to take care of him, sew on his missing buttons, comb his sandy hair. His English speech enchanted her.

"Tell about boating at Henley," she urged him. "Tell about climbing the Trossachs. Explain cricket." And while he described these things as fully as his inherent reserve would allow, the inflections of another voice fell across his. Jenny heard "fahncy dahnces." She heard "poor souls."

"Have you ever been to Atherleigh in Devon?" she asked him.

"That's Hatherleigh," he said.

If Jenny had written Edie, she would have said, "I love Massachusetts, I love my house, I can make scones, come and see us."

On a spring afternoon in 1948, Thomas Ransom called his children together in the same study where the aunts had read Cissy's letter of lament and recommendation. The tree his wife planted thirty years ago towered in green leaf outside the window.

The children had gathered from the outposts of the world—James from Paris, Eliza from the Mayan tropics, Jenny from snowed-in Boston. When he summoned them, they had assumed a crisis involving their father. Now they sat uneasily under the portrait of their mother, a girl years younger than themselves. Thomas Ransom offered them tea and sherry. He looked through the window at the tree.

At last he presented his news. "Edie is dying," he said. "She is in the hospital with cancer," as if cancer were a friend Edie had always longed to share a room with.

They visited her on a shining April morning, much like the one when they first met. With their first gray hairs and new lines at their eyes, they waited a moment on the hospital steps.

James took charge. "We'll go in one by one," he said.

So, as if they had rehearsed together, each of them stood alone outside the door that had a sign, No Visitors, stood there while carts of half-eaten lunches or patients prepared for surgery were wheeled past, stood and collected their childhood until a nurse noticed and said, "Go in. She wants to see you." Then, one after another, they pushed the door open, went to the high narrow bed, and said, "Edie."

She may not have known they were there. She had started to be a skeleton. Her skull was pulling her eyes in. Once they had spoken her name, there was nothing more to say. Before leaving, they touched the familiar, unrecognizable hand of shoe laces and hair ribbons and knew it, for the first time, disengaged.

After their separate visits, they assembled again on the hospital steps. It was now they remembered Lady Alice and Lady Anne.

"Where was that castle?" Eliza asked.

"In Kent," said Jenny.

All at one time, they imagined the girls in their tower after tea. Below them, swans pulled lengthening reflections behind them across the smooth surface of the lake. Lady Alice sat at her rosewood desk, Lady Anne at hers. They were still seven and eight years old. They wrote on thick paper with mother-of-pearl pens dipped into ivory ink-wells.

"Dear Edie," wrote Lady Alice.

"Dear Edie," wrote Lady Anne.

"I am sorry to hear you are ill," they both wrote.

Then, as if they were performing an exercise in penmanship, they copied "I am sorry" over and over in flowing script until they reached the bottom of the page. When there was no more room, they signed one letter, Alice, and the other letter, Anne.

In the midst of all this, Edie died.

Harriet Doerr's first novel, *Stones for Ibarra,* published when she was seventy-four years old, won the National Book Award. Born in Pasadena, California, she spent many years in Mexico, but now again makes her home in California. She studied in the Graduate Fiction program at Stanford University, and has published many stories. She is at work on a new novel.

CHARLES BAXTER

" 'Fenstad's Mother' began with a remark from a friend of mine. In a writing class he taught, someone wrote the following sentence: 'I, like most people, have a unique problem.' I was reminded of the adult-education classes I have taught, where I knew more about sentences than the students did, but they knew more about life.

"I began an early draft of the story, which was then called 'Composition'—Fenstad being a character who easily loses his composure. But I saw right away that the story was too funny, too much a surface story. I needed a character who saw through the situation, saw it in political and social terms, and I thought of the old radicals I had known in Minneapolis. My aunt Helen Baxter was not exactly a radical, but she was an enthusiastic letter-writer, and she, along with her friend Brenda Ueland (whose writing is now becoming better known), provided me with a kind of spiritual energy for the figure of Clara Fenstad.

"The landscapes are those of Minneapolis. York Follette is composited out of several students of mine at Wayne State University, and his name remembers that old-time Wisconsin political activist, 'Fighting Bob' La Follette. (People sometimes forget that the Midwest has a history of political activism.) Clara Fenstad's voice dominates the story: she's strong, intelligent, sympathetic, and a bit of a bully, all of which I liked about her. I enjoyed writing the scenes with her in them, and I still miss her. The panhandler in the restaurant is our current history and possibly our future. The climax of the story is tucked away in one sentence near the end."

FENSTAD'S MOTHER

ON Sunday morning after communion Fenstad drove across town to visit his mother. Behind the wheel, he exhaled with his hand flat in front of his mouth to determine if the wine on his breath could be detected. He didn't think so. Fenstad's mother was a lifelong social progressive who was amused by her son's churchgoing, and, wine or no wine, she could guess where he had been. She had spent her life in the company of rebels and deviationists, and she recognized all their styles.

Passing a frozen pond in the city park, Fenstad slowed down to watch the skaters, many of whom he knew by name and skating style. From a distance they were dots of color ready for flight, frictionless. To express grief on skates seemed almost impossible, and Fenstad liked that. He parked his car on a residential block and took out his skates from the back seat, where he kept them all winter. With his fingertips he touched the wooden blade guards, thinking of the time. He checked his watch; he had fifteen minutes.

Out on the ice, still wearing his churchy Sunday-morning suit, tie, and overcoat, but now circling the outside edge of the pond with his bare hands in his overcoat pockets, Fenstad admired the overcast sky and luxuriated in the brittle cold. He was active and alert in winter but felt sleepy throughout the summer. He passed a little girl in a pink jacket, pushing a tiny chair over the ice. He waved to his friend Ann, an off-duty cop, practicing her twirls. He waved to other friends. Without exception they waved back. As usual, he was impressed by the way skates improved human character.

Twenty minutes later, in the doorway of her apartment, his mother said, "Your cheeks are red." She glanced down at his trousers, damp with melted snow. "You've been skating." She kissed him on the cheek and turned to walk into her living room. "Skating after church? Isn't that some sort of doctrinal error?"

"It's just happiness," Fenstad said. Quickly he checked her apartment for any signs of memory loss or depression. He found none and immediately felt relief. The apartment smelled of soap and Lysol, the signs of an old woman who wouldn't tolerate nonsense. Out on her coffee table, as usual, were the letters she was writing to her congressman and to political dictators around the globe. Fenstad's mother pleaded for enlightened behavior and berated the dictators for their bad political habits.

She grasped the arm of the sofa and let herself down slowly. Only then did she smile. "How's your soul, Harry?" she asked. "What's the news?"

He smiled back and smoothed his hair. Martin Luther King's eyes locked into his from the framed picture on the wall opposite him. In the picture King was shaking hands with Fenstad's mother, the two of them surrounded by smiling faces. "My soul's okay, Ma," he said. "It's a hard project. I'm always working on it." He reached down for a chocolate-chunk cookie from a box on top of the television. "Who brought you these?"

"Your daughter Sharon. She came to see me on Friday." Fenstad's mother tilted her head at him. "You *want* to be a good person, but she's the real article. Goodness comes to her without any effort at all. She says you have a new girlfriend. A pharmacist this time. Susan, is it?" Fenstad nodded. "Harry, why does your generation always have to find the right person? Why can't you learn to live with the wrong person? Sooner or later everyone's wrong. Love isn't the most important thing, Harry, far from it. Why can't you see that? I still don't comprehend why you couldn't live with Eleanor." Eleanor was Fenstad's ex-wife. They had been divorced for a decade, but Fenstad's mother hoped for a reconciliation.

"Come on, Ma," Fenstad said. "Over and done with, gone and gone." He took another cookie.

"You live with somebody so that you're living with *somebody*, and then you go out and do the work of the world. I don't understand all this pickiness about lovers. In a pinch anybody'll do, Harry, believe me."

On the side table was a picture of her late husband, Fenstad's mild, middle-of-the-road father. Fenstad glanced at the picture and let the silence hang between them before asking, "How are you, Ma?"

"I'm all right." She leaned back in the sofa, whose springs made a strange, almost human groan. "I want to get out. I spend too much time in this place in January. You should expand my horizons. Take me somewhere."

"Come to my composition class," Fenstad said. "I'll pick you up at dinnertime on Tuesday. Eat early."

"They'll notice me," she said, squinting. "I'm too old."

"I'll introduce you," her son said. "You'll fit right in."

Fenstad wrote brochures in the publicity department of a computer company during the day, and taught an extension English-composition class at the downtown campus of the state university two nights a week. He didn't need the money; he taught the class because he liked teaching strangers and because he enjoyed the sense of hope that classrooms held for him. This hopefulness and didacticism he had picked up from his mother.

On Tuesday night she was standing at the door of the retirement apartment building, dressed in a dark blue overcoat—her best. Her stylishness was belied slightly by a pair of old fuzzy red earmuffs. Inside the car Fenstad noticed that she had put on perfume, unusual for her. Leaning back, she gazed out contentedly at the nighttime lights.

"Who's in this group of students?" she asked. "Working-class people, I hope. Those are the ones you should be teaching. Anything else is just a career."

"Oh, they work, all right." He looked at his mother and saw, as they passed under a streetlight, a combination of sadness and delicacy in her face. Her usual mask of tough optimism seemed to be deserting her. He braked at a red light and said, "I have a hairdresser and a garage mechanic and a housewife, a Mrs. Nelson, and three guys who're sanitation workers. Plenty of others. One guy you'll really like is a young black man with glasses who sits in the back row and reads *Workers' Vanguard* and Bakunin during class. He's brilliant. I don't know why he didn't test out of this class. His name's York Follette, and he's—"

"I want to meet him," she said quickly. She scowled at the moonlit snow. "A man with ideas. People like that have gone out of my life."

She looked over at her son. "What I hate about being my age is how *nice* everyone tries to be. I was never nice, but now everybody is pelting me with sugar cubes." She opened her window an inch and let the cold air blow over her, ruffling her stiff gray hair.

When they arrived at the school, snow had started to fall, and at the other end of the parking lot a police car's flashing light beamed long crimson rays through the dense flakes. Fenstad's mother walked deliberately toward the door, shaking her head mistrustfully at the building and the police. Approaching the steps, she took her son's hand. "I liked the columns on the old buildings," she said, "the old university buildings, I mean. I liked Greek Revival better than this Modernist-bunker stuff." Inside, she blinked in the light at the smooth, waxed linoleum floors and cement-block walls. She held up her hand to shade her eyes. Fenstad took her elbow to guide her over the snow melting in puddles in the entryway. "I never asked you what you're teaching tonight."

"Logic," Fenstad said.

"Ah." She smiled and nodded. "Dialectics!"

"Not quite. Just logic."

She shrugged. She was looking at the clumps of students standing in the glare of the hallway, drinking coffee from paper cups and smoking cigarettes in the general conversational din. She wasn't used to such noise: she stopped in the middle of the corridor underneath a wall clock and stared happily in no particular direction. With her eyes shut she breathed in the close air, smelling of wet overcoats and smoke, and Fenstad remembered how much his mother had always liked smoke-filled rooms, where ideas fought each other, and where some of those ideas died.

"Come on," he said, taking her hand again. Inside Fenstad's classroom six people sat in the angular postures of pre-boredom. York Follette was already in the back row, his copy of *Workers' Vanguard* shielding his face. Fenstad's mother headed straight for him and sat down in the desk next to his. Fenstad saw them shake hands, and in two minutes they were talking in low, rushed murmurs. He saw York Follette laugh quietly and nod. What was it that blacks saw and appreciated in his mother? They had always liked her—written to her, called her, checked up on her—and Fenstad wondered if they recognized something in his mother that he himself had never been able to see.

At seven thirty-five most of the students had arrived and were talking to each other vigorously, as if they didn't want Fenstad to start and thought they could delay him. He stared at them, and when they wouldn't quiet down, he made himself rigid and said, "Good evening. We have a guest tonight." Immediately the class grew silent. He held his arm out straight, indicating with a flick of his hand the old woman in the back row. "My mother," he said. "Clara Fenstad." For the first time all semester his students appeared to be paying attention: they turned around collectively and looked at Fenstad's mother, who smiled and waved. A few of the students began to applaud; others joined in. The applause was quiet but apparently genuine. Fenstad's mother brought herself slowly to her feet and made a suggestion of a bow. Two of the students sitting in front of her turned around and began to talk to her. At the front of the class Fenstad started his lecture on logic, but his mother wouldn't quiet down. This was a class for adults. They were free to do as they liked.

Lowering his head and facing the blackboard, Fenstad reviewed problems in logic, following point by point the outline set down by the textbook: *post hoc* fallacies, false authorities, begging the question, circular reasoning, *ad hominem* arguments, all the rest. Explaining these problems, his back turned, he heard sighs of boredom, boldly expressed. Occasionally he glanced at the back of the room. His mother was watching him carefully, and her face was expressing all the complexity of dismay. Dismay radiated from her. Her disappointment wasn't personal, because his mother didn't think that people as individuals were at fault for what they did. As usual, her disappointed hope was located in history and in the way people agreed with already existing histories.

She was angry with him for collaborating with grammar. She would call it unconsciously installed authority. Then she would find other names for it.

"All right," he said loudly, trying to make eye contact with someone in the room besides his mother, "let's try some examples. Can anyone tell me what, if anything, is wrong with the following sentence? 'I, like most people, have a unique problem.' "

The three sanitation workers, in the third row, began to laugh. Fenstad caught himself glowering and singled out the middle one.

"Yes, it is funny, isn't it?"

The man in the middle smirked and looked at the floor. "I was just thinking of my unique problem."

"Right," Fenstad said. "But what's wrong with saying, 'I, like most people, have a unique problem'?"

"Solving it?" This was Mrs. Nelson, who sat by the window so that she could gaze at the tree outside, lit by a streetlight. All through class she looked at the tree as if it were a lover.

"Solving what?"

"Solving the problem you have. What is the problem?"

"That's actually not what I'm getting at," Fenstad said. "Although it's a good *related* point. I'm asking what might be wrong logically with that sentence."

"It depends," Harold Ronson said. He worked in a service station and sometimes came to class wearing his work shirt with his name tag, HAROLD, stitched into it. "It depends on what your problem is. You haven't told us your problem."

"No," Fenstad said, "my problem is *not* the problem." He thought of Alice in Wonderland and felt, physically, as if he himself were getting small. "Let's try this again. What might be wrong with saying that most people have a unique problem?"

"You shouldn't be so critical," Timothy Melville said. "You should look on the bright side, if possible."

"What?"

"He's right," Mrs. Nelson said. "Most people have unique problems, but many people do their best to help themselves, such as taking night classes or working at meditation."

"No doubt that's true," Fenstad said. "But why can't most people have a unique problem?"

"Oh, I disagree," Mrs. Nelson said, still looking at her tree. Fenstad glanced at it and saw that it was crested with snow. It *was* beautiful.

No wonder she looked at it. "I believe that most people do have unique problems. They just shouldn't talk about them all the time."

"Can anyone," Fenstad asked, looking at the back wall and hoping to see something there that was not wall, "can anyone give me an example of a unique problem?"

"Divorce," Barb Kjellerud said. She sat near the door and knitted during class. She answered questions without looking up. "Divorce is unique."

"No, it isn't!" Fenstad said, failing in the crucial moment to control his voice. He and his mother exchanged glances. In his mother's face for a split second was the history of her compassionate, ambivalent attention to him. "Divorce is not unique." He waited to calm himself. "It's everywhere. Now try again. Give me a unique problem."

Silence. "This is a trick question," Arlene Hubbly said. "I'm sure it's a trick question."

"Not necessarily. Does anyone know what *unique* means?"

"One of a kind," York Follette said, gazing at Fenstad with dry amusement. Sometimes he took pity on Fenstad and helped him out of jams. Fenstad's mother smiled and nodded.

"Right," Fenstad crowed, racing toward the blackboard as if he were about to write something. "So let's try again. Give me a unique problem."

"You give *us* a unique problem," one of the sanitation workers said. Fenstad didn't know whether he'd been given a statement or a command. He decided to treat it as a command.

"All right," he said. He stopped and looked down at his shoes. Maybe it *was* a trick question. He thought for ten seconds. Problem after problem presented itself to him. He thought of poverty, of the assaults on the earth, of the awful complexities of love. "I can't think of one," Fenstad said. His hands went into his pockets.

"That's because problems aren't personal," Fenstad's mother said from the back of the room. "They're collective." She waited while several students in the class sat up and nodded. "And people must work together on their solutions." She talked for another two minutes, taking the subject out of logic and putting it neatly in politics, where she knew it belonged.

•

The snow had stopped by the time the class was over. Fenstad took his mother's arm and escorted her to the car. After letting her down on the passenger side and starting the engine, he began to clear the front windshield. He didn't have a scraper and had forgotten his gloves, so he was using his bare hands. When he brushed the snow away on his mother's side, she looked out at him, surprised, a terribly aged Sleeping Beauty awakened against her will.

Once the car had warmed up, she was in a gruff mood and repositioned herself under the seat belt while making quiet but aggressive remarks. The sight of the new snow didn't seem to calm her. "Logic," she said at last. "That wasn't logic. Those are just rhetorical tactics. It's filler and drudgery."

"I don't want to discuss it now."

"All right. I'm sorry. Let's talk about something more pleasant."

They rode together in silence. Then she began to shake her head. "Don't take me home," she said. "I want to have a spot of tea somewhere before I go back. A nice place where they serve tea, all right?"

He parked outside an all-night restaurant with huge front plate-glass windows; it was called Country Bob's. He held his mother's elbow from the car to the door. At the door, looking back to make sure that he had turned off his headlights, he saw his tracks and his mother's in the snow. His were separate footprints, but hers formed two long lines.

Inside, at the table, she sipped her tea and gazed at her son for a long time. "Thanks for the adventure, Harry. I do appreciate it. What're you doing in class next week? Oh, I remember. How-to papers. That should be interesting."

"Want to come?"

"Very much. I'll keep quiet next time, if you want me to."

Fenstad shook his head. "It's okay. It's fun having you along. You can say whatever you want. The students loved you. I knew you'd be a sensation, and you were. They'd probably rather have you teaching the class than me."

He noticed that his mother was watching something going on behind him, and Fenstad turned around in the booth so that he could see what it was. At first all he saw was a woman, a young woman with long hair wet from snow and hanging in clumps, talking in the aisle to two young men, both of whom were nodding at her. Then she moved on to the next table. She spoke softly. Fenstad couldn't hear her words, but he saw the solitary customer to whom she was speaking shake his head once, keeping his eyes down. Then the woman saw Fenstad and his mother. In a moment she was standing in front of them.

She wore two green plaid flannel shirts and a thin torn jacket. Like Fenstad, she wore no gloves. Her jeans were patched, and she gave off a strong smell, something like hay, Fenstad thought, mixed with tar and sweat. He looked down at her feet and saw that she was wearing penny loafers with no socks. Coins, old pennies, were in both shoes; the leather was wet and cracked. He looked in the woman's face. Under a hat that seemed to collapse on either side of her head, the woman's face was thin and chalk-white except for the fatigue lines under her eyes. The eyes themselves were bright blue, beautiful, and crazy. To Fenstad, she looked desperate, percolating slightly with insanity, and he was about to say so to his mother when the woman bent down toward him and said, "Mister, can you spare any money?"

Involuntarily, Fenstad looked toward the kitchen, hoping that the manager would spot this person and take her away. When he looked back again, his mother was taking her blue coat off, wriggling in the booth to free her arms from the sleeves. Stopping and starting again, she appeared to be stuck inside the coat; then she lifted herself up, trying to stand, and with a quick, quiet groan slipped the coat off. She reached down and folded the coat over and held it toward the woman. "Here," she said. "Here's my coat. Take it before my son stops me."

"Mother, you can't." Fenstad reached forward to grab the coat, but his mother pulled it away from him.

When Fenstad looked back at the woman, her mouth was open, showing several gray teeth. Her hands were outstretched, and he understood, after a moment, that this was a posture of refusal, a gesture saying no, and that the woman wasn't used to it and did it awkwardly. Fenstad's mother was standing and trying to push the coat toward the woman, not toward her hands but lower, at waist level, and she was saying, "Here, here, here, here." The sound, like a human birdcall, frightened Fenstad, and he stood up quickly, reached for his wallet, and removed the first two bills he could find, two twenties. He grabbed the woman's chapped, ungloved left hand.

"Take these," he said, putting the two bills in her icy palm, "for the love of God, and please go."

He was close to her face. Tonight he would pray for her. For a moment the woman's expression was vacant. His mother was still pushing the coat at her, and the woman was unsteadily bracing herself. The woman's mouth was open, and her stagnant-water breath washed over him. "I know you," she said. "You're my little baby cousin."

"Go away, please," Fenstad said. He pushed at her. She turned, clutching his money. He reached around to put his hands on his mother's shoulders. "Ma," he said, "she's gone now. Mother, sit down. I gave her money for a coat." His mother fell down on her side of the booth, and her blue coat rolled over on the bench beside her, showing the label and the shiny inner lining. When he looked up, the woman who had been begging had disappeared, though he could still smell her odor, an essence of wretchedness.

"Excuse me, Harry," his mother said. "I have to go to the bathroom."

She rose and walked toward the front of the restaurant, turned a corner, and was out of sight. Fenstad sat and tried to collect himself. When the waiter came, a boy with an earring and red hair in a flattop, Fenstad just shook his head and said, "More tea." He realized that his mother hadn't taken off her earmuffs, and the image of his mother in the ladies' room with her earmuffs on gave him a fit of uneasiness. After getting up from the booth and following the path that his mother had taken, he stood outside the ladies'-room door and, when no one came in or out, he knocked. He waited for a decent interval. Still hearing no answer, he opened the door.

His mother was standing with her arms down on either side of the first sink. She was holding herself there, her eyes following the hot water as it poured from the tap around the bright porcelain sink down into the drain, and she looked furious. Fenstad touched her and she snapped toward him.

"Your logic!" she said.

He opened the door for her and helped her back to the booth. The second cup of tea had been served, and Fenstad's mother sipped it in silence. They did not converse. When she had finished, she said, "All right. I do feel better now. Let's go."

At the curb in front of her apartment building he leaned forward and kissed her on the cheek. "Pick me up next Tuesday," she said. "I want to go back to that class." He nodded. He watched as she made her way past the security guard at the front desk; then he put his car into drive and started home.

That night he skated in the dark for an hour with his friend, Susan, the pharmacist. She was an excellent skater; they had met on the ice. She kept late hours and, like Fenstad, enjoyed skating at night. She listened attentively to his story about his mother and the woman in the restaurant. To his great relief she recommended no course of action. She listened. She didn't believe in giving advice, even when asked.

The following Tuesday, Fenstad's mother was again in the back row next to York Follette. One of the fluorescent lights overhead was flickering, which gave the room, Fenstad thought, a sinister quality, like a debtors' prison or a refuge for the homeless. He'd been thinking about such people for the entire week. For seven days now he had caught whiffs of the woman's breath in the air, and one morning, Friday, he thought he caught a touch of the rotten-celery smell on his own breath, after a particularly difficult sales meeting.

Tonight was how-to night. The students were expected to stand at the front of the class and read their papers, instructing their peers and answering questions if necessary. Starting off, and reading her paper in a frightened monotone, Mrs. Nelson told the class how to bake a cheese soufflé. Arlene Hubbly's paper was about mushroom hunting. Fenstad was put off by the introduction. "The advantage to mushrooms," Arlene Hubbly read, "is that they are delicious. The disadvantage to mushrooms is that they can make you sick, even die." But then she explained how to recognize the common shaggymane by its cylindrical cap and dark tufts; she drew a model on the board. She warned the class against the *Clitocybe illudens*, the Jack-o'-Lantern. "Never eat a mushroom like this one or *any* mushroom that glows in the dark. Take heed!" she said, fixing her gaze on the class. Fenstad saw his mother taking rapid notes. Harold Ronson, the mechanic, reading his own prose painfully and slowly, told the class how to get rust spots out of their automobiles. Again Fenstad noticed his mother taking notes. York Follette told the class about the proper procedures for laying down attic insulation and how to know when enough was enough, so that a homeowner wouldn't be robbed blind, as he put it, by the salesmen, in whose ranks he had once counted himself.

Barb Kjellerud had brought along a cassette player, and told the class that her hobby was ballroom dancing; she would instruct them in the basic waltz. She pushed the play button on the tape machine, and "Tales from the Vienna Woods" came booming out. To the accompaniment of the music she read her paper, illustrating, as she went, how the steps were to be performed. She danced alone in front of them, doing so with flair. Her blond hair swayed as she danced, Fenstad noticed. She looked a bit like a contestant in a beauty contest who had too much personality to win. She explained to the men the necessity of leading. Someone had to lead, she said, and tradition had given this responsibility to the male. Fenstad heard his mother snicker.

When Barb Kjellerud asked for volunteers, Fenstad's mother raised her hand. She said she knew how to waltz and would help out. At the front of the class she made a counterclockwise motion with her hand, and for the next minute, sitting at the back of the room, Fenstad watched his mother and one of the sanitation workers waltzing under the flickering fluorescent lights.

"What a wonderful class," Fenstad's mother said on the way home. "I hope you're paying attention to what they tell you."

Fenstad nodded. "Tea?" he asked.

She shook her head. "Where're you going after you drop me off?"

"Skating," he said. "I usually go skating. I have a date."

"With the pharmacist? In the dark?"

"We both like it, Ma." As he drove, he made an all-purpose gesture. "The moon and the stars," he said simply.

When he left her off, he felt unsettled. He considered, as a point of courtesy, staying with her a few minutes, but by the time he had this idea he was already away from the building and was headed down the street.

He and Susan were out on the ice together, skating in large circles, when Susan pointed to a solitary figure sitting on a park bench near the lake's edge. The sky had cleared; the moon gave everything a cold, fine-edged clarity. When Fenstad followed the line of Susan's finger, he saw at once that the figure on the bench was his mother. He realized it simply because of the way she sat there, drawn into herself, attentive even in the winter dark. He skated through the uncleared snow over the ice until he was standing close enough to speak to her. "Mother," he said, "what are you doing here?"

She was bundled up, a thick woolen cap drawn over her head, and two scarves covering much of her face. He could see little other than the two lenses of her glasses facing him in the dark. "I wanted to see you two," she told him. "I thought you'd look happy, and you did. I like to watch happiness. I always have."

"How can you see us? We're so far away."

"That's how I saw you."

This made no sense to him, so he asked, "How'd you get here?"

"I took a cab. That part was easy."

"Aren't you freezing?"

"I don't know. I don't know if I'm freezing or not."

He and Susan took her back to her apartment as soon as they could get their boots on. In the car Mrs. Fenstad insisted on asking Susan what kind of safety procedures were used to ensure that drugs weren't smuggled out of pharmacies and sold illegally, but she didn't appear to listen to the answer, and by the time they reached her building, she seemed to be falling asleep. They helped her up to her apartment. Susan thought that they should give her a warm bath before putting her into bed, and, together, they did. She did not protest. She didn't even seem to notice them as they guided her in and out of the bathtub.

Fenstad feared that his mother would catch some lung infection, and it turned out to be bronchitis, which kept her in her apartment for the first three weeks of February, until her cough went down. Fenstad came by every other day to see how she was, and one Tuesday, after work, he went up to her floor and heard piano music: an old recording, which sounded much-played, of the brightest and fastest jazz piano he had ever heard—music of superhuman brilliance. He swung open the door to her apartment and saw York Follette sitting near his mother's bed. On the bedside table was a small tape player, from which the music poured into the room.

Fenstad's mother was leaning back against the pillow, smiling, her eyes closed.

Follette turned toward Fenstad. He had been talking softly. He motioned toward the tape machine and said, "Art Tatum. It's a cut called 'Battery Bounce.' Your mother's never heard it."

"Jazz, Harry," Fenstad's mother said, her eyes still closed, not needing to see her son. "York is explaining to me about Art Tatum and jazz. Next week he's going to try something more progressive on me." Now his mother opened her eyes. "Have you ever heard such music before, Harry?"

They were both looking at him. "No," he said, "I never heard anything like it."

"This is my unique problem, Harry." Fenstad's mother coughed and then waited to recover her breath. "I never heard enough jazz." She smiled. "What glimpses!" she said at last.

After she recovered, he often found her listening to the tape machine that York Follette had given her. She liked to hear the Oscar Peterson Trio as the sun set and the lights of evening came on. She now often mentioned glimpses. Back at home, every night, Fenstad spoke about his mother in his prayers of remembrance and thanksgiving, even though he knew she would disapprove.

Charles Baxter has published a novel, *First Light,* a collection of poems, and three volumes of stories, including, most recently, *A Relative Stranger.* His stories have been anthologized in *Best American Short Stories* and *Prize Stories: The O. Henry Awards,* and have been published in a number of magazines. He lives in Ann Arbor, and teaches at the University of Michigan.

AMY TAN

" 'Rules of the Game' was at one time a jumbled thirteen-page manuscript which I submitted to my first writing workshop in 1985. It turned into a phenomenal bit of beginner's luck for me.

"I got the original idea for the story from an article in *Life* magazine about two Chinese-American chess prodigies. Since I didn't play chess, I figured the story was good material for fiction. As I began to write, the story kept veering from my original intentions—a cerebral piece about chess—to one that concerned the relationship between a girl and her greatest ally and adversary, her mother. In the end, I wrote a shapeless story about a woman from the ages of five to thirty-six and titled it 'Endgame.'

"At the workshop, Molly Giles (author of *Rough Translations*) told me that what I had written was not a story, but the beginnings of a dozen or more stories. She also pointed out that, although it was told in the first person, it had no one consistent voice but many voices. She suggested I rewrite, using each of the story fragments as a jumping-off point.

"Molly Giles liked the rewrite enough to recommend it to *FM Five*, a small literary magazine (later called *The Short Story Review*, and now, alas, defunct). Shortly after that, an editor at *Seventeen* read it in *FM Five* and decided to reprint it under the title 'Rules of the Game.' And then, lo and behold, an agent, Sandra Dijkstra, read the story in *Seventeen* and asked to represent me. . . .

"Eventually I reworked those other dozen or so beginnings into a collection of sixteen stories told by eight different first-person voices. The collection is now called *The Joy Luck Club*, and beyond any intentions I ever had in writing it, the book was received by reviewers and the public as a novel."

RULES OF THE GAME

I was six when my mother taught me the art of invisible strength. It was a strategy for winning arguments, respect from others, and eventually, though neither of us knew it at the time, chess games.

"Bite back your tongue," scolded my mother when I cried loudly, yanking her hand toward the store that sold bags of salted plums. At home, she said, "Wise guy, he not go against wind. In Chinese we say, Come from South, blow with wind—poom!—North will follow. Strongest wind cannot be seen."

The next week I bit back my tongue as we entered the store with the forbidden candies. When my mother finished her shopping, she quietly plucked a small bag of plums from the rack and put it on the counter with the rest of the items.

My mother imparted her daily truths so she could help my older brothers and me rise above our circumstances. We lived in San Francisco's Chinatown. Like most of the other Chinese children who played in the back alleys of restaurants and curio shops, I didn't think we were poor. My bowl was always full, three five-course meals every day, beginning with a soup full of mysterious things I didn't want to know the names of.

We lived on Waverly Place, in a warm, clean, two-bedroom flat that sat above a small Chinese bakery specializing in steamed pastries and dim sum. In the early morning, when the alley was still quiet, I could smell fragrant red beans as they were cooked down to a pasty sweetness. By daybreak, our flat was heavy with the odor of fried sesame balls and sweet curried chicken crescents. From my bed, I would listen as my father got ready for work, then locked the door behind him, one-two-three clicks.

At the end of our two-block alley was a small sandlot playground with swings and slides well-shined down the middle with use. The play area was bordered by wood-slat benches where old-country people sat cracking roasted watermelon seeds with their golden teeth and scattering the husks to an impatient gathering of gurgling pigeons. The best playground, however, was the dark alley itself. It was crammed with daily mysteries and adventures. My brothers and I would peer into the medicinal herb shop, watching old Li dole out onto a stiff sheet of white paper the right amount of insect shells, saffron-colored seeds, and pungent leaves for his ailing customers. It was said that he once cured a woman dying of an ancestral curse that had eluded the best of American doctors. Next to the pharmacy was a printer who specialized in gold-embossed wedding invitations and festive red banners.

Farther down the street was Ping Yuen Fish Market. The front window displayed a tank crowded with doomed fish and turtles struggling to gain footing on the slimy green-tiled sides. A hand-written sign informed tourists, "Within this store, is all for food, not for pet." Inside, the butchers with their bloodstained white smocks deftly gutted the fish while customers cried out their orders and shouted, "Give me your freshest," to which the butchers always protested, "All are freshest." On less crowded market days, we would inspect the crates of live frogs and crabs which we were warned not to poke, boxes of dried cuttlefish, and row upon row of iced prawns, squid, and slippery fish. The sanddabs made me shiver each time; their eyes lay on one flattened side and reminded me of my mother's story of a careless girl who ran into a crowded street and was crushed by a cab. "Was smash flat," reported my mother.

At the corner of the alley was Hong Sing's, a four-table café with a recessed stairwell in front that led to a door marked "Tradesmen." My brothers and I believed the bad people emerged from this door at night. Tourists never went to Hong Sing's, since the menu was printed only in Chinese. A Caucasian man with a big camera once posed me and my playmates in front of the restaurant. He had us move to the side of the picture window so the photo would capture the roasted duck with its head dangling from a juice-covered rope. After he took the picture, I told him he should go into Hong Sing's and eat dinner. When he smiled and asked me what they served, I shouted, "Guts and duck's feet and octopus gizzards!" Then I ran off with my friends, shrieking with laughter as we scampered across the alley and hid in the entryway grotto of the China Gem Company, my heart pounding with hope that he would chase us.

My mother named me after the street that we lived on: Waverly Place Jong, my official name for important American documents. But my family called me Meimei, "Little Sister." I was the youngest, the only daughter. Each morning before school, my mother would twist and yank on my thick black hair until she had formed two tightly wound pigtails. One day, as she struggled to weave a hard-toothed comb through my disobedient hair, I had a sly thought.

I asked her, "Ma, what is Chinese torture?" My mother shook her head. A bobby pin was wedged between her lips. She wetted her palm and smoothed the hair above my ear, then pushed the pin in so that it nicked sharply against my scalp.

"Who say this word?" she asked without a trace of knowing how wicked I was being. I shrugged my shoulders and said, "Some boy in my class said Chinese people do Chinese torture."

"Chinese people do many things," she said simply. "Chinese people do business, do medicine, do painting. Not lazy like American people. We do torture. Best torture."

My older brother Vincent was the one who actually got the chess set. We had gone to the annual Christmas party held at the First Chinese Baptist Church at the end of the alley. The missionary ladies had put together a Santa bag of gifts donated by members of another church. None of the gifts had names on them. There were separate sacks for boys and girls of different ages.

One of the Chinese parishioners had donned a Santa Claus costume and a stiff paper beard with cotton balls glued to it. I think the only children who thought he was the real thing were too young to know that Santa Claus was not Chinese. When my turn came up, the Santa man asked me how old I was. I thought it was a trick question; I was seven according to the American formula and eight by the Chinese calendar. I said I was born on March 17, 1951. That seemed to satisfy him. He then solemnly asked if I had been a very, very good girl this year and did I believe in Jesus Christ and obey my parents. I knew the only answer to that. I nodded back with equal solemnity.

Having watched the other children opening their gifts, I already knew that the big gifts were not necessarily the nicest ones. One girl my age got a large coloring book of biblical characters, while a less greedy girl who selected a smaller box received a glass vial of lavender toilet water. The sound of the box was also important. A ten-year-old boy had chosen a box that jangled when he shook it. It was a tin globe of the world with a slit for inserting money. He must have thought it was full of dimes and nickels, because when he saw that it had just ten pennies, his face fell with such undisguised disappointment that his mother slapped the side of his head and led him out of the church hall, apologizing to the crowd for her son who had such bad manners he couldn't appreciate such a fine gift.

As I peered into the sack, I quickly fingered the remaining presents, testing their weight, imagining what they contained. I chose a heavy, compact one that was wrapped in shiny silver foil and a red satin ribbon. It was a twelve-pack of Life Savers and I spent the rest of the party arranging and rearranging the candy tubes in the order of my favorites. My brother Winston chose wisely as well. His present turned out to be a box of intricate plastic parts; the instructions on the box proclaimed that when they were properly assembled he would have an authentic miniature replica of a World War II submarine.

Vincent got the chess set, which would have been a very decent present to get at a church Christmas party, except it was obviously used and, as we discovered later, it was missing a black pawn and a white knight. My mother graciously thanked the unknown benefactor, saying, "Too good. Cost too much." At which point, an old lady with fine white, wispy hair nodded toward our family and said with a whistling whisper, "Merry, merry Christmas."

When we got home, my mother told Vincent to throw the chess set away. "She not want it. We not want it," she said, tossing her head stiffly to the side with a tight, proud smile. My brothers had deaf ears.

They were already lining up the chess pieces and reading from the dog-eared instruction book.

I watched Vincent and Winston play during Christmas week. The chessboard seemed to hold elaborate secrets waiting to be untangled. The chessmen were more powerful than old Li's magic herbs that cured ancestral curses. And my brothers wore such serious faces that I was sure something was at stake that was greater than avoiding the tradesmen's door to Hong Sing's.

"Let me! Let me!" I begged between games when one brother or the other would sit back with a deep sigh of relief and victory, the other annoyed, unable to let go of the outcome. Vincent at first refused to let me play, but when I offered my Life Savers as replacements for the buttons that filled in for the missing pieces, he relented. He chose the flavors: wild cherry for the black pawn and peppermint for the white knight. Winner could eat both.

As our mother sprinkled flour and rolled out small doughy circles for the steamed dumplings that would be our dinner that night, Vincent explained the rules, pointing to each piece. "You have sixteen pieces and so do I. One king and queen, two bishops, two knights, two castles, and eight pawns. The pawns can only move forward one step, except on the first move. Then they can move two. But they can only take men by moving crossways like this, except in the beginning, when you can move ahead and take another pawn."

"Why?" I asked as I moved my pawn. "Why can't they move more steps?"

"Because they're pawns," he said.

"But why do they go crossways to take other men? Why aren't there any women and children?"

"Why is the sky blue? Why must you always ask stupid questions?" asked Vincent. "This is a game. These are the rules. I didn't make them up. See. Here. In the book." He jabbed a page with a pawn in his hand. "Pawn. P-A-W-N. Pawn. Read it yourself."

My mother patted the flour off her hands. "Let me see book," she said quietly. She scanned the pages quickly, not reading the foreign

English symbols, seeming to search deliberately for nothing in particular.

"This American rules," she concluded at last. "Every time people come out from foreign country, must know rules. You not know, judge say, Too bad, go back. They not telling you why so you can use their way go forward. They say, Don't know why, you find out yourself. But they knowing all the time. Better you take it, find out why yourself." She tossed her head back with a satisfied smile.

I found out about all the whys later. I read the rules and looked up all the big words in a dictionary. I borrowed books from the Chinatown library. I studied each chess piece, trying to absorb the power each contained.

I learned about opening moves and why it's important to control the center early on; the shortest distance between two points is straight down the middle. I learned about the middle game and why tactics between two adversaries are like clashing ideas; the one who plays better has the clearest plans for both attacking and getting out of traps. I learned why it is essential in the endgame to have foresight, a mathematical understanding of all possible moves, and patience; all weaknesses and advantages become evident to a strong adversary and are obscured to a tiring opponent. I discovered that for the whole game one must gather invisible strengths and see the endgame before the game begins.

I also found out why I should never reveal "why" to others. A little knowledge withheld is a great advantage one should store for future use. That is the power of chess. It is a game of secrets in which one must show and never tell.

I loved the secrets I found within the sixty-four black and white squares. I carefully drew a handmade chessboard and pinned it to the wall next to my bed, where at night I would stare for hours at imaginary battles. Soon I no longer lost any games or Life Savers, but I lost my adversaries. Winston and Vincent decided they were more interested in roaming the streets after school in their Hopalong Cassidy cowboy hats.

•

On a cold spring afternoon, while walking home from school, I detoured through the playground at the end of our alley. I saw a group of old men, two seated across a folding table playing a game of chess, others smoking pipes, eating peanuts, and watching. I ran home and grabbed Vincent's chess set, which was bound in a cardboard box with rubber bands. I also carefully selected two prized rolls of Life Savers. I came back to the park and approached a man who was observing the game.

"Want to play?" I asked him. His face widened with surprise and he grinned as he looked at the box under my arm.

"Little sister, been a long time since I play with dolls," he said, smiling benevolently. I quickly put the box down next to him on the bench and displayed my retort.

Lau Po, as he allowed me to call him, turned out to be a much better player than my brothers. I lost many games and many Life Savers. But over the weeks, with each diminishing roll of candies, I added new secrets. Lau Po gave me the names. The Double Attack from the East and West Shores. Throwing Stones on the Drowning Man. The Sudden Meeting of the Clan. The Surprise from the Sleeping Guard. The Humble Servant Who Kills the King. Sand in the Eyes of Advancing Forces. A Double Killing Without Blood.

There were also the fine points of chess etiquette. Keep captured men in neat rows, as well-tended prisoners. Never announce "Check" with vanity, lest someone with an unseen sword slit your throat. Never hurl pieces into the sandbox after you have lost a game, because then you must find them again, by yourself, after apologizing to all around you. By the end of the summer, Lau Po had taught me all he knew, and I had become a better chess player.

A small weekend crowd of Chinese people and tourists would gather as I played and defeated my opponents one by one. My mother would join the crowds during these outdoor exhibition games. She sat proudly on the bench, telling my admirers with proper Chinese humility, "Is luck."

A man who watched me play in the park suggested that my mother allow me to play in local chess tournaments. My mother smiled graciously, an answer that meant nothing. I desperately wanted to go, but

I bit back my tongue. I knew she would not let me play among strangers. So as we walked home I said in a small voice that I didn't want to play in the local tournament. They would have American rules. If I lost, I would bring shame on my family.

"Is shame you fall down nobody push you," said my mother.

During my first tournament, my mother sat with me in the front row as I waited for my turn. I frequently bounced my legs to unstick them from the cold metal seat of the folding chair. When my name was called, I leapt up. My mother unwrapped something in her lap. It was her *chang*, a small tablet of red jade which held the sun's fire. "Is luck," she whispered, and tucked it into my dress pocket. I turned to my opponent, a fifteen-year-old boy from Oakland. He looked at me, wrinkling his nose.

As I began to play, the boy disappeared, the color ran out of the room, and I saw only my white pieces and his black ones waiting on the other side. A light wind began blowing past my ears. It whispered secrets only I could hear.

"Blow from the South," it murmured. "The wind leaves no trail." I saw a clear path, the traps to avoid. The crowd rustled. "Shhh! Shhh!" said the corners of the room. The wind blew stronger. "Throw sand from the East to distract him." The knight came forward ready for the sacrifice. The wind hissed, louder and louder. "Blow, blow, blow. He cannot see. He is blind now. Make him lean away from the wind so he is easier to knock down."

"Check," I said, as the wind roared with laughter. The wind died down to little puffs, my own breath.

My mother placed my first trophy next to a new plastic chess set that the neighborhood Tao society had given to me. As she wiped each piece with a soft cloth, she said, "Next time win more, lose less."

"Ma, it's not how many pieces you lose," I said. "Sometimes you need to lose pieces to get ahead."

"Better to lose less, see if you really need."

At the next tournament, I won again, but it was my mother who wore the triumphant grin.

"Lost eight piece this time. Last time was eleven. What I tell you? Better off lose less!" I was annoyed, but I couldn't say anything.

I attended more tournaments, each one farther away from home. I won all games, in all divisions. The Chinese bakery downstairs from our flat displayed my growing collection of trophies in its window, amidst the dust-covered cakes that were never picked up. The day after I won an important regional tournament, the window encased a fresh sheet cake with whipped-cream frosting and red script saying "Congratulations, Waverly Jong, Chinatown Chess Champion." Soon after that, a flower shop, headstone engraver, and funeral parlor offered to sponsor me in national tournaments. That's when my mother decided I no longer had to do the dishes. Winston and Vincent had to do my chores.

"Why does she get to play and we do all the work," complained Vincent.

"Is new American rules," said my mother. "Meimei play, squeeze all her brains out for win chess. You play, worth squeeze towel."

By my ninth birthday, I was a national chess champion. I was still some 429 points away from grand-master status, but I was touted as the Great American Hope, a child prodigy and a girl to boot. They ran a photo of me in *Life* magazine next to a quote in which Bobby Fischer said, "There will never be a woman grand master." "Your move, Bobby," said the caption.

The day they took the magazine picture I wore neatly plaited braids clipped with plastic barrettes trimmed with rhinestones. I was playing in a large high school auditorium that echoed with phlegmy coughs and the squeaky rubber knobs of chair legs sliding across freshly waxed wooden floors. Seated across from me was an American man, about the same age as Lau Po, maybe fifty. I remember that his sweaty brow seemed to weep at my every move. He wore a dark, malodorous suit. One of his pockets was stuffed with a great white kerchief on which he wiped his palm before sweeping his hand over the chosen chess piece with great flourish.

In my crisp pink-and-white dress with scratchy lace at the neck, one of two my mother had sewn for these special occasions, I would clasp my hands under my chin, the delicate points of my elbows poised lightly on the table in the manner my mother had shown me for posing for the press. I would swing my patent leather shoes back and forth like an impatient child riding on a school bus. Then I would pause, suck in my lips, twirl my chosen piece in midair as if undecided, and then firmly plant it in its new threatening place, with a triumphant smile thrown back at my opponent for good measure.

I no longer played in the alley of Waverly Place. I never visited the playground where the pigeons and old men gathered. I went to school, then directly home to learn new chess secrets, cleverly concealed advantages, more escape routes.

But I found it difficult to concentrate at home. My mother had a habit of standing over me while I plotted out my games. I think she thought of herself as my protective ally. Her lips would be sealed tight, and after each move I made, a soft "Hmmmmph" would escape from her nose.

"Ma, I can't practice when you stand there like that," I said one day. She retreated to the kitchen and made loud noises with the pots and pans. When the crashing stopped, I could see out of the corner of my eye that she was standing in the doorway. "Hmmmph!" Only this one came out of her tight throat.

My parents made many concessions to allow me to practice. One time I complained that the bedroom I shared was so noisy that I couldn't think. Thereafter, my brothers slept in a bed in the living room facing the street. I said I couldn't finish my rice; my head didn't work right when my stomach was too full. I left the table with half-finished bowls and nobody complained. But there was one duty I couldn't avoid. I had to accompany my mother on Saturday market days when I had no tournament to play. My mother would proudly walk with me, visiting many shops, buying very little. "This my daughter Wave-ly Jong," she said to whoever looked her way.

One day after we left a shop I said under my breath, "I wish you wouldn't do that, telling everybody I'm your daughter." My mother stopped walking. Crowds of people with heavy bags pushed past us on the sidewalk, bumping into first one shoulder, then another.

"Aiii-ya. So shame be with mother?" She grasped my hand even tighter as she glared at me.

I looked down. "It's not that, it's just so obvious. It's just so embarrassing."

"Embarrass you be my daughter?" Her voice was cracking with anger.

"That's not what I meant. That's not what I said."

"What you say?"

I knew it was a mistake to say anything more, but I heard my voice speaking, "Why do you have to use me to show off? If you want to show off, then why don't you learn to play chess?"

My mother's eyes turned into dangerous black slits. She had no words for me, just sharp silence.

I felt the wind rushing around my hot ears. I jerked my hand out of my mother's tight grasp and spun around, knocking into an old woman. Her bag of groceries spilled to the ground.

"Aii-ya! Stupid girl!" my mother and the woman cried. Oranges and tin cans careened down the sidewalk. As my mother stooped to help the old woman pick up the escaping food, I took off.

I raced down the street, dashing between people, not looking back as my mother screamed shrilly, "Meimei! Meimei!" I fled down an alley, past dark, curtained shops and merchants washing the grime off their windows. I sped into the sunlight, into a large street crowded with tourists examining trinkets and souvenirs. I ducked into another dark alley, down another street, up another alley. I ran until it hurt and I realized I had nowhere to go, that I was not running from anything. The alleys contained no escape routes.

My breath came out like angry smoke. It was cold. I sat down on an upturned plastic pail next to a stack of empty boxes, cupping my chin with my hands, thinking hard. I imagined my mother, first walking briskly down one street or another looking for me, then giving up and returning home to await my arrival. After two hours, I stood up on creaking legs and slowly walked home.

The alley was quiet and I could see the yellow lights shining from our flat like two tiger's eyes in the night. I climbed the sixteen steps to the door, advancing quietly up each so as not to make any warning sounds. I turned the knob; the door was locked. I heard a chair moving, quick steps, the locks turning—click! click! click!—and then the door opened.

"About time you got home," said Vincent. "Boy, are you in trouble."

He slid back to the dinner table. On a platter were the remains of a large fish, its fleshy head still connected to bones swimming upstream in vain escape. Standing there waiting for my punishment, I heard my mother speak in a dry voice.

"We not concerning this girl. This girl not have concerning for us."

Nobody looked at me. Bone chopsticks clinked against the inside of bowls being emptied into hungry mouths.

I walked into my room, closed the door, and lay down on my bed. The room was dark, the ceiling filled with shadows from the dinnertime lights of neighboring flats.

In my head, I saw a chessboard with sixty-four black and white squares. Opposite me was my opponent, two angry black slits. She wore a triumphant smile. "Strongest wind cannot be seen," she said.

Her black men advanced across the plane, slowly marching to each successive level as a single unit. My white pieces screamed as they scurried and fell off the board one by one. As her men drew closer to my edge, I felt myself growing light. I rose up into the air and flew out the window. Higher and higher, above the alley, over the tops of tiled roofs, where I was gathered up by the wind and pushed up toward the night sky until everything below me disappeared and I was alone.

I closed my eyes and pondered my next move.

Amy Tan's first work of fiction, *The Joy Luck Club,* about Chinese-American daughters and their immigrant mothers, was published in 1989. It has since been translated into twenty foreign languages, and was a finalist for the National Book Award and the National Book Critics Circle Award. Her second book, *The Kitchen God's Wife,* published in 1991, also became an international best-seller.

Ms. Tan lives with her husband in San Francisco.

JOHN SAYLES

When the Bay of Pigs invasion occurred in 1961, John Sayles was eleven years old. He was raised Catholic, and he remembers the priests asking the children to pray for the invaders. He told *Publishers Weekly:* "When I was a kid I would visit my mother's parents in Hollywood, Florida, just north of Miami, and I saw that area change from 1954 to 1981. I saw it go from a dying Southern city to this thriving—with a lot of problems—international city. Most of that was through the exile of the Cubans, a lot of them resettling in Miami."

His novel *Los Gusanos* explores that Cuban American world, and what it would be like to be an exile in America rather than, as is true for most Americans or their ancestors, an immigrant. John Sayles learned Spanish in order to be able to read the diaries of some of the men who were part of the Bay of Pigs invasion.

The rhythms and richness of Spanish permeate his "The Halfway Diner" as well. In addition, says Sayles about this remarkable story, "I got a lot of the rhythm from listening to women talk (in Spanish and English) when I lived in Santa Barbara."

Sayles believes that "none of us has the whole story." He explores how one acts when one doesn't necessarily have all the information needed to act.

Lourdes, the Chicana through whose viewpoint "The Halfway Diner" is told, is a character who emerges from this fertile ground. "I don't write in first person much anymore (I do it all the time in movies), but now and then a Lourdes comes along and does half the work."

THE HALFWAY DINER

SOME of the other girls can read on the way but I get sick. I need somebody to talk to, it don't matter who so much, just someone to shoot the breeze with, pass time. *Si no puedes platicar, no puedes vivir,* says my mother and though I don't agree that the silence would kill me, twelve hours is a long stretch. So when Goldilocks climbs on all big-eyed and pale and almost sits herself in Renee's seat by the window I take pity and put her wise.

"You can't sit in that seat," I say.

Her face falls like she's a kid on the playground about to get whupped. "Pardon?" she says. *Pardon.*

"That's Renee's seat," I tell her. "She's got a thing about it. Something about the light."

"Oh. Sorry." She looks at the other empty seats like they're all booby-trapped. Lucky for her I got a soft heart and a mouth that needs exercise.

"You can sit here if you want."

She just about pees with relief and sits by me. She's not packing any magazines or books which is good cause like I said, I get sick. If the person next to me reads I get nosy and then I get sick plus a stiff neck.

"My name's Pam," she says.

"It would be. I'm Lourdes." We shake hands. I remember the first time I made the ride, four years ago, I was sure somebody was gonna cut me with a razor or something. I figured they'd all of them be women who'd done time themselves, a bunch of big tough mamas with tattoos on their arms who'd snarl out stuff like "Whatsit to you, sister?" Well, we're not exactly the Girl Scout Jamboree, but mostly people are pretty nice to each other, unless something happens like with Lee and Delphine.

"New meat?" I ask her.

"Pardon?"

"Is your guy new meat up there?" I ask. "Is this his first time inside?"

She nods and hangs her head like it's the disgrace of the century. Like we're not all on this bus for the same reason.

"You hear from him yet?"

"I got a letter. He says he doesn't know how he can stand it."

Now this is good. It's when they start to get comfortable up there you got to worry. We had this girl on the bus, her guy made parole first time up, only the minute he gets home he starts to mope. Can't sleep nights, can't concentrate, mutters to himself all the time, won't take an interest in anything on the outside. She lives with this a while, then one night they have a fight and really get down and he confesses how he had this kid in his cell, this little *mariquita,* and they got to doing it, you know, like some of the guys up there will do, only this guy fell in *love.* These things happen. And now he's *jealous,* see, cause his kid is still inside with all these *men,* right, and damn if a week later he doesn't go break his parole about a dozen different ways so he gets sent back up. She had to give up on him. To her it's a big tragedy, which is understandable, but I suppose from another point of view it's kind of romantic, like *Love Story,* only instead of Ali McGraw you got a sweetboy doing a nickel for armed robbery.

"What's your guy in for?" I ask.

Pam looks at her feet. "Auto theft."

"Not *that.* I mean how much *time.*"

"The lawyer says he'll have to do at least a year and a half."

"You don't go around asking what a guy's rap is in here," I tell her. "That's like *per*sonal, you know? But the length of sentence—hey, everybody counts the days."

"Oh."

"A year and a half is small change," I tell her. "He'll do that with his eyes closed."

The other girls start coming in then. Renee comes to her seat and sets up her equipment. She sells makeup, Renee, and her main hobby is wearing it. She's got this stand that hooks onto the back of the seat in front of her, with all these drawers and compartments and mirrors and stuff and an empty shopping bag for all the tissues she goes through during the trip. I made the mistake of sitting next to her once and she bent my ear about lip gloss for three hours straight, all the way to the Halfway Diner. You wouldn't think there'd be that much to say about it. Then after lunch she went into her sales pitch and I surrendered and bought some eye goop just so I wouldn't have to hear her say "our darker-complected customers" one more time. I mean it's all relative, right, and I'd rather be my shade than all pasty-faced like Renee, look like she's never been touched by the sun. She's seen forty in the rearview mirror though she does her best to hide it, and the big secret that everybody knows is that it's not her husband she goes to visit but her *son,* doing adult time. She just calls him "my Bobby."

Mrs. Tucker settles in front with her knitting, looking a little tired. Her guy is like the Birdman of Alcatraz or something, he's been in since back when they wore stripes like in the Jimmy Cagney movies, and she's been coming up faithfully every weekend for thirty, forty years, something incredible like that. He killed a cop way back when is what Yayo says the word on the yard is. She always sits by Gus, the driver, and they have these long lazy Mr. and Mrs. conversations while she knits and he drives. Not that there's anything going on between them off the bus, but you figure over the years she's spent more time with Gus than with her husband. He spaces out sometimes, Gus, the road is so straight and long, and she'll bring him back with a poke from one of her needles.

The ones we call the sisters go and sit in the back, talking nonstop. Actually they're married to brothers who are up for the same deal but they look alike and are stuck together like glue so we call them the sisters. They speak one of those Indio dialects from up in the mountains down south, so I can't pick out much of what they say. What my mother would call *mojadas.* Like she come over on the *Mayflower.*

Dolores comes in, who is a sad case.

"I'm gonna tell him this trip," she says. "I'm really gonna do it."

"Attagirl."

"No, I really am. It'll break his heart but I got to."

"It's the only thing to do, Dolores."

She has this boyfriend inside, Dolores, only last year she met some nice square Joe and got married. She didn't tell him about her guy inside and so far hasn't told her guy inside about the Joe. She figures he waits all week breathless for her visit, which maybe is true and maybe is flattering herself, and if she gives him the heave-ho he'll fall apart and kidnap the warden or something. Personally I think she likes to collect guilt, like some people collect stamps or coins or dead butterflies or whatever.

"I just feel so *guilty,*" she says and moves on down across from the sisters.

We got pretty much all kinds on the bus, black girls, white girls, Chicanas like me who were born here and new fish from just across the border, a couple of Indian women from some tribe down the coast, even one Chinese girl, whose old man is supposed to be a very big cheese in gambling. She wears clothes I would kill for, this girl, only of course they wouldn't look good on me. Most of your best clothes are designed for the flat-chested type, which is why the fashion pages are full of Orientals and anorexics like Renee.

This Pam is another one, the kind that looks good in a man's T-shirt, looks good in almost anything she throws on. I decide to be nice to her anyway.

"You gonna eat all that?"

She's got this big plastic sack of food under her feet, wrapped sandwiches and fruit and what looks like a pie.

"Me? Oh—no, I figure, you know—the food inside—"

"They don't let you bring food in."

Her face drops again. "No?"

"Only cigarettes. One carton a month."

"He doesn't smoke."

"That's not the point. Cigarettes are like money inside. Your guy wants anything, wants anything done, he'll have to pay in smokes."

"What would he want to have done?"

I figure I should spare her most of the possibilities, so I just shrug. "Whatever. We get to the Halfway you get some change, load up on Camels from the machine. He'll thank you for it."

She looks down at the sack of goodies. She sure isn't going to eat it herself, not if she worked at it for a month. I can picture her dinner plate alone at home, full of the kind of stuff my Chuy feeds his gerbil. A celery cruncher.

"You want some of this?" she says, staring into the sack.

"No thanks, honey," I tell her. "I'm saving myself for the Halfway Diner."

Later on I was struck by how it had already happened, the dice had already been thrown, only they didn't know it. So they took the whole trip up sitting together and talking and palling around unaware that they weren't friends anymore.

Lee and Delphine are as close as the sisters only nobody would ever mistake them for relatives, Lee being blonde and Delphine being one of our darker-complected customers. Lee is natural blonde, unlike certain cosmetics sales-women I could mention, with light blue eyes and a build that borders on the chunky although she would die to hear me say it. Del is thin and sort of elegant and black like you don't see too much outside of those documentaries on TV where people stick wooden spears in lions. *Negro como el fondo de la noche* my mother would say and on Del it looks great. The only feature they share is a similar nose, Del because she was born that way and Lee because of a field-hockey accident.

Maybe it was because they're both nurses or maybe just because they have complementary personalities, but somehow they found each other on the bus and since before I started riding they've been tight as ticks. You get the feeling they look forward to the long drive to catch up on each other's lives. They don't socialize off the bus, almost nobody does, but how many friends spend twelve hours a week together? Some of the black girls are friendly with some of the white girls, and us Chicanas can either spread around or sit together and talk home-talk, but black and white as tight as Lee and Del is pretty rare. Inside, well, inside you stay with your own, that's the beginning and the end of it. But inside is a world I don't even like to think about.

They plunk down across from us, Del lugging all these magazines—*Cosmo, People, Vogue, Essence*—that they sort of read and sort of make fun of, and Lee right away starts in on the food. Lee is obsessed with food the way a lot of borderline-chunky girls are, she can talk forever about what she didn't eat that day. She sits and gets a load of the sack at Pam's feet.

"That isn't food, is it?" she asks.

"Yeah," Pam apologizes. "I didn't know."

"Let's see it."

Obediently Pam starts shuffling through her sack, holding things up for a little show-and-tell. "I got this, and this," she says, "and this, I thought, maybe, they wouldn't have—I didn't know."

It's all stuff you buy at the bus station—sandwiches that taste like the cellophane they're wrapped in filled with that already-been-chewed kind of egg and chicken and tuna salad, stale pies stuffed with mealy applesauce, spotted fruit out of a machine. From all reports the food is better in the joint.

"How old are you, honey?" I ask.

"Nineteen."

"You ever cook at home?" Lee asks.

Pam shrugs. "Not much. Mostly I eat—you know, like salads. Maybe some fish sticks."

Del laughs. "I tried that fish-sticks routine once when Richard was home," she says. "He ask me, 'What is this?' That's their code for 'I don't like the look of it.' It could be something *bas*ic, right, like a fried egg starin up at em, they still say, 'What's this?' So I say, 'It's fish, baby.' He says, 'If it's fish, which end is the *head* and which is the *tail?*' When I tell him it taste the same either way he says he doesn't eat nothin with square edges like that, on account of inside they always be cookin everything in these big cake pans and serve it up in squares—square egg, square potato, square macaroni. That and things served out in ice-cream scoops. Unless it really *is* ice cream Richard don't want no *scoops* on his plate."

"Lonnie's got this thing about chicken bones," Lee says, "bones of any kind, but especially chicken bones. Can't stand to look at em while he's eating."

"Kind of rules out the Colonel, doesn't it?"

"Naw," she says. "He *loves* fried chicken. We come back with one of them buckets, you know, with the biscuits and all, and I got to go perform surgery in the kitchen before we can eat. He keeps callin in—'It ready yet, hon? It ready yet? I'm starvin here.' I'll tell you, they'd of had those little McNugget things back before he went up our marriage woulda been in a lot better shape."

They're off to the races then, Lee and Del, yakking away, and they sort of close up into a society of two. Blondie is sitting there with her tuna-mash sandwiches in her lap, waiting for orders, so I stow everything in the sack and kick it deep under the seat.

"We get to the Halfway," I tell her, "we can dump it."

Sometimes I wonder about Gus. The highway is so straight, cutting up through the Valley with the ground so flat and mostly dried up, like all its effort goes into those little square patches of artichokes or whatever you come past and after that it just got no more green in it. What can he be thinking about, all these miles, all these trips, up and down, year after year? He don't need to think to do his *yups* and *uh-huhs* at Mrs. Tucker, for that you can go on automatic pilot like I do with my Blanca when she goes into one of her stories about the tangled who-likes-who in her class. It's a real soap opera, *Dallas* for fifth-graders, but not what you need to concentrate on over breakfast. I wonder if Gus counts the days like we do, if there's a retirement date in his head, a release from the bus. Except to Mrs. Tucker he doesn't say but three things. When we first leave he says, "Headin out, ladies, take your seats." When we walk into the Halfway he always says, "Make it simple, ladies, we got a clock to watch." And when we're about to start the last leg, after dinner, he says, "Sweet dreams, ladies, we're bringin it home." Those same three things, every single trip. Like Mrs. Tucker with her blue sweater, always blue. Sometimes when I can't sleep and things are hard and awful and I can't see how they'll ever get better I'll lie awake and invent all these morbid thoughts, sort of torture myself with ideas, and I always start thinking that it's really the same exact sweater, that she goes home and pulls it apart stitch by stitch and starts from scratch again next trip. Not cause she wants to but cause she has to, it's her part of the punishment for what her husband done.

Other times I figure she just likes the color blue.

For the first hour or so Renee does her face. Even with good road and a fairly new bus this takes a steady hand, but she is an artist. Then she discovers Pam behind her, a new victim for her line of cosmetics, and starts into her pitch, opening with something tactful like, "You always let your hair go like that?" I'm dying for Pam to say, "Yeah, whatsit to you, sister?" but she is who she is and pretty soon Renee's got her believing it's at least a misdemeanor to leave the house without eye-liner on. I've heard all this too many times so I put my head back and close my eyes and aim my radar past it over to Lee and Del.

They talk about their patients like they were family. They talk about their family like they were patients. Both are RNs, they work at different hospitals but both on the ward. Lee has got kids and she talks about them, Del doesn't but wants some and she talks about that. They talk about how Del can eat twice as much as Lee but Del stays thin and Lee gets chunky. They talk about their guys, too, but usually not till we get pretty close to the facility.

"My Jimmy," Lee says, "is now convinced he's the man of the house. This is a five-year-old squirt, he acts like he's the Papa Bear."

"He remembers his father?"

"He likes to think he does, but he doesn't. His favorite saying these days is 'Why should I?' "

"Uh-oh."

"At least he doesn't go around saying he's an orphan like his sister. I introduce her, 'This is my daughter, Julie,' right, she says, 'Hi, I'm a orphan.' Cute."

"I used to do that," says Delphine. "Evertime my daddy spanked me that's what I'd spread round the neighborhood."

"So Julie says she's an orphan and Jimmy says his father works for the state."

Del laughs. "That's true enough."

"And he picks up all this stuff in the neighborhood. God I want to get out of there. Lonnie makes parole this rotation I'm gonna get him home and get his head straight and get us moved outa there."

"Like to the country or something?"

"Just anywheres it isn't so mean and he's not near his asshole so-called buddies."

"Yeah—"

"And I want—oh, I don't know, it sounds kinda stupid, really—"

"What?" Del says.

"I want a *dish*washer."

Del laughs again. Lee is embarrassed.

"You know what I mean—"

"Yeah, I know—"

"I want something in my life I just get it started and then it takes care of itself."

"I hear you *talk*in—"

"The other night Jimmy—now I know some of this is from those damn He-Man cartoons and all, but some of it is not having a father, I swear—he's in their room doing his prayers. He does this thing, the nuns told him praying is just talking to God, that's the new breed of nuns, right, so you'll go by their room and you'll hear Jimmy still up, having like these one-sided telephone conversations. 'Uh-huh, yeah, sure, I will, no problem, I'll try, uh-huh, uh-huh,' and he thinks he's talking with *God,* see, like a kid does with an imaginary friend. Or maybe he really *is* talking to God, how would I know? Anyhow, the other night I peek in and he's doing one of these numbers only now he's got that tough-guy look I hate so much pasted on his face like all the other little punks in the neighborhood and he's quiet for a long time, listening, and then he kind of sneers and says—'Why should I?' "

We all sort of pretend the food is better at the Halfway than it really is. Not that it's bad—it's okay, but nothing to write home about. Elvira, who runs the place, won't use a microwave, which makes me happy. I'm convinced there's vibes in those things that get into the food and ten years from now there'll be a national scandal. Whenever I have something from a microwave I get bad dreams, I swear it, so if something comes out a little lukewarm from her kitchen I don't complain.

The thing is, Elvira really seems to look forward to seeing us, looks forward to all the noise and hustle a busload of hungry women carry into the place, no matter what it is that brung them together. I imagine pulling into someplace different, with the name of the facility rolled up into the little destination window at the front of the bus, us flocking in and the waitresses panicking, the cooks ready to mutiny, the other customers sure we're pickpockets, prostitutes, baby-snatchers—no way José. So maybe the food here tastes better cause it comes through Elvira, all the square edges rounded off.

She's a big woman, Elvira, and if the country about here had a face it would look like hers. Kind of dry and cracked and worn, but friendly. She says she called the Halfway the Halfway because everyplace on earth is halfway between somewhere and somewhere else. I don't think being halfway between the city and the facility was what she had in mind, though.

When we bust in and spill out around the room there's only one other customer, a skinny old lizard in a Tecate cap and a T-shirt, never once looking up from his grilled-cheese sandwich.

"Make it simple, ladies," Gus says. "We got a clock to watch."

At the Halfway it's pretty hard to make it anything but simple. When they gave out the kits at Diner Central, Elvira went for bare essentials. She's got the fly-strip hanging by the door with a dozen little boogers stuck to it, got the cornflakes pyramided on a shelf, the specials hand-printed on paper plates stuck on the wall behind the counter, the morning's Danishes crusting over under their plastic hood, the lemon and chocolate cream pies with huge bouffants of meringue behind sliding glass, a cigarette machine, a phone booth, and a machine that tells your exact weight for a quarter which Lee feeds both coming in and going out.

"Have your orders ready, girls!" Elvira calls as we settle at the counter and in the booths, pretty much filling the place. "I want to hear numbers."

Elvira starts at one end of the counter and her girl Cheryl does the booths. Cheryl always seems like she's about to come apart, sighing a lot, scratching things out, breaking her pencil points. A nervous kid. What there is to be nervous about way out there in the middle of nowhere I couldn't tell you, but she manages. I'm sitting at the counter with Mrs. Tucker on one side, Pam on the other, then Lee and Del. Lee and Del get talking about their honeymoons while Pam goes off to pump the cigarette machine.

"So anyhow," says Lee, "he figures we'll go down to Mexico, that old bit about how your money travels further down there? I don't know how *far* it goes, but after that honeymoon I know how *fast.* He was just trying to be sweet, really, he figured he was gonna show me this wonderful time, cause he's been there and I haven't and he knows what to order and I don't and he knows where to go and all that, only he *doesn't,* you know, he just *thinks* he does. Which is the whole thing with Lonnie—he dreams things up and pretty soon he believes they're *true,* right, so he's more surprised than anybody when the shit hits the fan."

"Sounds familiar," says Del.

"So he's heard of this place—jeez, it's so long ago—Santa Maria de la Playa, something like that—" Lee looks to me for help. "You must know it, Lourdes. It's on the coast—"

"Lots of coast down there."

"There's like these mountains, and the ocean—"

"Sorry," I tell her. "I've never been to Mexico."

Delphine can't feature this. "You're shittin me," she says. *"You?"*

"You ever been to Africa?"

Del cracks up, which is one of the things I like about her. She's not oversensitive about that stuff. Usually.

"Anyway," says Lee, "he says to me, 'Baby, we're talkin Paradise here, we're talkin Honeymoon *Heav*en. I got this deal—' "

"They *al*ways got a deal," says Del.

Elvira comes by then with her pad, working fast but friendly all the time. "Hey, girls," she says, "how's it going? Mrs. Tucker?"

"Just the water," Mrs. Tucker says. "I'm not really hungry."

She doesn't look too good, Mrs. Tucker, kind of drawn around the eyes. Elvira shakes her head.

"Not good to skip lunch, Mrs. Tucker. You got a long ride ahead."

"Just the water, thank you."

Lee and Del get the same thing every week. "Let's see, we got a Number Three and a Number Five, mayo on the side," Elvira says. "Ice tea or lemonade?"

They both go for the lemonade and then Pam comes back dropping packs of Camels all over.

"How bout you, hon?"

"Um could I see a menu?" More cigarettes tumble from her arms. I see that Pam is one of those people who is accident-prone for life, and that her marrying a car thief is no coincidence. A catastrophe waiting to happen, this girl. Elvira jerks a thumb to the wall. Pam sees the paper plates. "Oh um—what are you having?"

"Number Three," says Lee.

"Number Five," says Delphine.

"Oh. I'll have a Number Four, please. And a club soda?"

"You know what a Number Four *is,* hon?"

"No, but I'll eat it."

Elvira thinks this is a scream but writes it down without laughing. "Four and a club," she says and moves on.

"So he's got this deal," says Del, getting back to the story.

"Right. He's got this deal where he brings these tapes down to San Miguel de los Nachos, whatever it was, and this guy who runs a brand-new resort down there is gonna give us the royal-carpet treatment in exchange—"

"Like cassette tapes?"

"Fresh from the K mart. Why they can't go to their own stores and buy these things I don't know—what's the story down there, Lourdes?"

"It's a mystery to me," I say.

"Anyhow, we got thousands of the things we're bringing through without paying duty, a junior version of the scam he finally went up for, only I don't know because they're under the back seat and he keeps laying this Honeymoon Heaven jazz on me."

"With Richard his deals always have to do with clothes," says Del. "Man come in and say, 'Sugar, what size dress you wear?' and my stomach just hits the *floor."*

"And he brings the wrong size, right?"

"Ever damn time." Del shakes her head. "We took our honeymoon in Jamaica, back when we was livin high. Girl, you never saw nobody with more fluff in her head than me back then."

"You were young."

"Young ain't no excuse for *stupid.* I had one of those posters in my head—soft sand, violins playing, rum and Coke on ice and I was the girl in the white bikini. I thought it was gonna be like that *always."* Del gets kind of distant then, thinking back. She smiles. "Richard gets outa there, gets his health back, we gonna *party,* girl. That's one thing the man knows how to do is party."

"Yeah, Lonnie too. They both get clear we should all get together sometime, do the town."

As soon as it's out Lee knows different. There's a silence then, both of them just smiling, uncomfortable. Guys inside, black and white, aren't likely to even know who each other is, much less get together outside and make friendly. It does that to you, inside. Yayo is the same, always on about *los gachos gavachos* this and *los pinches negros* that, it's a sickness you pick up there. Or maybe you already got it when you go in and the joint makes it worse. Lee finally breaks the silence.

"I bet you look great in a white bikini," she says.

Del laughs. "That's the *last* time I been to any *beach*, girl."

Cheryl shows with the food and Mrs. Tucker excuses herself to go to the ladies'. Lee has the diet plate, a scoop of cottage cheese with a cherry on top, Del has a BLT with mayo on the side, and Pam has the Number Four, which at the Halfway is a Monte Cristo—ham and cheese battered in egg, deep fried, and then rolled in confectioner's sugar. She turns it around and around on her plate, studying it like it fell from Mars.

"I think maybe I'll ask him this visit," says Del. "About the kids."

"You'd be a good mother," says Lee.

"You think so?"

"Sure."

"Richard with a baby in his lap . . ." Del grimaces at the thought. "Sometimes I think it's just what he needs—responsibility, family roots, that whole bit, settle him down. Then I think how maybe he'll just feel more *pres*sure, you know? And when he starts feelin pressure is when he starts messin up." Del lets the thought sit for a minute and then gives herself a little slap on the cheek as if to clear it away. "Just got to get him healthy first. Plenty of time for the rest." She turns to Pam. "So how's that Number Four?"

"It's different," says Pam. She's still working on her first bite, scared to swallow.

"You can't finish it," says Lee, "I might take a bite."

Del digs her in the ribs. "Girl, don't you even *look* at that Number

Four. Thing is just *evil* with carbohydrates. I don't wanta be hearing you bellyache about how you got no willpower all the way home."

"I got willpower," Lee says. "I'm a goddamn tower of strength. It's just my *ap*petite is stronger—"

"Naw—"

"My appetite is like God*zil*la, Del, you seen it at work, layin waste to everything in its path—"

"Hah-*haaah!*"

"But I'm gonna whup it—"

"That's what I like to hear."

"Kick its butt—"

"Tell it, baby—"

"I'm losin twenty pounds—"

"Go for it!"

"An I'm quittin smoking too—"

"You can do it, Lee—"

"And when that man makes parole he's gonna buy me a dishwasher!"

"Get *down!*"

They're both of them giggling then, but Lee is mostly serious. "You know," she says, "as much as I want him out, sometimes it feels weird that it might really happen. You get used to being on your own, get your own way of doing things—"

"I hear you talkin—"

"The trouble is, it ain't so bad that I'm gonna leave him but it ain't so good I'm dying to stay."

There's hardly a one of us on the bus hasn't said the exact same thing at one time or another. Del looks around the room.

"So here we all are," she says, "at the Halfway Diner."

Back on the road Pam gets quiet so I count dead rabbits for a while, and then occupy the time imagining disasters that could be happening with the kids at Graciela's. You'd be surprised at how entertaining this can be. By the time we pass the fruit stand Chuy has left the burners going on the gas stove and Luz, my baby, is being chewed by a rabid Doberman. It's only twenty minutes to the facility after the fruit stand

and you can hear the bus get quieter, everybody but Dolores. She's still muttering her good-bye speech like a rosary. The visits do remind me of confession—you go into a little booth, you face each other through a window, you feel weird afterward. I think about the things I don't want to forget to tell Yayo. Then I see myself in Renee's mirror and hit on her for some blush.

The first we know of it is when the guard at security calls Lee and Del's names and they're taken off in opposite directions. That sets everybody buzzing. Pam is real nervous, this being her first visit, and I think she is a little afraid of who her guy is going to be all of a sudden. I tell her not to ask too much of it, one visit. I can't remember me and Yayo just sitting and talking a whole hour that many times *before* he went up. Add to that the glass and the little speaker boxes and people around with rifles, and you have definitely entered Weird City. We always talk home-talk cause all the guards are Anglos and it's fun for Yayo to badmouth them under their noses.

"Big blowout last night in the mess," he says to me. "*Anglos contra los negros.* One guy got cut pretty bad."

I get a sick feeling in the pit of my stomach. The night Yayo got busted I had the same feeling but couldn't think of anything to keep him in the house. "Black or white?" I ask.

"A black dude got stabbed," he says. "This guy Richard. He was a musician outside."

"And the guy who cut him?" I say, although I already know without asking.

"This guy Lonnie, was real close to parole. Got him up in solitary now. *Totalmente jodido.*"

It was just something that kind of blew up and got out of control. Somebody needs to feel like he's big dick by ranking somebody else in front of the others and when you got black and white inside that's a fight, maybe a riot, and this time when the dust clears there's Lee's guy with his shank stuck in Del's guy. You don't ask it to make a lot of sense. I tell Yayo how the kids are doing and how they miss him a lot but I feel this weight pulling down on me, knowing about Lee and Del, I feel like nothing's any use and we're wasting our time squawking at each other over these microphones. We're out of rhythm, it's a long hour.

"I think about you all the time," he says as the guard steps in and I step out.

"Me too," I say.

It isn't true. Whole days go by when I hardly give him a thought, and when I do it's more an idea of him than really him in the flesh. Sometimes I feel guilty about this, but what the hell. Things weren't always so great when we were together. So maybe it's like the food at the Halfway, better to look forward to than to have.

Then I see how small he looks going back inside between the guards and I love him so much that I start to shake.

The bus is one big whisper when I get back on. The ones who have heard about Lee and Del are filling in the ones who haven't. Lee gets in first, pale and stiff, and sits by me. If I touched her with my finger she'd explode. Pam steps in then, looking shaky, and I can tell she's disappointed to see I'm already by someone. When Del gets on everybody clams up. She walks in with her head up, trying not to cry. If it had been somebody else cut her guy, somebody not connected with any of us on the bus, we'd all be around bucking her up and Lee would be first in line. As it is a couple of the black girls say something but she just zombies past them and sits in the very back next to Pam.

It's always quieter on the way home. We got things that were said to chew over, mistakes to regret, the prospect of another week alone to face. But after Del comes in it's like a morgue. Mrs. Tucker doesn't even knit, just stares out at the Valley going by kind of blank-eyed and sleepy. Only Pam, still in the dark about what went down inside, starts to talk. It's so quiet I can hear her all the way from the rear.

"I never thought about how they'd have those guns," she says, just opening up out of the blue to Del. "I never saw one up close, only in the movies or TV. They're *real*, you know? They look so heavy and like if they shot it would just take you *apart*—"

"White girl," says Del, interrupting, "I don't want to be hearin bout none of your problems."

After that all you hear is the gears shifting now and then. I feel sick, worse than when I try to read. Lee hardly blinks beside me, the muscles in her jaw working as she grinds something out in her head. It's hard to breathe.

I look around and see that the white girls are almost all up front but for Pam who doesn't know and the black girls are all in the back, with us Chicanas on the borderline between as usual. Everybody is just stewing in her own thoughts. Even the sisters have nothing to say to each other. A busload of losers slogging down the highway. If there's life in hell this is what the field trips are like. It starts to get dark. In front of me, while there is still a tiny bit of daylight, Renee stares at her naked face in her mirror and sighs.

Elvira and Cheryl look tired when we get to the Halfway. Ketchup bottles are turned on their heads on the counter but nothing is sliding down. Gus picks up on the mood and doesn't tell us how we got a clock to watch when he comes in.

Pam sits by me with Dolores and Mrs. Tucker on the other side. Dolores sits shaking her head. "Next time," she keeps saying. "I'll tell him next time." Lee shuts herself in the phone booth and Del sits at the far end of the counter.

Pam whispers to me, "What's up?"

"Big fight in the mess last night," I tell her. "Lee's guy cut Delphine's."

"My God. Is he okay?"

"He's alive if that's what you mean. I've heard Del say how he's got this blood problem, some old drug thing, so this ain't gonna help any."

Pam looks at the booth. "Lee must feel awful."

"Her guy just wrecked his parole but good," I say. "She's gettin it with both barrels."

Elvira comes by taking orders. "Rough trip, from the look of you all. Get your appetite back, Mrs. Tucker?"

"Yes, I have," she says. Her voice sounds like it's coming from the next room. "I'm very, very hungry."

"I didn't tell him," Dolores confesses to no one in particular. "I didn't have the heart."

We order and Elvira goes back in the kitchen. We know there is a cook named Phil but we have never seen him.

I ask Pam how her guy is making out. She makes a face, thinking. I can see her in high school, Pam, blonde and popular, and her guy, a good-looking charmer up to monkey business. An Anglo version of Yayo, full of promises that turn into excuses.

"He's okay, I guess. He says he's going to do his own time, whatever that means."

I got to laugh. "They all say that, honey, but not many manage. It means like mind your own business, stay out of complications."

"Oh."

Delphine is looking bullets over at Lee in the phone booth, who must be calling either her kids or her lawyer.

"Maybe that's how you got to be to survive in there," I say. "Hell, maybe out here, too. Personally I think it bites." Mrs. Tucker puts her head down into her arms and closes her eyes. It's been a long day. "The thing is," I say to Pam, "we're all of us doing time."

Lee comes out of the booth and goes to the opposite end of the counter from Del. It makes me think of me and Graciela. We used to be real jealous, her and me, sniff each other like dogs whenever we met, on account of her being Yayo's first wife. Not that I stole him or anything, they were bust long before I made the scene, but still you got to wonder what's he see in this bitch that I don't have? A natural human reaction. Anyhow, she's in the neighborhood and she's got a daughter by him who's ahead of my Chuy at the same school and I see her around but it's very icy. Then Yayo gets sent up and one day I'm stuck for a baby-sitter on visiting day. I don't know what possesses me, but desperation being the mother of a whole lot of stuff I ask Graciela. She says why not. When I get back it's late and I'm wasted and we get talking and I don't know why but we really hit it off. She's got a different perspective on Yayo of course, talks about him like he's her little boy gone astray which maybe in some ways he is, and we never get into sex stuff about him. But he isn't the only thing we got in common. Yayo, of course, thinks that's all we do, sit and gang up on him verbally, and he's not too crazy about the idea. We started shopping together and sometimes her girl comes over to play or we'll dump the kids with my mother and go out and it's fun, sort of like high school where you hung around not necessarily looking for boys. We go to the mall, whatever. There's times I would've gone right under without her, I mean I'd be *gonzo* today. I look at Lee and Del, sitting tight and mean inside themselves, and I think that's me and Graciela in reverse. And I wonder what happens to us when Yayo gets out.

"Mrs. Tucker, can you hear me? Mrs. Tucker?"

It's Gus who notices that Mrs. Tucker doesn't look right. He's shaking her and calling her name, and her eyes are still open but all fuzzy, the life gone out of them. The sisters are chattering something about cold water and Cheryl drops a plate of something and Pam keeps yelling, "Where's the poster? Find the poster!" Later she tells me she meant the anti-choking poster they're supposed to have up in restaurants, which Elvira kind of hides behind the weight-telling machine cause she says it puts people off their feed. Mrs. Tucker isn't choking, of course, but Pam doesn't know this at the time and is sure we got to look at this poster before we do anything wrong. Me, even with all the disasters I've imagined for the kids and all the rescues I've dreamed about performing, I've never dealt with this particular glassy-eyed-older-lady type of thing so I'm no help. Gus is holding Mrs. Tucker's face in his hands, her body gone limp, when Lee and Del step in.

"Move back!" says Lee. "Give her room to breathe."

"You got a pulse?" says Del.

"Not much. It's fluttering around."

"Get an ambulance here," says Del to Elvira and Elvira sends Cheryl running to the back.

"Any tags on her?"

They look around Mrs. Tucker's neck but don't find anything.

"Anybody ever hear her talk about a medical problem?" asks Del to the rest of us, while she holds Mrs. Tucker's lids up and looks deep into her eyes.

We rack our brains but come up empty, except for Gus. Gus looks a worse color than Mrs. Tucker does, sweat running down his face from the excitement. "She said the doctor told her to watch her intake," he says. "Whatever that means."

"She didn't eat lunch," says Elvira. "You should never skip lunch."

Lee and Del look at each other. "She got sugar, maybe?"

"Or something like it."

"Some orange juice," says Lee to Elvira and she runs off. Mrs. Tucker is kind of gray now, and her head keeps flopping if they don't hold it up.

"Usually she talks my ear off," says Gus. "Today she was like depressed or something."

Elvira comes back out. "I brung the fresh-squoze from the fridge," she says. "More vitamins."

Del takes it and feeds a little to Mrs. Tucker, tipping her head back to get it in. We're all of us circled around watching, opening our mouths in sympathy like when you're trying to get the baby to spoon-feed. Some dribbles out and some stays down.

"Just a little," says Lee. "It could be the opposite."

Mrs. Tucker takes another sip and smiles dreamily. "I like juice," she says.

"Here, take a little more."

"That's good," she says in this tiny, little-girl voice. "Juice is good."

By the time the ambulance comes we have her lying down in one of the booths covered by the lap blanket the sisters bring, her head pillowed on a couple of bags full of hamburger rolls. Her eyes have come clear and eventually she rejoins the living, looking up at all of us staring down around her and giving a little smile.

"Everybody's here," she says in that strange, far-off voice. "Everybody's here at the Halfway Diner."

The ambulance guys take some advice from Lee and Del and then drive her away. Just keep her overnight for observation is all. "See?" Elvira keeps saying. "You don't never want to skip your lunch." Then she bags up dinners for those who want them cause we have to get back on the road.

Nobody says anything, but when we get aboard nobody will take a seat. Everybody just stands around in the aisle talking about Mrs. Tucker and waiting for Lee and Del to come in and make their move. Waiting and hoping, I guess.

Lee comes in and sits in the middle. Pam moves like she's gonna sit next to her but I grab her arm. Delphine comes in, looks around kind of casual, and then like it's just a coincidence she sits by Lee. The rest of us settle in real quick then, pretending it's business as usual but listening real hard.

We're right behind them, me and Pam. They're not talking, not looking at each other, just sitting there side by side. Being nurses together might've cracked the ice but it didn't break it all the way through. We're parked right beneath the Halfway Diner sign and the neon makes this sound, this high-pitched buzzing that's like something about to explode.

"Sweet dreams, ladies," says Gus when he climbs into his seat. "We're bringin it home."

It's dark as pitch and it's quiet, but nobody is having sweet dreams. We're all listening. I don't really know how to explain this, and like I said, we're not exactly the League of Women Voters on that bus but there's a spirit, a way we root for each other and somehow we feel that the way it comes out between Lee and Delphine will be a judgment on us all. Nothing spoken, just a feeling between us.

Fifty miles go past and my stomach is starting to worry. Then, when Del finally speaks, her voice is so quiet I can hardly hear one seat away.

"So," she says. "San Luis Abysmal."

"Huh?" says Lee.

"Mexico," says Delphine, still real quiet. "You were telling me about your honeymoon down in San Luis Abysmal."

"Yeah," says Lee. "San Something-or-other—"

"And he says he speaks the language—"

You can feel this sigh like go through the whole bus. Most can't hear the words but just that they're talking. You can pick up the tone.

"Right," says Lee. "Only he learned his Spanish at Taco Bell. He's got this *deal,* right—"

"*Finalmente,*" one of the sisters whispers behind me.

"*¡Qué bueno!*" the other whispers. "*Todavía son amigas.*"

". . . so we get to the so-called resort and he cuts open the back seat and all these cas*settes* fall out, which I know nothing about—"

"Course not—"

"Only on account of the heat they've like *liq*uified, right—"

"*Naw*—"

"And this guy who runs the resort is roped off but so are we cause this so-called brand-new resort is so brand-new it's not *built* yet—"

"Don't *say* it, girl—"

"It's just a con*struc*tion site—"

"Hah-*haaah!*"

The bus kicks into a higher gear and out of nowhere Gus is whistling up front. He's never done this before, not once, probably because he had Mrs. Tucker talking with him, but he's real good, like somebody on a record. What he's whistling is like the theme song to some big romantic movie, I forget which, real high and pretty and I close my eyes and get that nice feeling like just before you fall to sleep and you know everything is under control and your body just relaxes. I feel good knowing there's hours before we got to get off, feel like as long as we stay on the bus, rocking gently through the night, we're okay, we're safe. The others are talking soft around me now, Gus is whistling high and pretty, and there's Del and Lee, voices in the dark.

"There's a beach," says Lee, "only they haven't brought in the *sand* yet and everywhere you go these little fleas are hoppin around and my ankles get bit and swole up like a balloon—"

"I been there, girl," says Del. "I hear you talkin—"

"Honeymoon Heaven, he says to me—"

Del laughs, softly. "Honeymoon *Heaven.*"

John Sayles, although best known as a film writer and director, has published three novels, including, most recently, *Los Gusanos* (meaning "The Worms," which is what Castro called those Cubans who left Cuba). He is also the author of a collection of stories, *The Anarchists' Convention*. Mr. Sayles lives in Hoboken, New Jersey, and upstate New York.

LAURIE COLWIN

"Although I am not an autobiographical writer, this story is a thinly disguised account of the birth of our daughter, now seven years old. As I lay on a gurney being rushed down the hall to have an emergency C-section some voice said to me: If you survive this it will doubtless be excellent material.

"We all survived. Our daughter is now the tallest person in her class. As I watch her play, which often involves a number of small objects over which she is artistic director, voice, scriptwriter and arranger, I realize that writers are grown-ups who never stopped playing in that way."

ANOTHER MARVELOUS THING

ON a cold, rainy morning in February, Billy Delielle stood by the window of her hospital room looking over Central Park. She was a week and a half from the time her baby was due to be born, and she had been put into the hospital because her blood pressure had suddenly gone up and her doctor wanted her constantly monitored and on bed rest.

A solitary jogger in bright red foul-weather gear ran slowly down the glistening path. The trees were black and the branches were bare. There was not another soul out. Billy had been in the hospital for five days. The first morning she had woken to the sound of squawking. Since her room was next door to the nursery, she assumed this was a sound some newborns made. The next day she got out of bed at dawn and saw that the meadow was full of sea gulls who congregated each morning before the sun came up.

The nursery was an enormous room painted soft yellow. When Billy went to take the one short walk a day allowed her, she found herself averting her eyes from the neat rows of babies in their little plastic bins, but once in a while she found herself hungry for the sight of them. Taped to each crib was a blue (I'M A BOY) or pink (I'M A GIRL) card telling mother's name, the time of birth, and birth weight.

At six in the morning the babies were taken to their mothers to be fed. Billy was impressed by the surprising range of noises they made: mewing, squawking, bleating, piping, and squealing. The fact that she was about to have one of these creatures herself filled her with a combination of bafflement, disbelief, and longing.

For the past two months her chief entertainment had been to lie in bed and observe her unborn child moving under her skin. It had knocked a paperback book off her stomach and caused the saucer of her coffee cup to jiggle and dance.

Billy's husband, Grey, was by temperament and inclination a naturalist. Having a baby was right up his street. Books on neonatology and infant development replaced the astronomy and bird books on his night table. He gave up reading mysteries for texts on childbirth. One of these books had informed him that babies can hear in the womb, so each night he sang "Roll Along Kentucky Moon" directly into Billy's stomach. Another suggested that the educational process could begin before birth. Grey thought he might try to teach the unborn to count.

"Why stop there?" Billy said. "Teach it fractions."

Billy had a horror of the sentimental. In secret, for she would rather have died than showed it, the thought of her own baby brought her to tears. Her dreams were full of infants. Babies appeared everywhere. The buses abounded with pregnant women. The whole process seemed to her one half miraculous and the other half preposterous. She looked around her on a crowded street and said to herself: "Every single one of these people was *born*."

Her oldest friend, Penny Stern, said to her: "We all hope that this pregnancy will force you to wear maternity clothes, because they will be so much nicer than what you usually wear." Billy went shopping for maternity clothes but came home empty-handed.

She said, "I don't wear puffed sleeves and frilly bibs and ribbons around my neck when I'm not pregnant, so I don't see why I should have to just because I am pregnant." In the end, she wore Grey's sweaters, and she bought two shapeless skirts with elastic waistbands. Penny forced her to buy one nice black dress, which she wore to teach her weekly class in economic history at the business school.

Grey set about renovating a small spare room that had been used for storage. He scraped and polished the floor, built shelves, and painted the walls pale apple green with the ceiling and moldings glossy white. They had once called this room the lumber room. Now they referred to it as the nursery. On the top of one of the shelves Grey put his collection of glass-encased bird's nests. He already had in mind a child who would go on nature hikes with him.

As for Billy, she grimly and without expression submitted herself to the number of advances science had come up with in the field of obstetrics.

It was possible to have amniotic fluid withdrawn and analyzed to find out the genetic health of the unborn and, if you wanted to know, its sex. It was possible to lie on a table and with the aid of an ultrasonic scanner see your unborn child in the womb. It was also possible to have a photograph of this view. As for Grey, he wished Billy could have a sonogram every week, and he watched avidly while Billy's doctor, a handsome, rather melancholy South African named Jordan Bell, identified a series of blobs and clouds as head, shoulders, and back.

Every month in Jordan Bell's office Billy heard the sound of her own child's heart through ultrasound and what she heard sounded like galloping horses in the distance.

Billy went about her business outwardly unflapped. She continued to teach and she worked on her dissertation. In between, when she was not napping, she made lists of baby things: crib sheets, a stroller, baby T-shirts, diapers, blankets. Two months before the baby was due, she and Penny went out and bought what was needed. She was glad she had not saved this until the last minute, because in her ninth month, after an uneventful pregnancy, she was put in the hospital, where she was allowed to walk down the hall once a day. The sense of isolation she had cherished—just herself, Grey, and their unborn child—was gone. She was in the hands of nurses she had never seen before, and she found herself desperate for their companionship because she was exhausted, uncertain, and lonely in her hospital room.

Billy was admitted wearing the nice black dress Penny had made her buy and taken to a private room that overlooked the park. At the bottom of her bed were two towels and a hospital gown that tied up the back. Getting undressed to go to bed in the afternoon made her feel like a child forced to take a nap. She did not put on the hospital gown. Instead, she put on the plaid flannel nightshirt of Grey's that she had packed in her bag weeks ago in case she went into labor in the middle of the night.

"I hate it here already," Billy said.

"It's an awfully nice view," Grey said. "If it were a little further along in the season I could bring my field glasses and see what's nesting."

"I'll never get out of here," Billy said.

"Not only will you get out of here," said Grey, "you will be released a totally transformed woman. You heard Jordan—all babies get born one way or another."

If Grey was frightened, he never showed it. Billy knew that his way of dealing with anxiety was to fix his concentration, and it was now fixed on her and on being cheerful. He had never seen Billy so upset before. He held her hand.

"Don't worry," he said. "Jordan said this isn't serious. It's just a complication. The baby will be fine and you'll be fine. Besides, it won't know how to be a baby and we won't know how to be parents."

Grey had taken off his jacket and he felt a wet place where Billy had laid her cheek. He did not know how to comfort her.

"A mutual learning experience," Billy said into his arm. "I thought nature was supposed to take over and do all this for us."

"It will," Grey said.

Seven o'clock began visiting hours. Even with the door closed Billy could hear shrieks and coos and laughter. With her door open she could hear champagne corks being popped.

Grey closed the door. "You didn't eat much dinner," he said. "Why don't I go downstairs to the delicatessen and get you something?"

"I'm not hungry," Billy said. She did not know what was in front of her, or how long she would be in this room, or how and when the baby would be born.

"I'll call Penny and have her bring something," Grey said.

"I already talked to her," Billy said. "She and David are taking you out to dinner." David was Penny's husband, David Hooks.

"You're trying to get rid of me," Grey said.

"I'm not," Billy said. "You've been here all day, practically. I just want the comfort of knowing that you're being fed and looked after. I think you should go soon."

"It's too early," said Grey. "Fathers don't have to leave when visiting hours are over."

"You're not a father yet," Billy said. "Go."

After he left she waited by the window to watch him cross the street and wait for the bus. It was dark and cold and it had begun to sleet. When she saw him she felt pierced with desolation. He was wearing his old camel's hair coat and the wind blew through his wavy hair. He stood back on his heels as he had as a boy. He turned around and scanned the building for her window. When he saw her, he waved and smiled. Billy waved back. A taxi, thinking it was being hailed, stopped. Grey got in and was driven off.

Every three hours a nurse appeared to take her temperature, blood pressure, and pulse. After Grey had gone, the night nurse appeared. She was a tall, middle-aged black woman named Mrs. Perch. In her hand she carried what looked like a suitcase full of dials and wires.

"Don't be alarmed," Mrs. Perch said. She had a soft West Indian accent. "It is only a portable fetal heart monitor. You get to say good morning and good evening to your baby."

She squirted a blob of cold blue jelly on Billy's stomach and pushed a transducer around in it, listening for the beat. At once Billy heard the sound of galloping hooves. Mrs. Perch timed the beats against her watch.

"Nice and healthy," Mrs. Perch said.

"Which part of this baby is where?" Billy said.

"Well, his head is back here, and his back is there and here is the rump and his feet are near your ribs. Or hers, of course."

"I wondered if that was a foot kicking," Billy said.

"My second boy got his foot under my rib and kicked with all his might," Mrs. Perch said.

Billy sat up in bed. She grabbed Mrs. Perch's hand. "Is this baby going to be all right?" she said.

"Oh my, yes," Mrs. Perch said. "You're not a very interesting case. Many others much more complicated than you have done very well and you will, too."

At four in the morning, another nurse appeared, a florid Englishwoman. Billy had spent a restless night, her heart pounding, her throat dry.

"Your pressure's up, dear," said the nurse, whose tag read "M. Whitely." "Dr. Bell has written orders that if your pressure goes up you're to have a shot of hydralazine. It doesn't hurt baby—did he explain that to you?"

"Yes," said Billy groggily.

"It may give you a little headache."

"What else?"

"That's all," Miss Whitely said.

Billy fell asleep and woke with a pounding headache. When she rang the bell, the nurse who had admitted her appeared. Her name was Bonnie Near and she was Billy's day nurse. She gave Billy a pill and then taped a tongue depressor wrapped in gauze over her bed.

"What's that for?" Billy said.

"Don't ask," said Bonnie Near.

"I want to know."

Bonnie Near sat down at the end of the bed. She was a few years older than Billy, trim and wiry with short hair and tiny diamond earrings.

"It's hospital policy," she said. "The hydralazine gives you a headache, right? You ring to get something to make it go away and because you have high blood pressure everyone assumes that the blood pressure caused it, not the drug. So this thing gets taped above your bed in the one chance in about fifty-five million that you have a convulsion."

Billy turned her face away and stared out the window.

"Hey, hey," said Bonnie Near. "None of this. I noticed yesterday that you're quite a worrier. Are you like this when you're not in the hospital? Listen. I'm a straight shooter and I would tell you if I was worried about you. I'm not. You're just the common garden variety."

Every morning Grey appeared with two cups of coffee and the morning paper. He sat in a chair and he and Billy read the paper together as they did at home.

"Is the house still standing?" Billy asked after several days. "Are the banks open? Did you bring the mail? I feel I've been here ten months instead of a week."

"The mail was very boring," Grey said. "Except for this booklet from the Wisconsin Loon Society. You'll be happy to know that you can order a record called 'Loon Music.' Would you like a copy?"

"If I moved over," Billy said, "would you take off your jacket and lie down next to me?"

Grey took off his jacket and shoes, and curled up next to Billy. He pressed his nose into her face and looked as if he could drift off to sleep in a second.

"Childworld called about the crib," he said into her neck. "They want to know if we want white paint or natural pine. I said natural."

"That's what I think I ordered," Billy said. "They let the husbands stay over in this place. They call them 'dads.' "

"I'm not a dad yet, as you pointed out," Grey said. "Maybe they'll just let me take naps here."

There was a knock on the door. Grey sprang to his feet and Jordan Bell appeared.

"Don't look so nervous, Billy," he said. "I have good news. I think we want to get this baby born if your pressure isn't going to go down. I think we ought to induce you."

Billy and Grey were silent.

"The way it works is that we put you on a drip of pitocin, which is a synthetic of the chemical your brain produces when you go into labor."

"We know," Billy said. "Katherine went over it in childbirth class." Katherine Walden was Jordan Bell's nurse. "When do you want to do this?"

"Tomorrow," Jordan Bell said. "Katherine will come over and give you your last Lamaze class right here."

"And if it doesn't work?"

"It usually does," said Jordan Bell. "And if it doesn't, we do a second-day induction."

"And if that doesn't work?"

"It generally does. If it doesn't, we do a cesarean, but you'll be awake and Grey can hold your hand."

"Oh what fun," said Billy.

When Jordan Bell left, Billy burst into tears.

"Why isn't anything normal?" she said. "Why do I have to lie here day after day listening to other people's babies crying? Why is my body betraying me like this?"

Grey kissed her and then took her hands. "There is no such thing as normal," he said. "Everyone we've talked to has some story or other—huge babies that won't budge, thirty-hour labors. A cesarean is a perfectly respectable way of being born."

"What about me? What about me getting all stuck up with tubes and cut up into little pieces?" Billy said, and she was instantly ashamed. "I hate being like this. I feel I've lost myself and some whimpering, whining person has taken me over."

"Think about how in two months we'll have a two-month-old baby to take to the park."

"Do you really think everything is going to be all right?" Billy said.

"Yes," said Grey. "I do. In six months we'll be in Maine."

Billy lay in bed with her door closed reading her brochure from the Loon Society. She thought about the cottage she and Grey rented every

August in Jewell Neck, Maine, on a lagoon. There at night with blackness all around them and not a light to be seen, they heard hoot owls and loons calling their night cries to one another. Loon mothers carried their chicks on their back, Billy knew. The last time she had heard those cries she had been just three months pregnant. The next time she heard them she would have a child.

She thought about the baby shower Penny had given her—a lunch party for ten women. At the end of it, Billy and Grey's unborn child had received cotton and wool blankets, little sweaters, tiny garments with feet, and two splendid Teddy bears. The Teddy bears had sat on the coffee table. Billy remembered the strange, light feeling in her chest as she looked at them. She had picked them both up and laughed with astonishment.

At a red light on the way home in a taxi, surrounded by boxes and bags of baby presents, she saw something that made her heart stop: Francis Clemens, who for two years had been Billy's illicit lover.

With the exception of her family, Billy was close only to Grey and Penny Stern. She had never been the subject of anyone's romantic passion. She and Grey, after all, had been fated to marry. She had loved him all her life.

Francis had pursued her: no one had ever pursued her before. The usual signs of romance were as unknown to Billy as the workings of a cyclotron. Crushes, she had felt, were for children. She did not really believe that adults had them.

Without her knowing it, she was incubating a number of curious romantic diseases. One day when Francis came to visit wearing his tweed coat and the ridiculously long paisley scarf he affected, she realized that she had fallen in love.

The fact of Francis was the most exotic thing that had ever happened in Billy's fairly stolid, uneventful life. He was as brilliant as a painted bunting. He was also, in marked contrast to Billy, beautifully dressed. He did not know one tree from another. He felt all birds were either robins or crows. He was avowedly urban and his pleasures were urban. He loved opera, cocktail parties, and lunches. They did not agree about economic theory, either.

Nevertheless, they spent what now seemed to Billy an enormous amount of time together. She had not sought anything like this. If her own case had been presented to her she would have dismissed it as messy, unnecessary, and somewhat sordid, but when she fell in love she fell as if backward into a swimming pool. For a while she felt dazed. Then Francis became a fact in her life. But in the end she felt her life was being ruined.

She had not seen Francis for a long time. In that brief glance at the red light she saw his paisley scarf, its long fringes flapping in the breeze. It was amazing that someone who had been so close to her did not know that she was having a baby. As the cab pulled away, she did not look back at him. She stared rigidly frontward, flanked on either side by presents for her unborn child.

The baby kicked. Mothers-to-be should not be lying in hospital beds thinking about illicit love affairs, Billy thought. Of course, if you were like the other mothers on the maternity floor and probably had never had an illicit love affair, you would not be punished by lying in the hospital in the first place. You would go into labor like everyone else, and come rushing into Maternity Admitting with your husband and your suitcase. By this time tomorrow she would have her baby in her arms, just like everyone else, but she drifted off to sleep thinking of Francis nonetheless.

At six in the morning, Bonnie Near woke her.

"You can brush your teeth," she said. "But don't drink any water. And your therapist is here to see you, but don't be long."

The door opened and Penny walked in.

"And how are we today?" she said. "Any strange dreams or odd thoughts?"

"How did you get in here?" Billy said.

"I said I was your psychiatrist and that you were being induced today and so forth," Penny said. "I just came to say good luck. Here's all the change we had in the house. Tell Grey to call constantly. I'll see you all tonight."

Billy was taken to the labor floor and hooked up to a fetal heart monitor whose transducers were kept on her stomach by a large elastic cummerbund. A stylish-looking nurse wearing hospital greens, a string of pearls, and perfectly applied pink lipstick poked her head through the door.

"Hi!" she said in a bright voice. "I'm Joanne Kelly. You're my patient today." She had the kind of voice and smile Billy could not imagine anyone's using in private. "Now, how are we? Fine? All right. Here's what we're going to do. First of all, we're going to put this IV into your arm. It will only hurt a little and then we're going to hook you up to something called pitocin. Has Dr. Bell explained any of this to you?" Joanne Kelly said.

"All," said Billy.

"Neat," Joanne Kelly said. "We *like* an informed patient. Put your arm out, please."

Billy stuck out her arm. Joanne Kelly wrapped a rubber thong under her elbow.

"Nice veins," she said. "You would have made a lovely junkie.

"Now we're going to start the pitocin," Joanne Kelly said. "We start off slow to see how you do. Then we escalate." She looked Billy up and down. "Okay," she said. "We're off and running. Now, I've got a lady huffing and puffing in the next room so I have to go and coach her. I'll be back real soon."

Billy lay looking at the clock, or watching the pitocin and glucose drip into her arm. She could not get a comfortable position and the noise of the fetal heart monitor was loud and harsh. The machine itself spat out a continual line of data.

Jordan Bell appeared at the foot of her bed.

"An exciting day—yes, Billy?" he said. "What time is Grey coming?"

"I told him to sleep late," Billy said. "All the nurses told me that this can take a long time. How am I supposed to feel when it starts working?"

"If all goes well, you'll start to have contractions and then they'll get stronger and then you'll have your baby."

"Just like that?" said Billy.

"Pretty much just like that."

But by five o'clock in the afternoon nothing much had happened.

Grey sat in a chair next to the bed. From time to time he checked the data. He had been checking it all day.

"That contraction went right off the paper," he said. "What did it feel like?"

"Intense," Billy said. "It just doesn't hurt."

"You're still in the early stages," said Jordan Bell when he came to check her. "I'm willing to stay on if you want to continue, but the baby might not be born till tomorrow."

"I'm beat," said Billy.

"Here's what we can do," Jordan said. "We can keep going or we start again tomorrow."

"Tomorrow," said Billy.

She woke up exhausted with her head pounding. The sky was cloudy and the glare hurt her eyes. She was taken to a different labor room.

In the night her blood pressure had gone up. She had begged not to have a shot—she did not see how she could go into labor feeling so terrible, but the shot was given. It had been a long, sleepless night.

She lay alone with a towel covering one eye, trying to sleep, when a nurse appeared by her side. This one looked very young, had curly hair, and thick, slightly rose-tinted glasses. Her tag read "Eva Gottlieb." Underneath she wore a button inscribed EVA: WE DELIVER.

"Hi," said Eva Gottlieb. "I'm sorry I woke you, but I'm your nurse for the day and I have to get you started."

"I'm here for a lobotomy," Billy said. "What are you going to do to me?"

"I'm going to run a line in you," Eva Gottlieb said. "And then I don't know what. Because your blood pressure is high, I'm supposed to wait until Jordan gets here." She looked at Billy carefully. "I know it's scary," she said. "But the worst that can happen is that you have to be sectioned and that's not bad."

Billy's head throbbed.

"That's easy for you to say," she said. "I'm the section."

Eva Gottlieb smiled. "I'm a terrific nurse," she said. "I'll stay with you."

Tears sprang in Billy's eyes. "Why will you?"

"Well, first of all, it's my job," said Eva. "And second of all, you look like a reasonable person."

Billy looked at Eva carefully. She felt instant, total trust. Perhaps that was part of being in hospitals and having babies. Everyone you came in contact with came very close, very fast.

Billy's eyes hurt. Eva was hooking her up to the fetal heart monitor. Her touch was strong and sure, and she seemed to know Billy did not want to be talked to. She flicked the machine on, and Billy heard the familiar sound of galloping hooves.

"Is there any way to turn it down?" Billy said.

"Sure," said Eva. "But some people find it consoling."

As the morning wore on, Billy's blood pressure continued to rise. Eva was with her constantly.

"What are they going to do to me?" Billy asked.

"I think they're probably going to give you magnesium sulfate to get your blood pressure down and then they're going to section you. Jordan does a gorgeous job, believe me. I won't let them do anything to you without explaining it first, and if you get out of bed first thing tomorrow and start moving around you'll be fine."

Twenty minutes later, a doctor Billy had never seen before administered a dose of magnesium sulfate.

"Can't you do this?" Billy asked Eva.

"It's heavy-duty stuff," Eva said. "It has to be done by a doctor."

"Can they wait until my husband gets here?"

"It's too dangerous," said Eva. "It has to be done. I'll stay with you."

The drug made her hot and flushed, and brought her blood pressure straight down. For the next hour, Billy tried to sleep. She had never been so tired. Eva brought her cracked ice to suck on and a cloth for her head. The baby wiggled and writhed, and the fetal heart monitor gauged its every move. Finally, Grey and Jordan Bell were standing at the foot of her bed.

"Okay, Billy," said Jordan. "Today's the day. We must get the baby out. I explained to Grey about the mag sulfate. We both agree that you must have a cesarean."

"When?" Billy said.

"In the next hour," said Jordan. "I have to check two patients and then we're off to the races."

"What do you think," Billy asked Grey.

"It's right," Grey said.

"And what about you?" Billy said to Eva.

"It has to be done," Eva said.

Jordan Bell was smiling a genuine smile and he looked dashing and happy.

"Why is he so uplifted?" Billy asked Eva after he had dashed down the hall.

"He loves the OR," she said. "He loves deliveries. Think of it this way: you're going to get your baby at last."

Billy lay on a gurney, waiting to be rolled down the hall. Grey, wearing hospital scrubs, stood beside her holding her hand. She had been prepped and given an epidural anesthetic, and she could no longer feel her legs.

"Look at me," she said to Grey. "I'm a mass of tubes. I'm a miracle of modern science." She put his hand over her eyes.

Grey squatted down to put his head near hers. He looked expectant, exhausted, and worried, but when he saw her scanning his face he smiled.

"It's going to be swell," Grey said. "We'll find out if it's little William or little Ella."

Billy's heart was pounding but she thought she ought to say something to keep her side up. She said, "I knew we never should have had sexual intercourse." Grey gripped her hand tight and smiled. Eva laughed. "Don't you guys leave me," Billy said.

Billy was wheeled down the hall by an orderly. Grey held one hand, Eva held the other. Then they left her to scrub.

She was taken to a large, pale green room. Paint was peeling on the ceiling in the corner. An enormous lamp hung over her head. The anesthetist appeared and tapped her feet.

"Can you feel this?" he said.

"It doesn't feel like feeling," Billy said. She was trying to keep her breathing steady.

"Excellent," he said.

Then Jordan appeared at her feet, and Grey stood by her head.

Eva bent down. "I know you'll hate this, but I have to tape your hands down, and I have to put this oxygen mask over your face. It comes off as soon as the baby's born, and it's good for you and the baby."

Billy took a deep breath. The room was very hot. A screen was placed over her chest.

"It's so you can't see," said Eva. "Here's the mask. I know it'll freak you out, but just breathe nice and easy. Believe me, this is going to be fast."

Billy's arms were taped, her legs were numb, and a clear plastic mask was placed over her nose and mouth. She was so frightened she wanted to cry out, but it was impossible. Instead she breathed as Katherine Walden had taught her to. Every time a wave of panic rose, she breathed it down. Grey held her hand. His face was blank and his glasses were fogged. His hair was covered by a green cap and his brow was wet. There was nothing she could do for him, except squeeze his hand.

"Now, Billy," said Jordan Bell, "you'll feel something cold on your stomach. I'm painting you with Betadine. All right, here we go."

Billy felt something like dull tugging. She heard the sound of foamy water. Then she felt the baby being slipped from her. She turned to Grey. His glasses had unfogged and his eyes were round as quarters. She heard a high, angry scream.

"Here's your baby," said Jordan Bell. "It's a beautiful, healthy boy."

Eva lifted the mask off Billy's face.

"He's perfectly healthy," Eva said. "Listen to those lungs." She took the baby to be weighed and tested. Then she came back to Billy. "He's perfect but he's little—just under five pounds. We have to take him upstairs to the preemie nursery. It's policy when they're not five pounds."

"Give him to me," Billy said. She tried to free her hands but they were securely taped.

"I'll bring him to you," Eva said. "But he can't stay down here. He's too small. It's for the baby's safety, I promise you. Look, here he is."

The baby was held against her forehead. The moment he came near her he stopped shrieking. He was mottled and wet.

"Please let me have him," Billy said.

"He'll be fine," Eva said. They then took him away.

The next morning Billy rang for the nurse and demanded that her IV be disconnected. Twenty minutes later she was out of bed slowly walking.

"I feel as if someone had crushed my pelvic bones," Billy said.

"Someone did," said the nurse.

Two hours later she was put into a wheelchair and pushed by a nurse into the elevator and taken to the Infant Intensive Care Unit. At the door the nurse said, "I'll wheel you in."

"I can walk," Billy said. "But thank you very much."

Inside, she was instructed to scrub with surgical soap and to put on a sterile gown. Then she walked very slowly and very stiffly down the hall. A Chinese nurse stopped her.

"I'm William Delielle's mother," she said. "Where is he?"

The nurse consulted a clipboard and pointed Billy down a hallway. Another nurse in a side room pointed to an isolette—a large plastic case with porthole windows. There on a white cloth lay her child.

He was fast asleep, his little arm stretched in front of him, an exact replica of Grey's sleeping posture. On his back were two discs the size of nickels hooked up to wires that measured his temperature and his heart and respiration rates on a console above his isolette. He was long and skinny and beautiful.

"He looks like a little chicken," said Billy. "May I hold him?"

"Oh, no," said the nurse. "Not for a while. He mustn't be stressed." She gave Billy a long look and said, "But you can open the windows and touch him."

Billy opened the porthole window and touched his leg. He shivered slightly. She wanted to disconnect his probes, scoop him up, and hold him next to her. She stood quietly, her hand resting lightly on his calf.

The room was bright, hot, and busy. Nurses came and went, washing their hands, checking charts, making notes, diapering, changing bottles of glucose solution. There were three other children in the room.

One was very tiny and had a miniature IV attached to a vein in her head. A pink card was taped on her isolette. Billy looked on the side of William's isolette. There was a blue card and in Grey's tiny printing was written "William Delielle."

Later in the morning, when Grey appeared in her room he found Billy sitting next to a glass-encased pump.

"This is the well-known electric breast pump. Made in Switzerland," Billy said.

"It's like the medieval clock at Salisbury Cathedral," Grey said, peering into the glass case. "I just came from seeing William. He's much *longer* than I thought. I called all the grandparents. In fact, I was on the telephone all night after I left you." He gave her a list of messages. "They're feeding him in half an hour."

Billy looked at her watch. She had been instructed to use the pump for three minutes on each breast to begin with. Her milk, however, would not be given to William, who, the doctors said, was too little to nurse. He would be given carefully measured formula, and Billy would eventually have to wean him from the bottle and onto herself. The prospect of this seemed very remote.

As the days went by, Billy's room filled with flowers, but she spent most of her time in the Infant ICU. She could touch William but not hold him. The morning before she was to be discharged, Billy went to William's eight o'clock feeding. She thought how lovely it would be to feed him at home, how they might sit in the rocking chair and watch the birds in the garden below. In William's present home, there was no morning and no night. He had never been in a dark room, or heard bird sounds or traffic noise, or felt a cool draft.

William was asleep on his side wearing a diaper and a little T-shirt. The sight of him seized Billy with emotion.

"You can hold him today," the nurse said.

"Yes?"

"Yes, and you can feed him today, too."

Billy bowed her head. She took a steadying breath. "How can I hold him with all this hardware on him?" she said.

"I'll show you," said the nurse. She disconnected the console, reached into the isolette, and gently untaped William's probes. Then she showed Billy how to change him, put on his T-shirt, and swaddle him in a cotton blanket. In an instant he was in Billy's arms.

He was still asleep, but he made little screeching noises and wrinkled his nose. He moved against her and nudged his head into her arm. The nurse led her to a rocking chair and for the first time she sat down with her baby.

All around her, lights blazed. The radio was on and a sweet male voice sang, "I want you to be mine, I want you to be mine, I want to take you home, I want you to be mine."

William opened his eyes and blinked. Then he yawned and began to cry.

"He's hungry," the nurse said, putting a small bottle into Billy's hand.

She fed him and burped him, and then she held him in her arms and rocked him to sleep. In the process she fell asleep, too, and was woken by the nurse and Grey, who had come from work.

"You must put him back now," said the nurse. "He's been out a long time and we don't want to stress him."

"It's awful to think that being with his mother creates stress," Billy said.

"Oh, no!" the nurse said. "That's not what I mean. I mean, in his isolette it's temperature controlled."

Once Billy was discharged from the hospital she had to commute to see William. She went to the two morning feedings, came home for a nap, and met Grey for the five o'clock. They raced out for dinner and came back for the eight. Grey would not let Billy stay for the eleven.

Each morning she saw Dr. Edmunds, the head of neonatology. He was a tall, slow-talking, sandy-haired man with horn-rimmed glasses.

"I know you will never want to hear this under any other circumstances," he said to Billy, "but your baby is very boring."

"How boring?"

"Very boring. He's doing just what he ought to do." William had gone to the bottom of his growth curve and was beginning to gain. "As soon as he's a little fatter he's all yours."

Billy stood in front of his isolette watching William sleep.

"This is like having an affair with a married man," Billy said to the nurse who was folding diapers next to her.

The nurse looked at her uncomprehendingly.

"I mean you love the person but can only see him at certain times," said Billy.

The nurse was young and plump. "I guess I see what you mean," she said.

At home William's room was waiting. The crib had been delivered and put together by Grey. While Billy was in the hospital, Grey had finished William's room. The Teddy bears sat on the shelves. A mobile of ducks and geese hung over the crib. Grey had bought a secondhand rocking chair and had painted it red. Billy had thought she would be unable to face William's empty room. Instead she found she could scarcely stay out of it. She folded and refolded his clothes, reorganized his drawers, arranged his crib blankets. She decided what should be his homecoming clothes and set them out on the changing table along with a cotton receiving blanket and a wool shawl.

But even though he did not look at all fragile and he was beginning to gain weight, it often felt to Billy that she would never have him. She and Grey had been told ten days to two weeks from day of birth. One day when she felt she could not stand much more Billy was told that she might try nursing him.

Touch him on his cheek. He will turn to you. Guide him toward the breast and the magical connection will be made.

Billy remembered this description from her childbirth books. She had imagined a softly lit room, a sense of peacefulness, some soft, sweet music in the background.

She was put behind a screen in William's room, near an isolette containing an enormous baby who was having breathing difficulties.

She was told to keep on her sterile gown, and was given sterile water to wash her breasts with. At the sight of his mother's naked bosom, William began to howl. The sterile gown dropped onto his face. Billy began to sweat. All around her, the nurses chatted, clattered, and dropped diapers into metal bins and slammed the tops down.

"Come on, William," Billy said. "The books say that this is the blissful union of mother and child."

But William began to scream. The nurse appeared with the formula bottle and William instantly stopped screaming and began to drink happily.

"Don't worry," the nurse said. "He'll catch on."

At night at home she sat by the window. She could not sleep. She had never felt so separated from anything in her life. Grey, to distract himself, was stenciling the wall under the molding in William's room. He had found an early American design of wheat and cornflowers. He stood on a ladder in his blue jeans carefully applying the stencil in pale blue paint.

One night Billy went to the door of the baby's room to watch him, but Grey was not on the ladder. He was sitting in the rocking chair with his head in his hands. His shoulders were shaking slightly. He had the radio on, and he did not hear her.

He had been so brave and cheerful. He had held her hand while William was born. He had told her it was like watching a magician sawing his wife in half. He had taken photos of William in his isolette and sent them to their parents and all their friends. He had read up on growth curves and had bought Billy a book on breast-feeding. He had also purloined his hospital greens to wear each year on William's birthday. Now *he* had broken down.

She made a noise coming into the room and then bent down and stroked his hair. He smelled of soap and paint thinner. She put her arms around him, and she did not let go for a long time.

Three times a day, Billy tried to nurse William behind a screen and each time she ended up giving him his formula.

Finally she asked a nurse, "Is there some room I could sit in alone with this child?"

"We're not set up for it," the nurse said. "But I could put you in the utility closet."

There amidst used isolettes and cardboard boxes of sterile water, on the second try William nursed for the first time. She touched his cheek. He turned to her, just as it said in the book. Then her eyes crossed.

"Oh, my God!" she said.

A nurse walked in.

"Hurts, right?" she said. "Good for him. That means he's got it. It won't hurt for long."

At his evening feeding he howled again.

"The course of true love never did run smooth," said Grey. He and Billy walked slowly past the park on their way home. It was a cold, wet night.

"I am a childless mother," Billy said.

Two days later William was taken out of his isolette and put into a plastic bin. He had no temperature or heart probes, and Billy could pick him up without having to disconnect anything. At his evening feeding when the unit was quiet, she took him out in the hallway and walked up and down with him.

The next day she was greeted by Dr. Edmunds.

"I've just had a chat with your pediatrician," he said. "How would you like to take your boring baby home with you?"

"When?" said Billy.

"Right now, if you have his clothes," Dr. Edmunds said. "Dr. Jacobson will be up in a few minutes and can officially release him."

She ran down the hall and called Grey.

"Go home and get William's things," she said. "They're springing him. Come and get us."

"You mean we can just walk out of there with him?" Grey said. "I mean, just take him under our arm? He barely knows us."

"Just get here. And don't forget the blankets."

A nurse helped Billy dress William. He was wrapped in a green and white receiving blanket and covered in a white wool shawl. On his head was a blue and green knitted cap. It slipped slightly sideways, giving him a raffish look.

They were accompanied in the elevator by a nurse. It was hospital policy that a nurse hold the baby, and hand it over at the door.

It made Billy feel light-headed to be standing out of doors with her child. She felt she had just robbed a bank and got away with it.

In the taxi, Grey gave the driver their address.

"Not door to door," Billy said. "Can we get out at the avenue and walk down the street just like everyone else?"

When the taxi stopped, they got out carefully. The sky was full of silver clouds and the air was blustery and cold. William squinted at the light and wrinkled his nose.

Then, with William tight in Billy's arms, the three of them walked down the street just like everyone else.

At the time of her death in the fall of 1992, Laurie Colwin had published four novels, including the very popular *Happy All the Time,* three short story collections, and a book of essays. She had been the recipient of a John Simon Guggenheim Memorial Fellowship and a grant from the National Foundation for the Endowment of the Arts. Her home was in New York City.

JANE SMILEY

" 'Lily' is a relic from my twenties, before I had children, which seems a lifetime ago and *is* two marriages ago. I did then what I now advise my students to do—I based the characters on people I knew (about whose identities I shall forever remain mum) but who never actually came together in this situation. Lily herself is based on a woman I knew who I thought was astoundingly beautiful, and many of her idiosyncrasies in the story I think grow out of her experience of other people reacting to her beauty. Beauty, though, is such a convention of literature and movies that readers often overlook Lily's beauty as a particular motivation in this story and then are somewhat perplexed by her—find her too removed or too shallow. Of Nancy and Kevin I will only say that I am rather fond of them, especially Nancy. I like how brazenly practical she is.

"More often than not, a short story hits me through a juxtaposition of unlike elements—for example my friends Nancy and Kevin next to my friend Lily, what would that be like, what might happen? I don't feel that I have developed my ideas or my craft in this particular form—I give more serious thought to novels and novellas. I also find that I can plan to write this or that novel or novella, and even plan when it might be finished, but that a story is an unexpected gift.

"Once a linguist from England told me that American Midwestern English had become, through demographics, standard English—the English, you might say, that is unaccented. Lots of TV anchorpersons do have their origins in the Midwest. Perhaps my voice is like theirs—unaccented, uncolorful, almost transparent. Certainly the concerns of my short stories and novellas have been fairly mainstream ones—the life and the sensibility of the educated middle class somewhere away from the coasts. I think it is also the voice of someone who feels at home. The fact is that my family has lived in the middle class and the middle of the country for generations. Yet I feel it was through writing my novel *The Greenlanders,* set in a remote place centuries ago, that I first truly found my voice.

"I consider my writing investigative rather than expressive. I always conceive a work as a way of imagining something that interests and mystifies me rather than as a way of expressing my own experiences. If my experiences flow into the subject, it is indirectly—more as an emotional reference point in my writing than as the goal of the work. I suppose the risk in such a method is that the work will get too abstract, but I find that the characters' experiences come to seem to me as real and as fraught with feeling as my own experiences."

LILY

CAREERING toward Lily Stith in a green Ford Torino were Kevin and Nancy Humboldt. Once more they gave up trying to talk reasonably; once more they sighed simultaneous but unsympathetic sighs; once more each resolved to stare only at the unrolling highway.

At the same moment, Lily was squeezing her mop into her bucket. Then she straightened up and looked out the window, eager for their arrival. She hadn't seen them in two years, not since having won a prestigious prize for her poems.

She was remarkably well made, with golden skin, lit by the late-afternoon sun, delicately defined muscles swelling over slender bones, a cloud of dark hair, a hollow at the base of her neck for some jewel. She was so beautiful that you could not help attributing to her all of your favorite virtues. To Lily her beauty seemed a senseless thing, since it gained her nothing in the way of passion, release, kinship, or intimacy. Now she was looking forward, with resolve, to making the

Humboldts confess really and truly what was wrong with her—why, in fact, no one was in love with her.

A few minutes later they pulled up to the curb. Nancy climbed the apartment steps bearing presents—a jar of dill pickles she had made herself, pictures of common friends, a cap knitted of rainbow colors for the winter. Lily put it on in spite of the heat. The rich colors Nancy had chosen lit up Lily's tanned face and flashing teeth. Almost involuntarily Nancy exclaimed, "You look better than ever!" Lily laughed and said, "But look at you! Your hair is below your hips now!" Nancy pirouetted and went inside before Kevin came up. He, too, looked remarkable, Lily thought, with his forty-eight-inch chest on his five-foot-nine-inch frame. Because of Nancy's hair and Kevin's chest, Lily always treasured the Humboldts more than she did her current friends. Kevin kissed her cheek, but he was trying to imagine where Nancy had gone; his eyes slid instantly past Lily. He patted her twice on the shoulder. She cried, "I've been looking for you since noon!" He said, "I always forget how far it is across Ohio," and stepped into the house.

That it had been two years—two years!—grew to fill the room like a thousand balloons, pinning them in the first seats they chose and forbidding conversation. Lily offered some food, some drink. They groaned, thinking of all they had eaten on the road (not convivially but bitterly, snatching, biting, swallowing too soon). Lily, assuming they knew what they wanted, did not ask again. Immediately Kevin's hands began to fidget for a glass to jiggle and balance and peer into, to turn slowly on his knee. Two years! Two days! Had they really agreed to a two-day visit?

Although the apartment was neat and airy, the carpet vacuumed and the furniture polished, Lily apologized for a bowl and a plate unwashed beside the sink. Actually, she often wondered whether cleanliness drove love away. Like many fastidious people, she suspected that life itself was to be found in dirt and disorder, in unknown dark substances that she was hesitant to touch. Lily overestimated her neatness in this case. The windowsills, for example, had not been vacuumed, and the leaves of the plants were covered with dust. She began to apologize for the lack of air-conditioning, the noise of cars and trucks through the open windows, the weather, the lack of air-conditioning again; then she breathed a profound sigh and let her hands drop limply between her knees.

Nancy Humboldt was moved by this gesture to remember how Lily always had a touch of the tragic about her. It was unrelated to anything that had ever happened, but it was distinct, always present. Nancy sat forward and smiled affectionately at her friend. Conversation began to pick up.

After a while they ate. Lily noticed that when Kevin carried his chest toward Nancy, Nancy made herself concave as she sidestepped him. Perhaps he did not exactly try to touch her; the kitchenette was very small. Jokes were much in demand, greeted with pouncing hilarity; a certain warmth, reminiscent of their early friendship, flickered and established itself. Conversation ranged over a number of topics. Nancy kept using the phrase "swept away." "That movie just swept me away!" "I live to be swept away!" "I used to be much more cautious than I am now; now I just want to be swept away!" Kevin as often used the word "careful." "I think you have to be really careful about your decisions." "I'm much more careful now." "I think I made mistakes because I wasn't careful." Lily listened most of the time. When the discussion became awkwardly heated, they leaped as one flesh on Lily and demanded to know about her prizewinning volume, her success, her work. Nancy wanted to hear some new pieces.

Lily was used to reading. Finishing the fourth poem, she wondered, as she often did, why men did not come up to her after readings and offer love, or at least ask her out. She had won a famous prize. With the intimacy of art she phrased things that she would not ordinarily admit to, discussed her soul, which seemed a perfectly natural and even attractive soul. People liked her work: they had bought more copies of her prizewinning volume than of any other in the thirteen-year series. But no one, in a fan letter, sent a picture or a telephone number. Didn't art or accomplishment make a difference? Was it all invisible? Lily said, "I think Kevin was bored."

"Not at all, really."

"I wasn't in the slightest," Nancy said. "They're very good. They don't have any leaves on them." Nancy grinned. She rather liked the occasional image herself.

Now was the time to broach her subject, thought Lily. The Humboldts had known her since college. Perhaps they had seen some little thing, spoken of it between themselves, predicted spinsterhood. Lily straightened the yellow pages and set them on the side table. "You know," she said with a laugh and a cough, "I haven't gone out in a month and a half. I mean, I realize it's summer and all, but anyway. And the last guy was just a friend, really, I—" She looked up and went on. "All those years with Ken, nobody even made a pass at me in a bus station. I didn't think it was important then, but now I've gotten rather anxious."

Kevin Humboldt looked straight at her, speculating. Yes, it must be the eyes. They were huge, hugely lashed, set into huge sockets. They were far more expressive and defenseless than anything else about her. The contrast was disconcerting. And the lids came down over them so opaquely, even when she blinked but especially when she lowered her gaze, that you were frightened into changing any movement toward her into some idle this or that. Guys he'd known in college had admired her from a distance and then dated plainer women with more predictable surfaces.

"Do you ever hear from Ken?" Nancy asked.

"I changed my number and didn't give him the new one. I think he got the message."

"I'll never understand why you spent—"

"Nine years involved with a married man, blah blah blah. I know."

"Among other things."

"When we were breaking up, I made up a lot of reasons, but now I remember what it was like before we met. It was just like it is now." Kevin thought of interrupting with his observation. He didn't.

"Everyone has dateless spells, honey," said Nancy, who'd had her first dateless spell after her marriage to Kevin. She had always attributed to Lily virginal devotion to her work. Nancy thought a famous prize certainly equaled a husband and three children. Love was like any activity, you had to put in the hours, but as usual Kevin was right there, so she didn't say this and shifted with annoyance in her chair. "Really," she snapped, "don't worry about it."

Kevin's jaws widened in an enormous yawn. Lily jumped up to find clean towels, saying, "Does it seem odd to you?" Kevin went into the bathroom and Nancy went into the bedroom with her suitcase. Lily followed her. "I have no way of knowing," she went on, but then she stopped. Nancy wasn't really listening.

In the morning Nancy braided and wound up her hair while Lily made breakfast. Kevin was still asleep. Nancy had always had long, lovely hair, but Lily couldn't remember her taking such pride in it as she was now, twisting and arranging it with broad, almost conceited motions. She fondled it, put it here and there, spoke about things she liked to do with it from time to time. She obviously cherished it. "You've kept it in wonderful shape," Lily said.

"My hair is my glory," Nancy replied, and sat down to her eggs. She was not kidding.

When Kevin staggered from bedroom to bathroom an hour later, Nancy had gone out to survey the local shops. Kevin looked for her in every room of the apartment and then said, "Nancy's not here?"

"She thought she'd have a look around."

Kevin dropped into his seat at the table and put his head in his arms. A second later he exclaimed, "Oh, God!" Lily liked Kevin better this visit than she had before. His chest, which had always dragged him aggressively into situations, seemed to have lost some of its influence. He was not as loud or blindingly self-confident as he had been playing football, sitting in the first row in class, barreling through business school, swimming two miles every day. Thus it was with sympathy rather than astonishment that Lily realized he was weeping. He wiped his eyes on his T-shirt. "She's going to leave me! When we get back to Vancouver, she's going to leave me for another guy!"

"Is that what she said?"

"I know."

"Did she say so?"

"I know."

"Look, sit up a second and have this piece of toast."

"He's just a dumb cowboy. I know she's sleeping with him."

She put food in front of him and he began to eat it. After a few bites, though, he pushed it away and put his head down. He moaned into the cave of his arms. Lily said, "What?"

"She won't sleep with me. She hasn't since Thanksgiving. She never says where she's going or when she'll be back. She can't stand me checking up on her."

"Do you check up on her?"

"I call her at work sometimes. I just want to talk to her. She never wants to talk to me. I miss her!"

"What do Roger and Fred say?" Roger and Fred were friends from college who also lived in Vancouver.

"They don't understand."

Lily nodded. Unlike Lily, Roger and Fred had wavered in their fondness for Nancy. Many times she had been selfish about certain things, which were perhaps purely feminine things. She thought people should come to the table when dinner was hot in spite of just-opened beers and half-smoked cigarettes or repair projects in the driveway. She had screamed, really screamed, about booted feet on her polished table. Roger and Fred especially found her too punctilious about manners, found her slightly shrill, and did not appreciate her sly wit or her generosity with food and lodging and presents (this liberality they attributed to Kevin, who was, simultaneously, a known tightwad). And they overlooked her capacity for work—willing, organized, unsnobbish bringing home of the bacon while all the men were looking for careers and worrying about compromising themselves. Lily and Kevin at least agreed that Nancy was a valuable article.

"Okay," Lily said, "who's just a dumb cowboy?"

"His name is Hobbs Nolan. She met him at a cross-country ski clinic last year. But he's not really outdoorsy or athletic; he just wears these pointy-toed cowboy boots and flannel cowboy shirts. Out there guys like him are a dime a dozen. . . ."

"You know him?"

"I've seen him. He knows people we know. They think he's a real jerk."

"You blame him for all of this, then?"

Kevin glanced at her and said, "No." After a moment he exclaimed "Oh, God!" again, and dropped his head on his arms. His hair grazed the butter dish, and Lily was suddenly repelled by these confidences. She turned and looked out the window, but Nancy was nowhere in sight. The freshness of the morning was gone, and the early blue sky had whitened. She looked at her watch. It was about ten-thirty. Any other morning she would already have sat down to her work with an apple and a cup of tea, or she would be strolling into town with her list of errands. She glanced toward the bedroom. The blanket was half off the bed and a corner of the contour sheet had popped off the mattress. Nancy's and Kevin's clothes were piled on the floor. They had left other items in the living room or the kitchen: Nancy's brush, a scarf, Kevin's running shoes and socks, two or three pieces of paper from Nancy's purse, the map on which they had traced their route. But hadn't she expected and desired such intimacy? He sat up. She smiled and said, "You know, you're the first people to spend the night here in ages. I'd forgotten—"

"I don't think you should worry about that. Like Nancy said, we all go through dry spells. Look at me, my—"

"Oh, that! I wasn't referring to that."

"My whole life was a dry spell before Nancy came along."

Lily sat back and looked at Kevin. He was sighing. "Hey," she said, "you're going to have a lot better luck if you lighten up a little."

"I know that, but I can't." He sounded petulant.

Lily said, "Well—"

"Well, now I'd better go running before it gets too hot." Kevin reached for his shoes and socks. But Nancy walked in and he sat up without putting them on. Nancy displayed her packages. "There was a great sale on halter tops, and look at this darling T-shirt!" She pulled out an example of the T-shirt Lily had seen on everyone all summer. It said, "If you live a good life, go to church, and say your prayers, when you die you will go to OHIO." Lily smiled. Nancy tossed the T-shirt over to Kevin, saying, "Extra extra large. I'm sure it will fit."

He held it up and looked at it and then said, glumly, "Thanks."

"Are you going for your run now?"

"Yeah."

But he didn't make a move. Everyone sat very still for a long time, maybe five minutes, and then Lily began clearing plates off the table and Nancy began to take down her hair and put it back up again. Kevin seemed to root himself in the chair. His face was impassive. Nancy glared at him, but finally sighed and said, "I got a long letter from Betty Stern not so long ago. She stopped working on her Chinese dissertation and went to business school last year."

"I heard that Harry got a job, but that it was in Newfoundland or someplace like that," Lily said.

"Who'd you hear that from?" Refusing even to look in Kevin's direction, Nancy combed her hair.

"Remember Meredith Lawlor? Did you know she was here? She's teaching in the pharmacy school here in Columbus. She raises all these poisonous tropical plants in a big greenhouse she and her husband built out in the country."

"Who's her husband?"

"She met him in graduate school, I think. He's from Arizona."

"I'd like to raise plants for a living. I don't know necessarily about poisonous ones." Nancy glanced at Kevin. Lily noticed that she had simply dropped her packages by her chair, that tissue paper and sales slips and the halter tops themselves were in danger of being stepped on. In college they had teased Nancy relentlessly about her disorderly ways, but Lily hadn't found them especially annoying then. Kevin said, "Why don't you pick that stuff up before you step on it?"

"I'm not going to step on it!"

"Well, pick it up anyway. I doubt that Lily wants your mess all over her place."

"Who are you to speak for Lily?"

"I'm speaking for society in general, in this case."

"Why don't you go running, for God's sake?"

"I'd rather not have a heart attack in the heat, thank you."

"Well, it's not actually that hot. It's not as hot as it was yesterday, and you ran seven miles."

"It's hot in here."

"Well, there's a nice breeze outside, and this town is very shady. When you get back we can have lunch after your shower. We can have that smoked turkey we got at the store last night. I still have some of the bread I made the day we left."

Kevin looked at her suspiciously, but all he said finally was, "Well, pick up that stuff, okay?"

Nancy smiled. "Okay."

Still Kevin was reluctant to go, tying his shoes with painful slowness, drinking a glass of water after letting the tap run and run, retying one of his shoes, tucking and untucking his shirt. He closed the door laboriously behind him, and Nancy watched out the window for him to appear on the street. When he did, she inhaled with sharp, exasperated relief. "Christ!" she exclaimed.

"He doesn't seem very happy."

"But you know he's always been into that self-dramatization. I'm not impressed. I used to be, but I'm not anymore."

Lily wondered how she was going to make it to lunch, and then through the afternoon to dinner and bedtime. Nancy turned toward her. "I shouldn't have let all these men talk to you before I did."

"What men?"

"Kevin, Roger, Fred."

"I haven't talked to Roger or Fred since late last winter, at least."

"They think I ought to be shot. But they really infuriate me. Do you know what sharing a house with Roger was like? He has the most rigid routine I have ever seen, and he drives everywhere, even to the quick shop at the end of the block. I mean, he would get in his car and drive out the driveway and then four houses down to pick up the morning paper. And every time he did the dishes, he broke something we got from our wedding, and then he would refuse to pay for it because we had gotten it for free anyway."

"Fred always said that being friends with Roger showed you could be friends with anyone."

"Fred and I get along, but in a way I think he's more disapproving than Roger is. Sometimes he acts as if I've shocked him so much that he can't bear to look at me."

"So how have you shocked him?"

"Didn't Kevin tell you about Hobbs Nolan?"

"He mentioned him."

"But Hobbs isn't the real issue, as far as I'm concerned. Men always think that other men are the real issue. You know, Roger actually sat me down one night and started to tell me off?"

"What's the real issue?"

"Well, one thing I can't bear is having to always report in whenever I go somewhere. I mean, I get in the car to go for groceries, and if I decide while I'm out to go to the mall, he expects me to call and tell him. Or if I have to work even a half hour late, or if the girl I work with and I decide to go out for a beer after work. I hate it. I hate picking up the goddamned telephone and dialing all the numbers. I hate listening to it ring, and most of all I hate that automatic self-justification you just slide into. I mean, I don't even know how to sound honest anymore, even when I'm being honest."

"Are you—"

"No, most of all I hate the image I have of Kevin the whole time I'm talking to him, sitting home all weekend with nothing to do, whining into the phone."

"I think Kevin is mostly upset because you don't sleep with him."

"Well—"

"I really don't see how you can cut him off like that."

"Neither does he."

"Why do you?"

"Don't you think he's strange-looking? And everything he does in bed simply repels me. It didn't used to but now it does. I can't help it. He doesn't know how big or strong he is and he's always hurting me. When I see him move toward me, I wince. I know he's going to step on me or poke me or bump into me."

"Well, you could go to a therapist. You ought to at least reassure Kevin that you're not sleeping with this other guy."

"We did go to a therapist, and he got so nervous he was even more clumsy, and I am sleeping with Hobbs."

"Nancy!"

"Why are you surprised? How can this be a reason for surprise? I'm a sexual person. Kevin always said that he thought I was promiscuous until I started with him, and then he just thought that I was healthy and instinctive."

"Well, Nancy—"

"I have a feeling you aren't very approving either."

"I don't know, I—"

"But that's all I want. I realized on the way here that all the time I've known you I've wanted you to approve of me. Not just to like me, or even respect me, but to approve of me. I still like being married to Kevin, but all of us should know by now that the best person for being married to isn't always the best person for sleeping with, and there's no reason why he should be." She glanced out the window. "Anyway, here he comes." A moment later the door slammed open. Lily thought Kevin was angry, until she realized that he had simply misjudged the weight of the door. Sweat was pouring off him, actually dripping on the carpet. Nancy said, "Jesus! Go take a shower." Lily wanted to tell him not to drip over the coffee table, with its bowl of fruit, but said nothing. He looked at them with studied ingenuousness and said, "Four miles in twenty-five minutes. Not bad, huh? And it's ninety-three. I just ran past the bank clock."

"Great." Nancy turned back to Lily and said, "Maybe I should try to call Meredith Lawlor while I'm here. We were pretty good friends junior year. I've often thought about her, actually." Kevin tromped into the bathroom.

Washing lettuce for the sandwiches, Lily watched Nancy slice the turkey. It was remarkable, after all, how the other woman's most trivial mannerisms continued to be perfectly familiar to her after two years, after not thinking about Nancy or their times together for days and even weeks at a stretch. It was as if the repeated movement of an arm through the air or the repeated cocking of a head could engrave itself willy-nilly on her brain, and her brain, recognizing what was already contained in it, would always respond with warmth. In fact, although she did feel this burr of disapproval toward Nancy, and sympathy for Kevin, Kevin's presence was oppressive and Nancy's congenial. Nancy got out the bread she had made, a heavy, crumbly, whole-grain production, and they stacked vegetables and meat on the slices and slathered them with mustard and catsup. The shower in the bathroom went off and Nancy sighed. Lily wondered if she heard herself.

Lily remembered that the kitchen workers in the college cafeteria had always teased Kevin about his appetite. Certainly he still ate with noise and single-minded gusto. His lettuce crunched, his bread fell apart, pieces of tomato dropped on his plate and he wiped them up with more bread. He drank milk. Lily tried to imagine him at work. Fifteen months before, he had graduated from business school near the top of his class and had taken a risky job with a small company. The owner was impressed with his confidence and imagination. In a year he'd gotten four raises, all of them substantial. Lily imagined him in a group of men, serious, athletic, well-dressed, subtly dominating. Was it merely Nancy's conversation about him that made him seem to eat so foolishly, so dependently, with such naked anxiety? To *be* so foolish, so dependent? When he was finished, Nancy asked him whether he was still hungry and said to Lily, "Isn't this good bread? I made up the recipe myself."

"It's delicious."

"I think so. I've thought of baking bread for the health-food store near us. In fact, they asked me to, but I'm not sure it would be very profitable."

"It's nice that they asked you."

"A couple of guys there really like it."

Kevin scowled. Lily wondered if one of these guys was Hobbs Nolan. Nancy went on, "I make another kind, too, an herb bread with dill and chives and tarragon."

"That sounds good."

"It is."

Lily was rather taken aback at Nancy's immodesty. This exchange, more than previous ones, seemed to draw her into the Humboldts' marriage and to implicate her in its fate. She felt a brief sharp relief that they would be gone soon. She finished her sandwich and stood up to get an apple. It was before one o'clock. More stuff—the towel Kevin had used on his hair, Nancy's sandals, Nancy's other hairbrush—was distributed around the living room. Lily had spent an especially solitary summer, with no summer school to teach and many of her friends away, particularly since the first of August. Some days the only people she spoke to were checkers at the grocery store or librarians. Her fixation on the Humboldts' possessions was a symptom that her solitary life certainly was unhealthy, that she was, after all, turning back into a virgin, as she feared. It was true that her apartment never looked "lived in" and that she preferred it that way. Suddenly she was envious of them; in spite of their suspicions and resentments their life together had a kind of chaotic richness. Their minds were full of each other. Just then Kevin said, with annoyance, "Damn!" and Nancy shrugged, perfectly taking his meaning.

"There's a great swimming pool here," Lily said. "I've spent practically the whole summer there. You must have brought your suits?"

Kevin had been diving off the high board steadily for at least forty-five minutes. At first, when Nancy and Lily had been talking about Kenneth Diamond and Lily's efforts to end that long relationship, Nancy had only glanced at Kevin from time to time. Lily remarked that she had slept with Ken fewer than twenty times in nine years. Nancy stared at her—not in disbelief but as if seeking to know the unfathomable. Then, for four dives, Nancy did not take her eyes off Kevin. He did a backward double somersault, tucked; a forward one-and-a-half lay-out; a forward one-and-a-half in pike position; and a double somersault with a half-gainer, which was astonishingly graceful. "I knew he dove in high school," she said, "but I've never seen this." A plump adolescent girl did a swan dive and Kevin stepped onto the board again. Other people looked up, including two of the lifeguards. Perhaps he was unaware that people were looking at him. At any rate, he was straightforward and undramatic about stepping into his dive. The board seemed to bend in two under his muscular weight and then to fling him toward the blue sky. He attempted a forward two-and-a-half, tuck position, but failed to untuck completely before entering the water. In a moment he was hoisting himself out and heading for the board to try again. Nancy said, "It's amazing how sexy he looks from a distance. All the pieces seem to fit together better. And he really is a good diver. I can't believe he hasn't practiced in all these years."

"Maybe he has."

"Maybe. I mean he looks perfect, and no older than twenty-one. That's how old he was when we first met—twenty-one. I was dating Sandy Ritter. And you were dating Murray Freed."

"I could have done worse than stick with Murray Freed. But he was so evasive that when Ken approached me in a grown-up, forthright way, I just gave up on Murray. He's got a little graphics company in Santa Barbara, and I hear he spends two or three months of the year living on the beach in Big Sur."

"Well, don't worry about it. I've always thought leisure and beauty were rather overrated, myself." She grinned. "But look at him! He did it! That one was nearly perfect, toes pointed and everything."

"I guess I'm sort of surprised that you think he's funny-looking. Everybody always thought he was good-looking in college."

"Did they? It's hard to remember what he looks like, even when I'm looking at him. I mean, I know what he looks like, but I don't know what I think about it. This diving sort of turns me on, if you can believe that."

"Really?" But Lily realized that she was vulnerable, too, and when Kevin came over, dripping and fit, toweling his hair and shoulders with Lily's own lavender towel, his smile seemed very white, his skin very rosy, and his presence rather welcome.

Actually, it was apparent that they all felt better. Lily had swum nearly half a mile, and Nancy had cooled off without getting her hair wet. Kevin was pleased with the dives he had accomplished and with Nancy's obvious admiration. All three of them had an appetite, and it was just the right time to begin planning a meal. "This is a nice park," Kevin said. "The trees are huge."

"We should get steak," Nancy said.

In the bedroom, putting on her clothes, Lily smiled to hear Nancy's laugh followed by a laugh from Kevin. Really, he was a good-humored sort of person, who laughed frequently. Although she could not have said how the visit had failed that morning, or why it was succeeding right then, she did sense their time filling up with possibilities of things they could do together. She heard Nancy say, "I think the coals must be ready by now," and the slam of the door. She pulled a cotton sweater over her head and went into the kitchen thinking fondly of the Humboldts' driving away the next morning with smiles on their faces and reconciliation in their hearts. She hadn't done anything, really, but something had done the trick. Kevin was sitting at the table wrapping onions and potatoes in foil. Lily opened the refrigerator and took out a large stalk of broccoli, which she began to slice for steaming. Kevin had put on a light-blue tailored shirt and creased corduroy slacks. His wet hair was combed back and he had shaved. He said, "Why did you stick with Diamond all those years? I mean"—he looked at her cautiously—"wasn't it obvious that you weren't going to get anything out of it?"

"I got a lot out of it. Ken's problem is that nobody thinks he's anything special but me. I do think he's quite special, though, and I think I got a good education, lots of attention, lots of affection, and lots of time to work. It wasn't what I expected but it wasn't so bad, though I wish there had been some way to practice having another type of relationship, or even just having dates."

"What did he think about your winning the prize?"

"I don't know. I broke up with him right after I applied for it, and I didn't read the letter he sent after I got it."

"Last night, when you were talking—" But the door opened and Nancy swept in. "The coals are perfect! Are these the steaks in here? I'm famished! Guess what? I got three big ears of corn from your neighbor, who was out in his garden. He's cute and about our age. What's his name? He was funny, and awfully nice to me."

"I've never even spoken to the guy," Lily said.

"What do you do? Cross the street when you see an attractive man?" Nancy teased.

"It's not that. It's that some curse renders me invisible. But Kevin was about to say something."

He shrugged.

"Put on you by Professor Kenneth Diamond, no doubt," Nancy said. She handed a potato back to Kevin. "Do that one better. The skin shows. Seriously, Lily"—Kevin took the potato back with a careful, restrained gesture—"you can't keep this up. It's impossible. You're the most beautiful woman anyone we know knows. You have to at least act like you're interested. I'm sure you act like you wouldn't go on a date for a million dollars. You don't prostitute yourself simply by being friendly." Kevin rewrapped the potato and handed it back to Nancy.

Then he smiled at Lily and she had a brief feeling that something dramatic and terrible had been averted, although she couldn't say what it was. Nancy ripped the paper off the rib eyes and dropped it on the table.

The wine was nearly finished. Kevin had chosen it, a California red that he'd tried in Vancouver. He kept saying, "I was lucky to find this so far east. That isn't a bad liquor store, really." Lily hadn't especially liked it at first because of its harsh flavor and thick consistency, but after three glasses she was sorry to see the second bottle close to empty. She set it carefully upright in the grass. There was a mystery to its flavor that made her keep wanting to try it again. Nancy was talking about the play she had been in, as the second lead, with a small theater group in Vancouver. She had loved everything about it, she said. "The applause most of all," Kevin said, smiling. "She got a lot of it, too. The third night, she got more than anyone in the cast. She was pretty funny."

"I was very funny."

"Yes, you were very funny."

Nancy lay back on the chaise longue. "The director said that he thought I should take acting classes at the university. They have a very good program. I had never acted before, and they gave me the second lead. You know, there are tons of professional actors in Vancouver."

"It wasn't exactly a professional show. Only the two leads were getting paid, and the guy wasn't even an Equity actor," Kevin said.

"I know that."

Lily took a deep breath. Neither Kevin nor Nancy had changed position in the past five minutes. Both were still leaning back, gazing into the tops of the trees or at the stars, but their voices were beginning to rise. She said, "It must be lovely to live in Vancouver." She thought of it vividly, as if for the first time: thick vegetation, brilliant flowers, dazzling peaks, lots to eat and do, the kind of paradise teaching would probably never take her to.

"It's expensive," Nancy said. "And I've found the people very self-satisfied."

"I don't think that's true," Kevin said.

"I know you don't. Kevin likes it there just fine. But the university is good, and they send acting students off to places like Yale and England and New York City all the time."

"By the time you could get into acting school, you would be thirty-one at the very least." Kevin had sat up now, but casually. He poured the last of the mysterious-tasting wine into his glass.

"How do you figure that?"

"Well, frankly, I don't see how you can quit working for another two years, until I get established." He looked at the wine in the glass and gulped it down. "And maybe thirty-one is a little old to start training for a profession where people begin looking for work before they're out of their teens. And what about having kids? You can't very well have any kids while you're going to school full time. That play had you going eighteen hours a day some days. Which is not to say that it wasn't worth it, but I don't know that you would even want to do it six or eight times a year."

Nancy was breathing hard. Lily leaned forward, alarmed that she hadn't averted this argument, and put her hand on Nancy's arm. Nancy shook it off. "Kids! Who's talking about kids? I'm talking about taking some courses in what I like to do and what some people think I'm good at doing. The whole time I was in that play you just acted like it was a game that I was playing. I have news for you—"

"It was a community-theater production! You weren't putting on Shakespeare or Chekhov, either. And it's not as if Bill Henry has directed in Toronto, much less in New York."

"He's done lights in New York! He did lights on *The Fantasticks!* And on *A Chorus Line!*"

"Big deal."

Nancy leaped to her feet. "I'll tell you something, mister. You owe it to me to put me through whatever school I want to go to, no matter what happens to our relationship or our marriage. I slaved in the purchasing department of that university for three years so that you could go to business school full time. I lived with those crummy friends of yours for four years so we could save on mortgage—"

Lily said, "Nancy—"

Kevin said, "What do you mean, 'no matter what happens to our relationship'? What do you mean by that?"

"You know perfectly well what I mean! Lily knows what I mean, too!"

Lily pressed herself deep into her chair, hoping that neither of them would address her, but Kevin turned to face her. In the darkness his deep-set eyes were nearly invisible, so that when he said, "What did she tell you?" Lily could not decide what would be the best reply to make. He stepped between her and Nancy and demanded, "What did she say?"

"I think you should ask her that."

"She won't tell me anything. You tell me." He took a step toward her. "You tell me whether she still loves me. I want to know that. That's all I want to know." The tone of his voice in the dark was earnest and nearly calm.

"That's between you and Nancy. Ask her. It's not my business."

"But you know. And I've asked her. She's said yes so many times to that question that it doesn't mean anything anymore. You tell me. Does she still love me?"

Lily tried to look around him at Nancy, but seeing the movement of her head, he shifted to block any communication between them. "Does she?"

"She hasn't told me anything."

"But you have your own opinion, don't you?"

"I can't see that that's significant in any way."

"Tell me what it is. Does she still love me?"

He seemed, with his chest, to be bearing down on her as she sat. She had lost all sense of where Nancy was, even whether she was still outside. Wherever she was, she was not coming to Lily's aid. Perhaps she too was waiting for Lily's opinion. Lily said, "No."

"No, what? Is that your opinion?"

Surely Nancy would have stepped in by now. "No, it doesn't seem to me that she loves you anymore." Lily broke into a sweat the moment she stopped speaking, a sweat of instant regret. Kevin stepped back and Lily saw that Nancy was behind him, still and silent on the chaise longue. "Oh, Lord," said Lily, standing up and taking her glass into the house.

The Humboldts stayed outside for a long time. Lily washed the dishes and got ready for bed; she was sitting on the cot in the guest room winding her clock when Nancy knocked on the door and came in. "We had a long talk," she said, "and things are all right."

"Did you—"

"I don't want to talk about it anymore. This may be the best thing. At least I feel that I've gotten some things off my chest. And I think we're going to leave very early in the morning, so I wish you wouldn't get up."

"But I—" Lily looked at Nancy for a moment, and then said, "Okay, I won't. Thanks for stopping."

"You can't mean that, but I'll write." She closed the door and Lily put her feet under the sheet. There were no sounds, and after a while she fell asleep. She awoke to a rhythmic knocking. She thought at first of the door, but remembered that Nancy had closed it firmly. Then she realized that the blows were against the wall beside her head. She tried to visualize the other room. It would be the bed, and they would be making love. She picked up her clock and turned it to catch light from the street. It was just after midnight. She had been asleep, although deeply, for only an hour. The knocking stopped and started again, and it was irregular enough to render sleep unlikely for the time being. She smoothed her sheet and blanket and slid farther into the bed. Even after her eyes had adjusted, the room was dark: the streetlight was ten yards down, and there was no moon. Nancy and Kevin's rhythmic banging was actually rather comforting, she thought. She lay quietly for a moment, and then sat up and turned on the light. She felt for her book under the bed. The banging stopped and did not start again, and Lily reached for the light switch, but as her hand touched it, Nancy cried out. She took her hand back and opened her book, and Nancy cried out again. Lily thought of the upstairs neighbor, whom she hadn't heard all evening, and hoped he wasn't in yet. The bed in the next room gave one hard bang against the wall, and Nancy cried out again. Lily grew annoyed at her lack of consideration, and then, inexplicably, alarmed. She put her feet on the floor. Once she had done that, she was afraid to do anything else. It was suddenly obvious to her that the cries had been cries of fear rather than of passion, and Lily was afraid to go out, afraid of what she might see in the next room. She thought of Nancy's comments about Kevin's strength, and of Nancy's carelessness about Kevin's feelings. She opened the door. Lights were on everywhere, shocking her, and the noise of some kind of tussle came from their bedroom. Lily crept around the door and peeked in. Kevin had his back to her and was poised with one knee on the bed. All the bedcovers were torn off the bed, and Nancy, who had just broken free, was backed against the window. She looked at Lily for a long second and then turned her head so that Lily could see that her hair had been jaggedly cut off. One side was almost to her shoulder, but the other side stopped at her earlobe. The skein of hair lay on the mattress. Lily recognized it now. Seeing Nancy's gaze travel past him, Kevin set down a pair of scissors, Lily's very own shears, that had been sitting on the shelf above the sewing machine. Lily said, "My God! What have you been doing?"

Looking for the first time at the hair on the bed, Nancy began to cry. Kevin bent down and retrieved his gym shorts from under the bed and stepped into them. He said to Lily rather than Nancy, "I'm going outside. I guess my shoes are in the living room."

Nancy sat on the bed beside the hair, looking at it. It was reddish and glossy, with the life of a healthy wild animal, an otter or a mink. Lily wished Nancy would say that she had been thinking of having it cut anyway, but she knew Nancy hadn't been. She thought of saying herself that Nancy could always grow it back, but that, too, was unlikely. Hair like that probably wouldn't grow again on a thirty-year-old head. Lily picked up the shears and put them back on the shelf above her sewing table and said, "You were making love?"

The door slammed. Nancy said, "Yes, actually. I wanted to. We decided to split up, earlier, outside." She looked at Lily. "And then when I got in bed I felt happy and free, and I just thought it would be nice."

"And Kevin?"

"He seemed fine! Relieved, even. We were lying there and he was holding me."

"I can't believe you—"

At once Nancy glared at her. "You can't? Why are you so judgmental? This whole day has been one long trial, with you the judge and me the defendant! What do you know, anyway? You've never even lived with anyone! You had this sterile thing with Kenneth Diamond that was more about editing manuscripts than screwing and then you tell my husband that I'm not in love with him anymore! Of course he was enraged. You did it! You hate tension, you hate conflict, so you cut it off, ended it. We could have gone on for years like this, and it wouldn't have been that bad!"

"I didn't say I knew anything. I never said I knew anything."

Nancy put her face in her hands and then looked up and said in a low voice, "What do I look like?"

"Terrible right now—it's very uneven. A good hairdresser can shape it, though. There's a lot of hair left." Nancy reached for her robe and put it on; she picked up the hair, held it for a moment, and then, with her usual practicality, still attractive, always attractive, dropped it into the wastebasket. She glanced around the room and said, "Well, let's clean up before he gets back, okay? And can you take me to the airport tomorrow?"

Lily nodded. They began to pick things up and put them gingerly away. When they had finished the bedroom, they turned out the light in there and began on the living room. It was difficult, Lily thought, to call it quits and go to bed. Kevin did not return. After a long silence Nancy said, "I don't suppose any of us are going to be friends after this." Lily shrugged, but really she didn't suppose so either. Nancy reached up and felt the ends of her hair, and said, "Ten years ago he wouldn't have done this to me."

Had it really been ten years that they'd all known each other? Lily looked around her apartment, virginal again, and she was frightened by it. She felt a sudden longing for Kevin so strong that it approached desire, not for Kevin as he was but for Kevin as he looked—self-confident, muscular, smart. Her throat closed over, as if she were about to cry. Across the room Nancy picked up one of her hairbrushes with a

sigh—and she was, after all, uninjured, unmarked. Lily smiled and said, "Ten years ago he might have killed you."

Jane Smiley teaches at Iowa State University and lives in Ames, Iowa. She studied at Vassar and the University of Iowa, where she received her Ph.D. She is the author of five novels, including, most recently, the celebrated *A Thousand Acres*, and of two collections of novellas and stories—*The Age of Grief*, and *Ordinary Love and Good Will.*

SANDRA CISNEROS

" 'One Holy Night' is the oldest story in *Woman Hollering Creek*. I began writing it in 1980 and I used to take it out each year to work on it. For many years it haunted me. It was published almost a decade after I began writing it, and then I finally felt I was finished with it. It is based on a newspaper story about a man in Peru who murdered young girls. I could only believe he had won their trust in some way, and I wondered who this character could be. I wanted to get inside the mind of a young girl, to write about how one falls in love at that age, irrevocably. I wanted to write about the power and danger of love. It is a story about a younger part of me. I fall in love a lot, and I transform the men I fall in love with into Mayan kings."

Born in Chicago, Cisneros is the daughter of a Mexican father and a Chicana mother; she and her parents and six brothers made long visits to Mexico City, where her paternal grandmother lived.

In an interview with Jim Sagel for *Publishers Weekly* she said, "I'm trying to write the stories that haven't been written. I feel like a cartographer; I'm determined to fill a literary void." At the Iowa Writers' Workshop, which she attended in the late 1970s, she had a breakthrough when her classmates spoke about the "house of the imagination," about the attics, stairways, and cellars of childhood. "Everyone seemed to have some communal knowledge which I did not have—and then I realized that the metaphor of *house* was totally wrong for me . . . I had no such house in my memories. . . . It was not until this moment when I separated myself, when I considered myself truly distinct, that my writing acquired a voice."

Her advice to young writers: "Imagine yourself at your kitchen table, in your pajamas. Imagine one person you'd allow to see you that way, and write in the voice you'd use to that friend. Write about what makes you different."

ONE HOLY NIGHT

About the truth, if you give it to a person, then he has power over you. And if someone gives it to you, then they have made themselves your slave. It is a strong magic. You can never take it back.

—CHAQ UXMAL PALOQUÍN

HE said his name was Chaq. Chaq Uxmal Paloquín. That's what he told me. He was of an ancient line of Mayan kings. Here, he said, making a map with the heel of his boot, this is where I come from, the Yucatán, the ancient cities. This is what Boy Baby said.

It's been eighteen weeks since Abuelita chased him away with the broom, and what I'm telling you I never told nobody, except Rachel and Lourdes, who know everything. He said he would love me like a revolution, like a religion. Abuelita burned the pushcart and sent me here, miles from home, in this town of dust, with one wrinkled witch woman who rubs my belly with jade, and sixteen nosy cousins.

I don't know how many girls have gone bad from selling cucumbers. I know I'm not the first. My mother took the crooked walk too, I'm told, and I'm sure my Abuelita has her own story, but it's not my place to ask.

Abuelita says it's Uncle Lalo's fault because he's the man of the family and if he had come home on time like he was supposed to and worked the pushcart on the days he was told to and watched over his goddaughter, who is too foolish to look after herself, nothing would've happened, and I wouldn't have to be sent to Mexico. But Uncle Lalo says if they had never left Mexico in the first place, shame enough would have kept a girl from doing devil things.

I'm not saying I'm not bad. I'm not saying I'm special. But I'm not like the Allport Street girls, who stand in doorways and go with men into alleys.

All I know is I didn't want it like that. Not against the bricks or hunkering in somebody's car. I wanted it come undone like gold thread, like a tent full of birds. The way it's supposed to be, the way I knew it would be when I met Boy Baby.

But you must know, I was no girl back then. And Boy Baby was no boy. Chaq Uxmal Paloquín. Boy Baby was a man. When I asked him how old he was he said he didn't know. The past and the future are the same thing. So he seemed boy and baby and man all at once, and the way he looked at me, how do I explain?

I'd park the pushcart in front of the Jewel food store Saturdays. He bought a mango on a stick the first time. Paid for it with a new twenty. Next Saturday he was back. Two mangoes, lime juice, and chili powder, keep the change. The third Saturday he asked for a cucumber spear and ate it slow. I didn't see him after that till the day he brought me Kool-Aid in a plastic cup. Then I knew what I felt for him.

Maybe you wouldn't like him. To you he might be a bum. Maybe he looked it. Maybe. He had broken thumbs and burnt fingers. He had thick greasy fingernails he never cut and dusty hair. And all his bones were strong ones like a man's. I waited every Saturday in my same blue dress. I sold all the mango and cucumber, and then Boy Baby would come finally.

What I knew of Chaq was only what he told me, because nobody seemed to know where he came from. Only that he could speak a strange language that no one could understand, said his name translated into boy, or boy-child, and so it was the street people nicknamed him Boy Baby.

I never asked about his past. He said it was all the same and didn't matter, past and the future all the same to his people. But the truth has a strange way of following you, of coming up to you and making you listen to what it has to say.

Night time. Boy Baby brushes my hair and talks to me in his strange language because I like to hear it. What I like to hear him tell is how he is Chaq, Chaq of the people of the sun, Chaq of the temples, and what he says sounds sometimes like broken clay, and at other times like hollow sticks, or like the swish of old feathers crumbling into dust.

He lived behind Esparza & Sons Auto Repair in a little room that used to be a closet—pink plastic curtains on a narrow window, a dirty cot covered with newspapers, and a cardboard box filled with socks and rusty tools. It was there, under one bald bulb, in the back room of the Esparza garage, in the single room with pink curtains, that he showed me the guns—twenty-four in all. Rifles and pistols, one rusty musket, a machine gun, and several tiny weapons with mother-of-pearl handles that looked like toys. So you'll see who I am, he said, laying them all out on the bed of newspapers. So you'll understand. But I didn't want to know.

The stars foretell everything, he said. My birth. My son's. The boy-child who will bring back the grandeur of my people from those who have broken the arrows, from those who have pushed the ancient stones off their pedestals.

Then he told how he had prayed in the Temple of the Magician years ago as a child when his father had made him promise to bring back the ancient ways. Boy Baby had cried in the temple dark that only the bats made holy. Boy Baby who was man and child among the great and dusty guns lay down on the newspaper bed and wept for a thousand years. When I touched him, he looked at me with the sadness of stone.

You must not tell anyone what I am going to do, he said. And what I remember next is how the moon, the pale moon with its one yellow eye, the moon of Tikal, and Tulum, and Chichén, stared through the pink plastic curtains. Then something inside bit me, and I gave out a cry as if the other, the one I wouldn't be anymore, leapt out.

So I was initiated beneath an ancient sky by a great and mighty heir—Chaq Uxmal Paloquín. I, Ixchel, his queen.

The truth is, it wasn't a big deal. It wasn't any deal at all. I put my bloody panties inside my T-shirt and ran home hugging myself. I thought about a lot of things on the way home. I thought about all the world and how suddenly I became a part of history and wondered if everyone on the street, the sewing machine lady and the *panadería* saleswomen and the woman with two kids sitting on the bus bench didn't all know. *Did I look any different? Could they tell?* We were all the same somehow, laughing behind our hands, waiting the way all women wait, and when we find out, we wonder why the world and a million years made such a big deal over nothing.

I know I was supposed to feel ashamed, but I wasn't ashamed. I wanted to stand on top of the highest building, the top-top floor, and yell, *I know.*

Then I understood why Abuelita didn't let me sleep over at Lourdes's house full of too many brothers, and why the Roman girl in the movies always runs away from the soldier, and what happens when the scenes in love stories begin to fade, and why brides blush, and how it is that sex isn't simply a box you check *M* or *F* on in the test we get at school.

I was wise. The corner girls were still jumping into their stupid little hopscotch squares. I laughed inside and climbed the wooden stairs two by two to the second floor rear where me and Abuelita and Uncle Lalo live. I was still laughing when I opened the door and Abuelita asked, Where's the pushcart?

And then I didn't know what to do.

It's a good thing we live in a bad neighborhood. There are always plenty of bums to blame for your sins. If it didn't happen the way I told it, it really could've. We looked and looked all over for the kids who stole my pushcart. The story wasn't the best, but since I had to make it up right then and there with Abuelita staring a hole through my heart, it wasn't too bad.

For two weeks I had to stay home. Abuelita was afraid the street kids who had stolen the cart would be after me again. Then I thought I might go over to the Esparza garage and take the pushcart out and leave it in some alley for the police to find, but I was never allowed to leave the house alone. Bit by bit the truth started to seep out like a dangerous gasoline.

First the nosy woman who lives upstairs from the laundromat told my Abuelita she thought something was fishy, the pushcart wheeled into Esparza & Sons every Saturday after dark, how a man, the same dark Indian one, the one who never talks to anybody, walked with me when the sun went down and pushed the cart into the garage, that one there, and yes we went inside, there where the fat lady named Concha, whose hair is dyed a hard black, pointed a fat finger.

I prayed that we would not meet Boy Baby, and since the gods listen and are mostly good, Esparza said yes, a man like that had lived there but was gone, had packed a few things and left the pushcart in a corner to pay for his last week's rent.

We had to pay $20 before he would give us our pushcart back. Then Abuelita made me tell the real story of how the cart had disappeared, all of which I told this time, except for that one night, which I would have to tell anyway, weeks later, when I prayed for the moon of my cycle to come back, but it would not.

When Abuelita found out I was going to *dar a luz,* she cried until her eyes were little, and blamed Uncle Lalo, and Uncle Lalo blamed this country, and Abuelita blamed the infamy of men. That is when she burned the cucumber pushcart and called me a *sinvergüenza* because I *am* without shame.

Then I cried too—Boy Baby was lost from me—until my head was hot with headaches and I fell asleep. When I woke up, the cucumber pushcart was dust and Abuelita was sprinkling holy water on my head.

Abuelita woke up early every day and went to the Esparza garage to see if news about that *demonio* had been found, had Chaq Uxmal Paloquín sent any letters, any, and when the other mechanics heard that name they laughed, and asked if we had made it up, that we could have some letters that had come for Boy Baby, no forwarding address, since he had gone in such a hurry.

There were three. The first, addressed "Occupant," demanded immediate payment for a four-month-old electric bill. The second was one I recognized right away—a brown envelope fat with cake-mix coupons and fabric-softener samples—because we'd gotten one just like it. The third was addressed in a spidery Spanish to a Señor C. Cruz, on paper so thin you could read it unopened by the light of the sky. The return address a convent in Tampico.

This was to whom my Abuelita wrote in hopes of finding the man who could correct my ruined life, to ask if the good nuns might know the whereabouts of a certain Boy Baby—and if they were hiding him it would be of no use because God's eyes see through all souls.

We heard nothing for a long time. Abuelita took me out of school when my uniform got tight around the belly and said it was a shame I wouldn't be able to graduate with the other eighth graders.

Except for Lourdes and Rachel, my grandma and Uncle Lalo, nobody knew about my past. I would sleep in the big bed I share with Abuelita same as always. I could hear Abuelita and Uncle Lalo talking in low voices in the kitchen as if they were praying the rosary, how they were going to send me to Mexico, to San Dionisio de Tlaltepango, where I have cousins and where I was conceived and would've been born had my grandma not thought it wise to send my mother here to the United States so that neighbors in San Dionisio de Tlaltepango wouldn't ask why her belly was suddenly big.

I was happy. I liked staying home. Abuelita was teaching me to crochet the way she had learned in Mexico. And just when I had mastered the tricky rosette stitch, the letter came from the convent which gave the truth about Boy Baby—however much we didn't want to hear.

He was born on a street with no name in a town called Miseria. His father, Eusebio, is a knife sharpener. His mother, Refugia, stacks apricots into pyramids and sells them on a cloth in the market. There are brothers. Sisters too of which I know little. The youngest, a Carmelite, writes me all this and prays for my soul, which is why I know it's all true.

Boy Baby is thirty-seven years old. His name is Chato which means fat-face. There is no Mayan blood.

I don't think they understand how it is to be a girl. I don't think they know how it is to have to wait your whole life. I count the months for the baby to be born, and it's like a ring of water inside me reaching out and out until one day it will tear from me with its own teeth.

Already I can feel the animal inside me stirring in his own uneven sleep. The witch woman says it's the dreams of weasels that make my child sleep the way he sleeps. She makes me eat white bread blessed by the priest, but I know it's the ghost of him inside me that circles and circles, and will not let me rest.

Abuelita said they sent me here just in time, because a little later Boy Baby came back to our house looking for me, and she had to chase him away with the broom. The next thing we hear, he's in the newspaper clippings his sister sends. A picture of him looking very much like stone, police hooked on either arm . . . *on the road to* Las Grutas de Xtacumbilxuna, *the Caves of the Hidden Girl . . . eleven female bodies . . . the last seven years . . .*

Then I couldn't read but only stare at the little black-and-white dots that make up the face I am in love with.

All my girl cousins here either don't talk to me, or those who do, ask questions they're too young to know *not* to ask. What they want to know really is how it is to have a man, because they're too ashamed to ask their married sisters.

They don't know what it is to lay so still until his sleep breathing is heavy, for the eyes in the dim dark to look and look without worry at the man-bones and the neck, the man-wrist and man-jaw thick and strong, all the salty dips and hollows, the stiff hair of the brow and sour swirl of sideburns, to lick the fat earlobes that taste of smoke, and stare at how perfect is a man.

I tell them, "It's a bad joke. When you find out you'll be sorry."

I'm going to have five children. Five. Two girls. Two boys. And one baby.

The girls will be called Lisette and Maritza. The boys I'll name Pablo and Sandro.

And my baby. My baby will be named Alegre, because life will always be hard.

Rachel says that love is like a big black piano being pushed off the top of a three-story building and you're waiting on the bottom to catch it.

But Lourdes says it's not that way at all. It's like a top, like all the colors in the world are spinning so fast they're not colors anymore and all that's left is a white hum.

There was a man, a crazy who lived upstairs from us when we lived on South Loomis. He couldn't talk, just walked around all day with this harmonica in his mouth. Didn't play it. Just sort of breathed through it, all day long, wheezing, in and out, in and out.

This is how it is with me. Love I mean.

Sandra Cisneros is the author of two collections of short fiction: *The House on Mango Street* and *Woman Hollering Creek*, and of a collection of poems, *My Wicked Wicked Ways*. She has taught at the Universities of California, Michigan, and New Mexico, and now makes her home in San Antonio, Texas.

DENNIS MCFARLAND

"'Nothing to Ask For' is based, closely in its physical details and less closely in its dramatic events, on an actual visit I paid a friend shortly before he died of AIDS. Writing the story was for me not only a way of grieving over the loss of my friend, but also a way of exorcising the haunting disease imagery surrounding the loss.

"I've been asked to say something about the voice of the narrator in this story, and perhaps something about narrative voice in general. More than one writer of fiction has told me that when he gets the voice of a thing right, the rest usually flows with comparative ease. Not a surprise, since narrative voice includes so many elements of storytelling—certainly point of view, but also tone and mood and diction and, in the case of first-person narratives, even characterization. Getting the voice right is nothing less than discovering the best general sound for the story, the best way to tell it. I think the nuts and bolts of voice are usually determined by the writer's intuition—the ear tells him what's right and wrong rhythmically, tonally, morally, and spiritually.

"When people have asked me what 'Nothing to Ask For' is about, I always say it's about a man whose best friend is dying of AIDS. That's because I identify so strongly with the narrator. But while it's true that the story is about him, the plight of the characters who are dying is the more dire, and it was necessary that he never let his concerns about himself upstage what's happening to Mack and Lester. And he had to be straightforward and reliable, because he needed to be ruthless in what he was willing to expose about the characters while always maintaining compassion. These considerations, I think, were the strongest influence on his voice, and they are more moral and spiritual than rhythmic or tonal.

"I didn't sit down and figure this out ahead of time. Every story is an investigation. As you investigate who a character is, you experiment with what he must sound like; and as you hear what he sounds like, you begin to understand more about who he is. Given this floundering process, it's a miracle that anything ever comes out right. And I think it's why our best stories are never entirely smooth, but tend to have rough edges."

NOTHING TO ASK FOR

INSIDE Mack's apartment, a concentrator—a medical machine that looks like an elaborate stereo speaker on casters—sits behind an orange swivel chair, making its rhythmic, percussive noise like ocean waves, taking in normal filthy air, humidifying it, and filtering out everything but the oxygen, which it sends through clear plastic tubing to Mack's nostrils. He sits on the couch, as usual, channel grazing, the remote-control button under his thumb, and he appears to be scrutinizing the short segments of what he sees on the TV screen with Zen-like patience. He has planted one foot on the bevelled edge of the long oak coffee table, and he dangles one leg—thinner at the thigh than my wrist—over the other. In the sharp valley of his lap, Eberhardt, his old long-haired dachshund, lies sleeping. The table is covered with two dozen medicine bottles, though Mack has now taken himself off all drugs except cough syrup and something for heartburn. Also, stacks of books and pamphlets—though he has lost the ability to read—on how to heal yourself, on Buddhism, on Hinduism, on dying. In one pamphlet there's a long list that includes most human ailments, the personality traits and character flaws that cause these ailments, and the affirmations that need to be said in order to overcome them. According to this well-intentioned misguidedness, most disease is caused by self-hatred, or rejection of reality, and almost anything can be cured by learning to love yourself—which is accomplished by saying, aloud and often, "I love myself." Next to these books are pamphlets and Xeroxed articles describing more unorthodox remedies—herbal brews, ultrasound, lemon juice, urine, even penicillin. And, in a ceramic dish next to these, a small, waxy envelope that contains "ash"—a very fine, gray-white, spiritually enhancing powder materialized out of thin air by Swami Lahiri Baba.

As I change the plastic liner inside Mack's trash can, into which he throws his millions of Kleenex, I block his view of the TV screen—which he endures serenely, his head perfectly still, eyes unaverted. "Do you remember old Dorothy Hughes?" he asks me. "What do you suppose ever happened to her?"

"I don't know," I say. "I saw her years ago on the nude beach at San Gregorio. With some black guy who was down by the surf doing cartwheels. She pretended she didn't know me."

"I don't blame her," says Mack, making bug-eyes. "I wouldn't like to be seen with any grownup who does cartwheels, would you?"

"No," I say.

Then he asks, "Was everybody we knew back then crazy?"

What Mack means by "back then" is our college days, in Santa Cruz, when we judged almost everything in terms of how freshly it rejected the status quo: the famous professor who began his twentieth-century-philosophy class by tossing pink rubber dildos in through the classroom window; Antonioni and Luis Buñuel screened each weekend in the dormitory basement; the artichokes in the student garden, left on their stalks and allowed to open and become what they truly were—enormous, purple-hearted flowers. There were no paving-stone quadrangles or venerable colonnades—our campus was the redwood forest, the buildings nestled among the trees, invisible one from the other—and when we emerged from the woods at the end of the school day, what we saw was nothing more or less than the sun setting over the Pacific. We lived with thirteen other students, in a rented Victorian mansion on West Cliff Drive, and at night the yellow beacon from the nearby lighthouse invaded our attic windows; we drifted to sleep listening to the barking of seals. On weekends we had serious softball games in the vacant field next to the house—us against a team of tattooed, long-haired townies—and afterward, keyed up, tired and sweating, Mack and I walked the north shore to a place where we could watch the waves pound into the rocks and send up sun-ignited columns of water twenty-five and thirty feet tall. Though most of what we initiated "back then" now seems to have been faddish and wrong-headed, our friendship was exceptionally sane and has endured for twenty years. It endured the melodramatic confusion of Dorothy Hughes, our beautiful short-stop—I loved her, but she loved Mack. It endured the subsequent revelation that Mack was gay—any tension on that count managed by him with remarks about what a homely bastard I was. It endured his fury and frustration over my low-bottom alcoholism, and my sometimes raging (and *en*raging) process of getting clean and sober. And it has endured the onlooking fisheyes of his long string of lovers and my two wives. Neither of us had a biological brother—that could account for something—but at recent moments when I have felt most frightened, now that Mack is so ill, I've thought that we persisted simply because we couldn't let go of the sense of *thoroughness* our friendship gave us; we constantly reported to each other on our separate lives, as if we knew that by doing so we were getting more from life than we would ever have been entitled to individually.

In answer to his question—was everybody crazy back then—I say, "Yes, I think so."

He laughs, then coughs. When he coughs these days—which is often—he goes on coughing until a viscous, bloody fluid comes up, which he catches in a Kleenex and tosses into the trash can. Earlier, his doctors could drain his lungs with a needle through his back—last time they collected an entire litre from one lung—but now that Mack has developed the cancer, there are tumors that break up the fluid into many small isolated pockets, too many to drain. Radiation or chemotherapy would kill him; he's too weak even for a flu shot. Later today, he will go to the hospital for another bronchoscopy; they want to see if there's anything they can do to help him, though they have already told him there isn't. His medical care comes in the form of visiting nurses, physical therapists, and a curious duo at the hospital: one doctor who is young, affectionate, and incompetent but who comforts and consoles, hugs and holds hands; another—old, rude, brash, and expert—who says things like "You might as well face it. You're going to die. Get your papers in order." In fact, they've given Mack two weeks to two months, and it has now been ten weeks.

"Oh, my God," cries Lester, Mack's lover, opening the screen door, entering the room, and looking around. "I don't recognize this hovel. And what's that wonderful smell?"

This morning, while Lester was out, I vacuumed and generally straightened up. Their apartment is on the ground floor of a building like all the buildings in this Southern California neighborhood—a two-story motel-like structure of white stucco and steel railings. Outside the door are an X-rated hibiscus (blood red, with its jutting, yellow powder-tipped stamen), a plastic macaw on a swing, two enormous yuccas; inside, carpet, and plainness. The wonderful smell is the turkey I'm roasting; Mack can't eat anything before the bronchoscopy, but I figure it will be here for them when they return from the hospital, and they can eat off it for the rest of the week.

Lester, a South Carolina boy in his late twenties, is sick, too—twice he has nearly died of pneumonia—but he's in a healthy period now. He's tall, thin, and bearded, a devotee of the writings of Shirley MacLaine—an unlikely guru, if you ask me, but my wife, Marilyn, tells me I'm too judgmental. Probably she is right.

The dog, Eberhardt, has woken up and waddles sleepily over to where Lester stands. Lester extends his arm toward Mack, two envelopes in his hand, and after a moment's pause Mack reaches for them. It's partly this typical hesitation of Mack's—a slowing of the mind, actually—that makes him appear serene, contemplative these days. Occasionally, he really does get confused, which terrifies him. But I can't help thinking that something in there has sharpened as well—maybe a kind of simplification. Now he stares at the top envelope for a full minute, as Lester and I watch him. This is something we do: we watch him. "Oh-h-h," he says, at last. "A letter from my mother."

"And one from Lucy, too," says Lester. "Isn't that nice?"

"I guess," says Mack. Then: "Well, yes. It is."

"You want me to open them?" I ask.

"Would you?" he says, handing them to me. "Read 'em to me, too."

They are only cards, with short notes inside, both from Des Moines.

Mack's mother says it just makes her *sick* that he's sick, wants to know if there's anything he needs. Lucy, the sister, is gushy, misremembers a few things from the past, says she's writing instead of calling because she knows she will cry if she tries to talk. Lucy, who refused to let Mack enter her house at Christmastime one year—actually left him on the stoop in sub-zero cold—until he removed the gold earring from his ear. Mack's mother, who waited until after the funeral last year to let Mack know that his father had died; Mack's obvious illness at the funeral would have been an embarrassment.

But they've come around, Mack has told me in the face of my anger.

I said better late than never.

And Mack, all forgiveness, all humility, said that's exactly right: much better.

"Mrs. Mears is having a craft sale today," Lester says. Mrs. Mears, an elderly neighbor, lives out back in a cottage with her husband. "You guys want to go?"

Eberhardt, hearing "go," begins leaping at Lester's shins, but when we look at Mack, his eyelids are at half-mast—he's half asleep.

We watch him for a moment, and I say, "Maybe in a little while, Lester."

Lester sits on the edge of his bed reading the newspaper, which lies flat on the spread in front of him. He has his own TV in his room, and a VCR. On the dresser, movies whose cases show men in studded black leather jockstraps, with gloves to match—dungeon masters of startling handsomeness. On the floor, a stack of gay magazines. Somewhere on the cover of each of these magazines the word "macho" appears; and inside some of them, in the personal ads, men, meaning to attract others, refer to themselves as pigs. "Don't putz," Lester says to me as I straighten some things on top of the dresser. "Enough already."

I wonder where he picked up "putz"—surely not in South Carolina. I say, "You need to get somebody in. To help. You need to arrange it now. What if you were suddenly to get sick again?"

"I know," he says. "He's gotten to be quite a handful, hasn't he? Is he still asleep?"

"Yes," I answer. "Yes and yes."

The phone rings and Lester reaches for it. As soon as he begins to speak I can tell, from his tone, that it's my four-year-old on the line. After a moment, Lester says, "Kit," smiling, and hands me the phone, then returns to his newspaper.

I sit on the other side of the bed, and after I say hello, Kit says, "We need some milk."

"O.K.," I say. "Milk. What are you up to this morning?"

"Being angry mostly," she says.

"Oh?" I say. "Why?"

"Mommy and I are not getting along very well."

"That's too bad," I say. "I hope you won't stay angry for long."

"We won't," she says. "We're going to make up in a minute."

"Good," I say.

"When are you coming home?"

"In a little while."

"After my nap?"

"Yes," I say. "Right after your nap."

"Is Mack very sick?"

She already knows the answer, of course. "Yes," I say.

"Is he going to die?"

This one, too. "Most likely," I say. "He's that sick."

"Bye," she says suddenly—her sense of closure always takes me by surprise—and I say, "Don't stay angry for long, O.K.?"

"You already said that," she says, rightly, and I wait for a moment, half expecting Marilyn to come onto the line; ordinarily she would, and hearing her voice right now would do me good. After another moment, though, there's the click.

Marilyn is back in school, earning a Ph.D. in religious studies. I teach sixth grade, and because I'm faculty adviser for the little magazine the sixth graders put out each year, I stay late many afternoons. Marilyn wanted me home this Saturday morning. "You're at work all week," she said, "and then you're over there on Saturday. Is that fair?"

I told her I didn't know—which was the honest truth. Then, in a possibly dramatic way, I told her that fairness was not my favorite subject these days, given that my best friend was dying.

We were in our kitchen, and through the window I could see Kit playing with a neighbor's cat in the back yard. Marilyn turned on the hot water in the kitchen sink and stood still while the steam rose into her face. "It's become a question of where you belong," she said at last. "I think you're too involved."

For this I had no answer, except to say, "I agree"—which wasn't really an answer, since I had no intention of staying home, or becoming less involved, or changing anything.

Now Lester and I can hear Mack's scraping cough in the next room. We are silent until he stops. "By the way," Lester says at last, taking the telephone receiver out of my hand, "have you noticed that he *listens* now?"

"I know," I say. "He told me he'd finally entered his listening period."

"Yeah," says Lester, "as if it's the natural progression. You blab your whole life away, ignoring other people, and then right before you die you start to listen."

The slight bitterness in Lester's tone makes me feel shaky inside. It's true that Mack was always a better talker than a listener, but I suddenly feel that I'm walking a thin wire, and that anything like collusion would throw me off balance. All I know for sure is that I don't want to hear any more. Maybe Lester reads this in my face, because what he says next sounds like an explanation: he tells me that his poor old backwoods mother was nearly deaf when he was growing up, that she relied almost entirely on reading lips. "All she had to do when she wanted to turn me off," he says, "was to just turn her back on me. Simple," he says, making a little circle with his finger. "No more Lester."

"That's terrible," I say.

"I was a terrible coward," he says. "Can you imagine Kit letting you get away with something like that? She'd bite your kneecaps."

"Still," I say, "that's terrible."

Lester shrugs his shoulders, and after another moment I say, "I'm going to the K mart. Mack needs a padded toilet seat. You want anything?"

"Yeah," he says. "But they don't sell it at K mart."

"What is it?" I ask.

"It's a *joke,* Dan, for Chrissake," he says. "Honestly, I think you've completely lost your sense of humor."

When I think about this, it seems true.

"Are you coming back?" he asks.

"Right back," I answer. "If you think of it, baste the turkey."

"How could I not think of it?" he says, sniffing the air.

In the living room, Mack is lying with his eyes open now, staring blankly at the TV. At the moment, a shop-at-home show is on, but he changes channels, and an announcer says, "When we return, we'll talk about tree pruning," and Mack changes the channel again. He looks at me, nods thoughtfully, and says, "Tree pruning. Interesting. It's just like the way they put a limit on your credit card, so you don't spend too much."

"I don't understand," I say.

"Oh, you know," he says. "Pruning the trees. Didn't the man just say something about pruning trees?" He sits up and adjusts the plastic tube in one nostril.

"Yes," I say.

"Well, it's like the credit cards. The limit they put on the credit cards is . . ." He stops talking and looks straight into my eyes, frightened. "It doesn't make any sense, does it?" he says. "Jesus Christ. I'm not making sense."

Way out east on University, there is a video arcade every half mile or so. Adult peepshows. Also a McDonald's, and the rest. Taverns—the kind that are open at eight in the morning—with clever names: Tobacco Rhoda's, the Cruz Inn. Bodegas that smell of cat piss and are really fronts for numbers games. Huge discount stores. Lester, who is an expert in these matters, has told me that all these places feed on addicts. "What do you think—those peepshows stay in business on the strength of the occasional customer? No way. It's a steady clientele of people in there every day, for hours at a time, dropping in quarters. That whole strip of road is *made* for addicts. And all the strips like it. That's what America's all about, you know. You got your alcoholics in the bars. Your food addicts sucking it up at Jack-in-the-Box—you ever go in one of those places and count the fat people? You got your sex addicts in the peepshows. Your shopping addicts at the K mart. Your gamblers running numbers in the bodegas and your junkies in the alley-ways. We're all nothing but a bunch of addicts. The whole fucking addicted country."

In the arcades, says Lester, the videos show myriad combinations and arrangements of men and women, men and men, women and women. Some show older men being serviced by eager, selfless young women who seem to live for one thing only, who can't get enough. Some of these women have put their hair into pigtails and shaved themselves—they're supposed to look like children. Inside the peepshow booths there's semen on the floor. And in the old days, there were glory holes cut into the wooden walls between some of the booths, so, if it pleased you, you could communicate with your neighbor. Not anymore. Mack and Lester tell me that some things have changed. The holes have been boarded up. In the public men's rooms you no longer read, scribbled in the stalls, "All faggots should die." You read, "All faggots should die of AIDS." Mack rails against the moratorium on fetal-tissue research, the most promising avenue for a cure. "If it was Legionnaires dying, we wouldn't have any moratorium," he says. And he often talks about Africa, where governments impede efforts to teach villagers about condoms: a social worker, attempting to explain their use, isn't allowed to remove the condoms from their foil packets; in another country, with a slightly more liberal government, a field nurse stretches a condom over his hand, to show how it works, and later villagers are found wearing the condoms like mittens, thinking this will protect them from disease. Lester laughs at these stories but shakes his head. In our own country, something called "family values" has emerged with clarity. "*Whose* family?" Mack wants to know, holding out his hands palms upward. "I mean we *all* come from families, don't we? The dizziest queen comes from a family. The axe-murderer. Even Dan *Quayle* comes from a family of some kind."

But Mack and Lester are dying, Mack first. As I steer my pickup into the parking lot at the K mart, I almost clip the front fender of a big, deep-throated Chevy that's leaving. I have startled the driver, a young Chicano boy with four kids in the back seat, and he flips me the bird—aggressively, his arm out the window—but I feel protected today by my sense of purpose: I have come to buy a padded toilet seat for my friend.

When he was younger, Mack wanted to be a cultural anthropologist, but he was slow to break in after we were out of graduate school—never landed anything more than a low-paying position assisting someone else, nothing more than a student's job, really. Eventually, he began driving a tour bus in San Diego, which not only provided a steady income but suited him so well that in time he was managing the line and began to refer to the position not as his job but as his calling. He said that San Diego was like a pretty blond boy without too many brains. He knew just how to play up its cultural assets while allowing its beauty to speak for itself. He said he liked being "at the controls." But he had to quit work over a year ago, and now his hands have become so shaky that he can no longer even manage a pen and paper.

When I get back to the apartment from my trip to the K mart, Mack asks me to take down a letter for him to an old high-school buddy back in Des Moines, a country-and-Western singer who has sent him a couple of her latest recordings. *"Whenever I met a new doctor or nurse,"* he dictates, *"I always asked them whether they believed in miracles."*

Mack sits up a bit straighter and rearranges the pillows behind his back on the couch. "What did I just say?" he asks me.

" 'I always asked them whether they believed in miracles.' "

"Yes," he says, and continues. *"And if they said no, I told them I wanted to see someone else. I didn't want them treating me. Back then, I was hoping for a miracle, which seemed reasonable.* Do you think this is too detailed?" he asks me.

"No," I say. "I think it's fine."

"I don't want to depress her."

"Go on," I say.

"But now I have lung cancer," he continues. *"So now I need not one but two miracles. That doesn't seem as possible somehow.* Wait. Did you write 'possible' yet?"

"No," I say. " 'That doesn't seem as . . .' "

"Reasonable," he says. "Didn't I say 'reasonable' before?"

"Yes," I say. " 'That doesn't seem as reasonable somehow.' "

"Yes," he says. "How does that sound?"

"It sounds fine, Mack. It's not for publication, you know."

"It's not?" he says, feigning astonishment. "I thought it was: 'Letters of an AIDS Victim.' " He says this in a spooky voice and makes his bug-eyes. Since his head is a perfect skull, the whole effect really is a little spooky.

"What else?" I say.

"Thank you for your nice letter," he continues, *"and for the tapes."* He begins coughing—a horrible, rasping seizure. Mack has told me that he has lost all fear; he said he realized this a few weeks ago, on the skyride at the zoo. But when the coughing sets in, when it seems that it may never stop, I think I see terror in his eyes: he begins tapping his breastbone with the fingers of one hand, as if he's trying to wake up his lungs, prod them to do their appointed work. Finally he does stop, and he sits for a moment in silence, in thought. Then he dictates: *"It makes me very happy that you are so successful."*

At Mrs. Mears' craft sale, in the alley behind her cottage, she has set up several card tables: Scores of plastic dolls with hand-knitted dresses, shoes, and hats. Handmade doll furniture. Christmas ornaments. A whole box of knitted bonnets and scarves for dolls. Also, some baked goods. Now, while Lester holds Eberhardt, Mrs. Mears, wearing a large straw hat and sunglasses, outfits the dachshund in one of the bonnets and scarves. "There now," she says. "Have you ever seen anything so *precious?* I'm going to get my camera."

Mack sits in a folding chair by one of the tables; next to him sits Mr. Mears, also in a folding chair. The two men look very much alike, though Mr. Mears is not nearly as emaciated as Mack. And of course Mr. Mears is eighty-seven. Mack, on the calendar, is not quite forty. I notice that Mack's shoelaces are untied, and I kneel to tie them. "The thing about reincarnation," he's saying to Mr. Mears, "is that you can't remember anything and you don't recognize anybody."

"Consciously," says Lester, butting in. "*Sub*consciously you do."

"Subconsciously," says Mack. "What's the point? I'm not the least bit interested."

Mr. Mears removes his houndstooth-check cap and scratches his bald, freckled head. "I'm not, either," he says with great resignation.

As Mrs. Mears returns with the camera, she says, "Put him over there, in Mack's lap."

"It doesn't matter whether you're interested or not," says Lester, dropping Eberhardt into Mack's lap.

"Give me good old-fashioned Heaven and Hell," says Mr. Mears.

"I should think you would've had enough of that already," says Lester.

Mr. Mears gives Lester a suspicious look, then gazes down at his own knees. "Then give me nothing," he says finally.

I stand up and step aside just in time for Mrs. Mears to snap the picture. "Did you ever *see* anything?" she says, all sunshades and yellow teeth, but as she heads back toward the cottage door, her face is immediately serious. She takes me by the arm and pulls me along, reaching for something from one of the tables—a doll's bed, white with a red strawberry painted on the headboard. "For your little girl," she says aloud. Then she whispers, "You better get him out of the sun, don't you think? He doesn't look so good."

But when I turn again, I see that Lester is already helping Mack out of his chair. "Here—let me," says Mrs. Mears, reaching an arm toward them, and she escorts Mack up the narrow, shaded sidewalk, back toward the apartment building. Lester moves alongside me and says, "Dan, do you think you could give Mack his bath this afternoon? I'd like to take Eberhardt for a walk."

"Of course," I say, quickly.

But a while later—after I have drawn the bath, after I've taken a large beach towel out of the linen closet, refolded it into a thick square, and put it into the water to serve as a cushion for Mack to sit on in the tub; when I'm holding the towel under, against some resistance, waiting for the bubbles to stop surfacing, and there's something horrible about it, like drowning a small animal—I think Lester has tricked me into this task of bathing Mack, and the saliva in my mouth suddenly seems to taste of Scotch, which I have not actually tasted in nine years.

There is no time to consider any of this, however, for in a moment

Mack enters the bathroom, trailing his tubes behind him, and says, "Are you ready for my Auschwitz look?"

"I've seen it before," I say.

And it's true. I have, a few times, helping him with his shirt and pants after Lester has bathed him and gotten him into his underwear. But that doesn't feel like preparation. The sight of him naked is like a powerful, scary drug: you forget between trips, remember only when you start to come on to it again. I help him off with his clothes now and guide him into the tub and gently onto the underwater towel. "That's nice," he says, and I begin soaping the hollows of his shoulders, the hard washboard of his back. This is not human skin as we know it but something already dead—so dry, dense, and pleasantly brown as to appear manufactured. I soap the cage of his chest, his stomach—the hard, depressed abdomen of a greyhound—the steep vaults of his armpits, his legs, his feet. Oddly, his hands and feet appear almost normal, even a bit swollen. At last I give him the slippery bar of soap. "Your turn," I say.

"My poor cock," he says as he begins to wash himself.

When he's done, I rinse him all over with the hand spray attached to the faucet. I lather the feathery white wisps of his hair—we have to remove the plastic oxygen tubes for this—then rinse again. "You know," he says, "I know it's irrational, but I feel kind of turned off to sex."

The apparent understatement of this almost takes my breath away. "There are more important things," I say.

"Oh, I know," he says. "I just hope Lester's not too unhappy." Then, after a moment, he says, "You know, Dan, it's only logical that they've all given up on me. And I've accepted it mostly. But I still have days when I think I should at least be given a chance."

"You can ask them for anything you want, Mack," I say.

"I know," he says. "That's the problem—there's nothing to ask for."

"Mack," I say. "I think I understand what you meant this morning about the tree pruning and the credit cards."

"You do?"

"Well, I think your mind just shifted into metaphor. Because I can see that pruning trees is like imposing a limit—just like the limit on the credit cards."

Mack is silent, pondering this. "Maybe," he says at last, hesitantly—a moment of disappointment for us both.

I get him out and hooked up to the oxygen again, dry him off, and begin dressing him. Somehow I get the oxygen tubes trapped between his legs and the elastic waistband of his sweatpants—no big deal, but I suddenly feel panicky—and I have to take them off his face again to set them to rights. After he's safely back on the living-room couch and I've returned to the bathroom, I hear him: low, painful-sounding groans. "Are you all right?" I call from the hallway.

"Oh, yes," he says, "I'm just moaning. It's one of the few pleasures I have left."

The bathtub is coated with a crust of dead skin, which I wash away with the sprayer. Then I find a screwdriver and go to work on the toilet seat. After I get the old one off, I need to scrub around the area where the plastic screws were. I've sprinkled Ajax all around the rim of the bowl and found the scrub brush when Lester appears at the bathroom door, back with Eberhardt from their walk. "Oh, Dan, really," he says. "You go too far. Down on your knees now, scrubbing our toilet."

"Lester, leave me alone," I say.

"Well, it's true," he says. "You really do."

"Maybe I'm working out my survivor's guilt," I say, "if you don't mind."

"You mean because your best buddy's dying and you're not?"

"Yes," I say. "It's very common."

He parks one hip on the edge of the sink. And after a moment he says this: "Danny boy, if you feel guilty about surviving . . . that's not irreversible, you know. I could fix that."

We are both stunned. He looks at me. In another moment, there are tears in his eyes. He quickly closes the bathroom door, moves to the tub and turns on the water, sits on the side, and bursts into sobs. "I'm sorry," he says. "I'm so sorry."

"Forget it," I say.

He begins to compose himself almost at once. "This is what Jane Alexander did when she played Eleanor Roosevelt," he says. "Do you remember? When she needed to cry she'd go in the bathroom and turn on the water, so nobody could hear her. Remember?"

In the pickup, on the way to the hospital, Lester—in the middle, between Mack and me—says, "Maybe after they're down there you could doze off, but on the *way* down, they want you awake." He's explaining the bronchoscopy to me—the insertion of the tube down the windpipe—with which he is personally familiar: "They reach certain points on the way down where they have to ask you to swallow."

"*He's* not having the test, is he?" Mack says, looking confused.

"No, of course not," says Lester.

"Didn't you just say to him that he had to swallow?"

"I meant *anyone,* Mack," says Lester.

"Oh," says Mack. "Oh, yeah."

"The general 'you,' " Lester says to me. "He keeps forgetting little things like that."

Mack shakes his head, then points at his temple with one finger. "My mind," he says.

Mack is on tank oxygen now, which comes with a small caddy. I push the caddy, behind him, and Lester assists him along the short walk from the curb to the hospital's front door and the elevators. Nine years ago, it was Mack who drove *me* to a different wing of this same hospital—against my drunken, slobbery will—to dry out. And as I watch him struggle up the low inclined ramp toward the glass-and-steel doors, I recall the single irrefutable thing he said to me in the car on the way. "You stink," he said. "You've puked and probably pissed your pants and you *stink,*" he said—my loyal, articulate, and best friend, saving my life, and causing me to cry like a baby.

Inside the clinic upstairs, the nurse, a sour young blond woman in a sky-blue uniform who looks terribly overworked, says to Mack, "You know better than to be late."

We are five minutes late to the second. Mack looks at her incredulously. He stands with one hand on the handle of the oxygen-tank caddy. He straightens up, perfectly erect—the indignant, shockingly skeletal posture of a man fasting to the death for some holy principle. He gives the nurse the bug-eyes, and says, "And you know better than to keep me waiting every time I come over here for some goddam procedure. But get over yourself: shit happens."

He turns and winks at me.

Though I've offered to return for them afterward, Lester has insisted on taking a taxi, so I will leave them here and drive back home, where again I'll try—successfully, this time—to explain to my wife how all this feels to me, and where, a few minutes later, I'll stand outside the door to my daughter's room, comforted by the music of her small high voice as she consoles her dolls.

Now the nurse gets Mack into a wheelchair and leaves us in the middle of the reception area; then, from the proper position at her desk, she calls Mack's name, and says he may proceed to the laboratory.

"Dan," Mack says, stretching his spotted, broomstick arms toward me. "Old pal. Do you remember the Christmas we drove out to Des Moines on the motorcycle?"

We did go to Des Moines together, one very snowy Christmas—but of course we didn't go on any motorcycle, not in December.

"We had fun," I say and put my arms around him, awkwardly, since he is sitting.

"Help me up," he whispers—confidentially—and I begin to lift him.

Dennis McFarland's first novel, *The Music Room,* published in 1990, was a national best-seller. His stories have appeared in a number of magazines, and "Nothing to Ask For" was included in both *Prize Stories: The O. Henry Awards* and *The Best American Short Stories*. Mr. McFarland lives near Boston with his wife and two children.

STEPHANIE VAUGHN

"Able, Baker, Charlie, Dog" is a remarkable story in which a daughter learns many things from her father, among them:

"He taught me the alphabet. Able, Baker, Charlie, Dog. It was the alphabet the military used to keep b's separate from v's and i's separate from y's. He liked the music of it, the way it sounded on his fine voice. I was four years old and my grandmother had not come to live with us yet . . ."

This story is an unforgettable portrait of a complex, tender, bedeviled man, and how he shaped the life of his young daughter. *The Voice Literary Supplement* referred to the "layered richness" of Stephanie Vaughn's writing about families, and said of Gemma, this story's heroine, "she is a whip-smart narrator who tells what it was like to be an army brat."

"Able, Baker, Charlie, Dog" is a favorite story of a number of people, including Bobbie Ann Mason, who said of Stephanie Vaughn's work: "these are some of the most honest and true stories about growing up and family life that I recall reading."

Wallace Stegner said, "There aren't five writers in the United States who could have written these stories, and maybe not even five; maybe only one. The mix of perception, irony and compassion is extraordinary, and she does it with such economy and sureness, and such apparent ease."

ABLE, BAKER, CHARLIE, DOG

WHEN I was twelve years old, my father was tall and awesome. I can see him walking across the parade ground behind our quarters. The wind blew snow into the folds of his coat and made the hem swoop around his legs. He did not lower his head, he did not jam his hands into the pockets. He was coming home along a diagonal that would cut the parade ground into perfect triangles, and he was not going to be stopped by any snowstorm. I stood at the kitchen door and watched him through a hole I had rubbed in the steamy glass.

My grandmother and mother fidgeted with pans of food that had been kept warm too long. It was one o'clock on Saturday and he had been expected home at noon.

"You want to know what this chicken looks like?" said my grandmother. "It looks like it died last year."

My mother looked into the pan but didn't say anything.

My grandmother believed my mother should have married a minister, not an Army officer. Once my mother had gone out with a minister, and now he was on the radio every Sunday in Ohio. My grandmother thought my father had misrepresented himself as a religious man. There was a story my mother told about their first date. They went to a restaurant and my father told her that he was going to have twelve sons and name them Peter, James, John, et cetera. "And I thought, Twelve sons!" said my mother. "Boy, do I pity your poor wife." My mother had two miscarriages and then she had me. My father named me Gemma, which my grandmother believed was not even a Christian name.

"You want to know what this squash looks like?" said my grandmother.

"It'll be fine," said my mother.

Just then the wind gusted on the parade ground, and my father veered to the left. He stopped and looked up. How is it possible you have caught me off guard, he seemed to ask. Exactly where have I miscalculated the velocities, how have I misjudged the vectors?

"It looks like somebody peed in it," my grandmother said.

•

"Keep your voice low," my father told me that day as we ate the ruined squash and chicken. "Keep your voice low and you can win any point."

We were living in Fort Niagara, a little Army post at the juncture of the Niagara River and Lake Ontario. We had been there through the fall and into the winter, as my father, who was second in command, waited for his next promotion. It began to snow in October. The arctic winds swept across the lake from Canada and shook the windows of our house. Snow drifted across the parade ground, and floes of ice piled up against each other in the river, so that if a person were courageous enough, or foolhardy enough, and also lucky, he could walk the mile across the river to Canada.

"And always speak in sentences," he told me. "You have developed a junior-high habit of speaking in fragments. Learn to come to a full stop when you complete an idea. Use semicolons and periods in your speech."

My mother put down her fork and knife. Her hands were so thin and light they seemed to pass through the table as she dropped them in her lap. "Zachary, perhaps we could save some of the lecture for dessert?" she said.

My grandmother leaned back into her own heaviness. "The poor kid never gets to eat a hot meal," she said. She was referring to the rule that said I could not cut my food or eat while I was speaking or being spoken to. My father used mealtimes to lecture on the mechanics of life, the how-tos of a civilized world. Normally I was receptive to his advice, but that day I was angry with him.

"You know, Dad," I said, "I don't think my friends are going to notice a missing semicolon."

I thought he would give me a fierce look, but instead he winked. "And don't say 'you know,' " he said.

He never said "you know," never spoke in fragments, never slurred his speech, even years later when he had just put away a fifth of scotch and was trying to describe the Eskimo custom of chewing up the meat before it was given to the elders, who had no teeth. He spoke with such calculation and precision that his sentences hung over us like high vaulted ceilings, or rolled across the table like ornaments sculptured from stone. It was a huge cathedral of a voice, full of volume and complexity.

He taught me the alphabet. Able, Baker, Charlie, Dog. It was the alphabet the military used to keep *b*'s separate from *v*'s and *i*'s separate from *y*'s. He liked the music of it, the way it sounded on his fine voice. I was four years old and my grandmother had not come to live with us yet. We were stationed in Manila, and living in a house the Army had built on squat stilts to protect us from the insects. There was a typhoon sweeping inland, and we could hear the hoarse sound of metal scraping across the Army's paved street. It was the corrugated roof of the house next door.

"Don't you think it's time we went under the house?" my mother said. She was sitting on a duffel bag that contained our tarps and food rations. The house had a loose plank in the living-room floor, so that if the roof blew away, or the walls caved in, we could escape through the opening and sit in the low space between the reinforced floor and the ground until the military rescue bus came.

My father looked at me and said, "Able, Baker, Charlie, Dog. Can you say it, Gemma?"

I looked up at the dark slope of our own metal roof.

"Can you say it?"

"Able, Baker, Charlie, Dog," I said.

The metal rumbled on the road outside. My mother lifted the plank.

"We will be all right," he said. "Easy, Fox, George, How."

"Anybody want to join me?" said my mother.

"Easy."

"Rachel, please put that plank back."

"Easy, Fox, George, How," I said.

My mother replaced the plank and sat on the floor beside me. The storm grew louder, the rain fell against the roof like handfuls of gravel.

"Item, Jig, King." My father's voice grew lower, fuller. We sat under the sound of it and felt safe. "Love, Mike, Nan."

But then we heard another sound—something that went *whap-whap*, softly, between the gusts of rain. We tilted our heads toward the shuttered windows.

"Well," said my father, standing up to stretch. "I think we are losing a board or two off the side of the house."

"Where are you going?" said my mother. "Just where do you think you're going?"

He put on his rain slicker and went into the next room. When he returned, he was carrying a bucket of nails and a hammer. "Obviously," he said, "I am going fishing."

We moved back to the States when I was six, and he taught me how to play Parcheesi, checkers, chess, cribbage, dominoes, and twenty questions. "When you lose," he told me, "don't cry. When you win, don't gloat."

He taught me how to plant tomatoes and load a shotgun shell. He showed me how to gut a dove, turning it inside out as the Europeans do, using the flexible breastbone for a pivot. He read a great many books and never forgot a fact or a technical description. He explained the principles of crop rotation and the flying buttress. He discussed the Defenestration of Prague.

When I was in elementary school, he was sent abroad twice on yearlong tours—once to Turkey and once to Greenland, both strategic outposts for America's Early Warning System. I wanted to, but I could not write him letters. His came to me every week, but without the rhythms of his voice the words seemed pale and flat, like the transparent shapes of cells under a microscope. He did not write about his work, because his work was secret. He did not send advice, because that he left to my mother and grandmother in his absence. He wrote about small things—the smooth white rocks he found on a mountainside in Turkey, the first fresh egg he ate in Greenland. When I reread the letters after he died, I was struck by their grace and invention. But when I read them as a child, I looked through the words—"eggs . . . shipment . . . frozen"—and there was nothing on the other side but the great vacuum of his missing voice.

"I can't think of anything to say," I told my mother the first time she urged me to write to him. He had already been in Turkey for three months. She stood behind me at the heavy library table and smoothed my hair, touched my shoulders. "Tell him about your tap lessons," she said. "Tell him about ballet."

"Dear Dad," I wrote. "I am taking tap lessons. I am also taking ballet." I tried to imagine what he looked like. I tried to put a face before my face, but it was gray and featureless, like the face of a statue worn flat by wind and rain. "And I hope you have a Happy Birthday next month," I concluded, hoping to evade the necessity of writing him again in three weeks.

The autumn I turned twelve, we moved to Fort Niagara, which was the administrative base for the missile sites strung along the Canadian border between Lake Erie and Lake Ontario. It was a handsome post, full of oak trees, brick buildings, and history. The French had taken the land from the Indians and built the original fort. The British took the fort from the French, and the Americans took it from the British. My father recounted the battles for us as we drove there along the wide sweep of the Niagara River, past apple orchards and thick pastures. My grandmother sat in the back seat and made a note of each red convertible that passed. I was supposed to be counting the white ones. When we drove through the gate and saw the post for the first time—the expanses of clipped grass, the tall trees, the row of Colonial houses overlooking the river—my grandmother put down her tablet and said, "This is some post." She looked at my father admiringly, the first indication she had ever given that he might be a good match for my mother after all. She asked to be taken to the far end of the post, where the Old Fort was. It sat on a point of land at the juncture of the lake and river, and looked appropriately warlike, with its moat and tiny gun windows, but it was surprisingly small—a simple square of yellow stone, a modest French château. "Is this all there is?" I said as my grandmother and I posed for pictures on the drawbridge near two soldiers dressed in Revolutionary War costumes. It was hard to imagine that chunks of a vast continent had been won and lost within the confines of a fortress hardly bigger than Sleeping Beauty's castle at Disneyland. Later, as we drove back along the river, my father said in his aphoristic way, "Sometimes the biggest battles are the smallest ones."

The week after we settled in our quarters, we made the obligatory trip to the Falls. It was a sultry day—Indian summer—and our eyes began to water as we neared the chemical factories that surrounded the city of Niagara Falls. We stopped for iced tea and my father explained how the glaciers had formed the escarpment through which the Falls had cut a deep gorge. *Escarpment*—that was the term he used, instead of *cliff.* It skidded along the roof of his mouth and entered the conversation with a soft explosion.

We went to the Niagara Falls Museum and examined the containers people had used successfully to go over the Falls early in the century, when there was a thousand-dollar prize given to survivors. Two were wooden barrels strapped with metal bands. One was a giant rubber ball reinforced with a steel cage. A fourth was a long steel capsule. On the walls were photographs of each survivor and plaques explaining who had been injured and how. The steel capsule was used by a man who had broken every bone in his body. The plaque said that he was in the hospital for twenty-three weeks and then took his capsule around the world on a speaking tour. One day when he was in New Zealand, he slipped on an orange peel, broke his leg, and died of complications.

We went next to Goat Island and stood on the open bank to watch the leap and dive of the white water. My mother held her handbag close to her breasts. She had a habit of always holding things this way—a stack of dinner plates, the dish towel, some mail she had brought in from the porch; she hunched over slightly, so that her body seemed at once to be protective and protected. "I don't like the river," she said. "I think it wants to hypnotize you." My father put his hands in his pockets to show how at ease he was, and my grandmother went off to buy an ice-cream cone.

At the observation point, we stood at a metal fence and looked into the frothing water at the bottom of the gorge. We watched bits and pieces of rainbows appear and vanish in the sunlight that was refracted off the water through the mist. My father pointed to a black shape in the rapids above the Horseshoe Falls. "That's a river barge," he said. He lowered his voice so that he could be heard under the roar of the water. "A long time ago, there were two men standing on that barge waiting to see whether in the next moment of their lives they would go over."

He told us the story of the barge then—how it had broken loose from a tug near Buffalo and floated downriver, gathering speed. The two men tore at the air, waved and shouted to people on shore, but the barge entered the rapids. They bumped around over the rocks, and the white water rose in the air. One man—"He was the thinking man," said my father—thought they might be able to wedge the barge among the rocks if they allowed the hull to fill with water. They came closer to the Falls—four hundred yards, three hundred—before the barge jerked broadside and stopped. They were there all afternoon and night, listening to the sound of the water pounding into the boulders at the bottom of the gorge. The next morning they were rescued, and one of the men, the thinking man, told the newspapers that he had spent the night playing poker in his head. He played all the hands, and he bluffed himself. He drew to inside straights. If the barge had torn loose from the rocks in the night, he was going to go over the Falls saying, "Five-card draw, jacks or better to open." The other man sat on the barge, his arms clasped around his knees, and watched the mist blow back from the edge of the Falls in the moonlight. He could not speak.

"The scream of the water entered his body," said my father. He paused to let us think about that.

"Well, what does that mean?" my grandmother said at last.

My father rested his arms on the fence and gazed pleasantly at the Falls. "He went insane."

The river fascinated me. I often stood between the yellow curtains of my bedroom and looked down upon it and thought about how deep and swift it was, how black under the glittering surface. The newspaper carried stories about people who jumped over the Falls, fourteen miles upriver from our house. I thought of their bodies pushed along the soft silt of the bottom, tumbling silently, huddled in upon themselves like fetuses—jilted brides, unemployed factory workers, old people who did not want to go to rest homes, teenagers who got bad grades, young women who fell in love with married men. They floated invisibly past my bedroom window, out into the lake.

•

That winter, I thought I was going to die. I thought I had cancer of the breasts. My mother had explained to me about menstruation, she had given me a book about the reproductive systems of men and women, but she had not told me about breasts and how they begin as invisible lumps that become tender and sore.

I thought the soreness had begun in a phys. ed. class one day in December when I was hit in the chest with a basketball. I didn't worry about it, and it went away by New Year's. In January, I found a pamphlet at the bus stop. I was stamping my feet in the cold, looking down at my boots, when I saw the headline—CANCER: SEVEN WARNING SIGNALS. When I got home, I went into the bathroom and undressed. I examined myself for enlarged moles and small wounds that wouldn't heal. I was systematic. I sat on the edge of the tub with the pamphlet by my side and began with my toenails, looking under the tips of them. I felt my soles, arches, ankles. I worked my way up my body and then I felt the soreness again, around both nipples. At dinner that night I didn't say anything all through the meal. In bed I slept on my back, with my arms stiff against my sides.

The next Saturday was the day my father came home late for lunch. The squash sat on the back of the stove and turned to ocher soup. The chicken fell away from the bones. After lunch he went into the living room and drank scotch and read a book. When I came down for supper, he was still sitting there, and he told my mother he would eat later. My grandmother, my mother, and I ate silently at the kitchen table. I took a long bath. I scrubbed my chest hard.

I went straight to my bedroom, and after a while my mother came upstairs and said, "What's wrong?"

I didn't say anything.

She stood in front of me with her hands clasped in front of her. She seemed to lean toward her own hands. "But you've been acting, you know"—and here she laughed self-consciously, as she used the forbidden phrase—"you know, you've been acting different. You were so quiet today."

I went to my chest of drawers and took the pamphlet out from under a stack of folded underpants and gave it to her.

"What's this?" she said.

"I think I have Number Four," I said.

She must have known immediately what the problem was, but she didn't smile. She asked me to raise my nightgown and she examined my chest, pressing firmly, as if she were a doctor. I told her about the soreness. "Here?" she said. "And here? What about here, too?" She told me I was beginning to "develop." I knew what she meant, but I wanted her to be precise.

"You're getting breasts," she said.

"But I don't *see* anything."

"You will."

"You never told me it would hurt."

"Oh, dear. I just forgot. When you're grown up you just forget what it was like."

I asked her whether, just to be safe, I could see a doctor. She said that of course I could, and I felt better, as if I had had a disease and already been cured. As she was leaving the room, I said, "Do you think I need a bra?" She smiled. I went to sleep watching the snow fall past the window. I had my hands cupped over my new breasts. When I awoke, I did not recognize the window. The snow had stopped and moonlight slanted through the glass. I could not make out the words, but I heard my father's voice filling up the house. I tiptoed down the back staircase that led to the kitchen and stood in the slice of shadow near the doorjamb. My grandmother was telling my mother to pack her bags. He was a degenerate, she said—she had always seen that in him. My mother said, "Why, Zachary, why are you doing this?"

"Just go pack your bags," my grandmother said. "I'll get the child."

My father said conversationally, tensely, "Do I have to break your arms?"

I leaned into the light. He was holding on to a bottle of scotch with one hand, and my mother was trying to pull it away with both of hers. He jerked his arm back and forth, so that she was drawn into a little dance, back and forth across the linoleum in front of him.

"The Lord knows the way of righteousness," said my grandmother.

"Please," said my mother. "Please, please."

"And the way of the ungodly shall perish," said my grandmother.

"Whose house is this?" said my father. His voice exploded. He snapped his arm back, trying to take the bottle from my mother in one powerful gesture. It smashed against the wall, and I stepped into the kitchen. The white light from the ceiling fixture burned across the smooth surfaces of the refrigerator, the stove, the white Formica countertops. It was as if an atom had been smashed somewhere and a wave of radiation was rolling through the kitchen. I looked him in the eye and waited for him to speak. I sensed my mother and grandmother on either side of me, in petrified postures. At last, he said, "Well." His voice cracked. The word split in two. "Wel-el." He said it again. His face took on a flatness.

"I am going back to bed," I said. I went up the narrow steps, and he followed me. My mother and grandmother came along behind, whispering. He tucked in the covers, and sat on the edge of the bed, watching me. My mother and grandmother stood stiff against the door. "I am sorry I woke you up," he said finally, and his voice was deep and soothing. The two women watched him go down the hall, and when I heard his steps on the front staircase I rolled over and put my face in the pillow. I heard them turn off the lights and say good-night to me. I heard them go to their bedrooms. I lay there for a long time, listening for a sound downstairs, and then it came—the sound of the front door closing.

I went downstairs and put on my hat, coat, boots. I followed his footsteps in the snow, down the front walk, and across the road to the riverbank. He did not seem surprised to see me next to him. We stood side by side, hands in our pockets, breathing frost into the air. The river was filled from shore to shore with white heaps of ice, which cast blue shadows in the moonlight.

"This is the edge of America," he said, in a tone that seemed to answer a question I had just asked. There was a creak and crunch of ice as two floes below us scraped each other and jammed against the bank.

"You knew all week, didn't you? Your mother and your grandmother didn't know, but I knew that you could be counted on to know."

I hadn't known until just then, but I guessed the unspeakable thing —that his career was falling apart—and I knew. I nodded. Years later, my mother told me what she had learned about the incident, not from him but from another Army wife. He had called a general a son of a bitch. That was all. I never knew what the issue was or whether he had been right or wrong. Whether the defense of the United States of America had been at stake, or merely the pot in a card game. I didn't even know whether he had called the general a son of a bitch to his face or simply been overheard in an unguarded moment. I only knew that he had been given a 7 instead of a 9 on his Efficiency Report and then passed over for promotion. But that night I nodded, not knowing the cause but knowing the consequences, as we stood on the riverbank above the moonlit ice. "I am looking at that thin beautiful line of Canada," he said. "I think I will go for a walk."

"No," I said. I said it again. "No." I wanted to remember later that I had told him not to go.

"How long do you think it would take to go over and back?" he said.

"Two hours."

He rocked back and forth in his boots, looked up at the moon, then down at the river. I did not say anything.

He started down the bank, sideways, taking long, graceful sliding steps, which threw little puffs of snow in the air. He took his hands from his pockets and hopped from the bank to the ice. He tested his weight against the weight of the ice, flexing his knees. I watched him walk a few yards from the shore and then I saw him rise in the air, his long legs scissoring the moonlight, as he crossed from the edge of one floe to the next. He turned and waved to me, one hand making a slow arc.

I could have said anything. I could have said "Come back" or "I love you." Instead, I called after him, "Be sure and write!" The last thing I heard, long after I had lost sight of him far out on the river, was the sound of his laugh splitting the cold air.

In the spring he resigned his commission and we went back to Ohio. He used his savings to invest in a chain of hardware stores with my uncle. My uncle arranged the contracts with builders and plumbers, and supervised the employees. My father controlled the inventory and handled the books. He had been a logistics officer, and all the skills he might have used in supervising the movement of land, air, and sea cargoes, or in calculating the disposition of several billion dollars' worth of military supplies, were instead brought to bear on the deployment of nuts and bolts, plumbers' joints and nipples, No. 2 pine, Con-Tact paper, acrylic paint, caulking guns, and rubber dishpans. He learned a new vocabulary—traffic builders, margins, end-cap displays, perfboard merchandisers, seasonal impulse items—and spoke it with the ostentation and faint amusement of a man who has just mastered a foreign language.

"But what I really want to know, Mr. Jenkins," I heard him tell a man on the telephone one day, "is why you think the Triple Gripper Vegetable Ripper would make a good loss-leader item in mid-winter." He had been in the hardlines industry, as it was called, for six months, and I was making my first visit to his office, and then only because my mother had sent me there on the pretext of taking him a midmorning snack during a busy Saturday. I was reluctant to confront him in his civilian role, afraid I would find him somehow diminished. In fact, although he looked incongruous among the reds, yellows, and blues that the previous owner had used to decorate the office, he sounded much like the man who had taught me to speak in complete sentences.

"Mr. Jenkins, I am not asking for a discourse on coleslaw."

When he hung up, he winked at me and said, "Your father is about to become the emperor of the building-and-housewares trade in Killbuck, Ohio."

I nodded and took a seat in a red-and-blue chair.

Then he looked at his hands spread upon the spotless ink blotter and said, "Of course, you know that I do not give a damn about the Triple Gripper Vegetable Ripper."

I had skipped a grade and entered high school. I saw less and less of him, because I ate dinner early so that I could go to play rehearsals, basketball games, dances. In the evenings he sat in a green chair and smoked cigarettes, drank scotch, read books—the same kinds of books, year after year. They were all about Eskimos and Arctic explorations—an interest he had developed during his tour in Greenland. Sometimes, when I came in late and was in the kitchen making a snack, I watched him through the doorway. Often he looked away from the book and gazed toward the window. He would strike a match and let it burn to his thumb and fingertip, then wave it out. He would raise the glass but not drink from it. I think he must have imagined himself to be in the Arctic during those moments, a warrior tracking across the ice for bear or seal. Sometimes he was waiting for me to join him. He wanted to tell me about the techniques the Eskimos had developed for survival, the way they stitched up skins to make them watertight vessels. He became obsessive on the subject of meat. The Eskimo diet was nearly all protein. "Eat meat," he said. Two professors at Columbia had tested the value of the Eskimo diet by eating nothing but caribou for a year and claimed they were healthier at the end of the experiment than they had been before.

Later, when I went to college, he developed the habit of calling me long distance when my mother and grandmother had gone to bed and he was alone downstairs with a drink. "Are you getting enough protein?" he asked me once at three in the morning. It was against dorm rules to put through calls after midnight except in cases of emergency, but his deep, commanding voice was so authoritative ("This is Gemma Jackson's father, and I must speak with her immediately") that it was for some time believed on my corridor that the people in my family were either accident-prone or suffering from long terminal illnesses.

He died the summer I received my master's degree. I had accepted a teaching position at a high school in Chicago, and I went home for a month before school began. He was overweight and short of breath. He drank too much, smoked too many cigarettes. The doctor told him to stop, my mother told him, my grandmother told him.

My grandmother was upstairs watching television and my mother and I were sitting on the front porch. He was asleep in the green chair, with a book in his lap. I left the porch to go to the kitchen to make a sandwich, and as I passed by the chair I heard him say, "Ahhhh. Ahhhhh." I saw his fist rise to his chest. I saw his eyes open and dilate in the lamplight. I knelt beside him.

"Are you okay?" I said. "Are you dreaming?"

We buried him in a small cemetery near the farm where he was born. In the eulogy he was remembered for having survived the first wave of the invasion of Normandy. He was admired for having been the proprietor of a chain of excellent hardware stores.

"He didn't have to do this," my mother said after the funeral. "He did this to himself."

"He was a good man," said my grandmother. "He put a nice roof over our heads. He sent us to Europe twice."

Afterward I went alone to the cemetery. I knelt beside the heaps of wilting flowers—mostly roses and gladiolus, and one wreath of red, white, and blue carnations. Above me, the maple pods spun through the sunlight like wings, and in the distance the corn trumpeted green across the hillsides. I touched the loose black soil at the edge of the flowers. Able, Baker, Charlie, Dog. I could remember the beginning of the alphabet, up through Mike and Nan. I could remember the end. X-ray, Yoke, Zebra. I was his eldest child, and he taught me what he knew. I wept then, but not because he had gone back to Ohio to read about the Eskimos and sell the artifacts of civilized life to homeowners and builders. I wept because when I was twelve years old I had stood on a snowy riverbank as he became a shadow on the ice, and waited to see whether he would slip between the cracking floes into the water.

Stephanie Vaughn was born in Millersburg, Ohio, and grew up on army posts in the United States and abroad. She was educated at Ohio State University, the University of Iowa, and Stanford University. Her stories have appeared in a number of magazines and were recently collected in her first book, *Sweet Talk*. She makes her home in Ithaca, New York.

ANDREA BARRETT

"I didn't start writing until I was in my mid-twenties, after I'd abandoned a career as a biologist; I was thirty before I published my first story and I felt, then, that I was just beginning to find my voice as a writer. I still feel that way. Each new novel or story demands its *own* voice, I think, and the genesis of each remains mysterious—a long, patient process of discovery.

"I began 'The Church of No Reason' in 1988, after a trip to St. Croix. My mother had once lived there briefly, and as I retraced some of her steps I found myself thinking how I might set a story in this place where we'd both visited, so many years apart. There would be a solitary woman, I thought, living in a rundown house with a parrot; there would be grown children visiting over the holidays. There would be talk about the long-ago events that had flung the family to the winds.

"Over the next two years, the story went through many incarnations. The visit, the island, and the grown children fell away bit by bit, leaving only the events of the family's past. Those events, I slowly came to see, *were* that family, and once I understood that, the story began to come together. The children's 'crimes' came to me while I was in London, working on something else. The 'Church of the New Reason' material came a few months later, when I was casting about for the symbolic wedge that splits the mother and her children. Queenie and Joan didn't appear until the next-to-last draft, when I was trying to understand what drove the family back together. Each of these discoveries altered the story's voice and tone as much as it did the plot.

"Who knows where stories come from? Each time I get hold of the tail end of one I am as mystified by the process as I was the first time. But I've learned to believe that the story will finally speak to me, if only I listen and wait."

THE CHURCH OF NO REASON

WHEN Taddy married his bookkeeper, and when the bookkeeper had a new baby, something snapped inside Mom and she turned to the Church of the New Reason, whose pamphlets had seduced her in the mail.

"What is this?" we said, the first time we found Mom sitting cross-legged on her narrow bed, poring over the cheap paperback that had become her Bible.

"It's a way to make sense of things," she said. The first change we saw in her was a strange detachment, which drained all her anger and joy and left her with a puppet's wooden face. "Nothing exists external to our own minds," she said. "Things are thoughts. The world is made up of our ideas. So if we change our ideas, we change the world. . . . I'm working on changing my ideas." She sat with her back straight and her hands folded loosely in her lap. "For instance," she said, "if I could lose the idea that we can't fly, I could float around this room."

My brother, Gene, stood staring at her. "But what's the *point?*" he said.

"The *point,*" Mom said, with a hint of her old distress, "is that there has to be something to life besides working and raising you. I hate my job, and you're all running wild. And there's nothing I can do about any of it."

She closed her eyes and chanted a string of phrases that excluded us entirely, and when we managed a peek at her new book a few days later, we found it full of words and charts that mystified us.

•

Two years earlier, in the June of 1966, Taddy had moved us from the Boston suburb of Natick to a big white house on the Cape. Taddy—a name easy enough for me and Gene to say, close enough to "Daddy" that Ellen didn't know the difference for years and strangers who overheard us thought we stumbled charmingly. Mom had married him six months after our other father died, when I was four and Gene was two and Ellen was the swelling of Mom's stomach against which we leaned our heads. Gene didn't remember our other father and I forgot him, and we trusted Taddy to be ours completely. "Taddy's not the father I made you with," Mom said, when we were old enough to need an explanation. "But he's the one who raised you, and that makes him your real father."

We'd spent six years together in Natick, in a boxy house in a neighborhood not far from the Carling Brewery. Taddy had adopted us, and so we all had the same last name; Taddy and Mom kept the house in which Gene and I had always lived. We had two parents and birthday parties and a school we could walk to, which was small and friendly and set in a hollow between two low hills. Taddy's plans to move us were a complete surprise.

"You'll love it," he said. "The house is right on the water. You can go fishing. We'll have a boat."

"I don't want to move," I told him. "My friends are here."

"Later, Evie," Mom said. She turned to Taddy and pled the only way she knew, appealing to his own comfort. "It's so far to commute," she said. "An hour and a half each way . . ."

Taddy said he'd do it gladly, for us. He'd found a wonderful house, he said, in a village not far from the Bourne Bridge. Cool, breezy summers. Balmy winters. Striped bass and small boats. For that, for us, he'd gladly give up three hours each day.

Mom couldn't seem to find anything else to say. "It'll be good," she told Gene and Ellen and me. "You'll see. It'll be fine." But her voice, even then, sounded unconvinced.

The Cape was farther from Boston than it is now; the superhighways that ring the city existed only in fragments. Taddy took our sole car each morning and left us as isolated as if we'd moved to Maine or Nova Scotia. It was dark each night when he returned, and within a few weeks of our move, his life had become so impossible that he was forced—"Forced," he said, frowning seriously, "to keep this family going"—to take a small apartment in Boston where he could camp for a few days each week.

By July, we'd become a weekend family. Our new house was large and had bedrooms enough for all of us, which was one of the things we were supposed to like. But Ellen and I had shared a room since her birth and we missed each other, as we missed every aspect of our old lives. We sulked and cried and longed for our friends, and Taddy pretended to be bewildered when he returned each weekend and found us curled together in one room.

"Why don't you *like* this?" he'd shout, exasperated by our refusal to enjoy the beach and the rowboat. "Why don't you act like kids?"

He dragged us fishing and clamming and swimming, organized picnics and helped us build a jetty. But the more he tried to entertain us the more sullen we grew, and each Monday he left grumbling about our ungratefulness. Mom withdrew; she rose and drank her coffee each morning in our bright, bare kitchen, and then she returned to her room or, on warm days, rowed the boat we were afraid to use out to Wily Island. Gene dragged out Taddy's binoculars so that he and Ellen and I could spy on Mom.

"Look at her," Gene said to me and Ellen one afternoon. "She's just *lying* there." He passed the binoculars to Ellen and me and we saw, stretched out on the far shore, a small figure wearing our mother's red cotton bathing suit with the baggy seat and the boned top. We watched her smoke a few cigarettes and then we made ourselves peanut-butter sandwiches and retired to the playroom, where we watched soap operas all afternoon and battled during the commercials.

There was no one around to watch over us, no other children to play with, and we fought like animals all that summer. Gene cracked me with a baseball bat and broke my left front tooth. I gave him a black eye and bit his ear so hard it bled. We experimented with half-nelsons, leg-locks, and Indian burns, and one day Gene pushed Ellen off a huge boulder and then stood staring in dark surprise at the gash above her eyebrow. Mom bound our wounds in disappointed silence, and then she retreated to her dark room and lay there with a cloth on her head. “You are more than I can manage,” she’d say. “This is more than I can stand.”

As soon as she closed her door, we’d start fighting again. We pushed each other down the stairs and closed doors on each other’s fingers, and when Taddy came home on the weekends he wanted to know what was going on.

“Jimmy and I were playing baseball and I got hit,” Gene said.

“I was playing dolls at the Harwells,” Ellen said sullenly. “I slipped.”

“Terry and I fell out of her treehouse,” I said.

“Who are the Harwells?” Taddy said. “Who’s Jimmy? Who’s Terry?”

We pointed in various vague directions, locating our imaginary friends. “Kids,” Ellen said.

“Kids we met at the beach,” Gene said.

I said nothing, because that was the summer I became convinced that some things had no explanations. Who could explain Taddy’s absences, or our mother’s sadness?

We had to go to school when September came. Mom was too distracted to take us shopping, and so we had no new book-bags or pencil cases or pink erasers or notebooks, and our arms and legs stuck out of our old clothes and made us look ridiculous. We were as shifty-eyed as stray dogs, frightened of everything: for the first time we could remember, our mother hadn’t woken us early for our special back-to-school breakfast. In fact, she hadn’t woken us at all. Gene had stolen an alarm clock from the drugstore and had woken Ellen and me, and then we’d packed our own lunches and left for the bus stop, where we were separated immediately.

Gene was entering fifth grade and Ellen third; they had to wait for the elementary-school bus on the east side of the road. I was starting seventh grade, but the middle school in our new town was so full that year that all the seventh-graders south of the beach were being bussed to the school on Otis Air Force Base. I had to wait on the road’s west side, while Gene and Ellen clung to a tree across the asphalt. The dip in the road held the morning mist, so that we could hardly see each other.

We stood silently until the white shack and the trailer crowning the hill behind us came alive and poured out a stream of girls we had never seen before. Five in all—three from the trailer and two from the shack. They ran down the hill, shouting and laughing, and they stopped dead at the sight of us.

"Hey," the tallest girl said mockingly. "New kids."

"New kids, new kids!" a smaller girl shrieked, tossing her tangled black hair.

"Dinks," said another, even smaller girl.

The tall girl swaggered up to me. "You," she said. "Where you live?"

I pointed out the dirt road that led over the railroad tracks to our small spit of sandy land. "Back there," I said.

"What's your name?"

"Evie," I said.

Her skin-tight lime green skirt stopped inches above her knees and was held up with a white plastic hip-hugger belt. She wore stockings and pointed flat shoes and a floppy-sleeved white shirt, beneath which I could see a proper bra. White lipstick, blue mascara; she was my age; she was twelve. There was nothing about her I did not envy and fear.

"You going to Otis?" she asked.

"I guess."

"Then you're going with me. And with Frankie." She whistled between her teeth and a red-haired girl ran over to join us. "I'm Nashoba," she continued. "You can call me Nash. This is my cousin Frankie."

Frankie grinned. Her clothes were tighter and tackier than Nash's; her belt was wider and her eyelids more blue. But she was nowhere near as pretty as Nash and looked not nearly as dangerous. Instantly I decided it was Nash I wanted for my friend.

Nash pointed across the road, where the three smaller girls were swarming around Ellen and Gene. "The blond one's my sister, Nicole," she said. "Nicky. She's in third. The others are Frankie's sisters. Darlene and Wanda."

I nodded dumbly.

"That your brother and sister?"

I admitted they were. "Ellen's going to third," I said. "With Nicky, I guess."

"Peebles," Nash said.

"Peebles is the elementary school," Frankie added helpfully. Her front teeth were folded together like the blades of an ivory fan. A bus rolled up just then, and I watched as Gene and Ellen boarded and disappeared. Nicky had already attached herself to Ellen's arm.

Nash looked up and down the road and then pulled a pack of Kents from her purse and stuck one in her white-lipped mouth. "You smoke?" she said.

I shook my head.

"Baby," she said scornfully. As soon as she lit up, our bus came into sight. She pinched the lit tip of her cigarette and stuck the butt back in her purse.

Everyone at school looked like Nash or Frankie or worse. In Natick I had gone to school with kids my own size, from families like mine, but at Otis there were service brats who'd lived in Japan and Korea and Texas, children of the Portuguese fishermen who caught the bluefish we ate, Wampanoag Indian kids from the Mashpee Reservation that bordered the base. All of them seemed older and taller and tougher than me, so I attached myself to Nash and Frankie in self-defense. They beat up my lockermate, who'd stolen my coat. They shepherded me through the terrors of lunch. They showed me how to roll my skirts so they'd be short enough not to be scorned, and all they wanted in return was my lunch money, my homework, an occasional bauble stolen from Kresge's, a steady supply of Mom's cigarettes, and the freedom to spend their afternoons at our house, which they found more comfortable than the trailer and the shack.

Ellen struck a similar bargain with Nicky, and Gene, tormented by the boys his own age, aligned himself with Darlene and Wanda. Our house gradually became home to all of them, and the eight of us circled aimlessly in the afternoons, waiting for Mom to return from the job she'd taken at an insurance agency. When Mom, speaking tiredly to none of us in particular, would ask, "How was school?" Nash would answer for all of us, lying wildly.

"Fantastic," she'd say. "We got ourselves quite an exclusive little click."

That was how she said it—"click"—and her tales were among the few things that made Mom smile. Mom seemed pleased that we'd found friends, and she didn't mind that we traded clothes, shared food, hacked at each other's hair with her scissors. She didn't mind what we did, as long as we left her alone.

"You're lucky," Nash said to us one day, when we were crouched on the beach below the house. "Having a mom like that. Bet she hardly ever belts you."

Gene and Ellen and I exchanged glances. We had met the girls' mothers by then: fat Queenie, whose huge bright housedresses strained over her bulk, and skinny, brittle Joan, whose eyes were rimmed with greasy dark lines. Both of them terrified us. They screamed, cried, threw things, laughed, rocketing from one extreme of emotion to the next. They swore and spoke like no adults we'd ever met. Still, we had not expected this.

"Your mother *hits* you?" Gene said.

"Belts us," Wanda said firmly. "Our mothers have this old leather belt they share. They keep it in the shed."

Gene turned his attention to her. "Where's your daddy?" he asked. "Doesn't he mind?"

"We don't have a daddy," Wanda said. She chipped at a flat stone with a trowel.

Ellen turned to Nicky. "Where's yours?" she asked.

"Don't have one neither," Nicky said. "None of us do. Our moms are sisters, and they get money from the Unemployment. We don't need a daddy. And anyway, my mom has boyfriends. Some nice ones."

"Ours too," Darlene and Wanda said. This was news to us; we'd assumed the girls' fathers were simply away, like ours. I looked at Nash, who shrugged and rolled her eyes.

"But," Gene said, "*everyone* has a daddy someplace . . ."

"Yuh?" Frankie said. "So where's yours?"

"Taddy will be home this weekend," Ellen said stoutly.

Wanda giggled. "Why do you call him that?" she asked.

"Because he likes it," I said. We told everyone that; we never mentioned that Taddy was not our natural father. "He comes home just on the weekends because he has a very, very important job in Boston that keeps him very busy."

"Yuh," Frankie said. "I bet." She smirked and pushed her right index finger through the circle she made of her left index finger and thumb. Poke, poke. And then she fell down on the sand and laughed hysterically.

Of course we spent all our time with them. We centered our lives on Nash and Frankie, their sisters and mothers, the tumble-down white shack and its companion on the hill, and through them we learned what we needed to get by. We came to understand the boyfriends to whom Nicky had referred, the ability of mothers to have children in the absence of fathers, the pleasures of liquor and cigarettes, the mysteries of Jim Morrison, the uses of forgery, the charms of darkness. We became expert at cheating, lying, hiding; and for a while we occupied ourselves by setting fires.

The boathouse was first, although Nash always swore afterwards that that had been an accident. But then we set fire to a couch in the basement of a summer home we'd broken into, and by the time we got it out the walls were streaked with smoke. We set fires in the woods and just barely contained them. We burned a rowboat once, and part of an abandoned dock, and when we tired of that we turned to stealing. When Ellen needed a new bathing suit, and when we couldn't get Mom to take her shopping and also couldn't get her to give us the money because she meant, every day, to make time to go, we began our careers as thieves.

We stole bathing suits first. Ellen and Frankie and Nash and Nicky and I crowded into the department-store dressing room, our arms heaped with suits, and we laughed and chattered and distracted the girl who guarded the door. We put the suits we liked over our underwear, under our clothes, and then we mashed the rejects together and marched out, still chattering. No one stopped us, and our success made us bold. Nash and I stole loose, full-bodied jackets with tight-knitted bands at the waists, and we taught ourselves how to use them. A carton of cigarettes or a bottle of gin fit under an armpit and was held between arm and chest beneath the concealing coat. Records and notebooks went in front, held by the coats' bottom bands; clothes went on in careful layers, and earrings—after we'd pierced our ears with sewing needles and recovered from our infections—slid into the pockets.

Other mothers, more acute, refused to let their children play with us, and our own mothers could not control us at all. Nash and Frankie shredded that infamous belt with a saw, and Gene and Ellen and I shredded Mom's authority just as surely.

"Do I have to stay home?" Mom would say. "To keep an eye on you? What do you expect me to do?"

We didn't know. Taddy vanished for good a year after our move, and by then we understood what Frankie had meant on the beach and we held our mother in some contempt for allowing it to happen. Taddy hadn't moved us to the Cape because he liked fishing and thought we should grow up near the water, nor because he'd found our house at a reasonable price. He'd moved us because he'd fallen in love with the bookkeeper at the chain of Boston shoe stores he managed, and because he'd known his daily commute would force him away from us.

Who could trust a mother fooled so easily? Who could resist trying to fool her again and again and again? We understood that we—our mother included—had been as stupid as fish. We had thought Taddy lived alone. We had thought our exile had some meaning, some purpose; that our mother wept the nights Taddy stayed in Boston because she was lonely. Our lives seemed to parallel those of our friends exactly, and our desperate misbehaviors seemed as justifiable as theirs.

Nash and Frankie and I finished our stint at Otis and entered eighth grade at the local school, where our classmates were smaller and more sedate. But the ways we'd learned in self-defense stuck with us long after we needed them, and we stood out at our new school like the criminals we were. The girls in the band and the pep squad and the debating club shunned us. Our teachers made us sit at the back of the room. We mocked everyone and redoubled our efforts to be bad.

We had no father, after all; this was our mother's fault. We told her we didn't know how the boathouse had burned—perhaps some old rags had caught fire by themselves. We said the teachers who sent home angry notes were insane. We told her the clothes that appeared in the absence of money were gifts, and that Nash's mother had pierced our ears. When we lied about our crimes, Mom closed her eyes and said, "Fine. Whatever you say." Then she went off to her dark room, which was empty by then except for a narrow bed and her new books and a stiff chair by the window.

Taddy married his bookkeeper; we referred to her, when we referred to her at all, as "our stepfather's new wife." Mom never spoke of her. She returned Taddy's checks uncashed and supported us on her small salary, and we learned only by accident that Taddy wrote us letters which she tore up and threw away. "He's not your father," Mom said then. "He never was."

When we told our friends that, Nicky said, "See? A daddy isn't necessary." We agreed; we thought we were better off without him. But we hadn't counted on the power of the pamphlets that came to our mother, like a virus, in the mail.

I was a freshman in high school by the time things with Mom turned serious. Gene was in seventh grade—he had to go to Otis, too—and Ellen was in fifth. Nash and Frankie and I did everything together, with Gene and the others not far behind, and somehow we survived the suspensions from school, the Dodge crashed in the dark, the drugs and the drink and the parties, the lost weekends, the lost years. We had a church of our own, which Nash had named in a drunken moment by twisting Mom's Church of the New Reason: the Church of No Reason, founded on amnesia and chaos and loss. We stole liquor and cigarettes and sold them to other kids, and with the money we got we bought hash and opium, uppers and downers, sleeping pills and mushrooms and mescaline and speed and anything else we could find. We stole a lava lamp and uncounted records, and we set perfumed candles on the window seat and called that our altar.

When Mom vanished for three-day retreats with her fellow believers, we filled the house with summer kids and we trashed everything. And on one of those occasions, Mom came home a few hours early to find the garbage cans smoking with pillows we'd accidentally set on fire, and the upstairs-bathroom window smashed, and Darlene, who was twelve then, throwing up on our living-room rug. Mom took one look at the overflowing ashtrays, the soiled walls, the broken records and half-filled cups, and she shook her head and smiled strangely and said, "This doesn't exist."

Nash and Frankie and Gene and I—those of us old enough to know what we were doing—froze in panic, fearing we might finally be punished for all we'd done. But Mom simply closed her eyes and walked out the way she'd come.

"Jesus," Gene said. "What do we have to *do?*" Which is probably the closest any of us came to understanding the way we were pushing, pushing, trying to get Mom to wake up and respond to us.

"I'm going after her," I said.

Nash tagged along behind me. We found Mom in the tall grass lining the mouth of the river that flowed into our bay. Birds often gathered there when the tide ebbed, and that day some ducks were feeding, upending themselves so abruptly that their heads seemed to turn without transition into fat pointed tails. Mom was sitting cross-legged, watching them and talking to herself: at first we thought she was repeating some of the phrases from her book. We had read it all the way through by then; the eight of us had sat near our altar while Mom was away, reading passages in mocking voices and making fun of them. *There is no pain,* we'd read. *There is no guilt. There is no blame. Life is what you believe it is. You are the source of your world.* We'd laughed, but our laughter was bitter; we knew how false that was.

Mom's eyes stayed on the ducks as we approached her. "What's she saying?" Nash whispered.

We strained our ears, expecting to hear one of her formulas, but what we heard instead was, "Heads. Tails. Heads. Tails. Heads." And when I touched Mom lightly on the arm, when I whispered, "Are you all right?" she pulled her arm away and closed her eyes and said, "I have nothing. Nothing is mine."

•

During that first year after Mom broke down, when she was in and out of the hospital and our lives were more chaotic than they'd ever been, Nash and Frankie persuaded their mothers to take us in. We stayed in that white shack and that broken-down trailer for weeks at a stretch, and Queenie and Joan, whom Gene and Ellen and I had always, secretly despised, fed us and lied to the snooping social workers and forged Mom's name on our report cards and on the checks Taddy occasionally sent. And when Gene and I got picked up for shoplifting, it was Queenie and Joan who came down to the record store and lied to the manager as boldly as Nash had once lied to Mom.

"They've never done it before," Queenie said. She looked at the tapes the manager had pulled from our pockets, and she shook her head.

"They'll never do it again," Joan said.

Gene and I looked at each other. "Never," we said to the manager, when Queenie poked us with her elbow, and by the time she and Joan were done with us, we meant it. Mom had come home that week—for good, as things turned out—but Queenie and Joan didn't take us to her. Instead, they drove us to an isolated spot near the railroad bridge, where they parked the car and lit into us.

"If you were my kids," Queenie said grimly, "I'd straighten you out in a hurry." Her own kids, I thought, were as twisted as taffy, but this didn't seem the moment to point that out. Queenie leaned back over the torn car seat, one fat arm lying in front of me like a sausage. Joan sat with her legs drawn up, her bleached head bobbing in agreement. In the back seat, between Gene and me, the splotched mongrel that Nash despised yawned and drew her lips back from her teeth and began nipping at the fleas on her belly.

"Juvie court," Queenie said. "You wanna end up in front of that weasel-faced judge?"

"The Welfare's gonna be in your face," Joan said. "Once they get hold of you, won't *nobody* see you again."

While Gene and I glared at the dog between us, Queenie and Joan laid out what would have happened to us if they'd failed to talk the record-store manager out of pressing charges: policemen in uniforms, and then an investigation; horny-handed men and hard-faced women from the county offices. Mom pried away from us and from Ellen too, and then Ellen and Gene and I separated from each other. Each of us off in a stranger's house, sharing meals and rooms with people bound to us only by legal papers. Interviews. Progress reports. And somewhere, Mom praying alone to a dim candle.

"What the hell's wrong with you?" Queenie said. "The three of you, you've got everything—that big house, and a mother who loves you. So she's having a little trouble. You could give her a break."

A tanker passed through the canal while Gene and I listened, and when I looked at him I knew we were thinking the same thing: that we could throw open the doors of Queenie's battered white Impala, hurl ourselves into the swift current, grab hold of the steel rings on the tanker's red stern and sail away. But instead we sat and listened until those mothers were done with us, and after they brought us home and we had a talk with Ellen, we changed our lives.

We had managed to lose both Taddy and our other father, and when we understood that we might lose Mom for good—not just her attention but her presence, her fine smooth hands, her back straight against a wooden chair—we struggled to ease her back into daily life. I made the grocery list for our first joint foray to the store: bread, potatoes, frozen fish sticks, milk, tuna, cookies, fruit. Mom drove. Gene pushed the shopping cart and Ellen held Mom's hand while Mom slowly, slowly, pulled items from the shelves. She turned a strange yellow under the fluorescent lights, and once she froze, paralyzed by my mistake: I had written "cookies" on the list when I should have specified "Oreos."

The next time we ventured out, I wrote down brand names and package sizes and we did better. We cooked together, we cleaned up and did the dishes and the laundry together, and we changed beds like a drill team, a person for each corner of the sheet. For a while we moved through our house like a four-bodied being, and we only split into our separate selves when Mom put the Church of the New Reason behind her and embraced the medieval mystics instead. She started keeping a diary, which she left out where we could read it. *We are guilty by nature,* she wrote, as if that might explain our acts. *Sinful from birth. Only in joyful union with God can we be forgiven.* She read Julian of Norwich and Walter Hilton and *The Cloud of Unknowing,* and when we asked her what was going on she told us not to worry. She was practicing the prayer of quiet, she said. The prayer of recollection. We huddled in corners and waited for her to disappear again.

But she was healed; or at least changed, at least safe. She seldom went out except to go to work and she never made any friends, but when she left the house in the morning we began to feel reasonably sure she'd return at night. Gene and Ellen and I were so grateful that we turned our backs on Nash and Frankie and their families, blaming them for what had happened to us. They had read the book that Mom believed in. They had watched her odd behavior. Nash had heard her flip between the yes and no of life like a gambler gone mad with a quarter. We couldn't let her and the others see any more, and we hoped with all our hearts that we'd never see Queenie and Joan again. Gene and Ellen and I took to walking along the railroad tracks to another bus stop, where we could wait with strangers, and as we did we told stories about Queenie and Joan and their houses and our former friends.

"Their dog sleeps in the cupboard," Ellen said. "In with the pots." She gnawed at the skin around her thumbnail, already bloody and torn. The strain had told on all of us.

"Queenie never washes," Gene said. His face was narrow and pinched. "She's so fat, I can't believe those men give her money."

"Nash and Frankie are really half-sisters," I said. "The same man made both of them, even though they have different mothers." I felt a cold pain in my chest when I betrayed that confidence, but it passed soon enough.

We saw Nash and the others at school, but we ignored them, and after the first few mocking encounters they ignored us back. Once, across a crowded hall, Nash laughed and gave me the finger when she saw me in the blouse and pleated skirt Mom and I had bought together. She danced off in her fringed buckskin vest, out of my sight, out of my life, and when she and her band took up with some other kids who lived closer to school, news of their exploits came to us like distant legends.

Andrea Barrett is the author of the novels *Lucid Stars, Secret Harmonies* and, most recently, *The Middle Kingdom.* Her stories have appeared in a number of magazines. She and her husband make their home in Rochester, New York.

RAYMOND CARVER

Two versions of "A Small, Good Thing" were actually published. The story first appeared as "The Bath," in Raymond Carver's second collection, *What We Talk About When We Talk About Love*. But he went back to the story because he considered it "unfinished business." "I wrote the story and I didn't go far enough with it," he told an interviewer. "I saw a place to stop it and I stopped it . . . but the notion of what could have happened stayed with me."* He worked further and what finally emerged was "A Small, Good Thing," which is more than twice the length of the first version. Of it, and of "Cathedral" and other later stories, Carver said, "These are fuller, more generous somehow. I went as far as I wanted to go with reducing the stories to bare bones minimums."

"Every good thing that has happened to me during the last several years has been an incentive to do more and do better," Carver told interviewers in 1984. "I know I've felt that recently in writing . . . poems, and it's affecting my fiction as well. I'm more sure of my voice, more sure of *something*. I felt a bit tentative when I started writing those poems, maybe partly because I hadn't written any for so long, but I soon found a voice—a voice that gave me confidence."

Another interviewer, Kasia Boddy, commented to Carver: "Anne Tyler wrote that the reason you write such good stories is because you're not

*** (The full interviews from which these quotes are taken appear in *Conversations with Raymond Carver*, edited by Marshall Bruce Gentry and William L. Stull, University Press of Mississippi, Jackson and London, 1990.)**

saving the best things up for writing a novel." He replied: "She said I was a 'spendthrift.' That's good. I think that a writer ought to spend himself on whatever he's doing, whether it's a poem or a story, because you have to feel like the well is not going to run dry; you have to feel that there's more where that came from. If a writer starts holding back, for any reason whatsoever, that can be a very bad thing. I've always squandered."

A SMALL, GOOD THING

SATURDAY afternoon she drove to the bakery in the shopping center. After looking through a loose-leaf binder with photographs of cakes taped onto the pages, she ordered chocolate, the child's favorite. The cake she chose was decorated with a space ship and launching pad under a sprinkling of white stars, and a planet made of red frosting at the other end. His name, SCOTTY, would be in green letters beneath the planet. The baker, who was an older man with a thick neck, listened without saying anything when she told him the child would be eight years old next Monday. The baker wore a white apron that looked like a smock. Straps cut under his arms, went around in back and then to the front again, where they were secured under his heavy waist. He wiped his hands on his apron as he listened to her. He kept his eyes down on the photographs and let her talk. He let her take her time. He'd just come to work and he'd be there all night, baking, and he was in no real hurry.

She gave the baker her name, Ann Weiss, and her telephone number. The cake would be ready on Monday morning, just out of the oven, in plenty of time for the child's party that afternoon. The baker was not jolly. There were no pleasantries between them, just the minimum exchange of words, the necessary information. He made her feel uncomfortable, and she didn't like that. While he was bent over the counter with the pencil in his hand, she studied his coarse features and wondered if he'd ever done anything else with his life besides be a baker. She was a mother and thirty-three years old, and it seemed to her that everyone, especially someone the baker's age—a man old enough to be her father—must have children who'd gone through this special time of cakes and birthday parties. There must be that between them, she thought. But he was abrupt with her—not rude, just abrupt. She gave up trying to make friends with him. She looked into the back of the bakery and could see a long, heavy wooden table with aluminum pie pans stacked at one end; and beside the table a metal container filled with empty racks. There was an enormous oven. A radio was playing country-Western music.

The baker finished printing the information on the special order card and closed up the binder. He looked at her and said, "Monday morning." She thanked him and drove home.

On Monday morning, the birthday boy was walking to school with another boy. They were passing a bag of potato chips back and forth and the birthday boy was trying to find out what his friend intended to give him for his birthday that afternoon. Without looking, the birthday boy stepped off the curb at an intersection and was immediately knocked down by a car. He fell on his side with his head in the gutter and his legs out in the road. His eyes were closed, but his legs moved back and forth as if he were trying to climb over something. His friend dropped the potato chips and started to cry. The car had gone a hundred feet or so and stopped in the middle of the road. The man in the driver's seat looked back over his shoulder. He waited until the boy got unsteadily to his feet. The boy wobbled a little. He looked dazed, but okay. The driver put the car into gear and drove away.

The birthday boy didn't cry, but he didn't have anything to say about anything either. He wouldn't answer when his friend asked him what it felt like to be hit by a car. He walked home, and his friend went on to school. But after the birthday boy was inside his house and was telling his mother about it—she sitting beside him on the sofa, holding his hands in her lap, saying, "Scotty, honey, are you sure you feel all right, baby?" thinking she would call the doctor anyway—he suddenly lay back on the sofa, closed his eyes, and went limp. When she couldn't wake him up, she hurried to the telephone and called her husband at work. Howard told her to remain calm, remain calm, and then he called an ambulance for the child and left for the hospital himself.

Of course, the birthday party was canceled. The child was in the hospital with a mild concussion and suffering from shock. There'd been vomiting, and his lungs had taken in fluid which needed pumping out that afternoon. Now he simply seemed to be in a very deep sleep—but no coma, Dr. Francis had emphasized, no coma, when he saw the alarm in the parents' eyes. At eleven o'clock that night, when the boy seemed to be resting comfortably enough after the many X-rays and the lab work, and it was just a matter of his waking up and coming around, Howard left the hospital. He and Ann had been at the hospital with the child since that afternoon, and he was going home for a short while to bathe and change clothes. "I'll be back in an hour," he said. She nodded. "It's fine," she said. "I'll be right here." He kissed her on the forehead, and they touched hands. She sat in the chair beside the bed and looked at the child. She was waiting for him to wake up and be all right. Then she could begin to relax.

Howard drove home from the hospital. He took the wet, dark streets very fast, then caught himself and slowed down. Until now, his life had gone smoothly and to his satisfaction—college, marriage, another year of college for the advanced degree in business, a junior partnership in an investment firm. Fatherhood. He was happy and, so far, lucky—he knew that. His parents were still living, his brothers and his sister were established, his friends from college had gone out to take their places in the world. So far, he had kept away from any real harm, from those forces he knew existed and that could cripple or bring down a man if the luck went bad, if things suddenly turned. He pulled into the driveway and parked. His left leg began to tremble. He sat in the car for a minute and tried to deal with the present situation in a rational manner. Scotty had been hit by a car and was in the hospital, but he was going to be all right. Howard closed his eyes and ran his hand over his face. He got out of the car and went up to the front door. The dog was barking inside the house. The telephone rang and rang while he unlocked the door and fumbled for the light switch. He shouldn't have left the hospital, he shouldn't have. "Goddamn it!" he said. He picked up the receiver and said, "I just walked in the door!"

"There's a cake here that wasn't picked up," the voice on the other end of the line said.

"What are you saying?" Howard asked.

"A cake," the voice said. "A sixteen-dollar cake."

Howard held the receiver against his ear, trying to understand. "I don't know anything about a cake," he said. "Jesus, what are you talking about?"

"Don't hand me that," the voice said.

Howard hung up the telephone. He went into the kitchen and poured himself some whiskey. He called the hospital. But the child's condition remained the same; he was still sleeping and nothing had changed there. While water poured into the tub, Howard lathered his face and shaved. He'd just stretched out in the tub and closed his eyes when the telephone rang again. He hauled himself out, grabbed a towel, and hurried through the house, saying, "Stupid, stupid," for having left the hospital. But when he picked up the receiver and shouted, "Hello!" there was no sound at the other end of the line. Then the caller hung up.

He arrived back at the hospital a little after midnight. Ann still sat in the chair beside the bed. She looked up at Howard, and then she looked back at the child. The child's eyes stayed closed, the head was still wrapped in bandages. His breathing was quiet and regular. From an apparatus over the bed hung a bottle of glucose with a tube running from the bottle to the boy's arm.

"How is he?" Howard said. "What's all this?" waving at the glucose and the tube.

"Dr. Francis's orders," she said. "He needs nourishment. He needs to keep up his strength. Why doesn't he wake up, Howard? I don't understand, if he's all right."

Howard put his hand against the back of her head. He ran his fingers through her hair. "He's going to be all right. He'll wake up in a little while. Dr. Francis knows what's what."

After a time, he said, "Maybe you should go home and get some rest. I'll stay here. Just don't put up with this creep who keeps calling. Hang up right away."

"Who's calling?" she asked.

"I don't know who, just somebody with nothing better to do than call up people. You go on now."

She shook her head. "No," she said, "I'm fine."

"Really," he said. "Go home for a while, and then come back and spell me in the morning. It'll be all right. What did Dr. Francis say? He said Scotty's going to be all right. We don't have to worry. He's just sleeping now, that's all."

A nurse pushed the door open. She nodded at them as she went to the bedside. She took the left arm out from under the covers and put her fingers on the wrist, found the pulse, then consulted her watch. In a little while, she put the arm back under the covers and moved to the foot of the bed, where she wrote something on a clipboard attached to the bed.

"How is he?" Ann said. Howard's hand was a weight on her shoulder. She was aware of the pressure from his fingers.

"He's stable," the nurse said. Then she said, "Doctor will be in again shortly. Doctor's back in the hospital. He's making rounds right now."

"I was saying maybe she'd want to go home and get a little rest," Howard said. "After the doctor comes," he said.

"She could do that," the nurse said. "I think you should both feel free to do that, if you wish." The nurse was a big Scandinavian woman with blond hair. There was the trace of an accent in her speech.

"We'll see what the doctor says," Ann said. "I want to talk to the doctor. I don't think he should keep sleeping like this. I don't think that's a good sign." She brought her hand up to her eyes and let her head come forward a little. Howard's grip tightened on her shoulder, and then his hand moved up to her neck, where his fingers began to knead the muscles there.

"Dr. Francis will be here in a few minutes," the nurse said. Then she left the room.

Howard gazed at his son for a time, the small chest quietly rising and falling under the covers. For the first time since the terrible minutes after Ann's telephone call to him at his office, he felt a genuine fear starting in his limbs. He began shaking his head. Scotty was fine, but instead of sleeping at home in his own bed, he was in a hospital bed with bandages around his head and a tube in his arm. But this help was what he needed right now.

Dr. Francis came in and shook hands with Howard, though they'd just seen each other a few hours before. Ann got up from the chair. "Doctor?"

"Ann," he said and nodded. "Let's just first see how he's doing," the doctor said. He moved to the side of the bed and took the boy's pulse. He peeled back one eyelid and then the other. Howard and Ann stood beside the doctor and watched. Then the doctor turned back the covers and listened to the boy's heart and lungs with his stethoscope. He pressed his fingers here and there on the abdomen. When he was finished, he went to the end of the bed and studied the chart. He noted the time, scribbled something on the chart, and then looked at Howard and Ann.

"Doctor, how is he?" Howard said. "What's the matter with him exactly?"

"Why doesn't he wake up?" Ann said.

The doctor was a handsome, big-shouldered man with a tanned face. He wore a three-piece blue suit, a striped tie, and ivory cufflinks. His gray hair was combed along the sides of his head, and he looked as if he had just come from a concert. "He's all right," the doctor said. "Nothing to shout about, he could be better, I think. But he's all right. Still, I wish he'd wake up. He should wake up pretty soon." The doctor looked at the boy again. "We'll know some more in a couple of hours, after the results of a few more tests are in. But he's all right, believe me, except for the hairline fracture of the skull. He does have that."

"Oh, no," Ann said.

"And a bit of a concussion, as I said before. Of course, you know he's in shock," the doctor said. "Sometimes you see this in shock cases. This sleeping."

"But he's out of any real danger?" Howard said. "You said before he's not in a coma. You wouldn't call this a coma, then—would you, doctor?" Howard waited. He looked at the doctor.

"No, I don't want to call it a coma," the doctor said and glanced over at the boy once more. "He's just in a very deep sleep. It's a restorative measure the body is taking on its own. He's out of any real danger, I'd say that for certain, yes. But we'll know more when he wakes up and the other tests are in," the doctor said.

"It's a coma," Ann said. "Of sorts."

"It's not a coma yet, not exactly," the doctor said. "I wouldn't want to call it coma. Not yet, anyway. He's suffered shock. In shock cases, this kind of reaction is common enough; it's a temporary reaction to bodily trauma. Coma. Well, coma is a deep, prolonged unconsciousness, something that could go on for days, or weeks even. Scotty's not in that area, not as far as we can tell. I'm certain his condition will show improvement by morning. I'm betting that it will. We'll know more when he wakes up, which shouldn't be long now. Of course, you may do as you like, stay here or go home for a time. But by all means feel free to leave the hospital for a while if you want. This is not easy, I know." The doctor gazed at the boy again, watching him, and then he turned to Ann and said, "You try not to worry, little mother. Believe me, we're doing all that can be done. It's just a question of a little more time now." He nodded at her, shook hands with Howard again, and then he left the room.

Ann put her hand over the child's forehead. "At least he doesn't have a fever," she said. Then she said, "My God, he feels so cold, though. Howard? Is he supposed to feel like this? Feel his head."

Howard touched the child's temples. His own breathing had slowed. "I think he's supposed to feel this way right now," he said. "He's in shock, remember? That's what the doctor said. The doctor was just in here. He would have said something if Scotty wasn't okay."

Ann stood there a while longer, working her lip with her teeth. Then she moved over to her chair and sat down.

Howard sat in the chair next to her chair. They looked at each other. He wanted to say something else and reassure her, but he was afraid, too. He took her hand and put it in his lap, and this made him feel better, her hand being there. He picked up her hand and squeezed it. Then he just held her hand. They sat like that for a while, watching the boy and not talking. From time to time, he squeezed her hand. Finally, she took her hand away.

"I've been praying," she said.

He nodded.

She said, "I almost thought I'd forgotten how, but it came back to me. All I had to do was close my eyes and say, 'Please God, help us—help Scotty,' and then the rest was easy. The words were right there. Maybe if you prayed, too," she said to him.

"I've already prayed," he said. "I prayed this afternoon—yesterday afternoon, I mean—after you called, while I was driving to the hospital. I've been praying," he said.

"That's good," she said. For the first time, she felt they were together in it, this trouble. She realized with a start that, until now, it had only been happening to her and to Scotty. She hadn't let Howard into it, though he was there and needed all along. She felt glad to be his wife.

The same nurse came in and took the boy's pulse again and checked the flow from the bottle hanging above the bed.

In an hour, another doctor came in. He said his name was Parsons, from Radiology. He had a bushy mustache. He was wearing loafers, a Western shirt, and a pair of jeans.

"We're going to take him downstairs for more pictures," he told them. "We need to do some more pictures, and we want to do a scan."

"What's that?" Ann said. "A scan?" She stood between this new doctor and the bed. "I thought you'd already taken all your X-rays."

"I'm afraid we need some more," he said. "Nothing to be alarmed about. We just need some more pictures, and we want to do a brain scan on him."

"My God," Ann said.

"It's perfectly normal procedure in cases like this," this new doctor said. "We just need to find out for sure why he isn't back awake yet. It's normal medical procedure, and nothing to be alarmed about. We'll be taking him down in a few minutes," this doctor said.

In a little while, two orderlies came into the room with a gurney. They were black-haired, dark-complexioned men in white uniforms, and they said a few words to each other in a foreign tongue as they unhooked the boy from the tube and moved him from his bed to the gurney. Then they wheeled him from the room. Howard and Ann got on the same elevator. Ann gazed at the child. She closed her eyes as the elevator began its descent. The orderlies stood at either end of the gurney without saying anything, though once one of the men made a comment to the other in their own language, and the other man nodded slowly in response.

Later that morning, just as the sun was beginning to lighten the windows in the waiting room outside the X-ray department, they brought the boy out and moved him back up to his room. Howard and Ann rode up on the elevator with him once more, and once more they took up their places beside the bed.

They waited all day, but still the boy did not wake up. Occasionally, one of them would leave the room to go downstairs to the cafeteria to drink coffee and then, as if suddenly remembering and feeling guilty, get up from the table and hurry back to the room. Dr. Francis came again that afternoon and examined the boy once more and then left after telling them he was coming along and could wake up at any minute now. Nurses, different nurses from the night before, came in from time to time. Then a young woman from the lab knocked and entered the room. She wore white slacks and a white blouse and carried a little tray of things which she put on the stand beside the bed. Without a word to them, she took blood from the boy's arm. Howard closed his eyes as the woman found the right place on the boy's arm and pushed the needle in.

"I don't understand this," Ann said to the woman.

"Doctor's orders," the young woman said. "I do what I'm told. They say draw that one, I draw. What's wrong with him, anyway?" she said. "He's a sweetie."

"He was hit by a car," Howard said. "A hit-and-run."

The young woman shook her head and looked again at the boy. Then she took her tray and left the room.

"Why won't he wake up?" Ann said. "Howard? I want some answers from these people."

Howard didn't say anything. He sat down again in the chair and crossed one leg over the other. He rubbed his face. He looked at his son and then he settled back in the chair, closed his eyes, and went to sleep.

Ann walked to the window and looked out at the parking lot. It was night, and cars were driving into and out of the parking lot with their lights on. She stood at the window with her hands gripping the sill, and knew in her heart that they were into something now, something hard. She was afraid, and her teeth began to chatter until she tightened her jaws. She saw a big car stop in front of the hospital and someone, a woman in a long coat, get into the car. She wished she were that woman and somebody, anybody, was driving her away from here to somewhere else, a place where she would find Scotty waiting for her when she stepped out of the car, ready to say *Mom* and let her gather him in her arms.

In a little while, Howard woke up. He looked at the boy again. Then he got up from the chair, stretched, and went over to stand beside her at the window. They both stared out at the parking lot. They didn't say anything. But they seemed to feel each other's insides now, as though the worry had made them transparent in a perfectly natural way.

The door opened and Dr. Francis came in. He was wearing a different suit and tie this time. His gray hair was combed along the sides of his head, and he looked as if he had just shaved. He went straight to the bed and examined the boy. "He ought to have come around by now. There's just no good reason for this," he said. "But I can tell you we're all convinced he's out of any danger. We'll just feel better when he wakes up. There's no reason, absolutely none, why he shouldn't come around. Very soon. Oh, he'll have himself a dilly of a headache when he does, you can count on that. But all of his signs are fine. They're as normal as can be."

"It is a coma, then?" Ann said.

The doctor rubbed his smooth cheek. "We'll call it that for the time being, until he wakes up. But you must be worn out. This is hard. I know this is hard. Feel free to go out for a bite," he said. "It would do you good. I'll put a nurse in here while you're gone if you'll feel better about going. Go and have yourselves something to eat."

"I couldn't eat anything," Ann said.

"Do what you need to do, of course," the doctor said. "Anyway, I wanted to tell you that all the signs are good, the tests are negative, nothing showed up at all, and just as soon as he wakes up he'll be over the hill."

"Thank you, doctor," Howard said. He shook hands with the doctor again. The doctor patted Howard's shoulder and went out.

"I suppose one of us should go home and check on things," Howard said. "Slug needs to be fed, for one thing."

"Call one of the neighbors," Ann said. "Call the Morgans. Anyone will feed a dog if you ask them to."

"All right," Howard said. After a while, he said, "Honey, why don't *you* do it? Why don't you go home and check on things, and then come back? It'll do you good. I'll be right here with him. Seriously," he said. "We need to keep up our strength on this. We'll want to be here for a while even after he wakes up."

"Why don't *you* go?" she said. "Feed Slug. Feed yourself."

"I already went," he said. "I was gone for exactly an hour and fifteen minutes. You go home for an hour and freshen up. Then come back."

She tried to think about it, but she was too tired. She closed her eyes and tried to think about it again. After a time, she said, "Maybe I *will* go home for a few minutes. Maybe if I'm not just sitting right here watching him every second, he'll wake up and be all right. You know? Maybe he'll wake up if I'm not here. I'll go home and take a bath and put on clean clothes. I'll feed Slug. Then I'll come back."

"I'll be right here," he said. "You go on home, honey. I'll keep an eye on things here." His eyes were bloodshot and small, as if he'd been drinking for a long time. His clothes were rumpled. His beard had come out again. She touched his face, and then she took her hand back. She understood he wanted to be by himself for a while, not have to talk or share his worry for a time. She picked her purse up from the nightstand, and he helped her into her coat.

"I won't be gone long," she said.

"Just sit and rest for a little while when you get home," he said. "Eat something. Take a bath. After you get out of the bath, just sit for a while and rest. It'll do you a world of good, you'll see. Then come back," he said. "Let's try not to worry. You heard what Dr. Francis said."

She stood in her coat for a minute trying to recall the doctor's exact words, looking for any nuances, any hint of something behind his words other than what he had said. She tried to remember if his expression had changed any when he bent over to examine the child. She remembered the way his features had composed themselves as he rolled back the child's eyelids and then listened to his breathing.

She went to the door, where she turned and looked back. She looked at the child, and then she looked at the father. Howard nodded. She stepped out of the room and pulled the door closed behind her.

She went past the nurses' station and down to the end of the corridor, looking for the elevator. At the end of the corridor, she turned to her right and entered a little waiting room where a Negro family sat in wicker chairs. There was a middle-aged man in a khaki shirt and pants, a baseball cap pushed back on his head. A large woman wearing a housedress and slippers was slumped in one of the chairs. A teenaged girl in jeans, hair done in dozens of little braids, lay stretched out in one of the chairs smoking a cigarette, her legs crossed at the ankles. The family swung their eyes to Ann as she entered the room. The little table was littered with hamburger wrappers and Styrofoam cups.

"Franklin," the large woman said as she roused herself. "Is it about Franklin?" Her eyes widened. "Tell me now, lady," the woman said. "Is it about Franklin?" She was trying to rise from her chair, but the man had closed his hand over her arm.

"Here, here," he said. "Evelyn."

"I'm sorry," Ann said. "I'm looking for the elevator. My son is in the hospital, and now I can't find the elevator."

"Elevator is down that way, turn left," the man said as he aimed a finger.

The girl drew on her cigarette and stared at Ann. Her eyes were narrowed to slits, and her broad lips parted slowly as she let the smoke escape. The Negro woman let her head fall on her shoulder and looked away from Ann, no longer interested.

"My son was hit by a car," Ann said to the man. She seemed to need to explain herself. "He has a concussion and a little skull fracture, but he's going to be all right. He's in shock now, but it might be some kind of coma, too. That's what really worries us, the coma part. I'm going out for a little while, but my husband is with him. Maybe he'll wake up while I'm gone."

"That's too bad," the man said and shifted in the chair. He shook his head. He looked down at the table, and then he looked back at Ann. She was still standing there. He said, "Our Franklin, he's on the operating table. Somebody cut him. Tried to kill him. There was a fight where he was at. At this party. They say he was just standing and watching. Not bothering nobody. But that don't mean nothing these days. Now he's on the operating table. We're just hoping and praying, that's all we can do now." He gazed at her steadily.

Ann looked at the girl again, who was still watching her, and at the older woman, who kept her head down, but whose eyes were now closed. Ann saw the lips moving silently, making words. She had an urge to ask what those words were. She wanted to talk more with these people who were in the same kind of waiting she was in. She was afraid, and they were afraid. They had that in common. She would have liked to have said something else about the accident, told them more about Scotty, that it had happened on the day of his birthday, Monday, and that he was still unconscious. Yet she didn't know how to begin. She stood looking at them without saying anything more.

She went down the corridor the man had indicated and found the elevator. She waited a minute in front of the closed doors, still wondering if she was doing the right thing. Then she put out her finger and touched the button.

She pulled into the driveway and cut the engine. She closed her eyes and leaned her head against the wheel for a minute. She listened to the ticking sounds the engine made as it began to cool. Then she got out of the car. She could hear the dog barking inside the house. She went to the front door, which was unlocked. She went inside and turned on lights and put on a kettle of water for tea. She opened some dogfood and fed Slug on the back porch. The dog ate in hungry little smacks. It kept running into the kitchen to see that she was going to stay. As she sat down on the sofa with her tea, the telephone rang.

"Yes!" she said as she answered. "Hello!"

"Mrs. Weiss," a man's voice said. It was five o'clock in the morning, and she thought she could hear machinery or equipment of some kind in the background.

"Yes, yes! What is it?" she said. "This is Mrs. Weiss. This is she. What is it, please?" She listened to whatever it was in the background. "Is it Scotty, for Christ's sake?"

"Scotty," the man's voice said. "It's about Scotty, yes. It has to do with Scotty, that problem. Have you forgotten about Scotty?" the man said. Then he hung up.

She dialed the hospital's number and asked for the third floor. She demanded information about her son from the nurse who answered the telephone. Then she asked to speak to her husband. It was, she said, an emergency.

She waited, turning the telephone cord in her fingers. She closed her eyes and felt sick at her stomach. She would have to make herself eat. Slug came in from the back porch and lay down near her feet. He wagged his tail. She pulled at his ear while he licked her fingers. Howard was on the line.

"Somebody just called here," she said. She twisted the telephone cord. "He said it was about Scotty," she cried.

"Scotty's fine," Howard told her. "I mean, he's still sleeping. There's been no change. The nurse has been in twice since you've been gone. A nurse or else a doctor. He's all right."

"This man called. He said it was about Scotty," she told him.

"Honey, you rest for a little while, you need the rest. It must be that same caller I had. Just forget it. Come back down here after you've rested. Then we'll have breakfast or something."

"Breakfast," she said. "I don't want any breakfast."

"You know what I mean," he said. "Juice, something. I don't know. I don't know anything, Ann. Jesus, I'm not hungry, either. Ann, it's hard to talk now. I'm standing here at the desk. Dr. Francis is coming again at eight o'clock this morning. He's going to have something to tell us then, something more definite. That's what one of the nurses said. She didn't know any more than that. Ann? Honey, maybe we'll know something more then. At eight o'clock. Come back here before eight. Meanwhile, I'm right here and Scotty's all right. He's still the same," he added.

"I was drinking a cup of tea," she said, "when the telephone rang. They said it was about Scotty. There was a noise in the background. Was there a noise in the background on that call you had, Howard?"

"I don't remember," he said. "Maybe the driver of the car, maybe he's a psychopath and found out about Scotty somehow. But I'm here with him. Just rest like you were going to do. Take a bath and come back by seven or so, and we'll talk to the doctor together when he gets here. It's going to be all right, honey. I'm here, and there are doctors and nurses around. They say his condition is stable."

"I'm scared to death," she said.

She ran water, undressed, and got into the tub. She washed and dried quickly, not taking the time to wash her hair. She put on clean underwear, wool slacks, and a sweater. She went into the living room, where the dog looked up at her and let its tail thump once against the floor. It was just starting to get light outside when she went out to the car.

She drove into the parking lot of the hospital and found a space close to the front door. She felt she was in some obscure way responsible for what had happened to the child. She let her thoughts move to the Negro family. She remembered the name Franklin and the table that was covered with hamburger papers, and the teenaged girl staring at her as she drew on her cigarette. "Don't have children," she told the girl's image as she entered the front door of the hospital. "For God's sake, don't."

She took the elevator up to the third floor with two nurses who were just going on duty. It was Wednesday morning, a few minutes before seven. There was a page for a Dr. Madison as the elevator doors slid open on the third floor. She got off behind the nurses, who turned in the other direction and continued the conversation she had interrupted when she'd gotten into the elevator. She walked down the corridor to the little alcove where the Negro family had been waiting. They were gone now, but the chairs were scattered in such a way that it looked as if people had just jumped up from them the minute before. The tabletop was cluttered with the same cups and papers, the ashtray was filled with cigarette butts.

She stopped at the nurses' station. A nurse was standing behind the counter, brushing her hair and yawning.

"There was a Negro boy in surgery last night," Ann said. "Franklin was his name. His family was in the waiting room. I'd like to inquire about his condition."

A nurse who was sitting at a desk behind the counter looked up from a chart in front of her. The telephone buzzed and she picked up the receiver, but she kept her eyes on Ann.

"He passed away," said the nurse at the counter. The nurse held the hairbrush and kept looking at her. "Are you a friend of the family or what?"

"I met the family last night," Ann said. "My own son is in the hospital. I guess he's in shock. We don't know for sure what's wrong. I just wondered about Franklin, that's all. Thank you." She moved down the corridor. Elevator doors the same color as the walls slid open and a gaunt, bald man in white pants and white canvas shoes pulled a heavy cart off the elevator. She hadn't noticed these doors last night. The man wheeled the cart out into the corridor and stopped in front of the room nearest the elevator and consulted a clipboard. Then he reached down and slid a tray out of the cart. He rapped lightly on the door and entered the room. She could smell the unpleasant odors of warm food as she passed the cart. She hurried on without looking at any of the nurses and pushed open the door to the child's room.

Howard was standing at the window with his hands behind his back. He turned around as she came in.

"How is he?" she said. She went over to the bed. She dropped her purse on the floor beside the nightstand. It seemed to her she had been gone a long time. She touched the child's face. "Howard?"

"Dr. Francis was here a little while ago," Howard said. She looked at him closely and thought his shoulders were bunched a little.

"I thought he wasn't coming until eight o'clock this morning," she said quickly.

"There was another doctor with him. A neurologist."

"A neurologist," she said.

Howard nodded. His shoulders were bunching, she could see that.

"What'd they say, Howard? For Christ's sake, what'd they say? What is it?"

"They said they're going to take him down and run more tests on him, Ann. They think they're going to operate, honey. Honey, they *are* going to operate. They can't figure out why he won't wake up. It's more than just shock or concussion, they know that much now. It's in his skull, the fracture, it has something, something to do with that, they think. So they're going to operate. I tried to call you, but I guess you'd already left the house."

"Oh, God," she said. "Oh, please, Howard, please," she said, taking his arms.

"Look!" Howard said. "Scotty! Look, Ann!" He turned her toward the bed.

The boy had opened his eyes, then closed them. He opened them again now. The eyes stared straight ahead for a minute, then moved slowly in his head until they rested on Howard and Ann, then traveled away again.

"Scotty," his mother said, moving to the bed.

"Hey, Scott," his father said. "Hey, son."

They leaned over the bed. Howard took the child's hand in his hands and began to pat and squeeze the hand. Ann bent over the boy and kissed his forehead again and again. She put her hands on either side of his face. "Scotty, honey, it's Mommy and Daddy," she said. "Scotty?"

The boy looked at them, but without any sign of recognition. Then his mouth opened, his eyes scrunched closed, and he howled until he had no more air in his lungs. His face seemed to relax and soften then. His lips parted as his last breath was puffed through his throat and exhaled gently through the clenched teeth.

The doctors called it a hidden occlusion and said it was a one-in-a-million circumstance. Maybe if it could have been detected somehow and surgery undertaken immediately, they could have saved him. But more than likely not. In any case, what would they have been looking for? Nothing had shown up in the tests or in the X-rays.

Dr. Francis was shaken. "I can't tell you how badly I feel. I'm so very sorry, I can't tell you," he said as he led them into the doctors' lounge. There was a doctor sitting in a chair with his legs hooked over the back of another chair, watching an early-morning TV show. He was wearing a green deliveryroom outfit, loose green pants and green blouse, and a green cap that covered his hair. He looked at Howard and Ann and then looked at Dr. Francis. He got to his feet and turned off the set and went out of the room. Dr. Francis guided Ann to the sofa, sat down beside her, and began to talk in a low, consoling voice. At one point, he leaned over and embraced her. She could feel his chest rising and falling evenly against her shoulder. She kept her eyes open and let him hold her. Howard went into the bathroom, but he left the door open. After a violent fit of weeping, he ran water and washed his face. Then he came out and sat down at the little table that held a telephone. He looked at the telephone as though deciding what to do first. He made some calls. After a time, Dr. Francis used the telephone.

"Is there anything else I can do for the moment?" he asked them.

Howard shook his head. Ann stared at Dr. Francis as if unable to comprehend his words.

The doctor walked them to the hospital's front door. People were entering and leaving the hospital. It was eleven o'clock in the morning. Ann was aware of how slowly, almost reluctantly, she moved her feet. It seemed to her that Dr. Francis was making them leave when she felt they should stay, when it would be more the right thing to do to stay. She gazed out into the parking lot and then turned around and looked back at the front of the hospital. She began shaking her head. "No, no," she said. "I can't leave him here, no." She heard herself say that and thought how unfair it was that the only words that came out were the sort of words used on TV shows where people were stunned by violent or sudden deaths. She wanted her words to be her own. "No," she said, and for some reason the memory of the Negro woman's head lolling on the woman's shoulder came to her. "No," she said again.

"I'll be talking to you later in the day," the doctor was saying to Howard. "There are still some things that have to be done, things that have to be cleared up to our satisfaction. Some things that need explaining."

"An autopsy," Howard said.

Dr. Francis nodded.

"I understand," Howard said. Then he said, "Oh, Jesus. No, I don't understand, doctor. I can't, I can't. I just can't."

Dr. Francis put his arm around Howard's shoulders. "I'm sorry. God, how I'm sorry." He let go of Howard's shoulders and held out his hand. Howard looked at the hand, and then he took it. Dr. Francis put his arms around Ann once more. He seemed full of some goodness she didn't understand. She let her head rest on his shoulder, but her eyes stayed open. She kept looking at the hospital. As they drove out of the parking lot, she looked back at the hospital.

At home, she sat on the sofa with her hands in her coat pockets. Howard closed the door to the child's room. He got the coffee-maker going and then he found an empty box. He had thought to pick up some of the child's things that were scattered around the living room. But instead he sat down beside her on the sofa, pushed the box to one side, and leaned forward, arms between his knees. He began to weep. She pulled his head over into her lap and patted his shoulder. "He's gone," she said. She kept patting his shoulder. Over his sobs, she could hear the coffee-maker hissing in the kitchen. "There, there," she said tenderly. "Howard, he's gone. He's gone and now we'll have to get used to that. To being alone."

In a little while, Howard got up and began moving aimlessly around the room with the box, not putting anything into it, but collecting some things together on the floor at one end of the sofa. She continued to sit with her hands in her coat pockets. Howard put the box down and brought coffee into the living room. Later, Ann made calls to relatives. After each call had been placed and the party had answered, Ann would blurt out a few words and cry for a minute. Then she would quietly explain, in a measured voice, what had happened and tell them about arrangements. Howard took the box out to the garage, where he saw the child's bicycle. He dropped the box and sat down on the pavement beside the bicycle. He took hold of the bicycle awkwardly so that it leaned against his chest. He held it, the rubber pedal sticking into his chest. He gave the wheel a turn.

Ann hung up the telephone after talking to her sister. She was looking up another number when the telephone rang. She picked it up on the first ring.

"Hello," she said, and she heard something in the background, a humming noise. "Hello!" she said. "For God's sake," she said. "Who is this? What is it you want?"

"Your Scotty, I got him ready for you," the man's voice said. "Did you forget him?"

"You evil bastard!" she shouted into the receiver. "How can you do this, you evil son of a bitch?"

"Scotty," the man said. "Have you forgotten about Scotty?" Then the man hung up on her.

Howard heard the shouting and came in to find her with her head on her arms over the table, weeping. He picked up the receiver and listened to the dial tone.

Much later, just before midnight, after they had dealt with many things, the telephone rang again.

"You answer it," she said. "Howard, it's him, I know." They were sitting at the kitchen table with coffee in front of them. Howard had a small glass of whiskey beside his cup. He answered on the third ring.

"Hello," he said. "Who is this? Hello! Hello!" The line went dead. "He hung up," Howard said. "Whoever it was."

"It was him," she said. "That bastard. I'd like to kill him," she said. "I'd like to shoot him and watch him kick," she said.

"Ann, my God," he said.

"Could you hear anything?" she said. "In the background? A noise, machinery, something humming?"

"Nothing, really. Nothing like that," he said. "There wasn't much time. I think there was some radio music. Yes, there was a radio going, that's all I could tell. I don't know what in God's name is going on," he said.

She shook her head. "If I could, could get my hands on him." It came to her then. She knew who it was. Scotty, the cake, the telephone number. She pushed the chair away from the table and got up. "Drive me down to the shopping center," she said. "Howard."

"What are you saying?"

"The shopping center. I know who it is who's calling. I know who it is. It's the baker, the son-of-a-bitching baker, Howard. I had him bake a cake for Scotty's birthday. That's who's calling. That's who has the number and keeps calling us. To harass us about that cake. The baker, that bastard."

They drove down to the shopping center. The sky was clear and stars were out. It was cold, and they ran the heater in the car. They parked in front of the bakery. All of the shops and stores were closed, but there were cars at the far end of the lot in front of the movie theater. The bakery windows were dark, but when they looked through the glass they could see a light in the back room and, now and then, a big man in an apron moving in and out of the white, even light. Through the glass, she could see the display cases and some little tables with chairs. She tried the door. She rapped on the glass. But if the baker heard them, he gave no sign. He didn't look in their direction.

They drove around behind the bakery and parked. They got out of the car. There was a lighted window too high up for them to see inside. A sign near the back door said THE PANTRY BAKERY, SPECIAL ORDERS. She could hear faintly a radio playing inside and something creak—an oven door as it was pulled down? She knocked on the door and waited. Then she knocked again, louder. The radio was turned down and there was a scraping sound now, the distinct sound of something, a drawer, being pulled open and then closed.

Someone unlocked the door and opened it. The baker stood in the light and peered out at them. "I'm closed for business," he said. "What do you want at this hour? It's midnight. Are you drunk or something?"

She stepped into the light that fell through the open door. He blinked his heavy eyelids as he recognized her. "It's you," he said.

"It's me," she said. "Scotty's mother. This is Scotty's father. We'd like to come in."

The baker said, "I'm busy now. I have work to do."

She had stepped inside the doorway anyway. Howard came in behind her. The baker moved back. "It smells like a bakery in here. Doesn't it smell like a bakery in here, Howard?"

"What do you want?" the baker said. "Maybe you want your cake? That's it, you decided you want your cake. You ordered a cake, didn't you?"

"You're pretty smart for a baker," she said. "Howard, this is the man who's been calling us." She clenched her fists. She stared at him fiercely. There was a deep burning inside her, an anger that made her feel larger than herself, larger than either of these men.

"Just a minute here," the baker said. "You want to pick up your three-day-old-cake? That it? I don't want to argue with you, lady. There it sits over there, getting stale. I'll give it to you for half of what I quoted you. No. You want it? You can have it. It's no good to me, no good to anyone now. It cost me time and money to make that cake. If you want it, okay, if you don't, that's okay, too. I have to get back to work." He looked at them and rolled his tongue behind his teeth.

"More cakes," she said. She knew she was in control of it, of what was increasing in her. She was calm.

"Lady, I work sixteen hours a day in this place to earn a living," the baker said. He wiped his hands on his apron. "I work night and day in here, trying to make ends meet." A look crossed Ann's face that made the baker move back and say, "No trouble, now." He reached to the counter and picked up a rolling pin with his right hand and began to tap it against the palm of his other hand. "You want the cake or not? I have to get back to work. Bakers work at night," he said again. His eyes were small, mean-looking, she thought, nearly lost in the bristly flesh around his cheeks. His neck was thick with fat.

"I know bakers work at night," Ann said. "They make phone calls at night, too. You bastard," she said.

The baker continued to tap the rolling pin against his hand. He glanced at Howard. "Careful, careful," he said to Howard.

"My son's dead," she said with a cold, even finality. "He was hit by a car Monday morning. We've been waiting with him until he died. But, of course, you couldn't be expected to know that, could you? Bakers can't know everything—can they, Mr. Baker? But he's dead. He's dead, you bastard!" Just as suddenly as it had welled in her, the anger dwindled, gave way to something else, a dizzy feeling of nausea.

She leaned against the wooden table that was sprinkled with flour, put her hands over her face, and began to cry, her shoulders rocking back and forth. "It isn't fair," she said. "It isn't, isn't fair."

Howard put his hand at the small of her back and looked at the baker. "Shame on you," Howard said to him. "Shame."

The baker put the rolling pin back on the counter. He undid his apron and threw it on the counter. He looked at them, and then he shook his head slowly. He pulled a chair out from under the card table that held papers and receipts, an adding machine, and a telephone directory. "Please sit down," he said. "Let me get you a chair," he said to Howard. "Sit down now, please." The baker went into the front of the shop and returned with two little wrought-iron chairs. "Please sit down, you people."

Ann wiped her eyes and looked at the baker. "I wanted to kill you," she said. "I wanted you dead."

The baker had cleared a space for them at the table. He shoved the adding machine to one side, along with the stacks of notepaper and receipts. He pushed the telephone directory onto the floor, where it landed with a thud. Howard and Ann sat down and pulled their chairs up to the table. The baker sat down, too.

"Let me say how sorry I am," the baker said, putting his elbows on the table. "God alone knows how sorry. Listen to me. I'm just a baker. I don't claim to be anything else. Maybe once, maybe years ago, I was a different kind of human being. I've forgotten, I don't know for sure. But I'm not any longer, if I ever was. Now I'm just a baker. That don't excuse my doing what I did, I know. But I'm deeply sorry. I'm sorry for your son, and sorry for my part in this," the baker said. He spread his hands out on the table and turned them over to reveal his palms. "I don't have any children myself, so I can only imagine what you must be feeling. All I can say to you now is that I'm sorry. Forgive me, if you can," the baker said. "I'm not an evil man, I don't think. Not evil, like you said on the phone. You got to understand what it comes down to is I don't know how to act anymore, it would seem. Please," the man said, "let me ask you if you can find it in your hearts to forgive me?"

It was warm inside the bakery. Howard stood up from the table and took off his coat. He helped Ann from her coat. The baker looked at them for a minute and then nodded and got up from the table. He went to the oven and turned off some switches. He found cups and poured coffee from an electric coffee-maker. He put a carton of cream on the table, and a bowl of sugar.

"You probably need to eat something," the baker said. "I hope you'll eat some of my hot rolls. You have to eat and keep going. Eating is a small, good thing in a time like this," he said.

He served them warm cinnamon rolls just out of the oven, the icing still runny. He put butter on the table and knives to spread the butter. Then the baker sat down at the table with them. He waited. He waited until they each took a roll from the platter and began to eat. "It's good to eat something," he said, watching them. "There's more. Eat up. Eat all you want. There's all the rolls in the world in here."

They ate rolls and drank coffee. Ann was suddenly hungry, and the rolls were warm and sweet. She ate three of them, which pleased the baker. Then he began to talk. They listened carefully. Although they were tired and in anguish, they listened to what the baker had to say. They nodded when the baker began to speak of loneliness, and of the sense of doubt and limitation that had come to him in his middle years. He told them what it was like to be childless all these years. To repeat the days with the ovens endlessly full and endlessly empty. The party food, the celebrations he'd worked over. Icing knuckle-deep. The tiny wedding couples stuck into cakes. Hundreds of them, no, thousands by now. Birthdays. Just imagine all those candles burning. He had a necessary trade. He was a baker. He was glad he wasn't a florist. It was better to be feeding people. This was a better smell anytime than flowers.

"Smell this," the baker said, breaking open a dark loaf. "It's a heavy bread, but rich." They smelled it, then he had them taste it. It had the taste of molasses and coarse grains. They listened to him. They ate what they could. They swallowed the dark bread. It was like daylight under the fluorescent trays of light. They talked on into the early morning, the high, pale cast of light in the windows, and they did not think of leaving.

Raymond Carver, who died in 1988, was the author of three influential collections of stories—*Will You Please Be Quiet, Please?*, *What We Talk About When We Talk About Love*, and *Cathedral*, in which "A Small, Good Thing" appeared. *Where I'm Calling From*, Mr. Carver's New and Selected Stories, appeared in 1988. He also published four volumes of poetry. Mr. Carver taught at the Universities of Iowa, Texas, California and Syracuse, New York. He grew up in a small town in the Pacific Northwest, and at the time of his death lived in Port Angeles, Washington.

ANDREA LEE

"I wrote my first story at fourteen, sitting in the study hall of the Baldwin School in Bryn Mawr, Pennsylvania. I can remember with great clarity the hard chair, the high brown desks in a grid dotted with the hunched figures of girls in blue uniforms, the *cum laude* lists on the walls, the glum March light through leaded windows, and the ancient female despot who sat surveying us like a marcelled sphinx. In the midst of this stasis was the magical sense of something coming alive under my pen. The story, which drew heavily on de Maupassant, was the ironical tale of a Breton fisherman who nets a mermaid, with unhappy consequences. It was full of carefully researched expletives in dialect, and caused a gratifying stir in my English class. Almost better than the praise was the pleasure of going beyond the poetry I'd written since the age of five. Like poetry, the new form was shapely, energetic, and as versatile as Proteus.

"After college, where I wrote poetry and prose fiction under the guidance of Robert Fitzgerald and William Alfred, I found myself once again in the enchanted gloom of a study hall. This was Reading Room Number One of the Lenin Library in Moscow, which I was entitled to use as a participant in a student exchange. As distinguished Soviet scholars snored around me and snow fell on the Kremlin domes outside, I alternately gorged myself on Russian literature and worked on two projects. The first was to record images of Russia in journal form, and the second, to create a 'novel in stories' based on my childhood. Writing about Russia—the pieces appeared in *The New Yorker* and became the book *Russian Journal*—I tried to render real events in an episodic, descriptive form close to that of short fiction. In the childhood stories, completed several years later as the book *Sarah Phillips,* I attempted to convey truth on a different level—truth of atmosphere—in rearranging and embellishing memories, sharpening their significance by adding imaginary material.

" 'New African' is the central story in *Sarah Phillips.* It delineates the tension between old ways and new in an African-American family, and the equivocal pleasures of freedom, whether religious, political, or personal. Curiously enough, I didn't originally intend it for *Sarah Phillips.* I had an idea, instead, of using my memories of the First African Baptist Church of Philadelphia—the model for New African—to create a *New Yorker* memoir that would also be a portrait of the minister: my father, Dr. Charles Sumner Lee. After Fran Kiernan, then fiction editor at *The New Yorker,* suggested that what I wanted to say might come through best in a story, First African became New African, new characters appeared, and Sarah confronted her father the way I never had mine. Making a story of it meant I had license to trim, to twist, to steal from other lives, to invent. Writing 'New African' I experienced more pleasure of creation than I did in that first study hall, simply because it was glorious fun to take part of my own life and shape it into something alive in its own right."

NEW AFRICAN

ON a hot Sunday morning in the summer of 1963, I was sitting restlessly with my mother, my brother Matthew, and my aunts Lily, Emma, and May in a central pew of the New African Baptist Church. It was mid-August, and the hum of the big electric fans at the back of the church was almost enough to muffle my father's voice from the pulpit; behind me I could hear Mrs. Gordon, a stout, feeble old woman who always complained of dizziness, remark sharply to her daughter that at the rate the air-conditioning fund was growing, it might as well be for the next century. Facing the congregation, my father—who was Reverend Phillips to the rest of the world—seemed hot himself; he mopped his brow with a handkerchief and drank several glasses of ice water from the heavy pitcher on the table by the pulpit. I looked at him critically. He's still reading the text, I thought. Then he'll do the sermon, then the baptism, and it will be an hour, maybe two.

I rubbed my chin and then idly began to snap the elastic band that held my red straw hat in place. What I would really like to do, I decided, would be to go home, put on my shorts, and climb up into the tree house I had set up the day before with Matthew. We'd nailed an old bushel basket up in the branches of the big maple that stretched above the sidewalk in front of the house; it made a sort of crow's nest where you could sit comfortably, except for a few splinters, and read, or peer through the dusty leaves at the cars that passed down the quiet suburban road. There was shade and wind and a feeling of high adventure up in the treetop, where the air seemed to vibrate with the dry rhythms of the cicadas; it was as different as possible from church, where the packed congregation sat in a near-visible miasma of emotion and cologne, and trolleys passing in the city street outside set the stained-glass windows rattling.

I slouched between Mama and Aunt Lily and felt myself going limp with lassitude and boredom, as if the heat had melted my bones; the only thing about me with any character seemed to be my firmly starched eyelet dress. Below the scalloped hem, my legs were skinny and wiry, the legs of a ten-year-old amazon, scarred from violent adventures with bicycles and skates. A fingernail tapped my wrist; it was Aunt Emma, reaching across Aunt Lily to press a piece of butterscotch into my hand. When I slipped the candy into my mouth, it tasted faintly of Arpège; my mother and her three sisters were monumental women, ample of bust and slim of ankle, with a weakness for elegant footwear and French perfume. As they leaned back and forth to exchange discreet tidbits of gossip, they fanned themselves and me with fans from the Byron J. Wiggins Funeral Parlor. The fans, which were fluttering throughout the church, bore a depiction of the Good Shepherd: a hollow-eyed blond Christ holding three fat pink-cheeked children. This Christ resembled the Christ who stood among apostles on the stained-glass windows of the church. Deacon Wiggins, a thoughtful man, had also provided New African with a few dozen fans bearing the picture of a black child praying, but I rarely saw those in use.

There was little that was new or very African about the New African Baptist Church. The original congregation had been formed in 1813 by three young men from Philadelphia's large community of free blacks, and before many generations had passed, it had become spiritual home to a collection of prosperous, conservative, generally light-skinned parishioners. The church was a gray Gothic structure, set on the corner of a run-down street in South Philadelphia a dozen blocks below Rittenhouse Square and a few blocks west of the spare, clannish Italian neighborhoods that produced Frankie Avalon and Frank Rizzo. At the turn of the century, the neighborhood had been a tidy collection of brick houses with scrubbed marble steps—the homes of a group of solid citizens whom Booker T. Washington, in a centennial address to the church, described as "the ablest Negro businessmen of our generation." Here my father had grown up aspiring to preach to the congregation of New African—an ambition encouraged by my grandmother Phillips, a formidable churchwoman. Here, too, my mother and her sisters had walked with linked arms to Sunday services, exchanging affected little catchphrases of French and Latin they had learned at Girls' High.

In the 1950s many of the parishioners, seized by the national urge toward the suburbs, moved to newly integrated towns outside the city, leaving the streets around New African to fill with bottles and papers and loungers. The big church stood suddenly isolated. It had not been abandoned—on Sundays the front steps overflowed with members who had driven in—but there was a tentative feeling in the atmosphere of those Sunday mornings, as if through the muddle of social change, the future of New African had become unclear. Matthew and I, suburban children, felt a mixture of pride and animosity toward the church. On the one hand, it was a marvelous private domain, a richly decorated and infinitely suggestive playground where we were petted by a congregation that adored our father; on the other hand, it seemed a bit like a dreadful old relative in the city, one who forced us into tedious visits and who linked us to a past that came to seem embarrassingly primitive as we grew older.

I slid down in my seat, let my head roll back, and looked up at the blue arches of the church ceiling. Lower than these, in back of the altar, was an enormous gilded cross. Still lower, in a semicircle near the pulpit, sat the choir, flanked by two tall golden files of organ pipes, and below the choir was a somber crescent of dark-suited deacons. In front, at the center of everything, his bald head gleaming under the lights, was Daddy. On summer Sundays he wore white robes, and when he raised his arms, the heavy material fell in curving folds like the ridged petals of an Easter lily. Usually when I came through the crowd to kiss him after the service, his cheek against my lips felt wet and gravelly with sweat and a new growth of beard sprouted since morning. Today, however, was a baptismal Sunday, and I wouldn't have a chance to kiss him until he was freshly shaven and cool from the shower he took after the ceremony. The baptismal pool was in an alcove to the left of the altar; it had mirrored walls and red velvet curtains, and above it, swaying on a string, hung a stuffed white dove.

Daddy paused in the invocation and asked the congregation to pray. The choir began to sing softly:

Blessed assurance,
Jesus is mine!
Oh what a foretaste
Of glory divine!

In the middle of the hymn, I edged my head around my mother's cool, muscular arm (she swam every day of the summer) and peered at Matthew. He was sitting bolt upright holding a hymnal and a pencil, his long legs inside his navy-blue summer suit planted neatly in front of him, his freckled thirteen-year-old face that was so like my father's wearing not the demonic grin it bore when we played alone but a maddeningly composed, attentive expression. "Two hours!" I mouthed at him, and pulled back at a warning pressure from my mother. Then I joined in the singing, feeling disappointed: Matthew had returned me a glance of scorn. Just lately he had started acting very superior and tolerant about tedious Sunday mornings. A month before, he'd been baptized, marching up to the pool in a line of white-robed children as the congregation murmured happily about Reverend Phillips's son. Afterward Mrs. Pinkston, a tiny, yellow-skinned old woman with a blind left eye, had come up to me and given me a painful hug, whispering that she was praying night and day for the pastor's daughter to hear the call as well.

I bit my fingernails whenever I thought about baptism; the subject brought out a deep-rooted balkiness in me. Ever since I could remember, Matthew and I had made a game of dispelling the mysteries of worship with a gleeful secular eye: we knew how the bread and wine were prepared for Communion, and where Daddy bought his robes (Ekhardt Brothers, in North Philadelphia, makers also of robes for choirs, academicians, and judges). Yet there was an unassailable magic about an act as public and dramatic as baptism. I felt toward it the slightly exasperated awe a stagehand might feel on realizing that although he can identify with professional exactitude the minutest components of a show, there is still something indefinable in the power that makes it a cohesive whole. Though I could not have put it into words, I believed that the decision to make a frightening and embarrassing backward plunge into a pool of sanctified water meant that one had received a summons to Christianity as unmistakable as the blare of an automobile horn. I believed this with the same fervor with which, already, I believed in the power of romance, especially in the miraculous efficacy of a lover's first kiss. I had never been kissed by a lover, nor had I heard the call to baptism.

For a Baptist minister and his wife, my father and mother were unusually relaxed about religion; Matthew and I had never been required to read the Bible, and my father's sermons had been criticized by some older church members for omitting the word "sin." Mama and Daddy never tried to push me toward baptism, but a number of other people did. Often on holidays, when I had retreated from the noise of the family dinner table and sat trying to read in my favorite place (the window seat in Matthew's room, with the curtains drawn to form a tent), Aunt Lily would come and find me. Aunt Lily was the youngest of my mother's sisters, a kindergarten teacher with the fatally overdeveloped air of quaintness that is the infallible mark of an old maid. Aunt Lily hoped and hoped again with various suitors, but even I knew she would never find a husband. I respected her because she gave me wonderful books of fairy tales, inscribed in her neat, loopy hand; when she talked about religion, however, she assumed an anxious, flirtatious air that made me cringe. "Well, Miss Sarah, what are you scared of?" she would ask, tugging gently on one of my braids and bringing her plump face so close to mine that I could see her powder, which was, in accordance with the custom of fashionable colored ladies, several shades lighter than her olive skin. "God isn't anyone to be afraid of!" she'd continue as I looked at her with my best deadpan expression. "He's someone nice, just as nice as your daddy"—I had always suspected Aunt Lily of having a crush on my father—"and he loves you, in the same way your daddy does!"

"You would make us all so happy!" I was told at different times by Aunt Lily, Aunt Emma, and Aunt May. The only people who said nothing at all were Mama and Daddy, but I sensed in them a thoughtful, suppressed wistfulness that maddened me.

After the hymn, Daddy read aloud a few verses from the third chapter of Luke, verses I recognized in the almost instinctive way in which I was familiar with all of the well-traveled parts of the Old and New Testaments. "Prepare the way of the Lord, make his paths straight," read my father in a mild voice. "Every valley shall be filled, and every mountain and hill shall be brought low, and the crooked shall be made straight, and the rough paths made smooth, and all flesh shall see the salvation of God."

He had a habit of pausing to fix his gaze on part of the congregation as he read, and that Sunday he seemed to be talking to a small group of strangers who sat in the front row. These visitors were young white men and women, students from Philadelphia colleges, who for the past year had been coming to hear him talk. It was hard to tell them apart: all the men seemed to have beards, and the women wore their hair long and straight. Their informal clothes stood out in that elaborate assembly, and church members whispered angrily that the young women didn't wear hats. I found the students appealing and rather romantic, with their earnest eyes and timid air of being perpetually sorry about something. It was clear that they had good intentions, and I couldn't understand why so many of the adults in the congregation seemed to dislike them so much. After services, they would hover around Daddy. "Never a more beautiful civil rights sermon!" they would say in low, fervent voices. Sometimes they seemed to have tears in their eyes.

I wasn't impressed by their praise of my father; it was only what everyone said. People called him a champion of civil rights; he gave speeches on the radio, and occasionally he appeared on television. (The first time I'd seen him on Channel 5, I'd been gravely disappointed by the way he looked: the bright lights exaggerated the furrows that ran between his nose and mouth, and his narrow eyes gave him a sinister air; he looked like an Oriental villain in a Saturday afternoon thriller.) During the past year he had organized a boycott that integrated the staff of a huge frozen-food plant in Philadelphia, and he'd been away several times to attend marches and meetings in the South. I was privately embarrassed to have a parent who freely admitted going to jail in Alabama, but the students who visited New African seemed to think it almost miraculous. Their conversations with my father were peppered with references to places I had never seen, towns I imagined as being swathed in a mist of darkness visible: Selma, Macon, Birmingham, Biloxi.

Matthew and I had long ago observed that what Daddy generally did in his sermons was to speak very softly and then surprise everyone with a shout. Of course, I knew that there was more to it than that; even in those days I recognized a genius of personality in my father. He loved crowds, handling them with the expert good humor of a man entirely in his element. At church banquets, at the vast annual picnic that was held beside a lake in New Jersey, or at any gathering in the backyards and living rooms of the town where we lived, the sound I heard most often was the booming of my father's voice followed by shouts of laughter from the people around him. He had a passion for oratory; at home, he infuriated Matthew and me by staging absurd debates at the dinner table, verbal melees that he won quite selfishly, with a loud crow of delight at his own virtuosity. "Is a fruit a vegetable?" he would demand. "Is a zipper a machine?" Matthew and I would plead with him to be quiet as we strained to get our own points across, but it was no use. When the last word had resounded and we sat looking at him in irritated silence, he would clear his throat, settle his collar, and resume eating, his face still glowing with an irrepressible glee.

When he preached, he showed the same private delight. A look of rapt pleasure seemed to broaden and brighten the contours of his angular face until it actually appeared to give off light as he spoke. He could preach in two very different ways. One was the delicate, sonorous idiom of formal oratory, with which he must have won the prizes he held from his seminary days. The second was a hectoring, insinuating, incantatory tone, full of the rhythms of the South he had never lived in, linking him to generations of thunderous Baptist preachers. When he used this tone, as he was doing now, affectionate laughter rippled through the pews.

"I know," he said, looking out over the congregation and blinking his eyes rapidly, "that there are certain people in this room—oh, I don't have to name names or point a finger—who have ignored that small true voice, the voice that is the voice of Jesus calling out in the shadowy depths of the soul. And while you all are looking around and wondering just who those 'certain people' are, I want to tell you all a secret: they are you and me, and your brother-in-law, and every man, woman, and child in this room this morning. All of us listen to our bellies when they tell us it is time to eat, we pay attention to our eyes when they grow heavy from wanting sleep, but when it comes to the sacred knowledge our hearts can offer, we are deaf, dumb, blind, and senseless. Throw away that blindness, that deafness, that sulky indifference. When all the world lies to you, Jesus will tell you what is right. Listen to him. Call on him. In these times of confusion, when there are a dozen different ways to turn, and Mama and Papa can't help you, trust Jesus to set you straight. Listen to him. The Son of God has the answers. Call on him. Call on him. Call on him."

The sermon was punctuated with an occasional loud "Amen!" from Miss Middleton, an excitable old lady whose eyes flashed defiantly at the reproving faces of those around her. New African was not the kind of Baptist church where shouting was a normal part of the service; I occasionally heard my father mock the staid congregation by calling it Saint African. Whenever Miss Middleton loosed her tongue (sometimes she went off into fits of rapturous shrieks and had to be helped out of the service by the church nurse), my mother and aunts exchanged grimaces and shrugged, as if confronted by incomprehensibly barbarous behavior.

When Daddy had spoken the final words of the sermon, he drank a glass of water and vanished through a set of red velvet curtains to the right of the altar. At the same time, the choir began to sing what was described in the church bulletin as a "selection." These selections were always arenas for the running dispute between the choirmaster and the choir. Jordan Grimes, the choirmaster, was a Curtis graduate who was partial to Handel, but the choir preferred artistic spirituals performed in the lush, heroic style of Paul Robeson. Grimes had triumphed that Sunday. As the choir gave a spirited but unwilling rendition of Agnus Dei, I watched old Deacon West smile in approval. A Spanish-American War veteran, he admitted to being ninety-four but was said to be older; his round yellowish face, otherwise unwrinkled, bore three deep, deliberate-looking horizontal creases on the brow, like carvings on a scarab. "That old man is as flirtatious as a boy of twenty!" my mother often said, watching his stiff, courtly movements among the ladies of the church. Sometimes he gave me a dry kiss and a piece of peppermint candy after the service; I liked his crackling white collars and smell of bay rum.

The selection ended; Jordan Grimes struck two deep chords on the organ, and the lights in the church went low. A subtle stir ran through the congregation, and I moved closer to my mother. This was the moment that fascinated and disturbed me more than anything else at church: the prelude to the ceremony of baptism. Deacon West rose and drew open the draperies that had been closed around the baptismal pool, and there stood my father in water to his waist. The choir began to sing:

We're marching to Zion,
Beautiful, beautiful Zion,
We're marching upward to Zion,
The beautiful city of God!

Down the aisle, guided by two church mothers, came a procession of eight children and adolescents. They wore white robes, the girls with white ribbons in their hair, and they all had solemn expressions of terror on their faces. I knew each one of them. There was Billy Price, a big, slow-moving boy of thirteen, the son of Deacon Price. There were the Duckery twins. There was Caroline Piggee, whom I hated because of her long, soft black curls, her dimpled pink face, and her lisp that ravished grownups. There was Georgie Battis and Sue Anne Ivory, and Wendell and Mabel Cullen.

My mother gave me a nudge. "Run up to the side of the pool!" she whispered. It was the custom for unbaptized children to watch the ceremony from the front of the church. They sat on the knees of the deacons and church mothers, and it was not unusual for a child to volunteer then and there for next month's baptism. I made my way quickly down the dark aisle, feeling the carpet slip under the smooth soles of my patent-leather shoes.

When I reached the side of the pool, I sat down in the bony lap of Bessie Gray, an old woman who often took care of Matthew and me when our parents were away; we called her Aunt Bessie. She was a fanatically devout Christian whose strict ideas on child-rearing had evolved over decades of domestic service to a rich white family in Delaware. The link between us, a mixture of hostility and grudging affection, had been forged in hours of pitched battles over bedtimes and proper behavior. Her worshipful respect for my father, whom she called "the Rev," was exceeded only by her pride—the malice-tinged pride of an omniscient family servant—in her "white children," to whom she often unflatteringly compared Matthew and me. It was easy to see why my mother and her circle of fashionable matrons described Bessie Gray as "archaic"—one had only to look at her black straw hat attached with three enormous old-fashioned pins to her knot of frizzy white hair. Her lean, brown-skinned face was dominated by a hawk nose inherited from some Indian ancestor and punctuated by a big black mole; her eyes were small, shrewd, and baleful. She talked in ways that were already passing into history and parody, and she wore a thick orange face powder that smelled like dead leaves.

I leaned against her spare bosom and watched the other children clustered near the pool, their bonnets and hair ribbons and round heads outlined in the dim light. For a minute it was very still. Somewhere in the hot, darkened church a baby gave a fretful murmur; from outside came the sound of cars passing in the street. The candidates for baptism, looking stiff and self-conscious, stood lined up on the short stairway leading to the pool. Sue Anne Ivory fiddled with her sleeve and then put her fingers in her mouth.

Daddy spoke the opening phrases of the ceremony: "In the Baptist Church, we do not baptize infants, but believe that a person must choose salvation for himself."

I didn't listen to the words; what I noticed was the music of the whole—how the big voice darkened and lightened in tone, and how the grand architecture of the Biblical sentences ennobled the voice. The story, of course, was about Jesus and John the Baptist. One phrase struck me newly each time: "This is my beloved son, in whom I am well pleased!" Daddy sang out these words in a clear, triumphant tone, and the choir echoed him. Ever since I could understand it, this phrase had made me feel melancholy; it seemed to expose a hard knot of disobedience that had always lain inside me. When I heard it, I thought enviously of Matthew, for whom life seemed to be a sedate and ordered affair: he, not I, was a child in whom a father could be well pleased.

Daddy beckoned to Billy Price, the first baptismal candidate in line, and Billy, ungainly in his white robe, descended the steps into the pool. In soft, slow voices the choir began to sing:

Wade in the water,
Wade in the water, children,
Wade in the water,
God gonna trouble
The water.

In spite of Jordan Grimes's efforts, the choir swayed like a gospel chorus as it sang this spiritual; the result was to add an eerie jazz beat to the minor chords. The music gave me gooseflesh. Daddy had told me that this was the same song that the slaves had sung long ago in the South, when they gathered to be baptized in rivers and streams. Although I cared little about history, and found it hard to picture the slaves as being any ancestors of mine, I could clearly imagine them coming together beside a broad muddy river that wound away between trees drooping with strange vegetation. They walked silently in lines, their faces very black against their white clothes, leading their children. The whole scene was bathed in the heavy golden light that meant age and solemnity, the same light that seemed to weigh down the Israelites in illustrated volumes of Bible stories, and that shone now from the baptismal pool, giving the ceremony the air of a spectacle staged in a dream.

All attention in the darkened auditorium was now focused on the pool, where between the red curtains my father stood holding Billy Price by the shoulders. Daddy stared into Billy's face, and the boy stared back, his lips set and trembling. "And now, by the power invested in me," said Daddy, "I baptize you in the name of the Father, the Son, and the Holy Ghost." As he pronounced these words, he conveyed a tenderness as efficient and impersonal as a physician's professional manner; beneath it, however, I could see a strong private gladness, the same delight that transformed his face when he preached a sermon. He paused to flick a drop of water off his forehead, and then, with a single smooth, powerful motion of his arms, he laid Billy Price back into the water as if he were putting an infant to bed. I caught my breath as the boy went backward. When he came up, sputtering, two church mothers helped him out of the pool and through a doorway into a room where he would be dried and dressed. Daddy shook the water from his hands and gave a slight smile as another child entered the pool.

One by one, the baptismal candidates descended the steps. Sue Anne Ivory began to cry and had to be comforted. Caroline Piggee blushed and looked up at my father with such a coquettish air that I jealously wondered how he could stand it. After a few baptisms my attention wandered, and I began to gnaw the edge of my thumb and to peer at the pale faces of the visiting college students. Then I thought about Matthew, who had punched me in the arm that morning and had shouted, "No punchbacks!" I thought as well about a collection of horse chestnuts I meant to assemble in the fall, and about two books, one whose subject was adults and divorces, and another, by E. Nesbit, that continued the adventures of the Bastable children.

After Wendell Cullen had left the water (glancing uneasily back at the wet robe trailing behind him), Daddy stood alone among the curtains and the mirrors. The moving reflections from the pool made the stuffed dove hanging over him seem to flutter on its string, "Dear Lord," said Daddy, as Jordan Grimes struck a chord, "bless these children who have chosen to be baptized in accordance with your teaching, and who have been reborn to carry out your work. In each of them, surely, you are well pleased." He paused, staring out into the darkened auditorium. "And if there is anyone out there—man, woman, child—who wishes to be baptized next month, let him come forward now." He glanced around eagerly. "Oh, do come forward and give Christ your heart and give me your hand!"

Just then Aunt Bessie gave me a little shake and whispered sharply, "Go on up and accept Jesus!"

I stiffened and dug my bitten fingernails into my palms. The last clash of wills I had had with Aunt Bessie had been when she, crazily set in her old southern attitudes, had tried to make me wear an enormous straw hat, as her "white children" did, when I played outside in the sun. The old woman had driven me to madness, and I had ended up spanked and sullen, crouching moodily under the dining-room table. But this was different, outrageous, none of her business, I thought. I shook my head violently and she took advantage of the darkness in the church to seize both of my shoulders and jounce me with considerable roughness, whispering, "Now, listen, young lady! Your daddy up there is calling you to Christ. Your big brother has already offered his soul to the Lord. Now Daddy wants his little girl to step forward."

"No, he doesn't." I glanced at the baptismal pool, where my father was clasping the hand of a strange man who had come up to him. I hoped that this would distract Aunt Bessie, but she was tireless.

"Your mama and your aunt Lily and your aunt May all want you to answer the call. You're hurting them when you say no to Jesus."

"No, I'm not!" I spoke out loud and I saw the people nearby turn to look at me. At the sound of my voice, Daddy, who was a few yards away, faltered for a minute in what he was saying and glanced over in my direction.

Aunt Bessie seemed to lose her head. She stood up abruptly, pulling me with her, and, while I was still frozen in a dreadful paralysis, tried to drag me down the aisle toward my father. The two of us began a brief struggle that could not have lasted for more than a few seconds but that seemed an endless mortal conflict—my slippery patent-leather shoes braced against the floor, my straw hat sliding cockeyed and lodging against one ear, my right arm twisting and twisting in the iron circle of the old woman's grip, my nostrils full of the dead-leaf smell of her powder and black skirts. In an instant I had wrenched my arm free and darted up the aisle toward Mama, my aunts, and Matthew. As I slipped past the pews in the darkness, I imagined that I could feel eyes fixed on me and hear whispers. "What'd you do, dummy?" whispered Matthew, tugging on my sash as I reached our pew, but I pushed past him without answering. Although it was hot in the church, my teeth were chattering: it was the first time I had won a battle with a grownup, and the earth seemed to be about to cave in beneath me. I squeezed in between Mama and Aunt Lily just as the lights came back on in the church. In the baptismal pool, Daddy raised his arms for the last time. "The Lord bless you and keep you," came his big voice. "The Lord be gracious unto you, and give you peace."

What was curious was how uncannily subdued my parents were when they heard of my skirmish with Aunt Bessie. Normally they were swift to punish Matthew and me for misbehavior in church and for breaches in politeness toward adults; this episode combined the two, and smacked of sacrilege besides. Yet once I had made an unwilling apology to the old woman (as I kissed her she shot me such a vengeful glare that I realized that forever after it was to be war to the death between the two of us), I was permitted, once we had driven home, to climb up into the green shade of the big maple tree I had dreamed of throughout the service. In those days, more than now, I fell away into a remote dimension whenever I opened a book; that afternoon, as I sat with rings of sunlight and shadow moving over my arms and legs, and winged yellow seeds plopping down on the pages of *The Story of the Treasure Seekers*, I felt a vague uneasiness floating in the back of my mind—a sense of having misplaced something, of being myself misplaced. I was holding myself quite aloof from considering what had happened, as I did with most serious events, but through the adventures of the Bastables I kept remembering the way my father had looked when he'd heard what had happened. He hadn't looked severe or angry, but merely puzzled, and he had regarded me with the same puzzled expression, as if he'd just discovered that I existed and didn't know what to do with me. "What happened, Sairy?" he asked, using an old baby nickname, and I said, "I didn't want to go up there." I hadn't cried at all, and that was another curious thing.

After that Sunday, through some adjustment in the adult spheres beyond my perception, all pressure on me to accept baptism ceased. I turned twelve, fifteen, then eighteen without being baptized, a fact that scandalized some of the congregation; however, my parents, who openly discussed everything else, never said a word to me. The issue, and the episode that had illuminated it, was surrounded by a clear ring of silence that, for our garrulous family, was something close to supernatural. I continued to go to New African—in fact, continued after Matthew, who dropped out abruptly during his freshman year in college; the ambiguousness in my relations with the old church gave me at times an inflated sense of privilege (I saw myself as a romantically isolated religious heroine, a sort of self-made Baptist martyr) and at other times a feeling of loss that I was too proud ever to acknowledge. I never went up to take my father's hand, and he never commented upon that fact to me. It was an odd pact, one that I could never consider in the light of day; I stored it in the subchambers of my heart and mind. It was only much later, after he died, and I left New African forever, that I began to examine the peculiar gift of freedom my father—whose entire soul was in the church, and in his exuberant, bewitching tongue—had granted me through his silence.

Andrea Lee grew up in a suburb of Philadelphia, was educated at Harvard University, and now makes her home in Milan, Italy. She published a series of short stories in *The New Yorker* in the early 1980s which formed the basis of her first novel, *Sarah Phillips*. She also published a book of nonfiction, *Russia Journal,* written after she and her husband had lived in the Soviet Union.

BOBBIE ANN MASON

" 'Shiloh' was the second story of mine to appear in *The New Yorker*. For me, it was a turning point in learning to write short stories, because I had been struggling with the problem of tone. The tone of a story tells you what attitude to take toward the characters. It's tricky to get just the right distance from the characters—not too close, not too far—so that they can be taken seriously. If you don't hit it just right, you can seem either overindulgent or too critical. The story was written rather innocently, in about eleven days, and it was the kind of story that is such a pleasure to write because there were no preconceptions about what it was going to be about or where it was going. So I didn't have to try to hammer it in place to make it fit some notion. As I wrote along then, I was able to get close to the textures of the characters' lives (Norma Jean's weight lifting and her English compositions, Leroy's Lincoln logs), so that gradually Leroy and Norma Jean became real to me, and the conflict in their marriage emerged as the center. I had no idea they would be going to Shiloh, the Civil War battleground, until all of a sudden Norma Jean's mother suggested it. It sounded good to me, so away they went. That is the pure pleasure of creation—the not knowing that leads you to the knowing."

SHILOH

LEROY Moffitt's wife, Norma Jean, is working on her pectorals. She lifts three-pound dumbbells to warm up, then progresses to a twenty-pound barbell. Standing with her legs apart, she reminds Leroy of Wonder Woman.

"I'd give anything if I could just get these muscles to where they're real hard," says Norma Jean. "Feel this arm. It's not as hard as the other one."

"That's 'cause you're right-handed," says Leroy, dodging as she swings the barbell in an arc.

"Do you think so?"

"Sure."

Leroy is a truckdriver. He injured his leg in a highway accident four months ago, and his physical therapy, which involves weights and a pulley, prompted Norma Jean to try building herself up. Now she is attending a body-building class. Leroy has been collecting temporary disability since his tractor-trailer jackknifed in Missouri, badly twisting his left leg in its socket. He has a steel pin in his hip. He will probably not be able to drive his rig again. It sits in the backyard, like a gigantic bird that has flown home to roost. Leroy has been home in Kentucky for three months, and his leg is almost healed, but the accident frightened him and he does not want to drive any more long hauls. He is not sure what to do next. In the meantime, he makes things from craft kits. He started by building a miniature log cabin from notched Popsicle sticks. He varnished it and placed it on the TV set, where it remains. It reminds him of a rustic Nativity scene. Then he tried string art (sailing ships on black velvet), a macramé owl kit, a snap-together B-17 Flying Fortress, and a lamp made out of a model truck, with a light fixture screwed in the top of the cab. At first the kits were diversions, something to kill time, but now he is thinking about building a full-scale log house from a kit. It would be considerably cheaper than building a regular house, and besides, Leroy has grown to appreciate how things are put together. He has begun to realize that in all the years he was on the road he never took time to examine anything. He was always flying past scenery.

"They won't let you build a log cabin in any of the new subdivisions," Norma Jean tells him.

"They will if I tell them it's for you," he says, teasing her. Ever since they were married, he has promised Norma Jean he would build her a new home one day. They have always rented, and the house they live in is small and nondescript. It does not even feel like a home, Leroy realizes now.

Norma Jean works at the Rexall drugstore, and she has acquired an amazing amount of information about cosmetics. When she explains to Leroy the three stages of complexion care, involving creams, toners, and moisturizers, he thinks happily of other petroleum products—axle grease, diesel fuel. This is a connection between him and Norma Jean. Since he has been home, he has felt unusually tender about his wife and guilty over his long absences. But he can't tell what she feels about him. Norma Jean has never complained about his traveling; she has never made hurt remarks, like calling his truck a "widow-maker." He is reasonably certain she has been faithful to him, but he wishes she would celebrate his permanent homecoming more happily. Norma Jean is often startled to find Leroy at home, and he thinks she seems a little disappointed about it. Perhaps he reminds her too much of the early days of their marriage, before he went on the road. They had a child who died as an infant, years ago. They never speak about their memories of Randy, which have almost faded, but now that Leroy is home all the time, they sometimes feel awkward around each other, and Leroy wonders if one of them should mention the child. He has the feeling that they are waking up out of a dream together—that they must create a new marriage, start afresh. They are lucky they are still married. Leroy has read that for most people losing a child destroys the marriage—or else he heard this on *Donahue.* He can't always remember where he learns things anymore.

At Christmas, Leroy bought an electric organ for Norma Jean. She used to play the piano when she was in high school. "It don't leave you," she told him once. "It's like riding a bicycle."

The new instrument had so many keys and buttons that she was bewildered by it at first. She touched the keys tentatively, pushed some buttons, then pecked out "Chopsticks." It came out in an amplified fox-trot rhythm, with marimba sounds.

"It's an orchestra!" she cried.

The organ had a pecan-look finish and eighteen preset chords, with optional flute, violin, trumpet, clarinet, and banjo accompaniments. Norma Jean mastered the organ almost immediately. At first she played Christmas songs. Then she bought *The Sixties Songbook* and learned every tune in it, adding variations to each with the rows of brightly colored buttons.

"I didn't like these old songs back then," she said. "But I have this crazy feeling I missed something."

"You didn't miss a thing," said Leroy.

Leroy likes to lie on the couch and smoke a joint and listen to Norma Jean play "Can't Take My Eyes Off You" and "I'll Be Back." He is back again. After fifteen years on the road, he is finally settling down with the woman he loves. She is still pretty. Her skin is flawless. Her frosted curls resemble pencil trimmings.

Now that Leroy has come home to stay, he notices how much the town has changed. Subdivisions are spreading across western Kentucky like an oil slick. The sign at the edge of town says "Pop: 11,500"—only seven hundred more than it said twenty years before. Leroy can't figure out who is living in all the new houses. The farmers who used to gather around the courthouse square on Saturday afternoons to play checkers and spit tobacco juice have gone. It has been years since Leroy has thought about the farmers, and they have disappeared without his noticing.

Leroy meets a kid named Stevie Hamilton in the parking lot at the new shopping center. While they pretend to be strangers meeting over a stalled car, Stevie tosses an ounce of marijuana under the front seat of Leroy's car. Stevie is wearing orange jogging shoes and a T-shirt that says CHATTAHOOCHEE SUPER-RAT. His father is a prominent doctor who lives in one of the expensive subdivisions in a new white-columned brick house that looks like a funeral parlor. In the phone book under his name there is a separate number, with the listing "Teenagers."

"Where do you get this stuff?" asks Leroy. "From your pappy?"

"That's for me to know and you to find out," Stevie says. He is slit-eyed and skinny.

"What else you got?"

"What you interested in?"

"Nothing special. Just wondered."

Leroy used to take speed on the road. Now he has to go slowly. He needs to be mellow. He leans back against the car and says, "I'm aiming to build me a log house, soon as I get time. My wife, though, I don't think she likes the idea."

"Well, let me know when you want me again," Stevie says. He has a cigarette in his cupped palm, as though sheltering it from the wind. He takes a long drag, then stomps it on the asphalt and slouches away.

Stevie's father was two years ahead of Leroy in high school. Leroy is thirty-four. He married Norma Jean when they were both eighteen, and their child Randy was born a few months later, but he died at the age of four months and three days. He would be about Stevie's age now. Norma Jean and Leroy were at the drive-in, watching a double feature *(Dr. Strangelove* and *Lover Come Back),* and the baby was sleeping in the back seat. When the first movie ended, the baby was dead. It was the sudden infant death syndrome. Leroy remembers handing Randy to a nurse at the emergency room, as though he were offering her a large doll as a present. A dead baby feels like a sack of flour. "It just happens sometimes," said the doctor, in what Leroy always recalls as a nonchalant tone. Leroy can hardly remember the child anymore, but he still sees vividly a scene from *Dr. Strangelove* in which the President of the United States was talking in a folksy voice on the hot line to the Soviet premier about the bomber accidentally headed toward Russia. He was in the War Room, and the world map was lit up. Leroy remembers Norma Jean standing catatonically beside him in the hospital and himself thinking: Who is this strange girl? He had forgotten who she was. Now scientists are saying that crib death is caused by a virus. Nobody knows anything, Leroy thinks. The answers are always changing.

When Leroy gets home from the shopping center, Norma Jean's mother, Mabel Beasley, is there. Until this year, Leroy has not realized how much time she spends with Norma Jean. When she visits, she inspects the closets and then the plants, informing Norma Jean when a plant is droopy or yellow. Mabel calls the plants "flowers," although there are never any blooms. She always notices if Norma Jean's laundry is piling up. Mabel is a short, overweight woman whose tight, brown-dyed curls look more like a wig than the actual wig she sometimes wears. Today she has brought Norma Jean an off-white dust ruffle she made for the bed; Mabel works in a custom-upholstery shop.

"This is the tenth one I made this year," Mabel says. "I got started and couldn't stop."

"It's real pretty," says Norma Jean.

"Now we can hide things under the bed," says Leroy, who gets along with his mother-in-law primarily by joking with her. Mabel has never really forgiven him for disgracing her by getting Norma Jean pregnant. When the baby died, she said that fate was mocking her.

"What's that thing?" Mabel says to Leroy in a loud voice, pointing to a tangle of yarn on a piece of canvas.

Leroy holds it up for Mabel to see. "It's my needlepoint," he explains. "This is a *Star Trek* pillow cover."

"That's what a woman would do," says Mabel. "Great day in the morning!"

"All the big football players on TV do it," he says.

"Why, Leroy, you're always trying to fool me. I don't believe you for one minute. You don't know what to do with yourself—that's the whole trouble. Sewing!"

"I'm aiming to build us a log house," says Leroy. "Soon as my plans come."

"Like *heck* you are," says Norma Jean. She takes Leroy's needlepoint and shoves it into a drawer. "You have to find a job first. Nobody can afford to build now anyway."

Mabel straightens her girdle and says, "I still think before you get tied down y'all ought to take a little run to Shiloh."

"One of these days, Mama," Norma Jean says impatiently.

Mabel is talking about Shiloh, Tennessee. For the past few years, she has been urging Leroy and Norma Jean to visit the Civil War battleground there. Mabel went there on her honeymoon—the only real trip she ever took. Her husband died of a perforated ulcer when Norma Jean was ten, but Mabel, who was accepted into the United Daughters of the Confederacy in 1975, is still preoccupied with going back to Shiloh.

"I've been to kingdom come and back in that truck out yonder," Leroy says to Mabel, "but we never yet set foot in that battleground. Ain't that something? How did I miss it?"

"It's not even that far," Mabel says.

After Mabel leaves, Norma Jean reads to Leroy from a list she has made. "Things you could do," she announces. "You could get a job as a guard at Union Carbide, where they'd let you set on a stool. You could get on at the lumberyard. You could do a little carpenter work, if you want to build so bad. You could—"

"I can't do something where I'd have to stand up all day."

"You ought to try standing up all day behind a cosmetics counter. It's amazing that I have strong feet, coming from two parents that never had strong feet at all." At the moment Norma Jean is holding on to the kitchen counter, raising her knees one at a time as she talks. She is wearing two-pound ankle weights.

"Don't worry," says Leroy. "I'll do something."

"You could truck calves to slaughter for somebody. You wouldn't have to drive any big old truck for that."

"I'm going to build you this house," says Leroy. "I want to make you a real home."

"I don't want to live in any log cabin."

"It's not a cabin. It's a house."

"I don't care. It looks like a cabin."

"You and me together could lift those logs. It's just like lifting weights."

Norma Jean doesn't answer. Under her breath, she is counting. Now she is marching through the kitchen. She is doing goose steps.

Before his accident, when Leroy came home he used to stay in the house with Norma Jean, watching TV in bed and playing cards. She would cook fried chicken, picnic ham, chocolate pie—all his favorites. Now he is home alone much of the time. In the mornings, Norma Jean disappears, leaving a cooling place in the bed. She eats a cereal called Body Buddies, and she leaves the bowl on the table, with the soggy tan balls floating in a milk puddle. He sees things about Norma Jean that he never realized before. When she chops onions, she stares off into a corner, as if she can't bear to look. She puts on her house slippers almost precisely at nine o'clock every evening and nudges her jogging shoes under the couch. She saves bread heels for the birds. Leroy watches the birds at the feeder. He notices the peculiar way goldfinches fly past the window. They close their wings, then fall, then spread their wings to catch and lift themselves. He wonders if they close their eyes when they fall. Norma Jean closes her eyes when they are in bed. She wants the lights turned out. Even then, he is sure she closes her eyes.

He goes for long drives around town. He tends to drive a car rather carelessly. Power steering and an automatic shift make a car feel so small and inconsequential that his body is hardly involved in the driving process. His injured leg stretches out comfortably. Once or twice he has almost hit something, but even the prospect of an accident seems minor in a car. He cruises the new subdivisions, feeling like a criminal rehearsing for a robbery. Norma Jean is probably right about a log house being inappropriate here in the new subdivisions. All the houses look grand and complicated. They depress him.

One day when Leroy comes home from a drive he finds Norma Jean in tears. She is in the kitchen making a potato and mushroom-soup casserole, with grated-cheese topping. She is crying because her mother caught her smoking.

"I didn't hear her coming. I was standing here puffing away pretty as you please," Norma Jean says, wiping her eyes.

"I knew it would happen sooner or later," says Leroy, putting his arm around her.

"She don't know the meaning of the word 'knock,' " says Norma Jean. "It's a wonder she hadn't caught me years ago."

"Think of it this way," Leroy says. "What if she caught me with a joint?"

"You better not let her!" Norma Jean shrieks. "I'm warning you, Leroy Moffitt!"

"I'm just kidding. Here, play me a tune. That'll help you relax."

Norma Jean puts the casserole in the oven and sets the timer. Then she plays a ragtime tune, with horns and banjo, as Leroy lights up a joint and lies on the couch, laughing to himself about Mabel's catching him at it. He thinks of Stevie Hamilton—a doctor's son pushing grass. Everything is funny. The whole town seems crazy and small. He is reminded of Virgil Mathis, a boastful policeman Leroy used to shoot pool with. Virgil recently led a drug bust in a back room at a bowling alley, where he seized ten thousand dollars' worth of marijuana. The newspaper had a picture of him holding up the bags of grass and grinning widely. Right now, Leroy can imagine Virgil breaking down the door and arresting him with a lungful of smoke. Virgil would probably have been alerted to the scene because of all the racket Norma Jean is making. Now she sounds like a hard-rock band. Norma Jean is terrific. When she switches to a Latin-rhythm version of "Sunshine Superman," Leroy hums along. Norma Jean's foot goes up and down, up and down.

"Well, what do you think?" Leroy says, when Norma Jean pauses to search through her music.

"What do I think about what?"

His mind has gone blank. Then he says, "I'll sell my rig and build us a house." That wasn't what he wanted to say. He wanted to know what she thought—what she *really* thought—about them.

"Don't start in on that again," says Norma Jean. She begins playing "Who'll Be the Next in Line?"

Leroy used to tell hitchhikers his whole life story—about his travels, his hometown, the baby. He would end with a question: "Well, what do you think?" It was just a rhetorical question. In time, he had the feeling that he'd been telling the same story over and over to the same hitchhikers. He quit talking to hitchhikers when he realized how his voice sounded—whining and self-pitying, like some teenage-tragedy song. Now Leroy has the sudden impulse to tell Norma Jean about himself, as if he had just met her. They have known each other so long they have forgotten a lot about each other. They could become reacquainted. But when the oven timer goes off and she runs to the kitchen, he forgets why he wants to do this.

•

The next day, Mabel drops by. It is Saturday and Norma Jean is cleaning. Leroy is studying the plans of his log house, which have finally come in the mail. He has them spread out on the table—big sheets of stiff blue paper, with diagrams and numbers printed in white. While Norma Jean runs the vacuum, Mabel drinks coffee. She sets her coffee cup on a blueprint.

"I'm just waiting for time to pass," she says to Leroy, drumming her fingers on the table.

As soon as Norma Jean switches off the vacuum, Mabel says in a loud voice, "Did you hear about the datsun dog that killed the baby?"

Norma Jean says, "The word is 'dachshund.' "

"They put the dog on trial. It chewed the baby's legs off. The mother was in the next room all the time." She raises her voice. "They thought it was neglect."

Norma Jean is holding her ears. Leroy manages to open the refrigerator and get some Diet Pepsi to offer Mabel. Mabel still has some coffee and she waves away the Pepsi.

"Datsuns are like that," Mabel says. "They're jealous dogs. They'll tear a place to pieces if you don't keep an eye on them."

"You better watch out what you're saying, Mabel," says Leroy.

"Well, facts is facts."

Leroy looks out the window at his rig. It is like a huge piece of furniture gathering dust in the backyard. Pretty soon it will be an antique. He hears the vacuum cleaner. Norma Jean seems to be cleaning the living room rug again.

Later, she says to Leroy, "She just said that about the baby because she caught me smoking. She's trying to pay me back."

"What are you talking about?" Leroy says, nervously shuffling blueprints.

"You know good and well," Norma Jean says. She is sitting in a kitchen chair with her feet up and her arms wrapped around her knees. She looks small and helpless. She says, "The very idea, her bringing up a subject like that! Saying it was neglect."

"She didn't mean that," Leroy says.

"She might not have *thought* she meant it. She always says things like that. You don't know how she goes on."

"But she didn't really mean it. She was just talking."

Leroy opens a king-sized bottle of beer and pours it into two glasses, dividing it carefully. He hands a glass to Norma Jean and she takes it from him mechanically. For a long time, they sit by the kitchen window watching the birds at the feeder.

Something is happening. Norma Jean is going to night school. She has graduated from her six-week body-building course and now she is taking an adult-education course in composition at Paducah Community College. She spends her evenings outlining paragraphs.

"First you have a topic sentence," she explains to Leroy. "Then you divide it up. Your secondary topic has to be connected to your primary topic."

To Leroy, this sounds intimidating. "I never was any good in English," he says.

"It makes a lot of sense."

"What are you doing this for, anyhow?"

She shrugs. "It's something to do." She stands up and lifts her dumbbells a few times.

"Driving a rig, nobody cared about my English."

"I'm not criticizing your English."

Norma Jean used to say, "If I lose ten minutes' sleep, I just drag all day." Now she stays up late, writing compositions. She got a B on her first paper—a how-to theme on soup-based casseroles. Recently Norma Jean has been cooking unusual foods—tacos, lasagna, Bombay chicken. She doesn't play the organ anymore, though her second paper was called "Why Music Is Important to Me." She sits at the kitchen table, concentrating on her outlines, while Leroy plays with his log house plans, practicing with a set of Lincoln Logs. The thought of getting a truckload of notched, numbered logs scares him, and he wants to be prepared. As he and Norma Jean work together at the kitchen table, Leroy has the hopeful thought that they are sharing something, but he knows he is a fool to think this. Norma Jean is miles away. He knows he is going to lose her. Like Mabel, he is just waiting for time to pass.

One day, Mabel is there before Norma Jean gets home from work, and Leroy finds himself confiding in her. Mabel, he realizes, must know Norma Jean better than he does.

"I don't know what's got into that girl," Mabel says. "She used to go to bed with the chickens. Now you say she's up all hours. Plus her a-smoking. I like to died."

"I want to make her this beautiful home," Leroy says, indicating the Lincoln Logs. "I don't think she even wants it. Maybe she was happier with me gone."

"She don't know what to make of you, coming home like this."

"Is that it?"

Mabel takes the roof off his Lincoln Log cabin. "You couldn't get *me* in a log cabin," she says. "I was raised in one. It's no picnic, let me tell you."

"They're different now," says Leroy.

"I tell you what," Mabel says, smiling oddly at Leroy.

"What?"

"Take her on down to Shiloh. Y'all need to get out together, stir a little. Her brain's all balled up over them books."

Leroy can see traces of Norma Jean's features in her mother's face. Mabel's worn face has the texture of crinkled cotton, but suddenly she looks pretty. It occurs to Leroy that Mabel has been hinting all along that she wants them to take her with them to Shiloh.

"Let's all go to Shiloh," he says. "You and me and her. Come Sunday."

Mabel throws up her hands in protest. "Oh, no, not me. Young folks want to be by theirselves."

When Norma Jean comes in with groceries, Leroy says excitedly, "Your mama here's been dying to go to Shiloh for thirty-five years. It's about time we went, don't you think?"

"I'm not going to butt in on anybody's second honeymoon," Mabel says.

"Who's going on a honeymoon, for Christ's sake?" Norma Jean says loudly.

"I never raised no daughter of mine to talk that-a-way," Mabel says.

"You ain't seen nothing yet," says Norma Jean. She starts putting away boxes and cans, slamming cabinet doors.

"There's a log cabin at Shiloh," Mabel says. "It was there during the battle. There's bullet holes in it."

"When are you going to *shut up* about Shiloh, Mama?" asks Norma Jean.

"I always thought Shiloh was the prettiest place, so full of history," Mabel goes on. "I just hoped y'all could see it once before I die, so you could tell me about it." Later, she whispers to Leroy, "You do what I said. A little change is what she needs."

"Your name means 'the king,' " Norma Jean says to Leroy that evening. He is trying to get her to go to Shiloh, and she is reading a book about another century.

"Well, I reckon I ought to be right proud."

"I guess so."

"Am I still king around here?"

Norma Jean flexes her biceps and feels them for hardness. "I'm not fooling around with anybody, if that's what you mean," she says.

"Would you tell me if you were?"

"I don't know."

"What does *your* name mean?"

"It was Marilyn Monroe's real name."

"No kidding!"

"Norma comes from the Normans. They were invaders," she says. She closes her book and looks hard at Leroy. "I'll go to Shiloh with you if you'll stop staring at me."

On Sunday, Norma Jean packs a picnic and they go to Shiloh. To Leroy's relief, Mabel says she does not want to come with them. Norma Jean drives, and Leroy, sitting beside her, feels like some boring hitchhiker she has picked up. He tries some conversation, but she answers him in monosyllables. At Shiloh, she drives aimlessly through the park, past bluffs and trails and steep ravines. Shiloh is an immense place, and Leroy cannot see it as a battleground. It is not what he expected. He thought it would look like a golf course. Monuments are everywhere, showing through the thick clusters of trees. Norma Jean passes the log cabin Mabel mentioned. It is surrounded by tourists looking for bullet holes.

"That's not the kind of log house I've got in mind," says Leroy apologetically.

"I know *that.*"

"This is a pretty place. Your mama was right."

"It's O.K.," says Norma Jean. "Well, we've seen it. I hope she's satisfied."

They burst out laughing together.

At the park museum, a movie on Shiloh is shown every half hour, but they decide that they don't want to see it. They buy a souvenir Confederate flag for Mabel, and then they find a picnic spot near the cemetery. Norma Jean has brought a picnic cooler, with pimiento sandwiches, soft drinks, and Yodels. Leroy eats a sandwich and then smokes a joint, hiding it behind the picnic cooler. Norma Jean has quit smoking altogether. She is picking cake crumbs from the cellophane wrapper, like a fussy bird.

Leroy says, "So the boys in gray ended up in Corinth. The Union soldiers zapped 'em finally. April 7, 1862."

They both know that he doesn't know any history. He is just talking about some of the historical plaques they have read. He feels awkward, like a boy on a date with an older girl. They are still just making conversation.

"Corinth is where Mama eloped to," says Norma Jean.

They sit in silence and stare at the cemetery for the Union dead and, beyond, at a tall cluster of trees. Campers are parked nearby, bumper to bumper, and small children in bright clothing are cavorting and squealing. Norma Jean wads up the cake wrapper and squeezes it tightly in her hand. Without looking at Leroy, she says, "I want to leave you."

Leroy takes a bottle of Coke out of the cooler and flips off the cap. He holds the bottle poised near his mouth but cannot remember to take a drink. Finally he says, "No, you don't."

"Yes, I do."

"I won't let you."

"You can't stop me."

"Don't do me that way."

Leroy knows Norma Jean will have her own way. "Didn't I promise to be home from now on?" he says.

"In some ways, a woman prefers a man who wanders," says Norma Jean. "That sounds crazy, I know."

"You're not crazy."

Leroy remembers to drink from his Coke. Then he says, "Yes, you *are* crazy. You and me could start all over again. Right back at the beginning."

"We *have* started all over again," says Norma Jean. "And this is how it turned out."

"What did I do wrong?"

"Nothing."

"Is this one of those women's lib things?" Leroy asks.

"Don't be funny."

The cemetery, a green slope dotted with white markers, looks like a subdivision site. Leroy is trying to comprehend that his marriage is breaking up, but for some reason he is wondering about white slabs in a graveyard.

"Everything was fine till Mama caught me smoking," says Norma Jean, standing up. "That set something off."

"What are you talking about?"

"She won't leave me alone—*you* won't leave me alone." Norma Jean seems to be crying, but she is looking away from him. "I feel eighteen again. I can't face that all over again." She starts walking away. "No, it *wasn't* fine. I don't know what I'm saying. Forget it."

Leroy takes a lungful of smoke and closes his eyes as Norma Jean's words sink in. He tries to focus on the fact that thirty-five hundred soldiers died on the grounds around him. He can only think of that war as a board game with plastic soldiers. Leroy almost smiles, as he compares the Confederates' daring attack on the Union camps and Virgil Mathis's raid on the bowling alley. General Grant, drunk and furious, shoved the Southerners back to Corinth, where Mabel and Jet Beasley were married years later, when Mabel was still thin and good-looking. The next day, Mabel and Jet visited the battleground, and then Norma Jean was born, and then she married Leroy and they had a baby, which they lost, and now Leroy and Norma Jean are here at the same battleground. Leroy knows he is leaving out a lot. He is leaving out the insides of history. History was always just names and dates to him. It occurs to him that building a house out of logs is similarly empty—too simple. And the real inner workings of a marriage, like most of history, have escaped him. Now he sees that building a log house is the dumbest idea he could have had. It was clumsy of him to think Norma Jean would want a log house. It was a crazy idea. He'll have to think of something else, quickly. He will wad the blueprints into tight balls and fling them into the lake. Then he'll get moving again. He opens his eyes. Norma Jean has moved away and is walking through the cemetery, following a serpentine brick path.

Leroy gets up to follow his wife, but his good leg is asleep and his bad leg still hurts him. Norma Jean is far away, walking rapidly toward the bluff by the river, and he tries to hobble toward her. Some children run past him, screaming noisily. Norma Jean has reached the bluff, and she is looking out over the Tennessee River. Now she turns toward Leroy and waves her arms. Is she beckoning to him? She seems to be doing an exercise for her chest muscles. The sky is unusually pale—the color of the dust ruffle Mabel made for their bed.

Bobbie Ann Mason, a native of Kentucky, is the author of two collections of stories, *Shiloh and Other Stories*, which won the PEN/Hemingway Award, and *Love Life*. She has also published two novels, In Country, which was made into a film, and *Spence + Lila*. In speaking of her work, her editor at HarperCollins said: "She has given voice to the previously voiceless."

CHRISTOPHER TILGHMAN

"Almost every story I have ever written begins with a place. Events and characters and voice seem to flow out of a single image—usually a visual image—of a landscape or a house, or of two people in a grove of trees or an abandoned cabin. Even if I think I have an idea and perhaps a character or two, I still have to go back and find the visual image that put the idea in my mind. The whole thing is odd: I have never had any visual memory for people, and I often fail to observe wonderful views, spectacular sunsets, and other common feasts for the eye. (I am a bit like the comic writer who is actually dour and gloomy in person.)

"Nevertheless, these visual images come to me. In a way they pull me back and force me to concentrate. Why am I drawn to this image? Why do I think something *happened* in this scene? Finding the story contained in the image can be a painfully slow process. Part of it is meditation; part is the excruciating experience of false starts. Yet the image remains.

"I don't really know why place and visual image work that way for me, but I do know that discovering this fact, after nearly a decade of writing fiction, was a breakthrough. My work before then, it seems to me, was simply dry rhetoric, with very little of the blood. It took me a few more years to learn that 'place' in literature encompasses history and spirit, and is, above all, something revealed and known through sensuous investigation.

" 'In a Father's Place' came to me by the usual route. I had sputtered around with similar material until I saw the image of a man standing on a dock in a gale, looking out into Chesapeake Bay. In this case, the world was familiar to me, as I had spent a good bit of time on the Eastern Shore of Maryland. But the story required more than my usual measure of pain and frustration. It took me a long time to find Patty, the person who puts everything in motion. Once she came on the scene, I could get on with the job of finding what the story meant for me.

"Gradually it became clear that the real place, the real ancestral house in the story, is Dan's mind. And it became clear also that the spirit haunting this house is my own father, and that many of Dan's thoughts and anxieties about his children are things that my father has told me over the years about raising me and my three brothers. Dan and his life are most emphatically *not* a portrait of my father; it is more accurate to say that my father helped to create him. Naturally, I'm grateful for the assistance."

IN A FATHER'S PLACE

DAN had fallen asleep waiting for Nick and this Patty Keith, fallen deep into the lapping rhythm of a muggy Chesapeake evening, and when he heard the slam of car doors the sound came first from a dream. In the hushed amber light of the foyer Dan offered Nick a dazed and disoriented father's hug. Crickets seemed to have come in with them out of the silken night, the trill of crickets and honeysuckle pollen sharp as ammonia. Dan finally asked about the trip down, and Nick answered that the heat in New York had forced whole families onto mattresses in the streets. It looked like New Delhi, he said. Then they turned to meet Patty. She stood there in her Bermuda shorts and shirt, her brown hair in a bun, smelling of sweat and powder and looking impatient. She fixed Dan in her eyes as she shook his hand, and she said, I'm so glad to meet *you.* Maybe she was just talking about the father of her boyfriend, and maybe no new lover ever walked into fair ground in this house, but Dan could not help thinking Patty meant the steward of this family's ground, the signer of the will.

"Nick has told me so much about this place," she said. Her look ran up the winding Georgian staircase, counted off the low, wide doorways, took note of a single ball-and-claw leg visible in the dining room, and rested on the highboy.

"Yes," said Dan. "It's marvelous." He could claim no personal credit for what Patty saw, no collector's eye, not even a decorator's hand.

Rachel had arrived from Wilmington earlier in the evening, and she appeared on the landing in her nightgown. She looked especially large up there after Dan had taken in Patty's compact, tight features; Rachel was a big girl, once a lacrosse defenseman. "Hey, honey," she yelled. There had been no other greeting for her younger brother since they were teenagers. Nick returned a rather subdued hello. Tired, thought Dan, he's tired from the trip and he's got this girl to think about. Rachel came down the stairs; Patty took her hand with the awkwardness young women often show when shaking hands with other young women, or was it, Dan wondered as he watched these children meet in the breathless hall, a kind of guardedness?

Dan said, "You'll be on the third floor." He remembered his own father standing in this very place, saying these same words to polite tired girls; he remembered the underarms and collar of his father's starched shirt, yellowed and brushed with salt. But it was different now: when Dan offered the third floor—and he had done so for some years now—he meant that Rachel or Nick could arrange themselves and their dates in the three bedrooms however they wished.

"The third floor?" said Patty. "Isn't your room on the second floor looking out on the water?" She appealed to Nick with her eyes.

"Actually, Dad . . ." he said.

Dan was still not alert enough to handle conversation, especially with this response that came from a place outside family tradition. "Of course," he said after a long pause. "Wherever you feel comfortable." She wants a room with a view, that's all, he cautioned himself. They had moved deeper into the hall, into a mildewed stillness that smelled of English linen and straw mats. They listened to the grandfather clock on the landing sounding eleven in an unhurried bass.

Dan turned to Patty. "It just means you'll have to share a bathroom with Ray, and she'll fight you to the last drop on earth."

But Patty did not respond to this attempt at charm, and fortunately did not notice Rachel's skeptical look. It was an old joke, or, at least, old for them. Dan remained standing in the hall, slowly recovering from his dense, inflamed sleep as Nick and Patty took their things to the room. Patty seemed pleased, in the end, with the arrangements, and after Dan had said good night and retired to his room, he heard them touring the house, stopping at the portrait of Edward, the reputed family ghost, and admiring the letters from General Washington in gratitude for service to the cause. Theirs wasn't a family of influence anymore, not even of social standing to those few who cared, but the artifacts in the house bracketed whole epochs in American history, with plenty of years and generations left over. He heard Patty saying "Wow" in her low but quite clear-timbred voice. Then he heard the door openings and closings, the run of toilets, a brief, muffled conversation in the hall, and then a calm that returned the house to its creaks and groans, to sounds either real or imagined, a cry across the fields, the thud of a plastic trash can outside being knocked over by raccoons, the pulse of the tree toads, the hollow splash of rockfish and rays still feeding in the sleepless waters of the bay.

A few years ago Dan had taken to saying that Rachel and Nick were his best friends, and even if he saw Nick rarely these days, he hoped it was largely the truth. He'd married young enough never to learn the art of adult friendship, and then Helen had died young enough for it to seem fate, though it was just a hit-and-run on the main street of Easton. Lucille Jackson had raised the kids. Since Helen died there had been three or four women in his life, depending on whether he counted the first, women he'd known all his life who had become free again one by one, girls he'd grown up with and had then discovered as he masturbated in his teens, or who had appeared with their young husbands at lawn parties in sheer cotton sundresses that heedlessly brushed those young thighs, or who now sat alone and distracted on bleachers in a biting fall wind and watched their sons play football. At some point Dan realized if you stayed in a small town all your life, you could end up making love with every woman you had ever known and truly desired. Sheila Frederick had been there year after year in his dreams, at the lawn parties, and at football games, almost, it seemed to Dan later, as if she were stalking him through time. When they actually came together Dan stepped freely into the fulfillment of his teenage fantasies, and then stood by helplessly as she ripped a jagged hole eight years wide out of the heart of his life. There had been one more woman since then, but it was almost as if he had lost his will, if not his lust; the first time he brought her to the house she asked him where he kept the soup bowls, and in that moment he could barely withstand the fatigue, the unbearable temptation to throw it all in, that this innocent question caused him.

He undressed in the heat and turned the fan to hit him squarely on the bed. The air it brought into the room was damp but no cooler, the fecund heat of greenhouses. He felt soft and pasty, flesh that had lost its tone, more spent than tired. He tried to remember if he had put a fan in Nick's room, knowing that Nick would not look for one but would blame him in the morning for the oversight; Rachel, in a similar place, would simply barge in and steal his. Dan knew better than to compare the two of them, and during adolescence boys and girls were incomparable anyway. But they were adults now, three years apart in their mid-twenties, and noticing their differences was something he did all the time. Rachel welcomed being judged among men; and her lovers, like the current Henry, were invariably cheerful, willing bores. This tough, assertive Patty Keith with those distrustful sharp eyes, there was something of Nick's other girls there, spiky, nursing some kind of damage, expecting fear. Patty would do better in the morning. They always did. As he fell asleep finally, he was drifting back into history and memory, and it was not Patty Keith, and not even Helen meeting his father, but generations of young Eastern Shore women he saw, coming to this house to meet and be married, the ones who were pretty and eager for sex, the ones who were silent, the ones the parents loved much too soon, and the ones who broke their children's hearts.

In the morning Dan and Rachel ate breakfast together in the dining room, under the scrutiny of cousin Oswald, who had last threatened his sinful parishioners in 1681. The portraitist had caught a thoroughly unpleasant scowl, a look the family had often compared to Lucille on off days. She had prepared a full meal with eggs, fried green tomatoes, and grits, a service reserved as a reward when they were all in the house. When Nick and the new girl did not come down, Lucille cleared their places so roughly that Dan was afraid she would chip the china.

"I'm done with mothering," she said, when Dan asked if she wasn't curious to meet Patty.

Dan and Rachel looked at each other and held their breath.

"I got six of my own to think about," she said. And then, as she had done for years, a kind of rebuke when Nick and Rachel were fighting or generally disobeying her iron commands, she listed their names in a single word. "LonFredMaryHennyTykeDerek."

"And you'd have six more if you could, besides Nick and me," said Rachel.

"And you better get started, *Miss* Rachel," she said.

"How about a walk," said Dan quickly.

August weather had settled in like a member of the family, part of the week's plans. The thick haze lowered a scorching dust onto the trees and fields, a blanched air that made the open pastures pitiless for the Holsteins, each of them solitary in the heat except for the white specks of cowbirds perched on their withers. Dan was following Rachel down a narrow alley of brittle, dried-out box bushes. She was wearing a short Mexican shift and her legs looked just as solid now as they did when she cut upfield in her Princeton tunic. He would not imagine calling her manly, because hers was a big female form in the most classic sense, but he could understand that colleagues and clients, predominantly men, would find her unthreatening. She gave off no impression that she was prone to periodic weaknesses; they could count on her stamina, which, the older he got, Dan recognized as the single key to business. Nick was slight and not very athletic, just like Helen.

"So what do you think?" she asked over her shoulder.

"If you're talking about Patty I'm not going to answer, I don't think anything."

She gave him an uncompromising shrug.

They came out of the box bush on the lower lawn at the edge of the water and fanned out to stand side by side. "The truth is," said Dan, "what I'm thinking about these days is Nick. I think I've made a hash of Nick."

"That's ridiculous." She stooped to pick a four-leaf clover out of an expanse of grass; she could do the same with arrowheads on the beach. They stood silently for a moment looking at the sailboat resting slack on its mooring. It was a heavy boat, a nineteen-foot fiberglass sloop with a high bow, which Dan had bought after a winter's deliberation, balancing safety and speed the way a father must. When it arrived Nick hadn't even bothered to be polite. He wanted a "racing machine," something slender and unforgiving and not another "beamy scow." He was maybe ten at the time, old enough to know he could charm or hurt anytime he chose. Rachel didn't care much one way or the other—life was all horses for her—and Dan was so disappointed and angry with them both that he went behind the toolshed and wept.

"It's not. I really don't communicate with him at all. I don't even know what his book is about. Do you?"

"Well, I guess what it's really about is you. Not really you, but a father, and this place."

"Just what I was afraid of," said Dan.

"I don't think any of it will hurt your feelings, at least not the pieces I've read."

"Stop being so reassuring. A kiss-and-tell is not my idea of family fun." But Dan was already primed to be hurt. He'd been to a cocktail party recently where a woman he hardly knew forced him to read a letter from her daughter. It was a kind of retold family history, shaped by contempt, a letter filled with the word "never." This woman was not alone. It seemed so many of the people he knew were just now learning that their children would never forgive things, momentary failures of affection and pride, mistakes made in the barren ground between trying to keep hands off and the sin of intruding too much, things that seemed so trivial compared to a parent's embracing love. And even at the time Dan had never been sure what kind of father Nick wanted, what kind of man Nick needed in his life. Instead, Dan remembered confusion, such as the telephone calls he made when he still traveled, before Helen died. Rachel came to the phone terse and quick—she really was a kind of disagreeable girl, but so easy to read. Nick never had the gift of summarizing; his earnest tales of friends and school went on and on, until Dan, tired, sitting in a hotel room in Chicago, could not help but drop his coaxing, nurturing tone and urge him to wrap it up. Too often, in those few short years, calls with Nick ended with the agreement that they'd talk about it more when he got home, which they rarely did.

"But that's really my point," said Dan after Rachel found nothing truly reassuring to say. "This has been going on for quite a while. I'm losing him. Maybe since your mother died, for all I know."

"Oh, give him time."

"He's changed. You can't deny that. He's lost the joy."

"No one wants to go through life grinning for everyone. It's like being a greeter in Atlantic City."

"I don't think he would have come at all this week if you weren't here." It felt good to say these things, even if he knew Rachel was about to tell him to stop feeling sorry for himself.

But Rachel cleared her throat, just the way her mother did when she had something important to say. "See," she said, "that's the thing. I've been waiting to tell you. I've got a job offer from a firm in Seattle, and I think I'm going to take it."

Dan stopped dead; the locusts were buzzing overhead like taut wires through the treetops. "What?"

"It's really a better job for me. It's general corporate practice, not just contracts."

"But you'll have to start all over again," he whined. "I'd really hate to see you go so far away."

"Well, that's the tough part."

Dan nodded, still standing in his footsteps. "I keep thinking, 'She can't do this, she's a girl.' I'm sorry."

He forced himself to resume walking, and then to continue the conversation with the right kinds of questions—the new firm, how many attorneys, prospects for making partner—the questions of a father who has taught his children to live their own lives. They didn't touch on why she wanted to go to Seattle; three thousand miles seemed its own reason for the move, to be taken well or badly, just like Nick's novel. Dan pictured Seattle as a wholesome and athletic place, as if the business community all left work on Fridays in canoes across Puget Sound. It sounded right for Rachel. They kept walking up toward the stable, and Dan hung back while Rachel went in for a peek at a loved, but now empty, place. When she came back she stood before him and gave him a long hug.

"I'm sorry, but you'll have to humor the old guy," he said.

She did her best; Dan and Lucille had raised a kind woman. But there was nothing further to say and they continued the wide arc along the hayfield fences heavy with honeysuckle, and back out onto the white road paved with oyster shells. They approached the house from the land side, past the old toolsheds and outbuildings, and Dan suddenly remembered the time, Rachel was ten, when they were taking down storm windows and she had insisted on carrying them around for storage in the chicken coop. He was up on the ladder and heard a shattering of glass, and jumped from too high to find her covered in blood. Dr. Stout pulled the shards from her head without permanent damage or visible scar before turning to Dan's ankle, which was broken. Helen was furious. But the next time Dan saw Dr. Stout was in the emergency room at Easton Hospital, and they were both covered with Helen's blood, and she was dead.

Patty and Nick had come down while they were gone, and Dan found her alone on the screened porch that had been once, and was still called, the summer kitchen. It was open on three sides, separated from the old smokehouse on the far end by a small open space, where Raymond, Lucille's old uncle, used to slaughter chickens and ducks. The yellow brick floor was hollowed by cooks' feet where the chimney and hearth had been; Dan could imagine the heat even in this broad, airy place. Patty was sitting on a wicker chair with her legs curled under her, wearing a men's strap undershirt and blue jogging shorts. She was reading a book, held so high that he could not fail to notice that it was by Jacques Derrida, a writer of some sort whose name Dan had begun to notice in the Sunday *New York Times*. Perhaps she had really not heard his approach, because she put the book down sharply when he called a good morning.

"Actually we've been up for hours," she said.

"Ah. Where's Nick?"

"He's working," she said with a protective edge on it.

Again, all Dan could find to say was "Ah." She smiled obscurely—

her smiles, he observed, seemed to be directed inward—and he stood for a few more seconds before asking her if she would like anything from the kitchen. There was no question in his mind now: he was going to have to work with this one.

Rachel had just broken her news to Lucille, and the wiry, brusque lady who was "done mothering" at breakfast was crying soundlessly into a paper towel.

"I don't know what it is about you children, moving so far away," she said finally. Dan knew at least one of her sons had moved to Salisbury, and she had daughters who had married and were gone even farther.

"We've gotten by, by ourselves," said Dan.

"But that was just for schooling, for training," she answered; training, if Dan understood her right, for coming back and assuming their proper places in the family tethers. She was leaning against the sink, a vantage point on her terrain, like Dan's desk chair in his Queensville office, the places where both of them were putting in their allotted time. Rachel was sitting at the kitchen table and she stayed there, much as she might have liked to come closer to Lucille and reach out to her.

Dan went back to the summer kitchen and sat beside the girl. "You'll have to excuse us. Rachel's just dropped a bit of a bombshell and we're all a little shaky."

"You mean about her moving to Seattle."

"Well, yes. That's right." He waited for her to offer some kind of vague sympathies, but she did not; it was asking too much of a young person to understand how much this news hurt.

"So," he said finally, "I hope you're comfortable here."

At this she brightened noticeably and put her book face-down on the table. "It's a museum! Nick was going to set up his computer on that pie crust table. Can you imagine?"

Dan could picture it well and he supposed it would be no worse than the time Nick had ascended the highboy, climbing from pull to pull, leaving deep sneaker scuffs on the mahogany burl as he struggled for purchase. But she was right, of course, and she had known enough to notice and identify a pie crust table. "You know antiques, then?"

Yes, she said, her mother was a corporate art consultant and her father, as long as Dan had asked, was a doctor who lived on the West Coast. She mentioned a few more pieces of furniture that caught her eye.

"My mother thinks Chippendales and Queen Anne have peaked, maybe for a long time."

"I wouldn't know," said Dan.

"But the graveyard!" she exclaimed at the end.

Dan was relieved that she had finally listed something of no monetary value, peak or valley, something that couldn't be sold by her mother to Exxon. "As they say in town," he answered, "when most people die they go to heaven; if you're a Williams you just walk across the lawn."

"That's funny."

"I guess," he said. It was all of it crap, he reflected, if he became the generation that lost its children. He'd be just as dead now as later.

"They're the essential past."

Essential past? Whatever could she mean, with her Derrida at her side, her antiques? "I'm not sure I understand what you mean, but to tell you the truth," he said, "I often think the greatest gift I could bestow on the kids is to bulldoze the place and relieve them of the burden."

"I think that's something for the two of them to decide."

"I suppose coming to terms with all this is what Nick is up to in his novel." The girl had begun to annoy him terribly and he could not resist this statement, even as he regretted opening himself to her answer.

"Oh," she said coyly, "I wouldn't say 'coming to terms.' No, I think just looking at it more reflexively. He's trying to deconstruct this family."

"Deconstruct? You mean destroy?" he said quickly, trying not to sound genuinely alarmed.

Patty gave him a patronizing look. "No. It's a critical term. It's very complicated."

Fortunately Nick walked in on this last line. It was Dan's first chance to get a look at him and he saw the full enthusiasm—and the smug satisfaction—of one who has worked a long morning while others took aimless walks. Nick was gangly, he would always be even if he gained weight, but surprisingly quick. As unathletic as he was, he had been the kind of kid who could master inconsequential games of dexterity; he once hit a pong paddle ball a thousand times without missing, and could balance on a teeter-totter until he quit out of boredom. All his gestures, even his expressions, came on like compressed air. And while Dan had to work not to speculate on what part of himself had been "deconstructed" today, this tall, pacing, energetic man was the boy he treasured in his heart.

"The Squire has been surveying the grounds?" said Nick.

"Someone has to work for a living," said Dan, quickly worrying that Nick might miss the irony.

"I was wondering what you called it," he answered.

Patty watched this exchange with a confused look. Any kind of humor, even very bad humor, seemed utterly to escape her. "Did you finish the chapter?" she asked.

"No, but I broke through. I'm just a scene away. Maybe two."

"Well," she said with a deliberate pause, "wasn't that what you said yesterday?"

Good God, thought Dan, the girl wants to marry a published novelist, a novelist with antiques. He said quickly, "But it seems you had a great"—too much accent on the great—"a really very productive morning of work."

Nick's face darkened slightly, as fine a change as a razor cut. "It's kind of a crucial chapter. It has to be right."

"Were you tired?" she asked.

"No. It's just slow, that's all."

During this conversation Rachel had shouted down that lunch was ready, and Dan hung back for the kids to go first, and he repeated this short conversation to himself. It was not such a large moment, he reflected, but nervous-making just the same, and during lunch Nick sat quietly while Patty filled the air with questions, questions about the family, about Lord Baltimore and the Calverts. They took turns answering her questions, but finally it fell back to Nick to unlace the strands of the family, to place ancestors prominently at the Battle of

Yorktown. He looked now and again to Dan for confirmation, and Dan knew how he felt reciting these facts that, even if true, could only sound like family puffery. Dan wanted to do better by his son and did try to engage himself back into the conversation, but by the time Lucille had cleared the plates he felt full of despair, gummy with some kind of sadness for all of them, for himself, for Rachel now off to Seattle in a place where maybe no one would marry her, for Nick with this girl, for Lucille so much older than she looked, and hiding, Dan knew it, her husband's bad health from everyone.

Patty ended the meal by offering flatteries all around the table, including compliments to Lucille that sent her back to the kitchen angrily—but loud enough only for Dan's practiced ear—mimicking the girl's awkward phrase, "So pleasant to have eaten such a good lunch." As they left the table finally, Dan announced he had to spend the afternoon in his office. At this point, he wasn't sure what he would less rather do. He changed quickly and left for town with the three of them discussing the afternoon in the summer kitchen, and he could hear Rachel laboring for every word.

He was so distracted as he drove to town that he nearly ran the single stoplight. Driving mistakes, of any kind, went right to his living memory; once he slightly rear-ended a car on Route 301, and he bolted to the bushes and threw up in front of the kids, in front of a very startled carload of hunters. He crawled to Lawyers' Row and came in the door pale enough for Mrs. McCready—it had always been *Mrs.* McCready—to comment on the heat and ask him if his car air conditioner was working properly. His client was waiting for him, Bobbie Perlee, one of those heavy, fleshy teenagers in Gimme caps and net football jerseys, with greasy long hair. The smell of frying oil and cigarettes filled his office. Whenever he had thought of Rachel joining his practice, he had reminded himself that she would spend her time with clients like this one, court-appointed, Bobbie Perlee in trouble with the law again, assaulting his friend Aldene McSwain with a broken fishing pole. McSwain could lose the eye yet. But Dan couldn't blame a thousand Perlees on anyone but himself; he had made the choice to practice in Queensville when it became clear that the kids needed him closer to home and not working late night after night across the bay in Washington. If she had lived, Helen would have insisted anyway.

"What do you have to say this time, Bobbie?"

Bobbie responded with the round twangy *O*'s of the Eastern Shore, a sound that for so long had spelled ignorance to Dan, living here on a parallel track. He said nothing in response to Bobbie's description of the events; he didn't really hear them. Bobbie Perlee pawed his fat feet into Dan's worn-out Persian rug. For a moment it all seemed so accidental to Dan; sitting in this office with the likes of Bobbie Perlee seemed both frighteningly new and endlessly rehearsed. He could only barely remember the time when escape from the Eastern Shore gave meaning and guided everything he did. It was there when he refused to play with the Baileys and the Pacas, children of family and history like himself. It was there when he refused to go to "the University," which, in the case of Maryland gentry, meant the University of Pennsylvania. It was there even the night he first made love, because it was with his childhood playmate, Molly Tobin. They had escaped north side by side for college, and came together out of loneliness, and went to bed as if breaking her hymen would shatter the last ring that circled them both on these monotonous farmlands and tepid waters.

But he'd come back anyway when his father was dying, and brought Helen with him, a Jew and a midwesterner who came with a sense of discovery, a fresh eye on the landscape. Helen had given the land back to Dan, and Sheila Frederick had chained him to it, coming back out of his youth like a lost bookend, with a phone call saying *I don't look the same, you know,* and because none of them did—it had been thirty years—it meant she was still pretty. She lived in a bright new river-shore condo in Chestertown. She was still pretty, but now when she relaxed, her mouth settled into a tight line of bitterness. Their last night, two years ago, after a year of fighting, she told Dan she worried about his aloneness, not his loneliness which was, she said, her problem and a female one at that, but his aloneness as he rattled around that huge house day after day, with no company but that harsh and unforgiving Lucille. From her, this talk and prediction of a solitary life was a threat; to Dan, at that moment, anyway, being alone was perfect freedom.

Dan finally waved Perlee out of his office without anything further said. These lugs, he could move them around like furniture and they'd never ask why. Dan looked out his office window onto the Queen Anne's County courthouse park, a crosshatching of herringbone brick pathways shaded under the broad leaves of the tulip trees. At the center gathering of the walks was a statue of Queen Anne that had been rededicated by Princess Anne herself. She was only a girl at the time but could have told that wildly enthusiastic crowd a thing or two about history, if they'd chosen to listen. Dan had done well by his children, if today was any indication. They were free not because they had to be, but because they wanted to be. Rachel won a job offer from three thousand miles away because she was that good. My God, how would he bear it when she was gone? And Nick was reaching adulthood with a passion, on the wings of some crazy notion about literary deconstruction that, who knew? could well be what they all needed to hear and understand. So, in many ways, his thoughts ended with this sad girl, this Patty Keith, who seemed the single part of his life that didn't have to be, yet it was she who had been tugging him into depression and ruminations on the bondages of family and place all afternoon.

On the way home he stopped at Mitchell Brothers Liquors, a large windowless block building with a sign on the side made of a giant *S* that formed the first letter of "Spirits, Subs, and Shells." The shells, of course, were the kind you put into shotguns and deer rifles. The Mitchells were clients of his and were very possibly the richest family in town. He bought a large bottle of Soave and at the last minute added a jug of Beefeaters, which was unusual enough for Doris Mitchell to ask if he was having a party. He answered that Nick was home with a girlfriend that looked like trouble, and he was planning to drink the gin himself.

The summer kitchen was empty when he stepped out, gin and tonic in hand. A shower and a first drink had helped. He might have hoped for the three of them, now fully relaxed, to be there trading stories, but instead they came out one by one, and everyone was carrying something to read. He supposed Patty was judging him for staring out at the trees and water, no obscure Eastern European novel in his hand. Nick was uncommunicative, sullen really, this sullenness in the place of the sparkling joy he used to bring into the house. Dinner passed quickly. Afterwards, Patty insisted that Nick take her to the dock and show her the stars and the lights of Kent Island the way, she said firmly, he *promised* he would. Rachel and Dan turned in before they got back, and Dan read *Newsweek* absently until the last of the doors had closed, and he slipped out of his room for one of his house checks, the changing of the guard from the mortals of evening and the ghosts of the midwatch. He was coming back to his room when he heard a cry from Nick's room. In shame and panic he realized that they were making love, but before he could flee he heard her say. "No. No." It wasn't that she was being forced, he could tell that immediately; instead, there was a harshness to it that, even as a father is repelled at the idea of listening to his son have sex, forced Dan to remain there. He had not taken a breath, had not shifted his weight off the ball of his left foot; if anyone had come to the door he would not have been able to move. There was more shuffling from inside, a creak as they repositioned in the old sleigh bed. "*That's* right," said Patty finally. "Like *that.* Like that." Her voice, at least, was softer now, clouded by the dreaminess of approaching orgasm. "Like that," she breathed one last time, and came with a thrust. But from Nick, this whole time, there had not been a word, not a grunt or a sound, so silent he was that he might not have been there at all.

"I think she's a witch," said Rachel. They were on their post-breakfast walk again, this time both of them digging in their heels in purposeful strides.

Dan let out a disgusted and fearful sigh.

"No. I mean it. I think she's using witchcraft on him."

"If you'll forgive the statement, it's cuntcraft if it's anything."

"That's pretty, Dad," she said. They had already reached the water and were turning into the mowed field. "But I'm telling you, it's spooky."

All night Dan had pictured Patty coming, her legs tight around Nick's body, her thin lips clenched pale, and her white teeth dripping blood.

"She controls him. She tells him what to do," said Rachel. "If this were Salem she'd be hanging as we speak."

They had now walked along the hayfield fence line through the brown grass, and said nothing more as they turned for the house, its lime-brushed brick soft and golden in the early morning sun.

"It won't last. He'll get over her," he said.

"Yes, but the older you are the longer it takes to grow out of things, wouldn't you say?"

Dan nodded; Rachel, as usual, was quite right about that. It had taken him six months to figure out that Sheila Frederick was one of the worst mistakes of his life, and another seven years to do something about it. It would not have been so bad if it weren't for the kids. He could admit and confess almost everything in his life except for the fact that he had known, for years, how much they hated her. They hated her so much that when it was over, Nick didn't even bother to comment except to tell Dan he'd seen her twice slipping family teaspoons into her purse.

They skirted the graveyard and without further discussion bypassed the house for another tour. As they went by, Dan glanced over his shoulder, and there she was, Derrida in hand, a small voracious lump that had taken over a corner of the summer kitchen. He looked up at the open window where Nick was working.

"I think I'd better marry Henry," said Rachel.

"He's a very nice guy. You know how fond of him I am," said Dan.

"Nice, but not very interesting. Is that what you mean?"

"Not at all. But as long as you put it this way, I think this Patty Keith is interesting."

"So what are we going to do about Miss Patty?" asked Rachel.

"Well, nothing. What can we do? Nick's already mad at me; I'm not going to give him reason to hate me by butting into his relationships."

"But someday Nick's going to wake up, maybe not for a year, or ten years, and he'll realize he's just given over years of his life to that witch, and then isn't he going to wonder where his sister and father were all that time?"

"It doesn't work that way. Believe me. You don't blame your mistakes in love on others."

Rachel turned to look at him fully with just the slightest narrowing of focus. It was an expression any lawyer, from the first client meeting to the last summary to the jury, had to possess. "Are you talking about Mrs. Frederick?" she said finally.

"I suppose I am. I'm not saying others don't blame you for the mistakes you make in love." Without any trouble, without even a search of his memory, Dan could list several things Sheila had made him do that the kids should never, ever forgive. What leads us to live our lives with people like that?

"No one blames you for her. The cunt."

Dan was certain that Rachel had never before in her whole life used that word. He laughed, and so did Rachel, and he put his arm on her shoulder for a few steps.

She said finally, with an air of summary, "I really think you're making a mistake. I believe she's programming him. I mean it. I think she's dangerous to him and to us. It happens to people a lot more resilient and less sensitive than Nick."

"We'll see." They walked for a few more minutes, in air that was so still the motion of their steps felt like relief. Again Rachel was right; he was a less sensitive man than his son but he had been equally powerless to resist the eight years he had spent with Sheila. Dan couldn't answer for his own life, much less Nick's, so they completed their dejected morning walk and climbed the brick steps to the back portico. As they reached the landing, he took his daughter in his arms again and said, "God, Rachel, I'm going to miss you."

When they came back Patty was in the kitchen talking to Lucille. From the sound of it she had been probing for details about Nick as a boy, which could have been a lovely scene if it hadn't been Patty, eyes sharp, brain calculating every monosyllabic response, as if, in the middle of it, she might take issue with Lucille and start correcting her memories. It's not the girl's fault, thought Dan; it's just a look, the way her face moves, something physical. There was no way for Patty to succeed with Lucille; no girl of Nick's could have done better. It's not Patty's fault, Dan said to himself; she's trying to be nice but she just doesn't have any manners; her parents haven't given her any grace. He said this to himself again later in the morning when she poked her head into his study and asked if his collection of miniature books was valuable. Mother obviously did not deal in miniatures although, Dan supposed, she would be eager to sell Audubons to IBM. Dan answered back truthfully that he didn't know, some of his books may be valuable, as a complete collection it could be of interest to someone. She took this information back with her to the summer kitchen. Dan watched her walk down the hall, a short sweatshirt that exposed the hollow of her back and a pair of those tight jersey pants that made her young body look solid as a brick.

Dan did not see Nick come down, did not hear whether he had finished his chapter and whether that was enough for Patty. At lunch Rachel noted that the Orioles were playing a day game, and Dan had to remind himself again that except for sailing, the athlete in the family was the girl, that she'd been not only older but much more physical than her brother. He remembered how he and Helen had despaired about Nick, a clinger, quick to burst into tears at the first furrowing of disapproval; how Dan had many times caught a tone from the voices in the school playground right across the street from his office, and how he had often stopped to figure out if it was Nick's wail he heard, or just the high-pitched squeals of the girls, or the screech of tires on some distant street. And how curious it was that with this softness also came irrepressible energy, the force of the family, as if he saved every idea and every flight of joy for Dan and Rachel. Yet it had been years now that Nick had turned it on for him.

For once, Patty seemed content to sit at the sidelines while Rachel and Nick continued with the Orioles. Name the four twenty-game winners in 1971, said Rachel, and Nick, of course, could manage only the obvious one, Jim Palmer. Rachel's manners—they were Lucille's doing as much as his, Dan reminded himself—compelled her to ask Patty if she could do any better; Patty made a disgusted look and went back to her crab salad. At that point Dan saw the chance he had been waiting for, and he turned to Nick and told him he had to go see a client's boat—a Hinckley—that was rammed by a drunk at Chestertown mooring. "Come on along and we'll catch up," he said offhandedly. He looked straight into Nick's eyes and would not allow him to glance toward Patty.

"Hey, great," said Nick after the slightest pause. "How about later in the afternoon?"

"Nope. Got to go at low tide. The boat sank." His tone was jocular, the right tone for cornering his son before Patty could move, before she started to break into the conversation with her "Wait a minute" and her "I don't understand." Rachel moved fast as well and quickly suggested, in a similar tone, that they, in the meantime, would go see the Wye Oak, the natural wonder of the Eastern Shore. "We can buy T-shirts," said Rachel.

"But . . ."

A few minutes later Dan and Nick were on the road in Dan's large Buick. There was considerable distance between them on the seat. "I hope Patty doesn't mind me stealing you like this," Dan said finally.

Nick could not hide his discomfort, but he waved it all off.

"Women," said Dan.

Nick let out a small laugh. He was sitting with his body turned slightly toward the door, gazing out at the familiar sights, the long chicken sheds of McCready's Perdue operation, the rustic buildings of the 4-H park under the cool shade of tall loblolly pines.

"So how's it going? The novel."

Good, he said. He'd finished his chapter.

"You know," said Dan, working to something he'd planned to say, "I'm interested to read it anytime you're ready to show it. I won't mention it again, just so long as you know. I can't wait to see what it's about."

"Oh," said Nick, "it's not really *about* anything, not a plot, anyway. I'm more interested in process. It's kind of part of a critical methodology."

Dan wanted to ask what in the world that meant, but could not. "Patty seems interested. I'm sure that's helpful."

"Patty's energy," Nick said, finally turning straight on the seat, "is behind every word."

"She certainly is a forceful girl." Dan realized his heart was pounding, and that it was breaking as he watched Nick come to life at the mention of her name.

"She tore the English department at Columbia *apart.*" He laughed at some private memory that Dan really did not want to hear. "I know she's not for everyone, but I've never known anyone who takes less shit in her life."

And I love her, he was saying. I'm in love with her because she doesn't take shit from anyone. Not like you, Dan heard him think, who is living out his life a prisoner of family history. Not like you who let Mrs. Frederick lock me out the night I ran away from my finals in freshman year. Dan supposed the list was endless.

And at this impasse something could well have ended for him and Nick. It would not come as a break, a quarrel, but it would also not come unexpectedly or undeserved. In the end, thought Dan, being Nick's father didn't mean he and his son couldn't grow apart; didn't mean a biological accident gave him any power over the situation. It meant only that it would hurt more. He could not imagine grieving over friends he once loved with all his heart and now never saw. The Hellmans, how he had loved them, and where in the world were they now? But Nick, even if he never spoke to him again, even if this Patty Keith took him away to some isolation of spirit, Dan would know where he was and feel the pain.

"So why so glum, Dad?" said Nick, a voice very far away from the place where Dan was lost in thought.

"What?"

"I mean, we're going to see a wreck, a Hinckley, for Christ's sake, and you're acting like you owned it yourself."

They were crossing the long bridge over the Chester, lined, as always, with market fishermen sitting beside plastic pails of bait and tending three or four poles apiece. Twenty years ago they'd all been black, now mostly white, but there had not been too much other change in this seventeenth-century town; Dan had never known how to take this place, old families jostling to the last brick even as they washed and sloshed their way down Washington Street on rivers of gin. But it was a lovely town, rising off the river on the backsides of gracious houses, brick and slate with sleeping porches resting out over the tulip trees in a line of brilliant white slats. Dan looked ahead at this pleasant scene while Nick craned his neck out to the moorings.

"Oh yes," he said. "There's a mast at a rather peculiar angle."

The boat was a mess, lying on its side on a sandbar in a confused struggle of lines, a tremendous fibrous gash opening an almost indecent view of the forward berths. Nick rowed them out in a dinghy no one knew who owned; he was full of cheer, free, no matter what, on the water. The brown sandbar came up under them at the edge of the mooring like a slowly breaching whale. As they came alongside, Nick jumped out and waded over to the boat, peered his head through the jagged scar, and then started hooting with laughter.

"What is it?" said Dan.

Nick backed his head out of the hull. "Porn videos. God, there must be fifty of them scattered over the deck."

Dan quickly flashed a picture of his rather proper Philadelphia client, who could have no idea that his most secret compartment had been burst in the crash.

"Jesus," said Nick. "Here's one that is actually called *Nick My Dick*. It's all-male."

"Stop it. It's none of your business," said Dan, but he could not help beaming widely as he said this, and together they plowed the long way back through the moorings, making loud and obnoxious comments about most of the boats they passed. Dan doubted any of these tasteless, coarse stinkpots, all of the new ones featuring a dreadful palette of purples and plums, contained a secret library to compare with the elegant white Hinckley's. After they returned the boat they strolled up Washington Street to the court square and stopped for an ice cream at one of the several new "quality" establishments that had begun to spring up here. Dan hoped, prayed, only that Sheila Frederick, who lived here, would not choose this moment to walk by, but if she did she would simply ignore him anyway, which would not be a bad thing for Nick to see.

But it was all bound by the return, as if Nick were on furlough. And it was certain to be bad, Dan could sense it by now as they turned through the gates back to the farm. This time, when they re-entered the summer kitchen, the Derrida remained raised. As far as Dan could tell she had made little headway in this book, but she stuck to it through Nick's stray, probing comments about their trip. For the first time she struck Dan as funny, touchingly adolescent, with her tight little frown and this pout that she seemed helpless, like a twelve-year-old, to control. No, she had *not* gone to see the Wye Oak. No, she did not wish for any iced tea.

This is how it went for the rest of the day and into the evening. She's in quite a snit, said Rachel when they passed in the front hall, both of them pretending not to be tiptoeing out of range of the summer kitchen, which had seemed to grow large and overpowering around that hard nub of rage. Nick also circled, spending some of the time reading alongside the girl, some of the time upstairs writing a whole new chapter, perhaps a whole new volume, as penance. It was Lucille's day off, and normally eating at the kitchen table gave the family leave to loosen up, a kind of relief from the strictures of life. Patty sat but did not eat, just made sure that everyone understood, as Nick might have said, that she wouldn't take this shit. Dan could not imagine what she was telling herself, how she had reconstructed the events of the afternoon to give her sufficient reason for all this. In the silence, everything in the kitchen, the pots and pans, the appliances and spices, seemed to close in, all this unnecessary clutter. The pork chops tasted like sand; the back of the chair cut into his spine. He tried to picture how she might describe this to friends, if she had any. He could not guess which one of them had earned the highest place in this madness, but he knew which one of them would pay. He'd seen it in couples all his life, these cycles of offense and punishment, had lived the worst of it himself with Sheila Frederick. When she finally left the table, and Nick followed a few minutes later—he gave a kind of shrug but his face was blank—Rachel tried to make a slight joke of it. "We are displeased," she said.

"No. This is tragic," said Dan. "She's mad."

They cleaned the dishes, and after Rachel kissed him good night he went out into the darkness of the summer kitchen. The air, so motionless all week, was still calm but was beginning to come alive; he could hear the muffled clang of the bell buoy a mile into the river. A break in the heat was coming; the wildlife that never stopped encroaching on this Chesapeake life always knew about the weather in advance, and the voices became shortened and sharp. The squirrels' movements through the trees or across the lawns became quick dashes from cover to cover; the beasts and beings were ready, even to a lone firefly, whose brief flashes gave only a staccato edginess to a darkening night. Dan felt old; he was tired. For a moment or two his unspoken words addressed the spirits of the house—they too never stopped encroaching—but he stopped abruptly because he knew, had known since a boy, that if he let them in he would never again be free of them. He wondered if Helen would be among them. He waited long enough, deep into this skittish night, for everyone to be asleep; he could not stand the thought of hearing a single sound from Nick's room. But when he finally did turn in he could not keep from hesitating for a moment at the door, much as he and Helen used to when the children were infants, and they needed only the sound of a moist breath to know all was well.

Under the door he saw that the light was on, and through it he heard the low mumble of a monotone. It was her, and it was just a steady drone, a break now and again, a slightly higher inflection once or twice. It was a sheet of words, sentences, if they were written, that would swallow whole paragraphs, and though Dan wanted to think this unemotional tone meant her anger was spent, he knew immediately that this girl was abusing his son. She was interrogating him without questions; she was damning him without accusations, just this litany, an endless rosary of rage. It could well have been going on for hours, words from her mad depths replacing Nick's, supplanting his thoughts. He could make out no phrase except, once, for a distinct "What we're discussing here . . ." that was simply a pause in the process as she forced him to accept not only her questions, but her answers as well. He did not know how long he stood there; he was waiting, he realized after a time, for the sound of Nick's voice, because as Dan swayed tired back and forth in the hall, he could imagine anything, even that she had killed him and was now incoherently continuing the battle over his body. When finally the voice of his son did appear, it was just two words. "Christ, Patty." There was only one way to read these two names: he was begging, pleading, praying for her to stop. And then the drone began again.

He closed his bedroom door carefully behind him, and sat by his bay window in an old wingback that had been Helen's sewing chair.

Her dark mahogany sewing table was empty now, the orderly rows of needles and spooled threads scattered over the years. The wide windows beckoned him. He could feel no breezes on his sweating forehead and neck, but the air was flavored now with manure, milk, gasoline, and rotting silage, a single essence of the farm that was seeping in from the northwest on the feet of change. He stared out into the dark for a long time before he undressed, and was still half awake when the first blades of moving air began to slice through the humidity. He was nodding off when later, on his pillow, he heard the crustacean leaves of the magnolias and beeches begin to clatter in the wind.

The house was awakened by the steady blow, an extravagance of air and energy after these placid weeks of a hot August. Dan could hear excited yips from the kitchen, as if the children were teenagers once again; he thought, after what he had heard and the hallucinations that plagued him all night long, that he was dreaming an especially cruel vision of a family now lost. But he went down to the kitchen and they were all there: Rachel, as usual grumpy and slow moving in the morning and today looking matronly and heavy in her long unornamented nightgown; Patty, standing on the other side by the refrigerator with a curiously unsure look; Lucille at her most abrupt, wry best; and Nick, wearing nothing but his bathing suit, pacing back and forth, filled with the joy and energy only a few hours ago Dan had given up as lost forever.

"A real wind," he said. "A goddamn hurricane."

"Shut your mouth with that," said Lucille happily.

"We're going to sail all the way to the *bridge,*" he continued, and poked Rachel in the side with a long wooden spoon until she snarled at him.

"I've got to wash my hair," said Rachel.

"Fuck your hair."

Lucille grabbed her own wooden spoon and began to move toward him, and he backed off toward Patty, who was maybe tired out from her efforts the night before, or maybe just so baffled by this unseen Nick that even she could not intrude. Nick picked her up by the waist and spun her around. She was in her short nightgown and when Nick grabbed her he hiked it over her underpants; even as Dan helplessly noticed how sexy her body was, he recoiled at the thought of Nick touching it. With mounting enthusiasm, Dan watched this nervy move and wondered whether it would work on her, but she struggled to get down and was clearly furious as she caught her footing.

"I agree with Rachel," she said. It was probably, Dan realized, the first time she'd ever used Rachel's name.

Nick persisted. "Wind like this happens once a year. It might blow out."

"It could be flat calm again by lunch," said Dan.

She turned quickly on Dan as if he hadn't the slightest right to give an opinion, to speak at all. "I *understand,*" she whined. "I just think this is a good chance for him to get work done."

It was "him," Dan noticed. He waited for Nick's next move and almost shouted with triumph when it came.

"Fuck work." As he said this, a quite large honey locust branch cracked off the tree outside the window and fell to a thud through a rustle of leaves.

Patty screwed her face into a new kind of scowl—she had more frowns, thought Dan, and scowls and pouts than any person he ever met—and announced, "Well I'm not going. I'm going to get *something* done."

"Derrida?" said Dan. He was still giddy with relief.

She glared.

"Oh, come on, sweetie," Nick coaxed. "You won't believe what sailing in wind like this is like." He tried cajoling in other ways, promises of unbroken hours of work, a chance to see the place from the water; he even made public reference to the fight of the day before when he told her a sail would "clear the air after that awful night." He could be worn down by this, Dan knew; he could still lose. But earlier in the conversation Rachel had slipped out and now, with a crash of the door that was probably calculated and intentional, she came back into the kitchen in her bathing suit—she really should watch her weight, Dan couldn't avoid thinking—and that was all the encouragement Nick needed.

Dan walked down to the water with them and sat on the dock as they rigged the boat. The Dacron sails snapped in slicing folds; the boom clanked on the deck like a road sign flattened to the pavement in a gale. "Is it too much?" he called out. Of course it was; under normal circumstances he would be arguing strenuously that it was dangerous. They all knew it was too much. Nick called back something, but he was downwind and the sound was ripped away as soon as he opened his mouth. They cast off and in a second had been blown a hundred feet up the creek. They struggled quickly to haul in the sails; Rachel was on the tiller and Dan wished she wasn't because she was nowhere near the sailor Nick was; she would have been better on the sheets where her brute strength could count. But she let the boat fall off carefully and surely, and all of a sudden the wind caught the sails with a hollow, dense thud, and as they powered past the dock upwind toward the mouth of the creek, Dan heard Nick yell, full voice and full of joy, "Holy shit!"

When he got back to the house she was in her place in the summer kitchen. How tired he was of her presence, of feeling her out there. All the time—it was maybe nothing more than a family joke, but it was true—she had been sitting in his chair. Nick may have told her, or she may have even sensed it. He walked through the house and was met, as he expected, as he had hoped, with an angry, hostile stare.

"You don't approve of water sports, I gather?" he said, ending curiously on a slightly British high point.

She fixed him in her gimlet eyes; this was the master of the Columbia English department.

"Not interested?" he asked again.

"As a matter of fact, I don't approve of very much around here."

"I'm sorry for that," he said. He still held open the possibility that the conversation could be friendly, but he would not lead it in that direction. "It hasn't seemed to have gone well for you."

"There's nothing wrong with *me.*"

"Ah-ha."

"I think you're all in a fantasy."

Dan made a show of looking around at the walls, the cane and wicker furniture, and ended by rapping his knuckles on the solid table. He shrugged. "People from the outside seem to make a lot more of this than we do," he said.

She leaned slightly forward; this was the master of his son. "It's not for me to say, but when you read Nick's novel you'll know where *he* stands."

The words exploded from him. "How dare you bring Nick's novel into this."

"Why do you think he wanted to come here, anyway?"

"Patty," said Dan, almost frightened by the rage that was now fevering his muscles, "when it comes to families, I really think you should let people speak for themselves. I think you should reconsider this conversation."

"You have attacked me. You have been sarcastic to me. I have nothing to apologize for." She made a slight show of returning to her book.

"Tell me something. What are your plans? What are you plans for Nick?"

"Nick makes his own plans."

It was not a statement of fact; it was a threat, a show of her larger power over him. "And you? What are your plans?"

"I'm going to live my own life and I'm not going to pretend that all this family shit comes to anything."

"Whose family? Yours or Nick's?"

"You mean do I plan to marry Nick? So I can get my hands on this?" She mimicked his earlier gesture. "I suppose that's why from the second, the very second I walked in, you have disapproved of me. Well, don't worry"—she said this with a patronizing tone, addressing a child, a pet—"the only thing I care about around here is Nick and . . ." She cut herself off.

"And what?"

"And his work. Not that it matters to you."

"Oh, cut the crap about his work. You want his soul, you little Nazi, you want any soul you can get your hands on."

She pounded the table with her small fist. "What we're talking about here . . ." she shouted, and Dan's body recoiled with this phrase, "is the shit you have handed out, and I'll cite chapter and verse, and—"

"Patty, Patty." He interrupted her with difficulty. "Stop this."

"I have some power, you know."

"Patty, I think it would be better for everyone if you left. Right now."

"What?"

"You heard me."

"You would throw me out?" She did, finally, seem quite stunned. "And just what do you think Nick's going to do when he gets back?"

"I don't know. But I will not tolerate you in my house for another minute."

She slammed her feet down on the brick floor and jumped up almost as if she planned to attack him, to take a swing at him. "O.K., I will. I'm not going to take this shit."

She marched through the kitchen, and a moment or two later he heard a door slam. He moved from his seat to his own chair; suddenly the view seemed right again, the pecan lined up with blue spruce by the water, and the corner of the smokehouse opened onto a hay land that had, from this vantage, always reminded him of the fields of Flanders. A few minutes later he heard a heavy suitcase being dragged over the yellow pine staircase, the steel feet striking like golf spikes into the Georgian treads. He heard a mumble as she came to the kitchen to say something tactical to Lucille, perhaps to give her a note for Nick or to play the part of the tearful girl unfairly accused. He heard the trunk of her car open and he pictured her hefting her large bag, packed with dresses and shorty nightgowns and diaphragms and makeup, over the lip of her BMW, and then she was off, coming into view at the last minute in a flash of red.

Dan heard Lucille's light step, and then saw her face peer out onto the summer kitchen. As many times as Dan had tried to make her change, she never liked to come into a room to say something, but would stand in the doorway and make everyone crane their necks to see her.

"Mister Dan?"

"Lucille, *please* come out."

She took two steps. "You're in a mess of trouble now."

He held his arms up. "What could I do?"

"You just gotta make sure you're picking a fight with the right woman."

Dan looked away as she said this, and hung his head slightly, as if he expected her to say plenty more. But when he glanced back up she was smiling, such a rare and precious event.

"I got six of my own to worry about," she said. The wind was singing through the screens in a single, sustained high note. "But I do hope to the good Lord that those babies are O.K. out in this storm."

Dan stayed in the summer kitchen all morning. The winds weren't going to die down this time—he knew that the moment he woke up—it was a storm with some power to it and it would bring rain later in the day. He ate lunch in his study, and around two went down to the dock. The water was black and the wind was slicing the wave tops into fine spray. No one should be out in this, and not his two children. He pictured them, taking turns at the tiller as the boat pounded on the bottoms and broke through the peaks in a shattering of foam. He wasn't worried yet; he'd selected that big boat for days like this. It would swamp before it would capsize and they could run for a sandy shore any time they wanted. The winds would send them back to this side; he'd sailed more than one submerged hulk home as a boy, and he'd left a boat or two on the beach and hiked home through the fields. This was the soul of the Chesapeake country, never far from land on the water, the water always meeting the land, always in flux. You could always run from one to the other. The water was there, in the end, with Sheila, because he had triumphed over her, had fought battles for months in telephone calls that lasted for hours and evenings drowned in her liquors, until one morning he had awakened and listened to the songs from the water and realized that he was free.

He lowered his legs over the dock planking and sat looking out into the bay. From this spot, he had watched the loblolly pines on Carpenter's Island fall one by one across the low bank into the irresistible tides. When the last of the pines had gone the island itself was next, and it sank finally out of sight during the hurricanes of the fifties. Across the creek Mr. McHugh's house stood empty, blindfolded by shutters. What was to become of the place now that the old man's will had scattered it among nieces and nephews? What was to happen to his own family ground if Rachel went to Seattle for good and Nick . . . and Nick left this afternoon, never to come back?

Dan tried to think again of what he would say to Nick, what his expression should be as they closed upon the mooring, what his first words should cover. But the wind that had already brought change brushed him clean of all that and left him naked, a man. He could not help the rising tide of joy that was coming to him. He was astonished by what had happened to him. By his life. By the work he had done, the wills, the clients, all of them so distant that he couldn't remember ever knowing them at all. By the wife he had loved and lost on the main street of Easton, and by the women who had since then come in and out of life, leaving marks and changes he'd never even bothered to notice. By the children he fathered and raised, those children looking out from photographs over mounds of Christmas wrappings and up from the water's edge, smiles undarkened even by their mother's death. By his mistakes and triumphs, from the slap of a doctor's hand to the last bored spadeful of earth. It was all his, it all accumulated back toward him, toward his body, part of a journey back through the flesh to the seed where it started, and would end.

Christopher Tilghman, a graduate of Yale University, lives outside Boston with his wife and two young sons. "In a Father's Place" is the title story of his first collection, published in 1990. His stories have appeared in a number of magazines.

Oxford Progressive English Readers
General Editor: D.H. Howe

Further Adventures of Sherlock Holmes

The *Oxford Progressive English Readers* series provides a wide range of reading for learners of English. It includes classics, the favourite stories of young readers, and also modern fiction. The series has five grades: the *Introductory Grade* at a 1400 word level, *Grade 1* at a 2100 word level, *Grade 2* at a 3100 word level, *Grade 3* at a 3700 word level and *Grade 4* which consists of abridged stories. Structural as well as lexical controls are applied at each level.

Wherever possible the mood and style of the original stories have been retained. Where this requires departure from the grading scheme, definitions and notes are given.

All the books in the series are attractively illustrated. Each book also has a short section containing questions and suggested activities for students.

Further Adventures of Sherlock Holmes

Sir Arthur Connan Doyle

Hong Kong
OXFORD UNIVERSITY PRESS
Oxford Singapore Tokyo

Oxford University Press

Oxford New York Toronto
Kuala Lumpur Singapore Hong Kong Tokyo
Delhi Bombay Calcutta Madras Karachi
Nairobi Dar es Salaam Cape Town
Melbourne Auckland

and associated companies in
Beirut Berlin Ibadan Nicosia

This edition first published 1981
Third impression 1985

Adapted by Philip Nolses
Illustrated by Alice Wolff
Cover illustration by Kathryn Blomfield

Simplified according to the language grading scheme
especially compiled by D.H. Howe

ISBN 0 19 581281 6

Printed in Hong Kong by Topman Printing Press Ltd.
Published by Oxford University Press, Warwick House, Hong Kong

Contents

1 The Man with the Twisted Lip

Late one night in June 1889, my wife and I were at home when the doorbell suddenly rang. I sat up in my chair, and my wife said disappointedly, 'It must be someone wanting a doctor. You'll have to go.'

I was not pleased, since I had just returned from a hard day of work. We heard the door open and then a woman dressed in black entered the room.

'Excuse this late visit,' she began. Then suddenly she ran forward to my wife and cried on her shoulder. 'Oh! I'm in such trouble. Please help me.'

'Why, it is Kate Whitney,' my wife said. They had been at school together, and Kate had been a friend for many years.

'I don't know what to do,' she explained. 'It's my husband – he has not been home for two days, Dr Watson, and I am so worried about him.'

In his college days Isa Whitney had developed the dangerous habit of using opium*, and in later years had been unable to stop it. Kate had spoken to us about her husband's trouble before. We tried to comfort her.

'Do you know where your husband is?' I asked anxiously.

'Yes. Recently he has been visiting an opium house in the East End of London, by the river. Usually he is away only during the day and returns in the evening, very, very tired. But this time he has been away for two days, and I'm sure he is still in that terrible place. A young woman like myself cannot go there among such evil men.'

'I am Isa's doctor,' I replied, 'and he listens to me. So I shall go there and send him home. I promise you this.'

Ten minutes later I was on my strange journey, though I did not yet know how strange it was to be.

I soon found the street. Between two dark buildings were

***opium**, a very dangerous drug which people smoke.

some steps which led down to the opium house. I entered a long, low room. The air was thick and heavy with opium smoke. Through the darkness I could see people lying about. Most were silent, but some whispered to themselves, and others spoke in strange, low voices. As I entered, an Indian* came up to me with a pipe and some opium.

'I have come to look for a friend, Isa Whitney,' I explained to him. And then I noticed Whitney, tired and dirty, looking at me through the darkness.

'Do you realize that you have been here for two days, man?' I said angrily. 'Your wife has been waiting for you. You should be ashamed of yourself!'

'You must be wrong, Watson,' he answered in a strange voice. 'I have been here a few hours, only three or four pipes. But I'll go home with you, for I don't want to worry Kate.'

I walked down a narrow hall to pay the Indian for the opium that Whitney had smoked. As I passed a thin old man smoking his opium pipe, I heard a low whisper.

'Walk past me, and then look back.'

I took two steps forward and looked back. I nearly cried out in surprise. In front of me was Sherlock Holmes himself in disguise*.

'Holmes!' I whispered. 'What are *you* doing in this evil place?'

'Quiet, Watson,' he answered. 'Send your friend home, and then wait for me outside.'

It was always difficult to refuse an order from Holmes. So I put Whitney in a carriage* for home, sent a note to my wife, and waited for Holmes.

Later that night Holmes and I were walking together down the street.

'I was very surprised to find you there,' I said.

'And I was surprised to see you, Watson,' he replied.

**Indian*, a person from the Asian country called India.
**in disguise*, wearing clothes, false hair, and other things to make one look like someone else.
**carriage*, an old kind of car, pulled by horses.

'I came to find a friend,' I explained.

'And I came to find an enemy,' Holmes replied. 'I am in the middle of an unusual case*. I hoped to find a clue* in that house. I went in disguise because no one must recognize me. My life depends on it. My enemy is the Indian. His opium house is the worst murder-trap in all of London. I fear that Neville Sinclair entered it and will never leave again. Now, Watson, I hope that you will come with me.'

'Of course,' I replied, 'if I can be of use.'

Holmes was staying at the house of Mrs Sinclair at Lee, seven miles away. As we travelled out there he explained matters to me.

'The case seems so simple, and yet I can make no progress. I'll tell the facts clearly. Perhaps you will see some light where all is dark to me.'

'What are the facts?' I asked.

'Five years ago Mr Neville Sinclair came to Lee. He seemed to be a rich man, and bought a large house in the village. After a few years he married the daughter of a local man, and now they have two children. He had no special job, but was interested in several London companies. So normally he travelled there each day on business, and returned on the five o'clock train. He has a large amount of money in the bank, and so I do not think money problems are part of the mystery.

'Last Monday Sinclair went to London as usual. By chance Mrs Sinclair also went to London later that day to visit some shops. At about half past four she was walking through the street where the opium house is. Do you understand me so far, Watson?'

'It is all very clear,' I replied.

'While she was walking down this street Mrs Sinclair suddenly heard a cry. She looked up and saw her husband at an upstairs window in the opium house. He appeared anxious and seemed to wave to her with his hands. Then he suddenly

**case*, a situation in which there is a problem of law.
**clue*, a fact or idea that suggests a possible answer to a problem.

disappeared, as if someone had pulled him from behind. One strange thing which Mrs Sinclair noticed was that some of her husband's clothes were different.

'She was certain that something was wrong, and so rushed down the steps to the house. But at the entrance she met the Indian. He pushed her out into the street. She quickly found some policemen and returned to the house with them. They went up to the room where she had seen her husband, but there was no one there. Apart from the Indian, the only person in the house was an ugly beggar, Hugh Boone, who seems to live there. Both men said no one else had been there that afternoon. But Mrs Sinclair noticed on a table a present which her husband had promised to buy for his son.

'This discovery caused the police to examine the house carefully. At the back of the house was a small bedroom which Boone used. There they found all of Sinclair's clothes, except his coat. And by the window were some drops of blood. All this pointed to an evil crime, Watson. The Indian said he had been downstairs all afternoon and knew nothing, but he could not speak for the beggar. Boone – certainly the last man to see Sinclair – is well known to the London police. He is a sad sight: a pale, dirty face with a terrible twisted lip and orange hair. But he is clever, and I think the police made a mistake by not arresting him immediately. For possibly it gave him a chance to pass something to the Indian. The police noticed that Boone had some blood on his shirt. He explained that he had cut his finger, which was quite true. Although he said he had never seen Sinclair and knew nothing about the clothes, he was taken away to the police station.'

'Were there any other clues?' I asked.

'Yes.' Holmes continued, 'Outside by the river, below Boone's window, the police found Sinclair's coat. The pockets were filled with pennies. I suppose that Boone was trying to throw away the dead Sinclair's clothes when the police came. He put the heavy coins in the pockets to make it sink. The police found no body, but the river current probably carried it away.'

'It certainly seems a probable solution*,' I said.

'We must use it until we have something better,' replied Holmes. 'But there are still too many questions which I cannot answer. What was Sinclair doing in the opium house? What happened to him there? Where is he now? What exactly connects* Boone and Sinclair's disappearance? This case seemed so simple at first, yet really it is so full of difficulties.'

By this time we had arrived at the Sinclair house. As we walked toward the house, the door opened and a small woman stood before us.

'Well, any news?' she anxiously asked Holmes.

'I am afraid not, Mrs Sinclair,' he replied. 'This is my friend, Dr Watson. He has been a great help to me in several of my cases. Luckily it is possible for me to bring him along this time as well.'

'I am delighted to see you,' she said, shaking my hand warmly. 'Now, Mr Holmes,' she said as we entered the room, 'I wish to ask you one or two plain questions.'

'Certainly, madam.'

'Do you truly believe that my husband is alive?' she asked.

'To tell the truth, no, I do not,' Holmes replied uncomfortably.

'Do you think he has been murdered?'

'I am not sure. Perhaps.'

'And on what day did he die?'

'On Monday,' answered Holmes.

'Then perhaps you will explain how I have received this letter from him today.'

'What!' Holmes shouted, jumping up from the chair.

She gave him a letter which he examined with great care. It had been posted on Friday. The envelope was not in Sinclair's writing, his wife explained, but the letter itself was.

'The envelope also contained my husband's ring, Mr Holmes. And I am certain the writing is Neville's. But it is the way he writes when he is in a hurry. The message reads:

**solution*, the answer to a problem.
**connects*, joins, has something in common.

"Dearest, do not be frightened. All will come well. There is a mistake which may take some time to set right. Neville."'

'It is possible that the letter itself was written on Monday, but it was not posted until today, Mrs Sinclair,' warned Holmes.

'You must not take any hope away from me,' she said. 'I am sure Neville is safe. We are so very close that I know when something happens to him. For example, on Monday morning he cut himself upstairs. Although I was downstairs at the time, I knew for certain that something had happened to him.'

'Tell me,' said Holmes. 'When you saw him at that house was the window open?'

'Yes.'

'Then he could have called to you?'

'I suppose so.'

'But instead he just cried out?'

'Yes, I thought it was a call for help.'

'And you thought he was pulled back?'

'He disappeared so suddenly.'

'Perhaps he jumped back,' suggested Holmes. 'Tell me, has your husband ever smoked opium?'

'Never.'

'Thank you, Mrs Sinclair. Now we must get some sleep, for Dr Watson and I may be busy tomorrow.'

When Holmes had a difficult case he used to go without rest for days, sometimes a whole week. He considered the facts over and over, arranging them in different ways until he reached a solution or else decided that he needed more facts. I soon realized that he was preparing for a sleepless night. He sat down in a comfortable chair with his pipe and a large pile of tobacco.

When I awoke in the morning Holmes was still sitting there. The room was full of smoke and the pile of tobacco had completely disappeared.

'Awake, Watson?' he asked.

'Yes.'

'Then get dressed. We have a journey to make.' He smiled as he spoke. He seemed different from the serious thinker of last night. 'I want to test a little idea,' he continued. 'I really have been very slow in this matter, but now I have the key to the problem.'

'And where is it?' I asked.

'In the wash-room,' was the strange answer. 'No, I am not joking.'

Soon we were on our way to London. Holmes spoke as we travelled along.

'In some ways it is a most unusual case. The facts were in front of me all the time, but I was so blind. Still, it is better to learn the solution late than never.'

We arrived at a police station in the centre of London. There Holmes asked to see Bradstreet, the officer in charge. A tall, heavy man came down the hall towards us.

'Please come into my office,' he said, and we entered a small room.

'Are you holding that beggar, Boone – the one connected with the disappearance of Neville Sinclair?' Holmes asked.

'Yes, he is being kept here,' the policeman replied.

'Is he quiet?'

'Oh, he gives us no trouble,' said Bradstreet. 'But he is such a dirty man. His face is as black as coal, but we cannot make him wash it.'

'I would very much like to see him,' said Holmes.

'Would you? That is easily done. Come this way.'

Bradstreet took us along a hall, through a door, down some stairs, and into another hall. There was a line of doors on each side. We stood outside one room, and through the window saw a man sleeping on a bed. He was badly-dressed, as beggars are, with a coloured shirt and a torn coat. He was indeed dirty, and beneath that dirt was a terribly ugly face. Because of his twisted lip several teeth were showing. Bright orange hair grew low over his eyes.

'He certainly needs a wash,' said Holmes, and to my surprise he brought out a face cloth. We then quietly entered

the prisoner's room. Holmes put some water on the cloth and began to wash the face of the sleeping man.

'Gentlemen,' my friend then said, 'allow me to introduce to you Mr Neville Sinclair.'

I have never seen such a change. Not only had the brown dirt disappeared from the face, but also the twisted lip and the bright hair. Before us there was a pale, sad man who looked very surprised. Realizing what had happened, he screamed and threw his face into the blankets.

'That is certainly the missing Sinclair,' said Bradstreet. 'I recognize him from the photograph we have.'

'There has been no murder,' Holmes explained, 'only a great mistake.' Turning to the man he said, 'You should have told your wife the truth.'

'But I did not want my children to be ashamed of their father,' the prisoner replied. 'What can I do?'

'You must now persuade the police that there was no crime. The matter will then go no further.'

'How can I thank you!' he cried, and then began his story. 'You are the first people to hear my story. When I was a young man I worked as a reporter for a newspaper. One day my chief asked me to write about beggars in London. That was the beginning of my adventures. For it was only by being a beggar myself that I could get the necessary information. Since I had once been an actor, I knew how to disguise my appearance. I painted my face brown, wore orange hair, and poor clothes. I became a beggar in the busiest part of London. In a single day I could earn as much as the newspaper paid me for a week's work. So I decided to give up reporting and spend all my time as a beggar.'

'Did anyone know your secret?' asked Holmes.

'Only one man,' replied Sinclair. 'He was the keeper of an opium house where I changed my disguise each morning and evening. I paid this man well, and knew my secret was safe with him. I was a very successful beggar, and as I became richer I bought a house and married. My dear wife knew that I had some business in London, but no more.

'Last Monday I had finished my day's begging and was taking off my disguise at the house when I had a great shock. I saw my wife in the street looking up at me. I gave a cry of surprise, and threw up my arms to cover my face. Quickly I jumped back and put on my disguise again. I was afraid that my wife might come in and recognize my ordinary clothes. So I decided to throw them out of the window into the river. At the window I opened a wound I had received that morning. I had time to throw only the coat away before my wife and the police entered. Then I was arrested on suspicion of murdering Neville Sinclair.

'Before the arrest I had managed to give the Indian a letter for my wife, together with my ring. I told her she had no cause to fear. I wanted to keep my disguise as long as possible. That is why I refused to wash my face.'

'The letter reached her only yesterday,' said Holmes.

'Good God!' cried Sinclair. 'What a terrible week for her. The Indian must have been slow to post it.'

'Things must stop here,' said Bradstreet. 'If the police are to remain quiet about this matter, then there must be no more Hugh Boone.'

'It shall be so,' promised Sinclair.

'Very well,' said Bradstreet. Turning to my friend he asked, 'Tell me, Mr Holmes, how did you solve this problem?'

'By sitting in a comfortable chair and smoking my pipe,' he replied with a smile. 'Come, Watson, let us return home.'

2 Silver Blaze

'I am afraid, Watson, that I shall have to go,' Holmes said to me one morning.

'Go! Where to?' I asked.

'To the west country – to Pyland,' was his reply.

'I am not surprised,' I said. 'Indeed, I only wonder that you did not start earlier on this unusual case. It is the one subject of conversation in all of England. For a whole day you have walked about the room, smoking that strong tobacco in your pipe and hardly listening to what I say. People have sent all the newspapers up to you. But even though you remained silent, I knew what was in your thoughts. Only one thing interested your powerful mind – the disappearance of the race-horse Silver Blaze and the murder of its trainer. And now you want to visit the scene of these events. I have been waiting and hoping for this. May I come along with you?'

'My dear Watson, I shall be most pleased. It will not be a waste of your time. There are several things which promise to make it no ordinary case.'

An hour later we were travelling west on the train to Devon.

'We are going well,' said Holmes, looking out of the window and then at his watch. 'We are travelling at fifty three and a half miles an hour.'

'I have not seen any quarter-mile posts,' I said.

'Nor have I, Watson,' he replied, 'but the telegram posts are sixty yards apart, which makes the matter simple. Now, I suppose you already know about Silver Blaze and the trainer?'

'I have read some of the newspapers.'

'It is a case where I must examine the known facts carefully rather than look for fresh material. Because the matter is so unusual and important, too many people have offered too many solutions. The difficulty is to set the actual facts apart from these solutions. Then we look to see where they lead us. On Tuesday I received telegrams from the owner, Colonel* Ross, and Gregory, the police detective*, asking for my help.'

'Tuesday!' I cried. 'But this is Thursday. Why did you not go down yesterday?'

'Because I made a mistake,' Holmes explained. 'I did not think it was possible for such a famous horse as Silver Blaze to remain unfound. But I was wrong. Now, let me state the main facts of the case to you, Watson.'

'Go ahead,' I replied.

'Before this business Silver Blaze was the favourite horse for the Wessex Cup, an important race next week. Large amounts of money have been bet* on him. So his disappearance is of advantage to many people. Therefore Colonel Ross has been anxious to guard him well. The trainer, Straker, had worked with the Colonel for many years. He had always shown himself to be an honest man. He was in charge of three stable boys*. Straker and his wife lived near the stables. The market town is two miles away. Also near are some other racing stables, at Capleton. In every other direction there is only field and forest.

'On Monday night one of the stable boys, Ned, was on duty. When Straker's cook took some curry out to him she noticed a stranger. He followed her to the stables, and offered the boy some money for information about the horses. Ned was angry at this and rushed across to get the dog. The cook is sure that she then saw the stranger leaning through the small stable window.'

'Was the stable door unlocked when the boy went to get the dog?' I asked.

**colonel*, title for an army officer.
**detective*, someone whose job is to solve crimes.
**bet*, risk money on guessing the result of a race or other event.
**stable boy*, boy who takes care of horses in a *stable*, which is a building where animals are kept.

'Excellent, Watson, excellent. I also wondered about that. A telegram from Pyland yesterday informed me that the boy did lock the door.

'Later that night,' continued Holmes, 'Straker got up and dressed – to see if all was well in the stables, he told his wife. In the morning he was still absent, so Mrs Straker went along to the stables. Ned was unconscious, and both the trainer and Silver Blaze were gone. Although the other two boys slept above the stables, they had heard nothing in the night.

'They went out to search for horse and trainer. About a quarter of a mile from the stables they found the dead body of the unlucky Straker. His head had been beaten in by some heavy weapon, and there was a wound in his leg from something sharp. Clearly Straker had fought back, for there was a small knife, covered in blood, in his right hand. In his left hand was a handkerchief. Both the cook and Ned are sure it belonged to the stranger. Ned also believes that the stranger secretly put some opium into his curry to make him unconscious. These, Watson, are the main facts.'

'What have the police done so far?' I asked.

'Gregory, the officer in charge of the case, is a man of great ability. But he doesn't have much imagination. As soon as he arrived at Pyland he arrested the man who was naturally suspected, the stranger. His name is Simpson and he comes from a good family, but wastes all his money on betting. It seems that he has bet five thousand pounds against Silver Blaze in the Wessex Cup. Simpson says he came down just to get information about the horses at Pyland and Capleton. He agrees that he was at the Pyland stables that night, but cannot say why Straker had his handkerchief. His wet clothes prove he was out that night. Also, he has a heavy walking-stick, which is possibly the weapon that killed Straker. But he has no knife wound.'

'Is it possible,' I asked, 'that Straker's wound was caused by his own knife during the fight?'

'Good, Watson. Yes, it is probable. But, if so, that goes against Simpson. I suppose that the police think Simpson made the stable boy unconscious with the opium. Then, with a second key he opened the stable door and led the horse away. Straker saw him do this and there was a fight. Simpson killed Straker, and then hid the horse somewhere – or else it escaped.'

It was evening when we arrived at the small market town near Pyland. At the station we were met by Gregory, the police detective, and Colonel Ross, the owner of Silver Blaze. They took us out to Pyland, and during the journey Holmes discussed the case with Gregory. The policeman's ideas were exactly as Holmes had supposed.

'Your explanation leaves too many unanswered questions, Gregory,' argued Holmes. 'Why did Simpson take the horse from the stables if he only wanted to hurt it? Have you found a second key? Where did he buy the opium? Where could he, a stranger, hide the horse?'

'The difficulties are not so great,' replied Gregory. 'He probably threw the key away. Opium can easily be bought in London. He has been to Pyland several times before. The horse may be hidden in the forest, or with a band of gipsies* – for we know they had a camp near the stables on Monday, and we are searching for them now.'

'There is another training stable quite close?' asked Holmes.

'Yes,' said Gregory. 'That is something we should not forget. At Capleton they have a horse which is second favourite in the Wessex Cup. So the disappearance of Silver Blaze is to their advantage. Silas Brown, the Capleton trainer, has large bets on his horse. However, we have searched the stables there and found nothing to connect him with this business. And Simpson is not connected with Capleton either.'

Here their conversation ended, and soon we reached Pyland. Holmes remained silent, looking thoughtfully into the sky. I touched his arm.

'Excuse me,' he said turning to Colonel Ross, who looked

gipsies, people with no definite home, who wander from place to place.

at him with some surprise. 'I was day-dreaming.' A smile on his face suggested to me that he had found a clue.

'Do you want to go immediately to the scene of the crime, Mr Holmes?' asked Gregory.

'I prefer to stay here a while and go into one or two questions in detail. May I see what Straker had in his pockets at the time of his death?'

We went into Straker's house and sat around a table. Gregory laid a pile of objects before us. There was a box of matches, a candle, a pipe, some tobacco, a silver watch, some coins, a few papers, and a small knife. Holmes picked the knife up and examined it carefully.

'This is an unusual knife. Do you recognize it, Watson?'

'Yes,' I replied. 'It is normally used for special medical work.'

'I thought so,' said Holmes. 'It has a very sharp blade. A strange thing for a man to carry with him; it does not even close inside a pocket. Now, what about these papers?'

'Nothing unusual,' said Gregory, 'except this one. It is a bill to a Mr Darbyshire from a London shop for a woman's dress. Mrs Straker says that Darbyshire was a friend of her husband's, and sometimes his letters came here.'

We then went outside and after a short walk arrived at the place where the body had been found. Holmes made a careful search of the ground.

'Hello!' he said suddenly, 'what is this?'

It was a half-burnt match which had been hidden in the ground. At first it had seemed to be just some thin piece of wood.

'I don't know why I didn't see that,' said Gregory a little angrily.

'It was out of sight, buried in the soil,' explained Holmes. 'I saw it only because I was looking for it.'

'What! You knew it was there?' asked Gregory surprised.

'I thought it was not unlikely,' Holmes replied.

By this time Colonel Ross was becoming rather annoyed by Holmes's manner. He and Gregory returned to Straker's house. Holmes then explained matters to me.

'For now, Watson, we need not worry about the murder of John Straker. We must discover what has happened to Silver Blaze. Suppose that he ran off and escaped. Where could he have gone to? A horse likes to be with other horses – that is their way. So perhaps he returned to Pyland or went across to the stables at Capleton. Certainly he did not run wild, since no one has seen him. And the gipsies have no reason to take him, for they are anxious to avoid any trouble with the police. Surely that is clear?'

'Where is he then?' I asked.

'As I said, it is natural for him to go to Pyland or Capleton. He is not at Pyland, therefore he is at Capleton. Let us go there and check. If I am right, then we shall probably discover some marks on the ground between here and Capleton.'

After a few minutes' walk we came to some wet, flat land. We each made a careful search of the ground. Soon I heard Holmes shout and saw him waving his hand to me. There were the marks of a horse clearly shown in the soft soil.

'See the value of the imagination,' said Holmes. 'It is a quality which Gregory doesn't have. We made a guess, imagined a possibility, and then tested it.'

We followed the marks for about a mile and came close to Capleton. Then we saw the footprints* of a man beside the marks of the horse.

'The horse was alone before,' I cried.

'Quite so, Watson,' answered Holmes. 'It *was* alone before.'

We followed the footprints. Our journey ended at the gates of the Capleton stables. A boy came out to meet us.

'Just one question,' Holmes said to him. 'Is your master, Silas Brown, up early in the mornings?'

'Yes, he is always the first. But I must go now, sir.'

Brown himself had appeared.

'We want no strangers here!' he shouted angrily. 'Go away or I shall get the dog!'

Holmes went forward and whispered into the trainer's

**footprints*, marks left in the ground by feet.

ear. The man became quiet. He and Holmes then went into the building for twenty minutes. When he came out, Silas Brown's face was pale and his hands were shaking.

'I shall do what you told me,' he said to Holmes.

'There must be no mistake,' my friend replied.

We left for Pyland. Holmes told me what had happened with Brown at Capleton.

'He has the horse then?' I asked.

'At first he said not. But because I described to him so exactly what he did on Tuesday morning, he now believes I actually watched him. I told Brown that he was the first person to be up and that he saw a horse running wild. Then, to his surprise, he recognized it as Silver Blaze. So he took it to Capleton to hide until after the Wessex Cup. When I told him every detail he admitted the truth. Now he is only anxious to escape more trouble.'

'But the police searched the Capleton stables,' I said.

'An old trainer knows many tricks. By the way, Watson, do not mention this to the Colonel. I wish to have a little joke with him. But of course all this is unimportant beside the murder of Straker.'

'You will attempt to solve that problem now?' I asked.

'No. We are returning to London by the night train.'

I was very surprised at this reply. We had been at Pyland only for a few hours. Why did Holmes not want to continue working on a case which he had begun so successfully? He said no more and we returned to Straker's house in silence. The Colonel and Gregory were waiting for us.

'Watson and I return to London tonight,' said Holmes. 'But keep Silver Blaze's name in the race.'

'So you cannot find Straker's murderer?' asked Colonel Ross.

'There are certainly great difficulties,' replied Holmes. 'But I hope that your horse will run in the Wessex Cup. Gregory, may I have a photograph of Straker?'

The policeman gave him a photograph from his pocket.

'I am rather disappointed in Holmes,' Colonel Ross said

roughly as we went out of the room.

Just before we left Pyland, Holmes suddenly seemed to have an idea. He spoke to one of the stable boys.

'Have you noticed anything strange about the local sheep recently?' he asked.

'Nothing much,' the youth replied, 'except that three have become lame, sir.'

Holmes seemed very pleased with this answer.

'Is there anything else of importance?' asked Gregory, who was interested.

'The strange behaviour of the dog in the night,' said Holmes.

'But the dog did nothing in the night,' replied Gregory.

'That was the strange behaviour.'

Four days later Holmes and I were again on the train. This time we were going to the Wessex Cup. Colonel Ross met us at the station, and his manner towards Holmes was very cold.

'I have not yet found my horse,' he said, 'but its name has remained in the race, as you ordered.'

'How is the betting?' asked Holmes.

'Very strange,' the Colonel replied. 'Silver Blaze still seems to be the favourite.'

'The race has begun!' I cried. 'All six are there.'

'Then Silver Blaze must be running,' said Ross, 'but I don't see him.' Then a powerful horse passed by wearing the Colonel's colours. 'That's not my horse! That animal has not a white hair on its body. What have you done, Holmes?'

'Well, let us see how he does,' said Holmes unworried.

From where we stood we had an excellent view. The six horses were close together, but half-way along the Capleton horse took the lead. However, before long it had tired itself out, and the Colonel's horse won easily.

'Well, it's my race,' said Colonel Ross. 'Don't you think you have kept up this mystery long enough, Holmes?'

We walked over to the winning horse and Holmes explained.

'You have only to wash his face and leg, and you will find

he is the same old Silver Blaze.'

'You have done well to find my horse,' replied the Colonel. 'You would do better to catch the murderer of John Straker.'

'I have done so,' said Holmes quietly.

The Colonel and I looked at Holmes in complete surprise.

'He is in my presence now,' continued my friend.

'Mr Holmes, this is a very bad joke indeed,' said the Colonel angrily.

Holmes laughed. 'I do not mean you, Colonel,' he explained. 'The real murderer stands right behind you,' and he placed his hand upon the horse. 'But I must say that he killed to save himself, and that Straker was not the honest man he appeared. But there's the bell for the next race. I shall tell you everything afterwards.'

During the train journey back to London, Holmes explained to us how he had solved* the mystery.

'Any solutions which I reached in London from the newspaper reports were completely wrong. I thought that Simpson was guilty, although I didn't know all the facts. But when I arrived at Pyland – you probably remember my "daydreaming" – I realized the importance of the stable boy's meal. Only a strong-tasting meal such as curry can hide the taste of opium. Now, Simpson was a stranger and could not know what the meal was to be. But clearly Straker knew it was curry, and he had a chance to put the opium in before the cook took it to the stables.'

'How does this connect with the dog's behaviour?' I asked.

'The dog's silence proved that it was not a stranger who took the horse away. Clearly the midnight visitor was someone the dog knew well,' Holmes explained. 'Already I suspected Straker. But why did he take the horse? The knife in his pocket provided the answer. Watson said it was used for exact medical work. By cutting the back of a horse's leg it is possible to make it lame. If the wound is small enough, then it will cause no suspicion.'

**solved*, found the answer to (a problem).

'The criminal*!' cried Colonel Ross.

'Straker took the horse into the fields to avoid any possible noise,' continued Holmes.

'Of course!' said the Colonel. 'That was why he needed the candle and matches.'

'Just so,' replied Holmes. 'And Straker's pockets also pro-

**criminal*, a person who does things the law does not allow.

vided the answer to the whole problem. For Straker was in fact Darbyshire, as I discovered when I took his photograph to the dress shop. It seems he had a lady friend in London, who liked expensive things. Straker needed money to pay his debts. To make Silver Blaze lame and then bet on another horse in the Wessex Cup was the solution to his problem. The rest of the story is clear. The bright candle frightened the

horse, and it kicked out at Straker. As he fell to the ground, the knife cut him.'

'What of Simpson's handkerchief?' I asked.

'Straker must have found it by pure chance.'

'Wonderful!' cried Colonel Ross. 'It's as if you were there yourself.'

'The final piece in the puzzle was provided by the lame sheep. Straker had practised on them with his knife.'

'You have made it perfectly clear, Mr Holmes,' said the Colonel, 'except for one thing. Where was the horse?'

'Ah, it escaped and was looked after by a neighbour. But no more of that. Here we are at the station.'

3 The Final Problem

It is with great sadness that I sit down to write these words. For this is the last story I shall ever be able to tell of the unusual gifts and abilities of my friend Sherlock Holmes. I have already written about some of the strange cases we have worked on since I first met Holmes ten years ago. But I decided to remain silent about the event which has made my life empty for the past two years. But the recent stories told by Colonel Moriarty about his dead brother have forced me to change my mind. I must give the public the facts exactly as they happened. Only I know the complete truth. So far there have been only three reports: in a foreign newspaper, in an English newspaper, and now by Colonel Moriarty. The first and second were very short, and the third is completely false. So now it is my duty to tell for the first time what really happened between Professor Moriarty and Sherlock Holmes.

Because of my marriage and busy medical work I saw less of Holmes. He still came to me sometimes when he wanted a companion for a particular case. But this happened more and more seldom. In 1890 I was with Holmes in only three cases. So I was surprised when he came to my house one Friday evening late in April 1891. I noticed that his face was whiter and thinner than usual.

'Yes, Watson, I have been rather tired recently,' he said, guessing my thoughts from the way I looked at him. 'I have been a little busy. May I pull the curtains together?' Holmes moved carefully round the room to the window.

'Are you afraid of something?' I asked.

'Well, I am,' he answered.

'Of what?'

'Of guns,' he replied.

'My dear Holmes, what do you mean?'

'I think you know me well enough, Watson, to understand that I am not easily frightened. But it is stupidity, not courage, to refuse to recognize a real danger. I am sorry to come visiting so late. Is your wife at home?'

'She is away on a visit,' I said.

'Indeed! You are alone?' he asked.

'Yes.'

'Will you come abroad with me, anywhere, for a week?'

There was something strange in all this. It was not usual for Holmes to take a holiday without good purpose. And he seemed so very tired. He read my thoughts, and began to explain matters to me.

'You have probably never heard of Professor Moriarty?' he said.

'Never,' I replied.

'That is the wonder of the thing!' he cried. 'The man is everywhere in London, and no one has heard of him. That is what makes him such a dangerous criminal. Truly, Watson, if I can free London of him then I shall feel that my life's work is done, and I can turn to more peaceful matters. But I cannot rest knowing that Moriarty walks freely through the streets of London.'

'What has he done, then?' I asked.

'His life has not been at all ordinary,' Holmes replied. 'He comes from a good family, and has a powerful and intelligent mind. At the age of twenty-one he wrote a small science book which made him famous all over the world. Because of it he became a mathematics professor at a small university. But there was something criminal in the man's blood, something made even more dangerous by his powerful mind. He was forced to give up his university position and he came down to London. Everyone knows this much.

'But what I tell you now is what I have discovered myself. As you realize, Watson, there is no one who knows the world of crime as well as I do. For many years now I have believed that there was some great, organizing power behind the ordinary criminal. Again and again I have felt the presence of this power in the most different crimes. For years I have tried to find out exactly what or who was this power, and finally the path has led me to Professor Moriarty.

'He is the evil prince of crime, Watson. He is the true cause of most of the evil in this great city. He has a really excellent brain. But he does little himself. Instead he is at the centre of everything, planning away. He has many agents*, and they are well organized. If someone wants a crime done, a message goes to the Professor and he organizes the matter. Sometimes the agent is caught, but never the controlling mind. This, Watson, is the organization which I have fought with all my powers.'

'Good God, Holmes! And have you succeeded?' I asked.

'At first it seemed impossible, for the Professor had made sure he was completely safe. You know my powers, my dear Watson, and yet after three months I believed I had met my equal. Although I thought his crimes were awful, I had to admire his brains and ability. But finally he made a mistake – only a very little mistake – but it was more than he could afford when I was so close behind him. This was my chance. I acted quickly and now the end of the Professor and his organization is near. In three days, on Monday, the Professor and all his group will be arrested by the police. It will be the greatest criminal trial of the century, the solution of over forty mysteries, and death for most of them.'

'Does Moriarty realize this?' I asked.

'Unfortunately, yes. He has watched every action of mine. Again and again he tried to get away, but each time I succeeded in getting closer to him. It has been one of the best fights in the history of detective work. Then, this morning, I was sitting in my room when the door opened and suddenly Moriarty stood before me.

'"Take a chair," I said. "I can give you five minutes if you have anything to say."

**agent*, a person who is paid to act for another.

‘“All that I have to say has already been through your mind,” he replied.

‘“Then possibly my answer has been through yours, Professor Moriarty.”

‘“You intend to go on with this?” he asked.

‘“Absolutely,” I said.

‘“By February you were becoming a problem to me. At the end of March you destroyed my plans. And now I am in danger of arrest. The situation is becoming impossible. You must leave me alone, Holmes. You really must.”

‘“After Monday,” I said.

‘“I have enjoyed watching you at work,” he continued. “I shall indeed be sorry if you force me to act. You smile, but it is true.”

‘“Danger is part of my job,” I said.

‘“This is not danger,” said Moriarty angrily. “It is certain death. You are fighting not just one man, Holmes, but a powerful organization. Even you do not realize its true size and greatness. You must get out of the way or be finished.”

‘“It's a shame our conversation must end here,” I said, “for I have other business now.”

‘“Well, well,” he said at last. “It seems a pity, but I have done all I can. I know all your plans. You can do nothing before Monday. You hope to beat me, but I tell you that you never will.”

‘That, Watson, was my strange meeting with Professor Moriarty. The memory of it is unpleasant.’

‘Can't the police make sure that you are safe from him?’ I asked.

‘I believe that it is not Moriarty but his agents who will attack me – and with good reason,’ my friend replied.

‘Have you been attacked already?’

‘My dear Watson, Moriarty is not a man who is slow to act. Today I went to do something in central London. As I passed the corner of a street, a cab* suddenly rushed directly towards me. Immediately I jumped back and only just saved

**cab*, a carriage that can be rented, with its driver, for short journeys.

myself. By then the cab had disappeared from sight. As I walked along another street, a brick came down from the roof of one of the houses and broke into pieces at my feet. I called the police and the place was searched. But I could prove nothing. As I came round to you this evening, Watson, I was attacked by some rough man with a heavy stick. I fought him off and he is now in the hands of the police. But I cannot prove any connection between him and Moriarty. So, you should not be surprised that I am anxious about the curtains. Also, I must not leave by the front door.'

'Will you sleep here tonight?' I asked.

'No, my friend. I am a dangerous visitor. But I have organized my plans and all will be well. The police can now arrest the Moriarty group without my help, although my presence will be necessary at the trial. Therefore it is best I get away for a few days. So it will be a pleasure if you can come abroad with me.'

'My medical work is not busy at present,' I replied, 'so I shall be glad to come.'

'And to start tomorrow morning?' Holmes asked.

'If necessary.'

'Oh, yes, it is most necessary. Here are my orders, Watson, and you must follow them exactly. For you are now playing a game with me against the cleverest and most powerful criminals in Europe. Now listen! Send your luggage – without an address – to the railway station tonight. Then, in the morning, take several different cabs and finally reach the station in time for the European train.'

'Where shall I meet you?' I asked.

'At the station, on the train. Go to the second car.'

Holmes refused to stay at my house that night because he wanted to avoid any danger to me. He came out into the garden with me, climbed over the back wall, and disappeared down a street.

In the morning I followed Holmes's orders. I arrived at the station and found the second car of the train. But I could not see my friend anywhere. I sat down beside an old foreigner and anxiously wondered about Holmes. The train was ready to leave.

'My dear Watson,' said a voice, 'you have not even said good morning.'

I turned round in complete surprise. The old foreigner was looking towards me. It was Holmes in disguise.

'Good God!' I cried.

'Such secrecy is still necessary,' Holmes whispered. 'They are following closely behind us. Ah, there is Moriarty.'

The train was already moving. Looking back I saw a tall man waving his hand as if he wanted to stop the train. However, it was too late, and soon we were out of the station. Holmes took off his disguise.

'Have you heard about my rooms in Baker Street, Watson?'

'No,' I replied.

'They set fire to them last night. Luckily no great damage was done.'

'This is terrible, Holmes,' I said.

'We must plan what to do about Moriarty now.'

'But this is an express* train,' I said. 'And the boat to Europe connects with it. So surely he cannot follow us.'

'My dear Watson, clearly you do not realize the great ability of this man. He can take a special train and follow us. This train stops at Canterbury; and there is always a delay of fifteen minutes at the port before the boat leaves. He will catch us there.'

'What shall we do then?' I asked.

'We shall leave this train at Canterbury.'

'And then?'

'We shall travel eighty miles to another port, and sail over to Europe from there. Moriarty will follow our luggage to Paris and wait for us there. But meanwhile we shall avoid Paris and go to Switzerland.'

At Canterbury we left our train. While we were waiting a special train passed quickly through the station.

'There he goes,' said Holmes as we secretly watched.

**express*, fast, making few stops.

We were in Europe that night, and then travelled slowly towards Switzerland. On Monday morning Holmes sent a telegram to the London police, and in the evening he received their reply.

'I should have realized,' he cried. 'He has escaped.'

'Moriarty!'

'They have arrested the whole group except him,' Holmes explained. 'He found a way to escape. Of course, when I left the country there was no one able to fight such a man. But I thought I had given the police all the help they needed for his arrest. You must return, Watson.'

'Why?' I asked.

'Because I am a dangerous companion now. Without his criminal organization Moriarty has no work, no interest in life. He cannot return to London for fear of arrest. I believe his only aim now will be to kill me. That is why you must leave now, Watson.'

I refused to leave my old friend in such danger. We argued over it for half an hour, but that night we continued our journey towards Switzerland. It was a pleasant week, and at the end of it we reached Meiringen. But I realized that Holmes never forgot the danger we were in. I could tell by the way he always watched so carefully all the people we passed, we could not escape this danger. One day in the mountains a rock fell down towards us. Holmes immediately rushed to a high point and looked around in every direction. Perhaps it really was an accident, but Holmes acted like he expected such things to happen. Yet during the whole journey he was quite cheerful. He often said that the arrest of Moriarty would be the end of his life's work.

'I think that my life has not been useless,' he said to me one day. 'Already I have done much. My presence has made London a better place. I have worked on over a thousand cases and have always been on the side of good. My work will end with the arrest or death of the most dangerous and clever criminal in Europe.'

The rest of my story will be short, but exact. I do not

really wish to write about this matter, but I know that I have a duty to include every detail.

On May 3rd we reached the little village of Meiringen among the mountains of Switzerland. There we stayed at the hotel of Peter Steiner. Steiner was a clever man who spoke good English, for he had once lived in London. The next day Holmes and I decided to cross the hills and see the next village. Steiner said we must visit the famous waterfall at Reichenbach on our way.

The Reichenbach Fall is a frightening place indeed. The melting snow from the mountains increases the size and speed of the river. When it reaches Reichenbach the rushing water crashes into the great depths of a huge valley with a terrible force. Holmes and I stood near the edge, looking down into the water and listening to the great noise which came up from the bottom. A small path there lets visitors have a better view of the waterfall. This ends suddenly, and so the traveller must return by the same way. As we walked back a boy ran up to me with a letter. It was a message from Steiner. Not long after we left the hotel an English woman had arrived. She was suffering from a terrible disease and was on a journey to visit some friends, but had suddenly become ill. She did not expect to live many more hours. She wanted to see an English doctor, and so Steiner asked me to return.

It was impossible to refuse to see an English woman who was dying in a foreign country. But I was anxious about leaving Holmes alone. We finally agreed that the boy could be his guide while I returned to Meiringen. I planned to meet with Holmes at the next village in the evening. As I turned to go I saw Holmes looking down into the rushing waters. It was the last time I ever saw him.

As I walked back to the hotel I noticed a man dressed in black. He was walking along the path which led to the Fall. But I soon forgot about him and continued my walk back. An hour later I arrived at Meiringen. Steiner was standing by the door of his hotel.

'Well,' I said as I hurried up. 'I hope that she is no worse.'

A look of surprise passed over his face. I suddenly became worried.

'You did not write this?' I asked, pulling the letter from my pocket. 'There is no sick English woman in the hotel?'

'Certainly not,' he cried. 'But the envelope has the hotel mark on it. The writer must be the tall Englishman who arrived after you left. He said –'

But I did not wait for Steiner's explanations. Filled with fear, I ran back the way I had just come. Finally at Reichenbach again, I found Holmes's walking-stick leaning against a rock. But I couldn't see Holmes anywhere, and no one answered my shouts.

The boy had gone. He was probably an agent of Moriarty. What had happened? I began to think of Holmes's own methods of solving a mystery, and tried to use them myself. It was not a difficult matter. Two lines of foot-prints were clearly marked along the far end of the path. We had not walked that far the first time, so it must be Holmes and someone else. But there were no foot-prints returning. I walked along the narrow path, with a steep wall of rock on one side and on the other a drop of several hundred feet. A few yards from the end of the path were signs of a fight. There were deep marks in the soil and grass at the edge was torn away. I shouted into the depths of the waterfall, but heard only the noise of the water.

But I still was allowed a last word from my old friend. By Holmes's walking-stick I noticed a piece of paper under a rock. It was addressed to me. The directions were as exact and the writing as clear and firm as if Holmes had written the note comfortably in his rooms at Baker Street.

My dear Watson, Professor Moriarty has kindly allowed me to write these few words to you. He has explained to me how he avoided arrest by the English police and at the same time knew of my actions. I made no mistake about his great ability. I am happy to rescue society from such a man, although the cost is great. But I have already explained to you that it is the best possible end to my life. I suspected that the message from the hotel was a trick, but I was anxious to complete this business. Tell the English police that the necessary papers for the trial of the Moriarty group are in my desk at Baker Street.

Your good friend,

Sherlock Holmes

There is little more to say. From the police examination it was certain that the two men fought and fell together into the waterfall. It was impossible to get the bodies back. So the greatest criminal and the best detective of our age will remain there for all time.

4 The Empty House

In the spring of 1894 all of London was interested in the murder of Ronald Adair. The facts of the case were unusual and quite impossible to explain. The public already knows some of the facts that the police discovered. But a great amount was kept secret, and it was unnecessary to mention it at the trial. Now, after nearly ten years, I am finally allowed to give all the details. The crime was certainly interesting in itself. But for me something else connected with it was even more important. This gave me the greatest shock and surprise in all my adventurous life. Even now, after this long time, the memory is still exciting.

Because of Sherlock Holmes, I had become deeply interested in crime. Even after his disappearance I still read with care about different cases. I sometimes tried to use Holmes's methods to solve these problems, though I was not as successful as him. Surely the most interesting case was the death of Ronald Adair. This case, more than any other, showed the great loss caused by Holmes's death. He would have been specially interested in such a strange matter. The careful methods and quick mind of the greatest detective in Europe would have helped the police greatly. I thought about the case quite a lot, but could find no possible explanation.

Ronald Adair was the son of a famous general who was abroad at the time. Adair and his mother were staying at 427 Park Lane, London. The youth's friends were gentle people from good families, and he seemed to have no enemies. He belonged to several London clubs, and on the day of his death had played a game of cards at the Bagatelle Club with Mr Murray, Sir John Hardy and Colonel Moran. They said that Adair probably lost about five pounds, which to him was nothing since he was so wealthy. Indeed, Adair and Colonel Moran had won £420 at a recent game.

On the evening of the crime, March 30th, Adair returned from the Bagatelle at exactly ten o'clock. The servant said he went upstairs to his room, where she had lit a fire and opened the window because of some smoke from it. Just before midnight, Adair's mother returned and went to say good-night to her son. But the door was locked and there was no answer. So the door was forced open. The young man was found lying near the table. A bullet* from a small gun had entered the side of his head, but the police could find no weapon. Several piles of coins were on the table, and a piece of paper with names of friends at the Bagatelle. This appeared to be a list of losses and winnings.

There were many questions the police could not answer. Why had Adair locked himself in the room? Had the murderer jumped from the window? Had the murderer climbed up into the room? There were no marks on the outside wall. Since it was impossible to aim a small gun from a distance, the murderer must have been in the room. Nobody had heard any noise. In addition to all this, what was the reason for killing Adair? Nothing had been stolen from the room.

All day I tried to understand these facts using Holmes's methods. But I made little progress. In the evening I walked across to Park Lane. A group on the pavement was looking up at the window of the Adair house. As I moved back I accidentally knocked into someone behind me. It was an old man with a bent back who was carrying some books which had fallen on to the ground. I picked them up for him and noticed their strange titles. I attempted to say sorry, but clearly the books were precious to their owner, for he angrily turned away and disappeared into the crowd.

What I saw at 427 Park Lane did not help me to discover how or why Adair had been murdered. It was impossible for anyone to climb up to that window. I returned home thinking over the problem. Not long after my return the servant said there was a visitor at the door. To my surprise it

******bullet*, **a shaped piece of metal that is fired from a gun.**

was the strange old man from Park Lane.

'You're surprised to see me, sir?' he said.

'Yes, I am,' I replied.

'Well, sir,' he explained, 'I felt bad about my behaviour in the street back there. So I decided to tell you that I'm sorry. Thank you for picking up my books.'

'It was nothing,' I said. 'How did you know who I was?'

'Well, I'm a neighbour of yours, sir. I have the bookshop at the corner of the next street. Perhaps you would like to buy some books from me, sir? Your shelves look quite empty.'

I moved round to look at my book-shelves. When I turned back Sherlock Holmes was standing smiling at me. I rose to my feet, looked at him for a few seconds, and then fainted. I awoke to find Holmes bending over me.

'My dear Watson,' said the very familiar voice, 'I am so sorry. I did not expect to have such a strong effect.'

'Holmes!' I cried, holding his arm. 'Is it really you? Can you truly be alive? I can hardly believe my eyes. How did you climb out of the terrible depths at Reichenbach? Tell me how you are still living, my dear fellow.'

He sat down and lit up his pipe in his old manner. He had taken off his disguise. From his thin and tired face I could tell that recently he had not been in very good health.

'Now, Watson,' he began, 'I need your help for a difficult and dangerous night's work. Perhaps it is better if I give you a full explanation afterwards.'

'I am most interested and prefer that you tell me now,' I replied.

'Very well. I had no serious difficulty in climbing out of the bottom of the Reichenbach Fall, for the very simple reason that I was never in it.'

'You were never in it?' I cried in surprise.

'No, Watson, although my note to you was real. When I saw the dark shadow of Moriarty in front of me, I believed it was the end. I saw in his grey eyes a purpose of complete certainty. He allowed me to write that short message to you, which I left under that rock. Then, when I had walked to the end of the path, Moriarty rushed at me and threw his arms around me. He knew that I had ruined his evil game, and wanted only the satisfaction of seeing me die as well. But I stepped aside quickly and he was moving too fast to prevent himself falling over the edge. I saw him fall a very long way before he hit a rock and crashed into the water below.'

'But the foot-marks, Holmes?' I said. 'There were only two lines, and they did not return from the end of that path.'

'I knew that Moriarty was not the only man who wanted my death,' Holmes began to explain. 'There were at least three others, and the death of their leader made them even more dangerous enemies. But if they believed me to be dead, then there was a chance for me. For here was a way to catch them when they did not expect it.

'I examined the cliff behind me. It was not completely impossible to climb, as you had thought, Watson. But it did seem difficult to climb all the way to the top. I decided to attempt it, and it was not a pleasant business. Beneath me I could hear the terrible noise of the Fall. Any mistake would mean sure death. I began to climb, and little by little I made my way to a small platform in the rock wall. I was hiding there when you came along. I listened to you describe my death.

'At last you went back to the hotel and I was alone. I thought this was the end of my adventure. But there was a most unwelcome surprise when a huge rock fell from above and almost hit me. At first I supposed it was an accident, but when I looked up I saw a man. Then another rock fell near my head. Clearly Moriarty had not been alone. This man was his companion.

'Quickly I climbed down to the path. It was much more dangerous than the journey up, and several times I nearly fell. After reaching the path I ran many miles over the mountains in the darkness. A week later I was in another country. I am sorry I did not tell you of my escape, Watson. But it was so important that you thought I was dead. It was necessary for you to write about my end. If you didn't think I had really died, you couldn't have written so well. You see, the trial of the Moriarty group in London was not completely successful. Two of the criminals escaped, and so I had to be very careful. At last I was certain that only one of my enemies was still alive. I decided to return to London. At this time I heard of the Park Lane mystery. I have been waiting for something like this to happen.'

'Your story is difficult to believe,' I said, 'but your presence here tonight proves it.'

'There is work for us now, Watson,' he replied. 'Success in this case will make all my recent dangerous adventures worth it. But come, first we have three years of our lives to discuss.'

It was just like the old days when we left my house later that evening. I did not know what wild animal we were hunting in the dark forest of criminal London. But I knew from Holmes's manner that the case was very important – and that we would succeed in solving it.

'Are we going to your rooms in Baker Street?' I asked.

'Not yet. Follow me carefully, Watson,' he replied.

We walked quickly and quietly along dark back streets and finally reached Blandford Street. Here we passed through a wooden gate into an empty yard. Holmes unlocked a door and we entered a house. The place was in complete darkness, but I knew it was empty. Holmes led me down a long hall and at the end we turned right into a large, square room. The window was so thick with dust that there was almost no light. We could hardly see each other. Holmes put his hand on my arm and whispered into my ear.

'Do you know where we are?'

'Surely that is Baker Street over there,' I answered, trying to see through the window.

'Exactly,' replied Holmes. 'We are in an empty house opposite my rooms in Baker Street.'

'But why are we here?' I asked.

'Because it is an excellent place to watch Baker Street, Watson. Now, be careful not to show yourself at the window, and look up to my old rooms. What do you see there?'

I moved forward and looked across. I gave a cry of surprise. Behind the closed curtain was a strong light in the room, and against the curtain was the shadow of a man. It looked exactly like Holmes!

'Well?' asked Holmes, laughing quietly. 'It's a wax* model.'

'Good God!' I said. 'It's excellently made.'

'I put it there myself,' Holmes explained, 'when I went to Baker Street this afternoon. I want certain people to think that I am there when really I am somewhere else.'

'Is someone watching your rooms?' I asked.

'My old enemies, Watson – that pleasant group of people whose leader lies at the bottom of the Reichenbach Fall. Only they know I am still alive. Sooner or later they expected me to return to Baker Street. They have watched continuously, and today they saw me arrive. Their leader now is a close friend of Moriarty. In fact, he was the man who dropped those rocks on me. The most able and dangerous criminal in London is after me tonight. But he does not know that we are after him.'

That night we waited together in the silent darkness of the room. Through the dusty window we saw many people pass by in the street. Once or twice I seemed to recognize the same person. I noticed two men hiding by the door of a house further up the street. I mentioned this to Holmes, but he was not interested. He became anxious. Was his plan working? Midnight passed and nothing had happened. I looked up to the window in Baker Street.

'Holmes, the shadow has moved!' I cried.

'Of course it has moved,' Holmes replied. 'We are trying to catch some of the cleverest men in Europe, not fools. In these two hours, my servant has moved that model eight times. Such were my orders.'

Suddenly Holmes pulled me back into the darkest corner of the room. Then a low sound came to my ears. It was not from the direction of Baker Street, but from the back of the

*wax, a soft, yellow material normally used for making candles.

same house where we were hiding. A door opened and shut, and someone crept quietly along the hall. I held a gun ready in my hand. A man dressed in black entered the room and came within ten feet of us. I was ready for his attack, but then realized that he did not even know we were there. He passed close by us over to the window, which he opened a little. The light from the street fell upon his face and I saw that he was an old, well-dressed man with a mean, wild face.

I thought he held a walking-stick in his hand, but when he placed it on the floor I heard the sound of metal. He then took something from his pocket and added it to the stick. I saw then that it was not a stick but some strange sort of gun. He rested it upon the edge of the window.

Suddenly there was a very quiet noise and then the sound of glass breaking. Holmes jumped upon the man and threw him to the ground, but the man caught my friend by the throat. I moved forward and hit him on the head with the handle of my gun. He fell to the floor. Holmes blew on a whistle and three policemen rushed into the room.

'It's good to see you back in London, sir,' said one of them to Holmes.

'I thought you needed a little help, Lestrade,' he replied with a smile.

By now the prisoner was held by two large policemen. Holmes closed the window and lit some candles. I was able at last to have a good look at the man. He had a strong, yet evil, face and cruel blue eyes. He did not notice us, but looked directly at Holmes.

'You devil! You clever devil!' he shouted in a voice that showed both hate and surprise.

'Ah, Colonel,' said Holmes easily, 'I don't think we have met since that pleasant adventure at Reichenbach. Gentlemen, I present to you Colonel Sebastian Moran, once of the Indian Army, and one of the most accurate men in the world with a gun. You have no equal in a tiger hunt, I believe.'

The old man said nothing but stared wildly at Holmes, looking almost like a tiger himself.

'I am surprised that my simple trick has caught such an old hunter,' said Holmes. 'Have you not often tied up a small animal and then hid in the tree above to wait for the tiger? Well, this empty house is my tree, the wax model is my small animal, and you are my tiger, Colonel. But there was one surprise for me. I did not expect you to use this house. I thought you worked from the street, where the police were hiding. Except for that, everything has happened just as I expected.'

Holmes picked up the gun from the floor and examined it carefully.

'A well-made and unusual weapon,' he said. 'It is noiseless and very powerful. I knew that Moriarty had ordered it to be

made. Look carefully at the bullets, Lestrade. Tell me, for what crime will you arrest him?'

'Why, attempting to murder you of course, Mr Holmes,' replied the puzzled policeman.

'Not so, Lestrade. You have in your hands the man who shot Ronald Adair through the open window of 427 Park Lane. Come, Watson, let us go to my rooms, if you do not mind a broken window.'

Holmes's old rooms in Baker Street had not been changed at all during his long absence. Everything was in its place. There was the corner where he did his chemistry experiments, the book-shelves, the pipes. I saw all these as I looked around. I noticed a hole in the head of the wax model. Holmes picked something up from the floor and showed it to me.

'See, this is the sort of bullet normally used in a small gun such as yours. But it has in fact been fired from a powerful, large gun from a great distance. Who would expect that? The bullet entered the back of the head and went straight through the brain. He was the best hunter in India, and there are few better in London. Have you heard of the name, Watson?'

'No, I have not,' I said.

'Well, well. But then you had not heard of Moriarty, who had one of the great criminal brains of the century. Take down my book of criminals from the shelf and pass it to me.'

He turned over the pages lazily and sat back in the big chair, sending out clouds of smoke from his pipe.

'M is a good letter. Moriarty himself is enough to make any letter famous. Morgan who murdered with poison. Matthews, who once knocked out a tooth of mine. Ah, here is our friend. Colonel Sebastian Moran. Born 1840, the son of Sir Augustus Moran. Educated at Oxford University. Indian Army 1861-1886. And at the side I have written "the second most dangerous man in London." '

'How unusual,' I said. 'The man comes from a good family, had the best education England can give, and has been an excellent army officer.'

'It is true, Watson,' Holmes replied. 'He did very well so

far. In India people still speak of his great courage. But for some reason Moran began to go wrong. Because of this he was forced to leave the army and India, so he returned to London. Moriarty discovered him and used him as his chief helper. The Colonel was so clever that he escaped even when the rest of the Moriarty group were arrested in 1891. Do you remember my fear of guns when I visited you that April night? Even then I knew about Moran's shooting ability and the powerful long gun he used. When we went to Switzerland he and Moriarty followed us, and I am sure it was Moran who threw the rocks down at me.

'During these last three years I knew that London was too dangerous for me so long as Moran was there. But what could I do? I could not kill him. I did not have enough proof for the police to arrest him. So I could not act. But I knew that in the end I would catch him. Then came the murder of Ronald Adair. My chance had finally arrived! I was certain that Moran had done it. He had played cards with Adair, had followed him home from his club, and shot him through the open window. There was no doubt about it. I returned to England at once. I was sure that Moran would become anxious at my presence and try to kill me. So I placed the model in my room and warned the police – it was they whom you saw hiding by that door. But I had not supposed that Moran would use that same room. Now, my dear Watson, does anything remain for me to explain?'

'Yes,' I said. 'Why did Moran kill Ronald Adair?'

'Ah, I cannot be certain about that. But I have made a guess which at least explains all the known facts. Moran and Adair played together at the card table and won quite a lot of money. I know that Moran used to cheat at cards. I believe that Adair discovered this and told Moran he must leave the Bagatelle Club. Moran could not possibly leave the club, for card playing was the only way he got his money. So he murdered Adair, who at the time was trying to see how much money to return to the people Moran had cheated. He locked the door because he did not want his mother to know about the matter. Is that a sensible explanation?'

'I have no doubt that is the truth,' I replied.

'Well, perhaps the trial will make it certain,' said Holmes. 'And now, once again Sherlock Holmes is free to spend his time examining those interesting little problems which London presents.'

5 The Norwood Builder

'London has become a most uninteresting city since the death of Professor Moriarty,' said Sherlock Holmes.

'I don't think that many ordinary people will agree with you,' I answered.

'I suppose London is better without Moriarty,' he said with a smile, 'but the detective without any cases to solve is not. When Moriarty was alive, there was some small mark of his activity in the newspaper every day – some clue as to what his evil brain was doing. A man who realized this could connect together most of the crimes in the city. For the student of crime London was better than any other European capital. But now –'

At this time I had returned to Baker Street and was again sharing rooms with Holmes. Our life was not really so uninteresting as he suggested. Recently there had been two important and exciting cases. But Holmes did not always allow me to mention his methods and the successes they brought. Indeed, it is not until ten years later that I now write about the strange case of the Norwood builder*.

After these words Holmes leaned back into his comfortable chair to read the morning newspaper. Suddenly there was a loud ring on the door-bell. Seconds later a frightened and rather wild young man rushed into the room.

'I am sorry, Mr Holmes,' he cried. 'You mustn't blame me for this sudden entrance. I'm nearly mad with worry. Mr Holmes, I am the unhappy John McFarlane.'

Clearly he expected us to recognize the name and so understand his visit and manner. But I could tell from Holmes's face that he knew as little as I did.

'Please sit down, Mr McFarlane,' said Holmes. 'Tell us slowly and quietly who you are and what you want. For I

**builder*, a person who makes money building houses for other people.

know nothing about you except that you are unmarried and a lawyer.'

The man looked surprised. But I knew Holmes's methods: the man's untidy clothes and the legal* papers in his pockets provided the clues.

'Mr Holmes, I am the most unlucky man in London. Please help me! Let me tell you my whole story before they arrest me. I will go happily to prison if I know you are working for me.'

'Why do you expect to be arrested?' asked Holmes who was showing some interest now.

'For murdering Jonas Oldacre,' he replied. 'There is a report in today's newspaper. I have been followed from the railway station, and I am certain they will arrest me soon.'

I looked with interest at this man who was said to be a murderer. He had yellow hair, frightened blue eyes, and a weak mouth. I guessed his age was about twenty-seven.

'Watson, will you read out what the paper says about this matter?' asked Holmes.

I read the report:

It is feared that a serious crime took place last night in Norwood. Mr Jonas Oldacre, a builder, has lived at Dene House for many years. He is 52 years old and unmarried. He is said to be a very wealthy man, although in recent years he has given up his building business. However, at the back of the house there is still a small wood-yard. Last night a pile of wood caught fire. By the time the police arrived it was completely destroyed. At first they thought it was an accident, but fresh clues suggest a serious crime. Mr Oldacre has disappeared. In his bedroom it looks like there was a fight and spots of blood were found, some on a walking-stick. The stick belongs to a young lawyer, Mr John McFarlane.

LATER: There have been more developments in the Norwood case. Burnt clothes and bones have been found among the ashes from the fire. The police believe that Oldacre was killed, and the murderer then set fire to the body

**legal*, having to do with law.

to disguise his crime. The police are now searching for McFarlane.

'Thank you, Watson,' said Holmes. 'The case is certainly of interest. Have you anything to add—'

The door-bell rang and a police detective entered the room. It was Lestrade, an old friend of ours.

'Mr John McFarlane, I arrest you for the murder of Jonas Oldacre of Norwood.'

'Wait a while, Lestrade,' said Holmes. 'Half an hour can make no difference. The gentleman wishes to tell me some details about the matter which may be useful.'

'Very well, Mr Holmes,' the policeman replied. 'You have helped me in the past, and so I owe you something. I'll give you half an hour.'

'I want you to hear the truth,' began McFarlane. 'I knew nothing of Mr Jonas Oldacre, but my parents had known him many years ago. Yesterday afternoon he came into my London office. I was most surprised when he told me the purpose of his visit. He placed some hand-written notes upon my table and explained that it was his will. He wanted me, as a lawyer, to make a proper legal form. To my shock I saw that he wished to give all his property to me on his death. He explained that he had no family, but had known my parents when he was a young man. He had heard that I was a worthy person, and he wanted to help me. So I wrote out a proper will and he signed it. Here it is, and these are the original notes he brought into my office.

'Oldacre then said that at his home there were some business papers which I must see. So he asked me to come out to his house at Norwood that night, to finish the matter. He asked me not to mention anything to my parents. This I promised, since I was naturally anxious not to refuse him anything. So yesterday evening, at half past nine, I arrived at his house.'

'One moment!' said Holmes. 'Who opened the door?'

'A woman – Oldacre's servant, I suppose.'

'Continue.'

'After a meal, Oldacre led me into a bedroom. He took some papers from a metal box and I studied them with him. We finished this work about half past eleven. I then left through a large open window – his bedroom was downstairs. I could not find my walking-stick, but Oldacre told me not to worry. He would find it and return it later. It was too late to reach my parents' home in Blackheath, so I spent the night at a hotel. Then this morning I read of these terrible events.'

'Anything more you want to know, Mr Holmes?' asked Lestrade.

'Not until I have been to Blackheath,' he replied.

'Surely you mean Norwood?'

'Oh yes, I suppose I do,' said Holmes with a smile on his face. He then looked at Oldacre's notes. 'Have you noticed anything strange about these, Lestrade?'

'Well,' replied the puzzled policeman, 'I can read the first few lines, and those in the middle of the second page, and one or two at the end. But the writing in between is very bad, and there are three places where I cannot read it at all.'

'How do you explain it?' asked Holmes.

'How do *you* explain it?' was the reply.

'The notes were written in a train,' said Holmes. 'The clear writing was done at a station, most of the rest during the ordinary journey, but some when the train crossed onto a new railway line.'

'What difference does that make to the case?' asked Lestrade.

'It is strange for a man to write an important thing like a will in such a careless manner as during a train journey. It suggests perhaps that he did not consider it important – that he did not want this to be his real will.'

'Well, the case is clear enough to me,' the policeman replied. 'A young man suddenly learns that he will get an old man's money on his death. So he secretly goes out to his house. Then, late at night, he murders him and burns the body. Surely this is all clear.'

'It seems to be a little too clear, Lestrade,' said Holmes. 'It is a pity that you lack imagination. Is this explanation really likely? To kill a man on the same day the will is made? To do the murder when you know a servant is in the house? To leave your walking-stick behind for the police to discover? I can give you a whole list of possibilities which will explain the facts equally well.'

Lestrade shook his head but he seemed less sure than before. After he and his prisoner had gone, Holmes began to prepare for his day's work.

'My first move, Watson, is to go out to Blackheath, as I said.'

'And why not to Norwood?' I asked.

'Because in this case one strange event has been followed by another. The police are mistaken to consider only the second, because it alone is a crime. I think we must first explain the earlier event – the unusual will. I shall return this evening, and I hope I can help this unlucky young man.'

Holmes returned late to Baker Street that night. I could tell by his face that he had not been successful. For an hour he sat silently in his chair smoking his pipe. At last he spoke.

'It's all going wrong, Watson, all as wrong as it can go. Perhaps Lestrade is right.'

'Did you go out to Blackheath?' I asked.

'Yes, I went there. And I soon discovered what an unpleasant fellow Oldacre was. McFarlane's father was out, so I talked with his mother. She spoke of Oldacre with great hate – which hardly helps her son's case. She knew Oldacre well at one time. Indeed, they were going to be married. But she realized how cruel Oldacre was. Once she saw him purposely set a cat loose among some birds. So she changed her mind about the marriage, and later married McFarlane's father instead. On her wedding day Oldacre sent her a photograph of herself. It was all cut up and terrible-looking. Although she was glad he is dead, she refuses to believe in her son's guilt.

'I made no progress, so went next to Oldacre's house in Norwood. It is a big modern house in the middle of a large garden. The wood-yard, where the fire was, is away from the road behind the house. Among the ashes the police found some buttons which certainly belong to Oldacre's clothes.

'I went into the bedroom, but was unable to find any new clues. However, I examined Oldacre's papers, which were still in piles on the table from last night. Surprisingly, they were of not much value, and there was not much money around either. But some papers seemed to be missing. The most valuable ones appeared to be missing. If McFarlane is guilty, why did he steal something he is certain to get?'

'Did you speak to the servant?' I asked.

'Yes,' Holmes replied, 'and I am sure she is not telling everything she knows. She said she let McFarlane in at half past nine and then went to bed an hour later. The fire woke her. She is certain that the buttons found in the fire belonged to the clothes Oldacre was wearing last night. Also, she says she smelt a burning body in the fire.

'So, my dear Watson, I have failed. And yet I *know* it's all wrong. I feel it in my bones. It's hard to find the smallest mistake in the police explanation. But there was one strange thing about the papers in Oldacre's room. I noticed from Oldacre's bank book that large amounts of money have been paid to Mr Cornelius during the last year. Is it possible that this Mr Cornelius has a part in the matter? The next thing is to visit Oldacre's bank and ask about Cornelius. But I am afraid that this time success belongs to the police and not to us, Watson.'

The next morning Holmes looked pale and tired. He had dark shadows around his bright eyes. An open telegram lay upon the table.

'What do you think of this, Watson?' he asked, passing it over to me.

It was from Norwood, and read: 'Important new clue. McFarlane's guilt now certain. Suggest you give up. Lestrade.'

'This sounds serious,' I said.

'I am not sure,' Holmes replied. 'The same clue can mean different things to different persons. After our meal we shall go out to Norwood and see what it is.'

An hour later we were at Dene House. A smiling Lestrade met us at the gates.

'Come this way, gentlemen. I think I can prove to you that McFarlane is the murderer.' Lestrade seemed to be in an unusually good mood. He led us into a dark hall and lit a match.

'This is where McFarlane must have come out to get his hat after the crime. Look on the wall – the mark of a thumb made in blood. You know, Mr Holmes, that no two thumbmarks are the same?'

'I have heard something like that,' said my friend, a little angry at Lestrade's behaviour.

'Well, then,' continued Lestrade. 'Compare that mark with this print of McFarlane's right thumb which I took this morning. The two are without doubt from the same thumb. I am afraid the case is over. This is final, Mr Holmes.'

'So it seems, Lestrade,' said Holmes, who did not appear as disappointed as I expected. 'By the way, who made this important discovery?'

'Mrs Lexington, the servant. We hadn't noticed it yesterday,' said Lestrade, and he went off to write his report for the police.

'I still have some hope for McFarlane,' said Holmes to me. 'There is one really serious fault with this proof here.'

'Indeed Holmes! What is it?'

'I *know* that the mark was not there yesterday when I examined the hall. Come, Watson, let us take a walk around the garden.'

We went outside, and Holmes spent some time examining the outside walls of the house with great care. He then returned inside and searched the whole house from bottom to top, even the empty rooms. On the top floor he seemed to find something exciting.

'Well, Watson, I think it is time we spoke to Lestrade. He has had his fun with us. Now we shall have our joke.'

We went into the room where Lestrade sat writing.

'Ah, Lestrade, before you finish your report I have some

new information for you.'

'What do you mean, Mr Holmes?' he asked.

'An important witness. Shall I try to produce him?'

'Certainly,' Lestrade replied, puzzled by this.

'Tell your policemen to bring in some of that wood from the back yard. I believe you have some matches in your pocket, Watson. Now, will you all come to the top of the house with me.'

On the top floor there was a wide central hall. We all stood at one end. Lestrade's face had begun to grow red and angry.

'Are you playing a game with us, Mr Holmes? If you know anything important, then surely you can say it without all this foolishness.'

'I have an excellent reason for everything I do, Lestrade,' Holmes replied. 'Perhaps you remember your own happy mood a few hours ago, when you thought you had solved the case. Now it is my turn. Watson, open that window and then light the pile of wood.'

I did so, and clouds of smoke rushed down the hall.

'Everyone shout "Fire!" as loud as possible,' ordered Holmes.

This we did several times. After the third cry came our surprise. A door suddenly flew open out of the wall at the end of the hall. A small frightened man ran out.

'Excellent!' said Holmes. 'Watson, put the fire out. Lestrade, let me present the missing witness, Mr Oldacre.'

The policeman was completely surprised. I looked at Oldacre. His face looked cruel and clever in an evil way.

'I have done no harm,' he cried.

'No harm?' asked Lestrade. 'You have tried to send a guiltless man to his death. You failed only because of Mr Holmes here.'

'But it was just a joke,' Oldacre insisted.

'Well, you won't be laughing, I promise you. Take him away,' Lestrade said to the other policemen. Then he looked at my friend. 'That is the cleverest thing you've done yet, Mr Holmes. It is all a mystery to me. You have saved not just McFarlane, but my name as a policeman.'

'Just make a few changes to your report, Lestrade,' said Holmes. 'Now, let us see where he has been hiding.'

Six feet before the real end of the passage, a false wall with a secret door had been built. Behind this was a small room with some furniture and a supply of food and books.

'Because he was a builder Oldacre could make this room himself,' Holmes explained. 'No one else knew about it, except the servant. Make sure you arrest her, Lestrade. I realized that Oldacre was hiding somewhere in the house. When I measured this hall, I discovered it was six feet shorter than the one below. So it was clear where he was.'

'But how did you know he was in the house at all?' asked Lestrade.

'The thumb-mark. You said it was final; and so it was, but in a different way. I knew it was not there yesterday. Therefore it had been put on during the night.'

'But how?'

'Very simply. Oldacre and McFarlane went through many papers the other night. Afterwards they were fastened up with string and soft wax. McFarlane's thumb-mark most probably went on one of the pieces of wax. Later Oldacre realized that such a thumb-mark could be used as the final proof of McFarlane's guilt.'

'Wonderful!' said Lestrade. 'Wonderful! But why did he do all this, Mr Holmes?'

'A desire for revenge* which had remained with him for thirty years. As a young man he was refused in marriage by McFarlane's mother – I told you I went to Blackheath first. During the last year or two Oldacre's business has done badly, and he owes large amounts of money. So he decided to cheat the bank who lent him money. He sent a lot of money to a Mr Cornelius, who is himself, I suspect. His plan was to disappear and start a new life somewhere else under the name of Cornelius. But he decided to get his revenge on McFarlane's mother at the same time. He wanted McFarlane to be arrested and punished for murder. His clever plan included the false will (the reason for the murder), the secret evening visit, keeping the walking-stick, the blood, and the burnt animals and buttons in the fire. Then he hid in the secret room, keeping with him the most valuable papers. But Oldacre did not know when to stop. He destroyed a perfect plan with that unnecessary thumb-mark.'

We went downstairs. Oldacre was being held in the hall by two policemen.

'It was a joke, sir, nothing more. I didn't want any harm to come to young Mr McFarlane,' he cried.

'That will be decided at your trial,' said Holmes. 'And I suspect that your bank will get control of Mr Cornelius' money.'

'I'll get my revenge on you one day!' Oldacre shouted fiercely at Holmes.

'You will be a busy man for many years,' my friend replied. 'By the way, was it a dog or some other animal that you put in the fire with your old clothes? I ask because Watson likes to write up these cases of mine, and he prefers to get the details exact.'

******revenge*, hurting someone who has hurt you in the past.**

6 The Devil's Foot

In the spring of 1897 Holmes's usual good health began to fail because of months of hard work without stop. A well-known London doctor warned him that there was a risk of a serious illness – he must give up all his cases and take a complete rest. My friend never showed any great interest in his own health. But he was worried that a serious illness might truly end his work. Therefore he agreed to take a holiday. So we travelled down to the western part of Cornwall and stayed in a small house.

Holmes liked the place. The house was on high ground and we could look down on the whole of Mount's Bay, so dangerous to ships because of the rocks. The land side of the house was as lonely as the sea. In that direction there were miles of empty waste land, with only a few churches and villages. Holmes enjoyed the dark mystery of the place and spent much of his time on long, lonely walks. He was interested in the ancient language of Cornwall, and used to read about it. But then, to my sorrow but Holmes's delight, came the case of the devil's foot. For my friend it was a more interesting and difficult problem than any of those he had recently worked on in London. It broke suddenly into our simple and peaceful life, and became famous not just in Cornwall but through the whole of western England.

There were a few local villages, and the nearest of these was Tredannick. Holmes had become a friend of a lawyer there, Mr Roundhay. He was a pleasant, middle-aged man with a deep knowledge of local history. With him lived Mr Mortimer Tregennis, a thin dark man with a rather bent back. From time to time we used to visit them and found the lawyer most friendly, though Tregennis was a more silent fellow.

Early one Tuesday morning Holmes and I were preparing

for a walk. Suddenly these two men entered the house.

'Mr Holmes,' said Roundhay in an anxious voice, 'a most unusual and sad event has taken place in the night. It is indeed lucky that you are in Cornwall now, for you are the one man in all England whom we need.'

Holmes took the pipe from his mouth and sat up with interest.

'I shall say a few words first,' continued the lawyer, 'and then you can either get more details from Mr Tregennis or go immediately to Trelew. Mr Tregennis spent yesterday evening with his brothers, Owen and George, and his sister, Brenda, at their house, Trelew, not far away. When he left them at ten o'clock they were still playing cards around the table. Then, this morning he woke early and went for a walk in that direction. On the way he met Dr Richards who had been called suddenly to Trelew. Naturally Mr Tregennis went with him. At Trelew he found his brothers and sister round the table, exactly as he had left them. But the sister was dead, and the brothers were laughing and shouting like madmen. All three had on their faces a look of the greatest horror*. No one else was in the house except the woman servant, who had heard no sound during the night. Nothing has been stolen. There seems to be no explanation of the horror which killed the woman and made the two men mad. Such are the facts, Mr Holmes, and if you can help to solve the mystery, you will have done a great thing.'

Holmes sat in silence for a while and smoked his pipe as he thought about this unexpected mystery.

'I will work on the matter,' he said finally. 'It does appear to be very unusual. Have you been out to Trelew, Mr Roundhay?'

'No. I came here as soon as Mr Tregennis returned.'

'Then we shall walk over together,' said Holmes. 'But first I must ask you a few questions, Mr Tregennis. Tell me about last night.'

'Well, Mr Holmes,' he replied, 'I went to Trelew for supper

**horror*, a feeling of terrible fear or dislike.

and afterwards George suggested a game of cards. We sat down about nine o'clock, and it was a quarter past ten when I left.'

'Who let you out of the house?' asked Holmes.

'The servant had gone to bed, so I let myself out. This morning the door and the windows were exactly as when I left last night. But my brothers had gone mad and Brenda was dead of fright. I'll never forget the sight of that room so long as I live.'

'The facts as you tell them are certainly unusual,' said Holmes. 'Have you any explanation yourself?'

'It's the work of the devil*, Mr Holmes!' cried Tregennis.

'First, I think, we must consider natural explanations,' said Holmes. 'Why did you not live at Trelew?'

'There was a quarrel many years ago. The family business was sold and the money divided between us. But that was all forgotten, and we were the best of friends in recent years.'

'Was there anything at all unusual about last night?' asked Holmes. 'Think carefully, Mr Tregennis.'

'There is only one thing,' he replied. 'I looked out of the window once and I seemed to see something dark in the garden. I cannot say whether it was a man or an animal. George saw it as well, but we did not go out to look.'

'And how did you hear the news so early?' asked Holmes.

'I usually take an early walk. I met the doctor and he told me the servant at Trelew had sent a message. When we arrived we saw what had happened. The doctor said Brenda had been dead at least six hours. There were no signs of a fight or that they'd been attacked by anyone. George and Owen were singing and shouting madly. It was terrible for us, and the doctor almost fell unconscious.'

'Most unusual,' said Holmes. 'Come, let us go to Trelew now. I have never known a case which at first sight presented a more difficult problem.'

Our first morning we discovered no new important clues. At the start was an event which left an unpleasant memory.

**devil*, the spirit of evil.

As we made our way to Trelew, a carriage came down from the house. It was taking the two brothers to the mad-house at Helston. Those frightened faces looking through the carriage's narrow window made a terrible sight.

Trelew was a large white house with a big garden. Holmes examined the ground carefully before we entered. Inside we were met by the servant, who answered all of Holmes's questions. She had heard nothing in the night. In the morning she almost fell unconscious when she entered the room where the brothers and sister were, but she felt better after she opened the window. We went to the room where these terrible events had taken place. Holmes searched everything, but I saw no sign of hope on his face.

'Why did they have a fire in this small room on a spring evening?' he asked, looking at the ashes.

'It was a cold, wet night,' replied Mortimer Tregennis.

Back at our house Holmes sat in his chair thoughtfully smoking his pipe and sending clouds of blue smoke into the air. Finally he laid it down and stood up.

'Let us take a walk by the sea, Watson,' he said with a smile. And as we walked along the shore he talked. 'I cannot work without enough clues. Let us consider exactly what we do know. First, when did this terrible business happen? If Tregennis's report is true, then it happened immediately after he left. That is very important. The cards were still on the table and the three had not changed their positions. So the strange event took place soon after Tregennis left, and certainly not later than eleven o'clock. From the foot-prints outside Trelew I know that Tregennis went directly back to Roundhay's house.

'We need not consider the servant,' Holmes continued. 'She is unimportant. Tregennis mentioned some movement in the garden. It was a dark, wet night, and so anyone wanting to frighten them needed to be very close to the window. But there are no foot-prints outside that window, or even near to it. Also, there seems to be no reason for a stranger to act in such a way. You see the difficulties, Watson?'

'They are only too clear,' I answered.

'Yet with a few more facts a solution is perhaps possible.'

By this time we had returned to our house, where we found a visitor. He had a huge body, rough face, wild eyes and a large red beard. I realized that this was Dr Leon Sterndale, the great African explorer and lion hunter. I knew that he lived not far away, and sometimes we had seen him on our walks. But he was not a friendly man and preferred to be alone. Therefore I was surprised at his visit.

'Mr Holmes,' he said, 'I have come to ask you about this mystery. I know the Tregennis family well – they are my cousins – and this has naturally been a great shock for me. I was seventy miles away at Plymouth when I heard the news. So I returned immediately instead of going on a ship to Africa, as I had planned.'

'How did you hear of this matter?' asked Holmes. 'It was not in the newspapers.'

'Mr Roundhay sent me a telegram,' Sterndale replied, a little angrily.

'Thank you. Now I shall answer your question. The case is not completely clear yet, but I am hopeful of a solution.'

'Do you suspect anyone?' our visitor asked Holmes.

'I cannot answer that.'

'Then I have wasted my time,' Sterndale said roughly, and left the house in a bad temper. Within five minutes Holmes left to follow him. He returned in the evening, but from his face I knew he was no nearer success.

'Sterndale certainly seems very interested, Watson,' he said. 'There is a clue here which I do not yet understand, but which may lead to a solution. I am sure that more facts will present themselves. When they do, our difficulties will be over.'

The next morning Holmes's words were proved true. Roundhay rushed up to our house. He could hardly speak.

'It's the devil's work, Mr Holmes!' he cried. Finally he shot out his terrible message. 'Mortimer Tregennis died during the night, in exactly the same way as his sister.'

Holmes jumped to his feet, and we went immediately to Roundhay's house. The police and the doctor had not yet arrived, so nothing had been moved. The air in Tregennis' room was thick and difficult to breathe. Luckily a maid had opened the window. An oil-lamp on the table was still burning. In a chair beside the table sat the dead man with a look of complete horror on his face. He had clearly dressed quickly as his clothes were untidy. He must have died in the early morning, for he had slept in his bed.

As soon as we entered the room Holmes's behaviour became more lively. He quickly examined the garden, downstairs, and Tregennis's second room upstairs. He seemed to find something important by the bedroom window. He rushed downstairs and out into the garden, where he again examined the ground before returning upstairs. He was specially interested in the oil-lamp. From the top of it he took some burnt dust and put it into an envelope. As the police arrived, he spoke to Roundhay.

'I may have discovered something important,' he said, 'but I cannot stay to talk with the police. Please tell them to look carefully at the bedroom window and at the oil-lamp. Each suggests something, and together they make it certain. Come, Watson, we must go now.'

For the next two days Holmes spent his time smoking in the house and going off on long walks alone. But one afternoon he suggested an experiment.

'You remember, Watson,' he said, 'that in these two cases there has been something similar. Tregennis told us that when the doctor entered the room at Trelew he almost fell unconscious. And the same thing happened to the servant there. In the second case – that of Mortimer Tregennis himself – you cannot have forgotten how thick the air was in the sitting-room, even though the window was opened. I later discovered that the servant who opened it was so ill that she had gone to her bed. So in each case there is a suggestion of something poisonous in the air. Also, at Trelew there had

been a fire, at Roundhay's house an oil-lamp. The fire was possibly necessary, but not the oil-lamp for it was daylight. These three things – the burning, the air in the room, and the deaths – must be connected.'

'It seems so,' I replied.

'Let us suppose that something was burned which produced a poisonous effect. At Trelew some of the poisonous air clearly escaped with the smoke from the fire. That is why only the woman was killed. But in the other case there was no chance for any such escape. I thought this was a possible solution. On the edge of the oil-lamp in Tregennis's room I noticed some half-burnt dust and put some of it into an envelope. Will you join me now in an experiment, Watson?'

'Certainly,' I said with interest.

'We will light this lamp, but keep the windows open. We do not want the experiment to be too successful! Sit on this chair near the lamp, and leave the door open. I shall put some dust on the lamp. So! Now, Watson, let us sit down and wait for developments.'

Soon I began to sense a thick smell in the room. I could no longer control my brain or imagination. A heavy black cloud was before my eyes. Dark shapes appeared. A terrible, cold horror took hold of me. I tried to scream, but could make only a small, distant noise. I could see Holmes's face, white with fear. With a sudden burst of strength I rushed over to Holmes and we dragged ourselves to the door.

'I am indeed sorry, Watson,' said Holmes at last. 'It was a dangerous experiment for myself, and I should not have let a friend take part. I did not realize the effect was so sudden and strong. Now do you know how those deaths happened?'

'Yes, I do,' I answered.

'Everything suggests that Tregennis was the criminal in the first case, but he himself died in the second. We were told of a family quarrel many years ago. Perhaps it lived on in his mind – he did not seem the sort of man to forgive easily. Remember it was he who spoke of a movement in the garden. He had reason to give us a false clue. And if he did not throw the poison on the fire when he left, then who did? There was nothing to suggest another visitor. Everything makes me believe that Tregennis was guilty.'

'Then do you think he killed himself?' I asked.

'It is not impossible, Watson. Perhaps his own guilt caused him to do so. But there are strong reasons against it. Luckily there is one man in England who knows all about it, and so we shall speak with him.'

Later that day Dr Sterndale came to see us.

'You sent for me, Mr Holmes,' he said. 'I received your note earlier today, though I am not sure why I came.'

'Thank you,' replied Holmes. 'I want to discuss the killing of Mortimer Tregennis.'

For a moment I wished I had my gun with me. Sterndale's face grew red with anger and he moved fiercely towards Holmes. Then he stopped himself and became quieter. This behaviour seemed to me even more dangerous.

'Africa is a wild place, Mr Holmes. It has changed me. I don't pay much attention to law any more. Do not forget that, for I have no desire to hurt you.'

'Nor do I desire to hurt you, Dr Sterndale. That is why I sent for you and not for the police.'

Sterndale sat down in silence. He had finally met someone who was his equal.

'What do you mean?' he asked at last.

'My future actions depend wholly upon what you tell me.'

'About what?'

'About Mortimer Tregennis's murder,' replied Holmes.

'You must be joking. I know nothing of the matter.'

'Any joke is on your part, Dr Sterndale,' said Holmes. 'Let me tell you some facts. When I refused to tell you whom I suspected, you went quickly to Roundhay's house. You waited outside it for some time, and finally returned home.'

'How do you know that?' demanded the explorer.

'I followed you,' explained Holmes.

'But I saw no one.'

'That is what you can expect to see when I follow you.

You left your house early the next morning. From your garden you picked up some small red stones.'

Sterndale looked at Holmes in complete surprise.

'You then walked to Roundhay's house, wearing those same shoes you have on now. You threw the stones up at Tregennis's bedroom window. He dressed quickly and you went in to talk with him. You left after a short discussion, but remained in the garden for a while. After Tregennis's death you returned to your house. Now, Dr Sterndale, perhaps you will explain matters to me.

Our visitor's face turned grey as he listened to Holmes. He sat thinking for a time, and then he suddenly took a photograph out of his pocket.

'That is why I have done it.' The picture was of a very beautiful woman. 'Brenda Tregennis. For years I have loved her and she has loved me. But I could not marry her because I have a wife, although she left me long ago. The marriage laws of this country are cruel, Mr Holmes. So for years Brenda and I waited – and now this has happened! Mr Roundhay knew about Brenda and me, and that is why he sent me the telegram.'

Sterndale took an envelope from his pocket. On the outside was written 'Devil's-foot root', with a red sign for poison beneath it.

'Devil's-foot root, Mr Holmes. No one else in Europe has any of it, except a scientist in Budapest. It is used in parts of West Africa, and I was given it when I was travelling there.

'There was a Tregennis family quarrel about some money many years ago. As a result Mortimer left the family home. Everone thought that the quarrel was over, but I was always suspicious about Mortimer. A few weeks ago he visited me and I showed him several things I had brought back from Africa. I told him of the devil's-foot root and its power to kill people or make them mad. I also said that its presence in a dead body cannot be discovered. I am certain now that he stole some when I was not looking. I remember he asked many questions about it.

'I thought no more about the matter until Roundhay's telegram reached me. Clearly Tregennis expected me to be at sea by that time. I returned immediately, and when I heard the details I realized that the poison had been used. I was sure that Mortimer Tregennis was the murderer. I suppose he did it to get control of their money.

'What could I do? I had no proof. My heart cried out for revenge. I decided that he must die the same terrible death which he had given to others. Your report of my movements is right, Mr Holmes. I took some stones from my garden to throw up at Tregennis' window to wake him. He came down and I told him I knew about the murder. I lit his lamp and placed some of the poison on it. I then waited outside the window, ready to shoot him if he left the room. In five minutes he died. My God! How he died! But I felt no sorrow after the evil he had done. There is my story. You can do what you like. I have no fear of death.'

Holmes sat in silence for some time.

'What were your plans?' he asked at last.

'I wanted to return to Central Africa,' replied Sterndale. 'My work there is only half finished.'

'Go and do the other half,' said Holmes. 'I shall not prevent you.'

Sterndale left the room quietly.

'Well, Watson,' my friend said, 'I have never loved. But if I did and the woman I loved was killed like that, maybe I would have done what Sterndale did. Anyway I will not make you angry by explaining what is clear. The small stones by the window of Tregennis's bedroom were my first clue. They were unlike anything in Roundhay's garden, but I did notice such stones at Sterndale's house. The oil-lamp burning in daylight and the half-burnt poison were clearly connected. And now, my dear Watson, I think we can have some less powerful smoke.'

Holmes leaned back comfortably in his chair and began to fill his pipe with tobacco.

7 The Creeping Man

One Sunday evening early in September 1903 I received this message from Holmes: 'Come at once if you can – if you cannot, still come. S.H.' Holmes was a man of strong habits, and I had become one of them. In his mind I was like his pipes, his tobacco, his chemistry experiments. When there was work to do he needed me. Like Holmes, I was not easily frightened, and so he could depend on me even for the most dangerous jobs. But I had other uses too. Holmes used to discuss his cases with me, and often this helped him to reach a solution. He also liked to think aloud in my presence. Such was my part in our friendship.

When I arrived at Baker Street I found him sitting comfortably in his chair, smoking his pipe and looking thoughtfully into the fire. It was clear that he was in the middle of a difficult problem. For half an hour he took no notice of me. Then at last he looked over and greeted me as usual.

'Please excuse my behaviour, Watson,' he said. 'Some strange facts have been presented to me in the last twenty-four hours. And they have caused some general thoughts to cross my mind. I am considering writing a small book on the use of dogs in the detective's work.'

'But surely, Holmes,' I said, 'there are books on this already – how to use dogs to find criminals and so on.'

'No, no, Watson. That side of the matter is, of course, clear. But there is another, which is less understood. A dog can tell you things about a house. Who ever saw a happy dog in a sad family, or a sad dog in a happy family? And dangerous people have dangerous dogs.'

Holmes sat down and filled his pipe again.

'The exact problem I am working on is this: why does Professor Presbury's dog try to bite him?'

I was disappointed with Holmes. Had he taken me away

from my work to ask such an unimportant question? He looked across at me.

'The same old Watson!' he said. 'You never learn that the most serious matters can depend on the smallest things. Presbury, the famous Camford scientist, has been attacked twice by his own dog. What do you think of that?'

'The dog is ill,' I suggested.

'Of course we must consider that. But he attacks no one else, and his master only sometimes. It is strange, Watson, very strange.'

There was a knock at the door and a young man entered. He was about thirty, well dressed, and there was something of the student in his manner. Holmes greeted him.

'Ah, Mr Bennett. This is my old friend, Dr Watson. I think we shall need some help in this matter. Watson, this is Mr Bennett, Professor Presbury's secretary. Soon he and the Professor's daughter will marry.'

'Does Dr Watson know the situation?' asked the young man.

'No, but I will explain matters to him now,' replied Holmes, 'and you can make sure that I have events in the right order. Presbury, Watson, is one of the most able scientists in Europe. His wife died many years ago, but he lives with his daughter, Edith. He has always been a man of strong will, and forceful behaviour. But no one ever suspected him of doing anything wrong or improper.

'A few months ago things began to change. At the age of sixty one Presbury suddenly fell in love with the youngest daughter of Professor Morphy. It was not the quiet, gentle love of an old man, but the wild, almost mad, love of a youth. Presbury's family thought his behaviour not very proper. But he is a rich man, and so Morphy did not try to stop the marriage. But Morphy's daughter, although she liked Presbury, decided he was much too old to marry.

'At about this time a little mystery entered the story. The Professor did something he had never done before. He left home and told no one where he was going. He was away for two weeks and returned rather tired. By chance Mr Bennett received a letter from a friend in Prague. The friend said he had been glad to see Professor Presbury there recently. Only in this way did his family learn where he had been.

'From that time a strange change came over the Professor. He appeared to be keeping a secret. His family felt he was not the same man they had known. He seemed to be under some dark shadow. His mind was no different – the classes he gave at the university were as excellent as ever. But there was something new in the Professor's behaviour, something dark and suspicious. And now, Mr Bennett, tell Watson about the letters.'

'Certainly,' Bennett replied. 'The Professor has always placed the greatest confidence in me. Part of my work as his secretary is to open all his letters. But soon after his return from Prague this changed. He told me not to open any envelopes marked with a cross. Several of these have arrived at the house. I do not even know if he answers them.'

'And the box,' said Holmes.

'Ah, yes, the box,' said Bennett. 'The Professor brought back a small box, made of wood and probably from Germany. He kept it in his library. One day I was looking for something, and I picked the box up. To my surprise he became very angry. It was the first time such a thing has happened. I tried to explain that it was an accident, but he continued to be angry with me for some time.' Mr Bennett looked in a little notebook he carried. 'That was on July 2nd, Mr Holmes.'

'You are certainly an excellent witness,' my friend replied. 'Dates are always useful.'

'Since then I have made a careful study of Professor Presbury's strange behaviour. It was on the same day – July 2nd – that the dog attacked the Professor. This happened again on July 11th and July 20th. He used to be such a gentle animal, but since this we have kept him tied in the stables.'

'Most unusual,' said Holmes to himself. 'Have there been any fresh developments?'

'Yes, on the night before last – September 4th,' replied Bennett, who looked more serious than ever. 'I was lying awake about two o'clock in the morning when I heard a sound in the hall. I opened the door and looked out. I could see something moving along. Then suddenly it came into the light, and I could see it was Professor Presbury. He was crawling, Mr Holmes – crawling! He was on his hands and feet. It was such a strange position, yet he moved quite naturally. I stepped forward to help him. He jumped up, shouted roughly at me, and rushed down the stairs. I waited there for an hour, but he did not return.'

'Well, Watson, what do you think of that?' asked Holmes.

'Perhaps he has an illness which prevents him walking properly,' I suggested.

'Possibly, Watson, but he was able to stand up immediately and rush off.'

'His health has never been better,' said Bennett. 'He is stronger than ever before. But these are the facts, Mr Holmes. We have no reason to call the police, and yet we do not know what to do. Edith – Miss Presbury – and I believe that we must do something.'

'It is a most unusual case,' said Holmes. 'What do you think, Watson?'

'As a doctor,' I replied, 'I think the trouble is medical. Presbury's mind has been upset* by his love for the young woman. He travelled abroad to forget it. His letters and the box are probably connected with something else – some money matters possibly.'

'And I suppose the dog does not like commerce?' said Holmes with a smile. 'No, Watson, there is more –'

A young lady rushed into the room and ran towards Bennett.

'Miss Presbury, I suppose?' asked Holmes. 'Have there been some new developments?'

'Oh, Mr Holmes, can't you help my poor father?' she cried.

'I have hopes, but the case is still not completely clear.

**upset*, seriously troubled.

Now, tell me your story.'

'Well,' she began, 'my father's behaviour was strange all day yesterday. Then, in the night I was awoken by noise from the dog. My bedroom is on the second floor. As I lay in bed looking toward the window I was surprised to see my father's face. Mr Holmes, I nearly died of surprise and horror. I was unable to move, and just watched the face for about half a minute. Then it disappeared. I lay awake until morning. At breakfast-time he seemed angry but didn't mention last night. I did not say anything myself, but made an excuse to come to London – and here I am.'

'Is there a long ladder in the garden?' asked Holmes.

'No,' replied Miss Presbury. 'There is no possible way of reaching the window. Yet he was there.'

'The date was September 5th,' said Holmes. 'That makes things difficult. Well, Mr Bennett, I think the next thing is for Watson and me to visit Professor Presbury. If I am right, then there is a strong reason for us coming as soon as possible. We shall be in Camford tomorrow.'

On Monday morning we travelled by train to Camford. Holmes did not talk about the case until we had arrived at our hotel.

'I think, Watson, we will see the Professor before lunch.'

'What possible excuse have we for our visit?' I asked.

Holmes looked at a piece of paper.

'From the dates Bennett gave me, I see there was some strange behaviour on August 26th. Probably the Professor's memory of that day is a little unclear. We can pretend he made an arrangement to meet us.'

We went past the ancient colleges of the university towards the southern edge of the town. Professor Presbury lived in a large house surrounded by a lovely garden. We entered the house and went into the library of this mysterious scientist. There was nothing unusual about his manner or appearance. He was a large, tall, serious man. His eyes were the most noticeable thing about him; they were sharp, clear and clever.

'Sit down, gentlemen. What can I do for you?' he asked.

'I was going to ask you the same question, Professor,' said Holmes.

'Me, sir!'

'Perhaps there is some mistake. Someone told me you wished to see me.'

'Oh, indeed?' the sharp grey eyes were shining angrily at Holmes. 'Who told you this?'

'I am sorry, Professor, but it was in confidence,' replied Holmes. 'There must have been a mistake.'

'I want to know more,' Presbury demanded. 'Do you have a letter or telegram to prove what you say?'

'No,' answered Holmes.

Presbury walked to the door and called his secretary.

'Come in, Bennett. This gentleman says he has been called to Camford to see me. Do you remember a letter to a person called Holmes?'

'No, sir,' said the anxious secretary.

'That is final,' said the Professor, looking angrily at Holmes. 'Now, sir,' he screamed, 'I want an explanation!'

Presbury moved between us and the door, shaking his hands at us fiercely. His face was twisted with a wild anger. We were afraid we'd have to fight our way out of the room.

'My dear Professor,' Bennett cried, 'consider your position! Mr Holmes is a well-known man. You cannot treat him like this.'

Presbury finally moved away from the door. We were glad to leave the house and get into the garden. Holmes seemed greatly amused. Bennett came running after us.

'I am so sorry, Mr Holmes. I have never seen him act so dangerously. His behaviour grows darker. Now you can understand why we are worried. And yet his mind is perfectly clear.'

'Too clear!' said Holmes. 'That was my mistake. Before we go can we see the window of Miss Presbury's bedroom?'

Bennett took us to the side of the house.

'It is up there,' he said, pointing at it. 'It really does seem impossible to reach. There is a large vine* which grows up the wall. But I certainly could not climb it, and it would be dangerous for any man to try. There is one other thing, Mr Holmes. Here is the name and address of the man in London who writes to the Professor. I saw it on an envelope this morning.'

Holmes looked at the paper Bennett gave him.

'Dorak – a strange name. From Czechoslovakia, I expect. Well, it is an important part of the chain. Watson and I shall return to London early tomorrow morning. We cannot act yet, Mr Bennett.'

'Then what on earth are we to do?' asked the secretary.

'Have patience, Mr Bennett. Things will soon develop. I suspect next Tuesday will be an important day. We shall be in Camford then. Meanwhile Miss Presbury must remain away from home.'

On our way back to the hotel Holmes sent off a telegram. In the evening he received a reply.

'It is from an agent of mine in London,' he explained. 'Dorak is a chemist from Czechoslovakia. This seems to connect with Presbury's visit to Prague.'

'At last something connects up with something,' I said. 'We seem to have before us a large number of unconnected events and no possible connection: an angry dog, a visit to a capital in central Europe, a man who crawls along the hall at night, and all those dates.'

Holmes smiled and lit his pipe.

'Well, now, let us take the dates first,' he said. 'With only one small exception, there is trouble every nine days. It cannot be a chance, for it has happened eight times now.'

I was forced to agree.

'My guess is this,' continued Holmes. 'Every ninth day Presbury takes some strong sort of medicine which has an immediate poisonous effect. He is by nature a fierce sort of man, and this makes him worse. He discovered the medicine in Prague, and is now supplied with it by a Czechoslovakian

**vine*, a kind of plant that grows up the side of houses.

in London.'

'But the dog, the face at the window, the creeping man?'

'We have made a start, Watson. Meanwhile let us enjoy this beautiful English town.'

After our return to London I did not see Holmes for a few days. But on Monday evening I received a note. He asked me to meet him at the railway station the next day. We travelled up to Camford in the afternoon and were met by Bennett.

'Things have been peaceful this last week,' he said, 'and the Professor's behaviour normal. A letter and a small package arrived today from Dorak. But there has been nothing else.'

'That is probably quite enough,' said Holmes seriously. 'I think the mystery will be solved tonight. We must watch the Professor carefully. Therefore I suggest you remain awake. If you hear Presbury in the hall, do not stop him, but follow quietly. Dr Watson and I will not be far away. We can do no more until we see how things develop. Goodbye – but I expect we shall see you before morning.'

It was nearly midnight when Holmes and I hid ourselves among some bushes across from the front door of Presbury's house. The night was clear but cold, and we were glad of our warm coats. Holmes was sure that we would soon find out the explanation for this mystery.

'If my nine-day idea is right,' said Holmes, 'then the Professor will be at his worst tonight. His strange behaviour began after his visit to Prague. He writes secretly to a Czechoslovakian in London, who is probably an agent for someone in Prague. And now this man has sent him a package. It all points in one direction, Watson. But we still do not know what he takes and why. Did you notice his hands?'

'No, I did not,' I replied.

'They were unusually thick and rough. Always look at the hands first. They were like –.' Holmes stopped for a moment and put his hand to his head. 'Oh, Watson, what a fool I have been! It's so hard to believe, but it must be true. Why did I not connect the ideas? The hands – how did I forget the hands? And the dog! And that vine growing up the wall! Look out, Watson. Here he is! We can now see for ourselves.'

The front door had slowly opened, and we saw Professor Presbury in his night-shirt. As he stepped forward there was a terrible change. He leaned down towards the ground and began to move along on his hands and feet. He crept along the front of the house and then round the corner. Bennett was following him.

'Come, Watson, come!' cried Holmes, and we moved to where we could see the side of the house. Presbury was looking at the vine which grew up the side of the house. As we watched him he suddenly began to climb it quickly and easily. He seemed to be enjoying his own ability to climb rather than trying to get anywhere.

Soon the Professor grew tired of this. He dropped to the ground and moved towards the stables. He crept along in the same strange way. The dog was out now, and making much noise. Presbury sat just out of the dog's reach. Then he picked up some small stones and threw them in the dog's face. Then he hit it with a long stick. The dog became wild beyond control. I do not think I have ever seen a stranger sight than this famous scientist, on his hands and feet, attacking a wildly angry dog.

And then in a moment it happened! The chain which held the dog suddenly broke. Immediately dog and man were rolling together on the ground. Presbury screamed, and it was a very narrow thing for his life. The animal had him by the throat and he was unconscious when we reached him. Bennett managed to get the dog under control.

We carried Presbury up to his bedroom where I examined him and put a bandage on his throat. The dog's teeth had done terrible damage. But in half an hour the immediate danger was over.

'He must go to a hospital,' I said.

'For God's sake, no!' cried Bennett. 'At present only those in the house know about this matter. But if people outside

find out, his position in the university will be ruined. And you must consider his daughter also.'

'Very well,' said Holmes. 'We shall remain silent. And now we must prevent this happening again. Let us see what we can find in that box of the Professor's.'

There was not much in the box, but it was enough. We found an empty medicine bottle and some letters. Most of these were from Anton Dorak about the supply of the bottles. But there was one other letter with a Prague postmark.

'Here we have our final clue!' cried Holmes and he opened it.

Dear Sir, Since your last visit I have thought much about your case. I know you have special reasons, but I warn you to be careful. My experiments have shown that there are possible dangers. As you know, there are two groups of monkeys that I could have used – the Anthropoid, or man-like, and the Langur. But at present I can send only medicine from the Langur's body. The Langur monkey is a crawler and a climber and so it is less like man. Dorak is my agent in London. He will supply you – Hans Lowenstein.

Lowenstein! I remembered a newspaper report about this Prague scientist who was searching for the secret of youth. The universities of Europe had been suspicious because he refused to say where his medicine came from. Here was the answer.

'The real cause,' explained Holmes, 'was Presbury's hopeless love for Miss Morphy. He thought a younger man was more likely to be successful. So he took the medicine. The dog, of course, realized the changes before we did. It was the monkey who threw things at the dog, and the monkey whom the dog attacked. Climbing up the wall was just a game. Come, Watson, we have a train to catch.'

8 Shoscombe Old Place

'Do you know anything about horse racing, Watson?' Holmes asked me one day.

'I ought to,' I replied. 'Too much of my money disappears on bets.'

'Then what do you know about Sir Robert Norberton?'

'He lives at Shoscombe Old Place in Berkshire. I know it well, for I used to spend summers near there. He nearly provided you with a case once.'

'How was that?' asked Holmes.

'It was when he attacked Sam Brewer, the well-known money-lender, at Newmarket races,' I explained. 'He almost killed the man.'

'Ah, he sounds interesting. Does he often act like that?'

'Well, they say he is a dangerous man. He rides without fear. In fact he came second in the Grand National races recently. He loves a good fight almost as much as he loves beautiful women. But I heard he has serious money problems these days.'

'An excellent short description, Watson!' Holmes said. 'I feel I almost know the man. Now, what can you tell me about Shoscombe Old Place?'

Only that it is in the centre of Shoscombe Park,' I replied, 'and that the famous Shoscombe stables are there.'

'And the trainer,' said Holmes, 'is John Mason. You need not look surprised, Watson. I have here a letter from Mason. But first, tell me more about Shoscombe.'

'There are the Shoscombe dogs,' I continued, 'which are famous over all England. The lady of Shoscombe Old Place is especially proud of these dogs.'

'The lady is Sir Robert's wife, I suppose?' asked Holmes.

'No, Norberton was never married,' I explained. 'He lives with his sister, Lady Beatrice Falder. The place belonged to the family of her dead husband. She can continue to live there during her life. But on her death all the property will go to her husband's younger brother. So at present she lives there and receives all profits from the Shoscombe property. And Sir Robert spends them all. They say she loves him dearly. But what is wrong at Shoscombe?'

'Ah, that is just what I want to know,' said Holmes. 'And here, I expect, is the man who can tell us.'

The door had opened and in walked a tall, serious man. Mr John Mason greeted us and sat down.

'I am here to explain my note, Mr Holmes,' he began. 'I think that my employer*, Sir Robert Norberton, is mad.'

Holmes looked surprised. 'Mr Mason, I am a detective, not a doctor. But why do you say this?'

'Well, sir,' Mason explained, 'when a man does one odd thing, or even two, there is probably an explanation. But when everything he does is strange, then I begin to wonder. I believe Shoscombe Prince and the Grand National races are making him mad.'

'Shoscombe Prince is the horse you are training for the Derby next month?' asked Holmes.

'The best in England, Mr Holmes. And I know. Sir Robert must win this Derby. He owes the bank huge amounts of money, and this is his only chance to pay them back. He has bet a lot of money on his horse. The public do not know how good the horse is. For when I pretend to take the horse out from Shoscombe, it is not really the Prince, but a similar horse which is slower. Everything Sir Robert has depends upon the Prince.'

'It seems a dangerous risk,' said Holmes. 'But why do you say he is mad?'

'Well, for a start there is his wild, tired appearance. I don't believe he sleeps at night. He spends all his time in the stables. Then there is his behaviour to Lady Beatrice.'

'Ah! What is that?' asked Holmes with interest.

'They have always been such good friends. They had the

**employer*, someone who pays people to do work for him or her.

same interests, and she loved the horses as much as he did. Every day she went to see them, and she loved the Prince above all. But that is over now. She seems to have lost interest. For a whole week now she has not entered the stables.'

'Do you think there has been a quarrel?' asked Holmes.

'Yes, a terrible quarrel,' the trainer replied. 'Why else did he give away her favourite dog to the owner of a local hotel? And he used to spend each evening in her room, for she is an ill woman and unable to walk much. But now he never goes near her. She must be greatly disappointed, Mr Holmes, for she drinks much now – often a bottle a day. It's all changed and there is something strange.'

'Is there anything else?' asked Holmes, who had clearly become most interested in the matter.

'In the park at Shoscombe there is an old ruined church, about a quarter of a mile from the main house. Many of the Falder family are buried there. Stephens – who also works for Sir Robert – saw him go there one night. So the next night we followed him. Beneath the church is a crypt*, a dark place that frightens most people. We saw Sir Robert go there and meet a man. What was my master doing there in the middle of the night?'

'Wait!' said Holmes. 'You said there was another man there. Did you recognize him?'

'No,' Mason replied. 'After Sir Robert returned to the house, we went up to this man to ask him what he was doing. But immediately he ran off into the darkness. All I saw was his unpleasant face.'

Holmes sat for some time lost in thought.

'Has Mrs Falder a servant-companion?' he asked at last.

'Yes, Carrie Evans. She has been with her for five years. I suspect there is something between her and Sir Robert, but that is not my business.'

'Is it possible that this is the cause of the quarrel between Sir Robert and his sister?' suggested Holmes. 'But I suppose

*_crypt_, an underground room, where dead bodies may be kept.

that does not explain the visits to the crypt.'

'No, sir,' replied Mason. 'And there is something more that I can't fit in. Why does Sir Robert want to dig up a dead body?'

Holmes suddenly sat up. 'What?'

'We only found it yesterday – after I had written to you,' explained Mason. 'Sir Robert had gone up to London, so Stephens and I went down to the crypt. Everything was normal, except that in one corner was part of a human body.'

'You told the police?' said Holmes.

'Well, sir, I don't think it will interest them. It is probably several hundred years old. But it wasn't there before, I'm sure. That corner had always been empty. We left the body just as we found it.'

'When did Sir Robert give away his sister's dog?' asked Holmes.

'A week ago today. It was making a noise in the garden. Sir Robert seemed very angry that morning. I half expected him to kill it. But instead he gave it to old Barnes at "The Green Dragon" hotel in the village.'

Holmes sat for some time in silent thought. He was smoking the oldest and least pleasant of his many pipes.

'This is all rather unclear, Mr Mason,' he said at last. 'Can you give me something more exact?'

'Perhaps this is more exact, Mr Holmes,' said our visitor. He took a small package from his pocket. Inside it was a burnt piece of bone. Holmes examined it with interest.

'Where did you get it?' he asked.

'There is a large fire used for the heating of the whole house,' explained Mason. 'It is directly beneath Mrs Falder's room. Normally the fire is not lit in the late spring. But recently Sir Robert said it was cold and he ordered it to be used. This morning the boy found this piece of bone among the remains of the fire.'

'It is the bone from a human leg,' I said.

'Exactly!' Holmes had become very serious. 'When does the boy light the fire?' he asked.

'In the evening,' answered Mason, 'and then he leaves it until the next morning.'

'So anyone can go there in the night? How many entrances are there to the room?'

'One from outside, and another by some stairs which go up to a passage by Mrs Falder's room.'

'Was Sir Robert at home last night?' asked Holmes.

'No, so someone else must have burnt the bones.'

'This is a serious matter, Mr Mason,' said Holmes. 'Is there good fishing in Berkshire?'

Mr Mason looked surprised. 'Why, yes.'

'Watson and I need a fishing holiday. We shall go to Berkshire tonight and stay at "The Green Dragon". We shall meet again when I find out more about this matter.'

It was a bright May evening when Holmes and I travelled by train to the small village of Shoscombe. From the station it was only a short walk to "The Green Dragon". The owner, Barnes, and Holmes discussed the question of fishing.

'Are there any fish in the lake by Shoscombe Old Place?' asked Holmes.

Barnes' expression changed. 'Don't go there, sir. You might find yourself thrown in the lake! Sir Robert is a suspicious man, and he doesn't like strangers.'

'I hear that his horse will run in the Grand National,' said Holmes.

'Yes, and a good horse too,' replied Barnes. And then, looking at us thoughtfully, he asked, 'You aren't racing fellows yourselves, are you?'

'No indeed, just two tired men from London who want a holiday in Berkshire.'

'Well, that's all right. But remember what I said about Sir Robert. Stay away from the park,' warned Barnes.

'Certainly, Mr Barnes,' said Holmes. 'By the way, that is a most beautiful dog you have.'

'It is indeed, sir. A real Shoscombe dog – none better.'

'And how much does a dog like that cost?' asked Holmes.

'More than I can afford. Sir Robert gave me this one,'

replied Barnes. 'I must tie it up to prevent it returning to the big house.'

'I'm learning a few things, Watson,' said Holmes after Barnes had left us. 'It's a difficult case, but I think I may solve it in a day or two. Since Sir Robert is still in London, perhaps we can safely enter Shoscombe Park. There are certain things I want to check.'

'Do you have any ideas about the case?' I asked.

'Only this, Watson: that something of great importance happened at the house a week ago. What was that something? We can only guess from its effects. The brother no longer visits his sister. He gives away her favourite dog. Her dog, Watson! Does that suggest anything to you?'

'His anger?' I suggested.

'Possibly. But there is another explanation. But, to continue – Mrs Falder remains in her room, changes her habits, avoids the stables, drinks a lot. This is the first group of strange events.'

'What about the crypt?' I asked.

'That is part of the second group. Sir Robert is anxious to win the Grand National. He is afraid that his bank will take all his property. He is a clever man. Most of his money comes from his sister. His sister's servant is also under his control. Now, let us suppose – only suppose, Watson – that Sir Robert has murdered his sister.'

'My dear Holmes!' I cried in shock.

'I know he comes from an excellent family, but such things do happen sometimes. Remember Colonel Moran, Watson, and Moriarty himself. So let us suppose what I have suggested is true. Norberton cannot escape until after the race, which he hopes Shoscombe Prince will win. So he must remain here. Therefore he must destroy the body and get someone to take his sister's place. The servant helps him, and they hide the body in the crypt until he can burn it at night. What do you think?'

'Well, I suppose it is all possible. But I cannot believe Sir Robert is a murderer.'

'I think there is a small experiment which we can try tomorrow,' said Holmes. 'Meanwhile let us go fishing.'

About eleven o'clock the next morning, Holmes and I went for a walk towards Shoscombe Park. We took with us the black dog which we had borrowed from Barnes.

'This is the place,' said Holmes, as we came to the high gates at the entrance to the park. 'About mid-day, Barnes says, Mrs Falder comes out in her carriage. It stops while the gates are opened. When it comes through I want you to ask the driver something. I shall hide by this bush.'

We did not wait long. After fifteen minutes we saw the open carriage come down from the big house. Someone ran to open the gates. In the carriage were a young woman, probably the servant, and an older woman with a blanket around herself. I moved forward and asked if Sir Robert was at Shoscombe.

At the same moment Holmes stepped out and let the dog go. It rushed happily up to the carriage. When it got close to the old woman, it suddenly stopped, and made low, angry noises.

'Drive on! Drive on!' screamed a voice, and the carriage quickly disappeared down the road.

'Well, Watson,' said Holmes with a smile, 'the dog thought it was Mrs Falder, but discovered it was a stranger. Dogs don't make mistakes.'

'But her voice was the voice of a man!' I cried.

'Exactly. Now we have another clue.'

My companion seemed to have no further plans for the day. In the afternoon we actually caught some fish for our meal. But after supper Holmes showed he was ready for some activity. Soon we were walking to the park gates again. There we met Mason, the trainer.

'Good evening, gentlemen,' he said. 'I got your note, Mr Holmes. Sir Robert has not yet returned, but he will be back later tonight.'

'I think we can safely examine the crypt,' said Holmes. 'Will you lead the way, Mr Mason.'

There was no moon that night and so everything was in complete darkness. Mason led us across some fields until we reached the ancient ruined church. The roof and the top part of the walls had fallen down long ago. In one corner of the building were stone stairs leading down to the crypt. We went down into the wet, unpleasant room. I lit a lamp and saw coffins* all around, some on the floor, some on shelves reaching up to the stone ceiling.

'You spoke of some bones, Mr Mason,' said Holmes. 'Can you show them to me?'

'They are here in this corner,' replied the trainer. 'But they are gone!'

'As I expected,' answered Holmes. 'You will probably find their remains in the fire at the house.'

'But why burn the bones of a man who died several hundred years ago?' asked the puzzled trainer.

'That is what we are here to discover. It will be a long search, but I think we shall find the solution.'

When Mason had left Holmes began a careful examination

**coffins*, wooden boxes in which dead people are buried.

of all the coffins. After an hour or more he came to a coffin near the stairs, and I heard a cry of success from him. He was looking in detail at the lid. He had only just begun to open up the coffin when we had an unexpected visitor.

Someone was walking in the church above. It was obviously a person who knew the place well, for his steps were quick and sure. Soon a man came down the stairs. He was huge and had a wild appearance. He looked angrily round the crypt, finally seeing us.

'Who the devil are you?' he shouted. 'And what are you doing on my property?'

Holmes made no answer. The man came forward and lifted his heavy stick.

'Do you hear me?' he continued fiercely. 'Who are you? What are you doing?'

Holmes walked forward to meet him.

'I also have a question, Sir Robert,' he said seriously. 'Who is this? And what is she doing here?'

He turned and tore open the coffin behind him. Inside was a body dressed in a white sheet. Its face was the colourless face of an old woman.

Sir Robert fell back in surprise.

'How do you know of this?' he cried. 'And what business is it of yours?'

'My name is Sherlock Holmes,' said my companion. 'Perhaps you have heard of it. My business is that of every honest man – to keep the law. I think you have an explanation to give.'

Sir Robert became much quieter.

'Well, if I must tell, I must. Come up to the house and you can decide matters for yourself.'

Fifteen minutes later we were in the library at Shoscombe Old Place. Sir Robert called two others to join us: the young woman we had seen in the carriage and a small man with an unpleasant face.

'These,' said Sir Robert, 'are my sister's servant and her husband. They are my witnesses and can prove the truth of what I shall tell you. You probably know that I am running a horse for the Grand National next month. Everything depends on my success. All the money I have comes from my sister. But most people know that when she dies all the Shoscombe property returns to the Falder family. I owe very large amounts of money. And when my sister dies, then the bank will take all my property because they know I shall have no more money to repay them. Well, Mr Holmes, my sister *did* die a week ago.'

'And you told no one?' asked Holmes.

'What could I do? I was completely ruined. But three weeks could make all the difference. So the servant's husband, who is an actor, disguised himself as my sister. My sister died naturally from a long illness. Her doctor will tell you that she had been ill for many months and death was certain.'

'And the body?' asked Holmes.

'It could not remain in the house. At first we hid it in the garden-house. But we were followed by her dog. He made such a noise that I decided a safer place was needed. So I gave the dog away and carried the body to the crypt. We put the body in a coffin and burnt the old bones in the fire at night. That is my story, Mr Holmes.'

'There is just one thing wrong, Sir Robert,' said Holmes. 'Your bets on the race will remain safe even if the bank takes your property.'

'No, Mr Holmes. For the Prince is a part of the property, and they will take him also. And they will probably not even run him in the race. For the bank person who lent me money is my worst enemy – Sam Brewer, whom I once attacked at Newmarket. Do you think he would try to save me?'

'Well, Sir Robert,' said Holmes, 'I must report this to the police. My work ends here. It is not for me to judge your behaviour. Come, Watson, we must return to "The Green Dragon".'

This strange matter ended successfully for Sir Robert – perhaps more so than it should have. Shoscombe Prince did win the Derby that year, and won eighty thousand pounds for his owner. Sir Robert had enough money to pay back the bank and still keep a large amount for himself. The police finally decided to take no action against him for hiding his sister's body. People even say that as Sir Robert grows older he is becoming a quiet sort of man.

Questions

The Man with the Twisted Lip

1. Explain why Watson first went to the opium house.
2. What was Sherlock Holmes doing in the opium house?
3. Why were Mrs Sinclair and the police sure a terrible crime had taken place?
4. What new clue came to Mrs Sinclair, and how did she know it was not a fake?
5. Why did Holmes say the answer to the mystery was 'in the wash-room'?
6. Tell in your own words the unusual story of how Mr Neville Sinclair became Hugh Boone.

Silver Blaze

1. Why wasn't Holmes interested in the disappearance of Silver Blaze at first?
2. What clues made the police sure that Simpson, the stranger, did the crime?
3. Which things from the dead man's pockets proved to be important clues? Tell why.
4. How did Holmes find out where Silver Blaze was hidden?
5. Why did the colonel become angry when Holmes told him that Straker's killer was 'in his presence'?
6. Why was the chicken curry an important clue?

The Final Problem

1. Was Moriarty an ordinary criminal? Explain your answer.
2. Describe the conversation between Holmes and Moriarty.

3. How did Holmes and Watson get to Europe?
4. What caused Watson to leave Holmes alone at the Reichenbach Fall?
5. What did Watson discover when he returned to the Fall?

The Empty House

1. Why was the murder of Ronald Adair such a mystery?
2. Why did Watson fall unconscious when he turned back to look at the funny old man who had come to see him?
3. What really happened at the Reichenbach Fall?
4. What was the man with the gun trying to do? Why did he not succeed?
5. Who was Moran?
6. What is the probable reason Moran killed Ronald Adair?

The Norwood Builder

1. Why didn't Holmes know who John McFarlane was at first?
2. Did Holmes believe McFarlane's story? Why?
3. Why did Holmes first go to Blackheath and not Norwood?
4. What did the 'final clue' of the thumbprint prove to Lestrade? To Holmes?
5. Explain how Holmes used fire to bring out Oldacre.
6. Describe Oldacre's plan.

The Devil's Foot

1 What was the strange thing that happened at Trelew to Tregennis's brothers and sister?
2. Mr Tregennis said it was 'the work of the devil'. Knowing the answer to the mystery, what is interesting about this statement?
3. Why was Holmes interested in the oil-lamp in the room where Tregennis died?
4. Describe the experiment Watson and Holmes did.

5. Why was Sterndale so interested in the Tregennis family fate? What was his role in the deaths?
6. Why did Holmes decide not to tell the police what he knew?

The Creeping Man

1. What was Watson to Holmes?
2. When and how did things begin to change for Professor Presbury?
3. What happened to him after his mysterious trip?
4. How did Holmes and Watson get in to see the Professor?
5. Why was the dog's behaviour an important clue?
6. What was the Professor becoming? How?

Shoscombe Old Place

1. What kind of man was Sir Robert Norberton?
2. Why did the trainer think Sir Robert and his sister Lady Beatrice had quarrelled?
3. What strange things had been happening around the crypt?
4. What was the piece of burnt bone Mason showed to Holmes and where did it come from?
5. Why did Holmes let Lady Falder's dog into her stopped carriage? What did he find out?
6. Describe the meeting between Holmes and Sir Robert in the crypt.
7. Why did Sir Robert do as he had done?

Oxford Progressive English Readers

Introductory Grade

Vocabulary restricted to 1400 headwords
Illustrated in full colour

The Call of the Wild and Other Stories	Jack London
Emma	Jane Austen
Jungle Book Stories	Rudyard Kipling
Life Without Katy and Seven Other Stories	O. Henry
Little Women	Louisa M. Alcott
The Lost Umbrella of Kim Chu	Eleanor Estes
Stories from Vanity Fair	W.M. Thackeray
Tales from the Arabian Nights	Retold by Rosemary Border
Treasure Island	R.L. Stevenson

Grade 1

Vocabulary restricted to 2100 headwords
Illustrated in full colour

The Adventures of Sherlock Holmes	Sir Arthur Conan Doyle
Alice's Adventures in Wonderland	Lewis Carroll
A Christmas Carol	Charles Dickens
The Dagger and Wings and Other Father Brown Stories	G.K. Chesterton
The Flying Heads and Other Strange Stories	Retold by C. Nancarrow
The Golden Touch and Other Stories	Retold by R. Border
Great Expectations	Charles Dickens
Gulliver's Travels	Jonathan Swift
Hijacked!	J.M. Marks
Jane Eyre	Charlotte Brontë
Lord Jim	Joseph Conrad
Oliver Twist	Charles Dickens
The Stone Junk	Retold by D.H. Howe
Stories of Shakespeare's Plays 1	Retold by N. Kates
Tales from Tolstoy	Retold by R.D. Binfield
The Talking Tree and Other Stories	David McRobbie
The Treasure of the Sierra Madre	B. Traven
True Grit	Charles Portis

Grade 2

Vocabulary restricted to 3100 headwords
Illustrated in colour

The Adventures of Tom Sawyer	Mark Twain
Alice's Adventures through the Looking Glass	Lewis Carroll
Around the World in Eighty Days	Jules Verne
Border Kidnap	J.M. Marks
David Copperfield	Charles Dickens
Five Tales	Oscar Wilde
Fog and Other Stories	Bill Lowe
Further Adventures of Sherlock Holmes	Sir Arthur Conan Doyle

Grade 2 (cont.)

The Hound of the Baskervilles	Sir Arthur Conan Doyle
The Missing Scientist	S.F. Stevens
The Red Badge of Courage	Stephen Crane
Robinson Crusoe	Daniel Defoe
Seven Chinese Stories	T.J. Sheridan
Stories of Shakespeare's Plays 2	Retold by Wyatt & Fullerton
A Tale of Two Cities	Charles Dickens
Tales of Crime and Detection	Retold by G.F. Wear
Two Boxes of Gold and Other Stories	Charles Dickens

Grade 3

Vocabulary restricted to 3700 headwords
Illustrated in colour

Battle of Wits at Crimson Cliff	Retold by Benjamin Chia
Dr Jekyll and Mr Hyde and Other Stories	R.L. Stevenson
From Russia, with Love	Ian Fleming
The Gifts and Other Stories	O. Henry & Others
The Good Earth	Pearl S. Buck
Journey to the Centre of the Earth	Jules Verne
Kidnapped	R.L. Stevenson
King Solomon's Mines	H. Rider Haggard
Lady Precious Stream	S.I. Hsiung
The Light of Day	Eric Ambler
Moonraker	Ian Fleming
The Moonstone	Wilkie Collins
A Night of Terror and Other Strange Tales	Guy De Maupassant
Seven Stories	H.G. Wells
Stories of Shakespeare's Plays 3	Retold by H.G. Wyatt
Tales of Mystery and Imagination	Edgar Allan Poe
20,000 Leagues Under the Sea	Jules Verne
The War of the Worlds	H.G. Wells
The Woman in White	Wilkie Collins
Wuthering Heights	Emily Brontë
You Only Live Twice	Ian Fleming

Grade 4

Vocabulary within a 5000 headwords range
Illustrated in black and white

The Diamond as Big as the Ritz and Other Stories	F. Scott Fitzgerald
Dragon Seed	Pearl S. Buck
Frankenstein	Mary Shelley
The Mayor of Casterbridge	Thomas Hardy
Pride and Prejudice	Jane Austen
The Stalled Ox and Other Stories	Saki
The Thimble and Other Stories	D.H. Lawrence